HANNAH AND SORAYA'S FULLY MAGIC GENERATION-Y *SNOWFLAKE* ROAD TRIP ACROSS AMERICA

Hannah and Soraya's Fully Magic Generation-Y *Snowflake* Road Trip across America

James Ward

Copyright © 2020 James Ward

The excerpt from Elise Cowen's poetry is used by kind permission of the Cowen estate.

The moral right of the author has been asserted.

Apart from any fair dealing for the purposes of research or private study, or criticism or review, as permitted under the Copyright, Designs and Patents Act 1988, this publication may only be reproduced, stored or transmitted, in any form or by any means, with the prior permission in writing of the publishers, or in the case of reprographic reproduction in accordance with the terms of licences issued by the Copyright Licensing Agency. Enquiries concerning reproduction outside those terms should be sent to the publishers.

This is a work of fiction. Names, characters, businesses, places, events and incidents are either the products of the author's imagination or used in a fictitious manner. Any resemblance to actual persons, living or dead, or actual events is purely coincidental.

Matador
9 Priory Business Park,
Wistow Road, Kibworth Beauchamp,
Leicestershire. LE8 0RX
Tel: 0116 279 2299
Email: books@troubador.co.uk
Web: www.troubador.co.uk/matador
Twitter: @matadorbooks

ISBN 978 1838595 340

British Library Cataloguing in Publication Data.
A catalogue record for this book is available from the British Library.

Printed and bound in Great Britain by 4edge Limited
Typeset in 11pt Minion Pro by Troubador Publishing Ltd, Leicester, UK

Matador is an imprint of Troubador Publishing Ltd

To my wife

God *is* hidden
And not for picture postcards.
ELISE COWEN

PART ONE

I'm the One Who First Suggested the Idea

OUR HOTEL WAS TYPICAL OF WHAT PASSED FOR LUXURY in Venice. Walls of fashionably cracked plaster and too many mirrors, enclosing a room just big enough to accommodate a sofa, two chairs, a dresser, a double bed, plus gaps to squeeze in between when you needed to go to the bathroom. Only the balcony was what you'd truly call spacious, and, because it had a sea view, we'd spent the whole first day there, sipping cocktails and ignoring comments from a succession of creepy guys down on the *fondamente*, where the paparazzi had gathered. The afternoon sunshine made a rectangle on the wall and a breeze billowed the curtains. Vases of flowers stood on every available surface, all gifts from fans and admirers, with more downstairs in reception.

All this was before Julia's galaxy-shattering phone call and the crisis meeting in Verona. I was sitting up in bed with my new laptop, wearing white-wire earbuds, navigating the TJN site and listening to retro. I clicked on pause. "Maybe we should road trip across the USA," I said. 'Road trip' like a verb.

Soraya lay in her underwear on the sofa. She nursed a glass of orange and looked indifferently across and said nothing. She wore her headphones, so maybe she hadn't even heard me.

"What are you listening to?" I said.

She lifted her left ear cushion and threw me a 'what?' look.

"What are you listening to?" I asked again.

She sighed like it was the dullest question ever. "*All of the Stars*. Ed Sheeran."

We returned to our separate worlds. Outside, a man shouted 'Soraya!' in a wheedling, hopeless voice. Then, 'Please to come out… *per uno momento!*' She yawned, then I did. An ocean liner parped. Half a dozen seagulls quarrelled close by, presumably devouring the bread we'd put out earlier. 'Soraya!' another desperate male called. *'Soraya!'* Like listening to ghosts.

"Just the two of us?" she asked after five minutes. "I mean, your American road trip?"

"Unless *you* want to bring someone?"

"I'm not judging, but we spend less and less time together nowadays."

"Untrue. And don't make out you're jealous of Tim, because I know you can't be." I spooled my earphones and put them on the bedside table. "That was a joke, by the way."

"Ho, ho. Not funny."

"We're supposed to be having a holiday," I said, trying to affect a conciliatory tone. "Why so grouchy?"

"*This?*" She leaned so far forward, pointing manically to her scalp, that she almost fell off the sofa.

Aha. Okay. I chuckled.

We both had them. San Marco, two minutes on a rickety wooden chair, fifty euros a pop. We'd been lucky: others had paid twice that and knelt for the privilege. A bald rectangle courtesy of a dead painter no one really knows anything about, except that hers is the glowering face on a million T-shirts.

"It's itchy," she went on. "*Really* itchy. And the *heat*. I can't sleep at night."

"It got us the cover of *Harper's Bazaar*."

"Too high a price. And I've no idea what the fuss is about Whatshername who allegedly started it all off."

It wasn't the only thing we were in Venice for. We'd extended our stay a few days because we thought it'd be cool to be here when the charts were announced: Tuesday for the Billboard, Friday for the UK Singles. *Top of My Tower* was probably Coal Tar's best track to date, yet Tuesday had come and gone, and it had stayed #6 in the US. We were hoping for better tomorrow in Britain. In the intervening period, Venice's famous melancholy seemed to have got to us. Too many violet sunsets, maybe, too much grandeur, too many vague echoes of all the historical debauchery, real or imagined.

Anyway, the rock 'n' roll lifestyle's identical everywhere: if you're any good, the public incarcerates you indefinitely in a hotel room. Why we'd imagined it'd be any different in Venice defeats me. We were trying to take our minds off everything with a succession of castles in the air. Things like *Let's go on a road trip*.

Clearly Soraya was interested, though. When I thought more about it, I seemed to remember her broaching something like the same idea a while ago; could have been last year.

Or maybe the year before.

Pre- or post-Trump? It made a difference. America wasn't the land of *Give me your tired, your poor, your huddled masses* any more. So people said.

Mind you, that wasn't just the USA. It was the whole world.

I closed the laptop.

A road trip across the USA. Like Jack Kerouac and Dean Moriarty, or Thelma and Louise, or any number of high school seniors in teen movies, driving pink convertibles across the endless Arizona Desert. And diners, flashing red neon signs saying 'Motel', rap, new jack swing, jazz, timber-framed suburban houses with stars and stripes hanging from the balcony, rodeos, Jacob Lawrence, Elvis, yellow school buses. Another world.

But Soraya was right. It was a pipe dream. Obviously, we'd *been* to America, lots of times, but only in an *If it's Tuesday, This Must Be Belgium* kind of way. *No time for sightseeing, we've got to be in Kansas City tomorrow morning.* Those words usually coming out of my mouth, no one else's. I'm the manager, after all. It's part of my job to arrange schedules, fix deadlines, see everything's done properly, be the sergeant-major everyone loathes. Most of the time, we could be anywhere.

Anyway, I'll be thirty-eight next birthday, nine years older than Soraya. I'm thin, long blonde hair, and people say I've a pleasant face; but you can't hide the signs of encroaching middle-age. Not that I would. Botox isn't something you do in the rock business, not unless you're some kind of *poseur*. Grow old brazenly, that's the ideal: like a budget-price melting candle. Keith Richards, Patti Smith, Iggy.

Party People

That night, we went to Marinello's party. A go-fast boat picked us up just outside the hotel. We were served the predictable champagne at seventy knots.

When we reached the yacht, the music and mingling had long since started. I wouldn't say everyone with a capital E was there, but Harlinne Vobrosky was, and since she'd invited us to Venice for the *Harper's* gig, we could hardly avoid her. Born and bred in Wisconsin, sixty-ish, tall with a grey bouffant and a worsted skirt-suit (even to something like this, where you'd imagine evening wear would be obligatory), she chain-smoked cheroots and drank rum and lemonade from a plastic mug with camels on the side.

Soraya behaved respectably for a change and, after about an hour, the three of us sat on our own at the prow and talked about life and purpose. Harlinne is one of those people who believes the end of the world is imminent: Google's making us stupider, the falcon can't hear the falconer, that sort of thing. I think Soraya was a little scared of her. Nevertheless, after about an hour, they went off somewhere alone. I was on my sixth or tenth champagne, so I made no attempt to follow them. I was tired, if I'm honest. I wanted to lie on a mattress with my cheek on a cool white pillow.

And depressed. *At number six for the second week running, Fully Magic Coal Tar Lounge and...* Our best song. You stayed still for a week and people stopped believing in you. You hardly ever recouped the loss. Next week, you'd be twelfth.

Please, Britain, please come through for us. We'd been seventh in the UK Singles Chart last Friday. Right now, I'd have settled for fourth this week. Fifth or sixth would be a loss of momentum, given that we'd been twentieth the week before.

Fourth, bloody hell. What happened to the days when we'd release a song and it'd go straight to number one? Me, praying for *fourth!* Maybe we'd reached the end of the line, success-wise.

No one from further up the boat came and sat with me. One of those times when you realise you don't have as many friends as you think. Or maybe no one knew I was here. Either way, it was just as well, because frankly, I was having a minor meltdown. I was actually shaking (mind you, it *was* cold). *Seventh.* We were in seventh place! And I was hoping for *fourth!* That was how careers ended in this business: washed up on fourth, desperately praying for a miracle.

Soraya and Harlinne came back. They didn't look like they'd been doing much. But they must have been up to something. Perhaps Harlinne had fancied her professional chances. *You're losing momentum, Soraya. Just look at the Billboard. You need a solo career and a new manager.* If so, she didn't know what she was up against. Again, I found myself not particularly caring. Partly, I suppose, because I knew Soraya would never leave me.

Most of the women here were flaunting their bald patches, sunburn and all, but Harlinne didn't even have one. Too special a bouffant, clearly. I wondered what she was doing working for *Harper's*, her being such a mixture of conservatism and bizarreness. Then I remembered: she was an agent, so not on their payroll. Just a go between.

Still, *Harper's* must respect her.

I can't remember what happened in the last three hours. I know it sounds clichéd, but after a while, all those occasions feel the same. Enjoyable in a way, but not something you'd make a detour for. Like work, really. Soraya and I held hands, and she kept asking if I was okay, like she felt guilty about having left me alone. I do remember we were back at the hotel, in bed, no later than four.

And we hadn't mentioned the road trip at any point that evening.

A Paranoid Confession

This sounds like it might be a pointless aside, but I promise you, it *is* relevant to what comes later. The truth is, Soraya and I are a majorly odd couple. Even we can see it. She's lead singer in, and I'm the manager of, the world's biggest rock band (if 'rock' is still a word – she says it isn't): Fully Magic Coal Tar Lounge, *four great guys, one stellar woman!* You'd expect our musical tastes to be the same; or at least similar.

Not at all. She's into Overmono, Rihanna, Cardi B, Drake, MIA, Lucy Ward, Ariana Grande, Connie Constance, Jay-Z, Cupcakke, Stone Broken, Koyo, Beyoncé, Laura Marling, The Furrow Collective. Eclectic up to a point, but nothing older than a few years. I love all the above – some more than others, obviously – but my major tastes lie elsewhere. A motley collection of ancients too embarrassing to list here.

The point is, if we did go on a road trip across the US, we'd have to play our music *on* something. Radio, CD, MP3 player, you've got to share it. How to do that when you only ever manage to avoid fighting by retreating into your own phones and orbiting completely different playlists? Unfortunately – here's the quandary – music is pretty much the most important thing in the world to both of us.

And it's more powerful than people usually imagine. Yes, maybe it could unite the world, but it could also drive it apart. It's tribal, especially when people start getting snobby about it, which they always do. *My playlist's better than yours. In fact, to be honest, yours is pants.* Pride. Hundreds of years ago, one of the seven deadly sins.

Nowadays, when Soraya asks me what I'm listening to, I'll likely as not make something up.

Hey, I've built a career on being the coolest cat on the block. I don't want people to know what I'm *actually* listening to. And I can't change it. My tastes are my tastes.

Which explains how and why I decided that a road trip across the USA was out of the question. I mean, driving across Britain would be bad enough: South Shields to Skinburness, ninety miles, give or take. *How the hell can you listen to that stuff? Turn it off, it's making my ears bleed!* Three thousand miles would be the end of us, on all levels. I'm not sure I could stand that.

I wish I'd kept my stupid trap shut. It'd be the perfect pretext for her to go off with Harlinne.

Also, I Wish I'd Never Written That

Now that I've written that down, I can see how crazy it is. And let's say Soraya and I *were* to go on a road trip across the USA, I could just *make up* a playlist. Load a bunch of up-to-the-minute stuff onto my phone, pretend I think it's all freaking wonderful.

Couldn't I?

Truth is, I don't know. Driving across America without Joni Mitchell and Alanis Morissette and David Bowie and Lindisfarne –

There, I've said it now.

And unfortunately, there's much more where that came from.

To complete the sentence, however: it would seem like sacrilege.

And the weird thing is, none of the above are even *from* the USA.

How Things Suddenly Got Taken Out of My Hands

How do I remember that it was 4am when Soraya and I got to bed, that night in Venice? Good question. God knows, I shouldn't have: we'd had enough to drink. What I *can* say is that my phone rang at five, and at that point, I reckon I'd had less than an hour's sleep.

Not unusual, the early hours phone call. I've lots of friends who've no idea when to call it a night, and insufficient brains to realise that, since it's dark and five o'clock in the morning, you might not actually be awake, let alone primed for a conversation. If *they* are, *you* are: that's their logic. Or they're in some completely different time zone, and they don't understand the implications of *that* either.

I looked at the screen expecting *Gaz, Paul, Elliot, Brian, Laura, Lulu*… Before I'd exhausted the possibilities, I read the actual name. *Julia*.

The Julia? The *My Little Sister* Julia?

It was my address book, so yes, J.U.L.I.A. meant Julia.

Not good. She wouldn't be ringing me unless… I picked up. "Is everything okay?"

"Very definitely not." No preliminaries, no reassuring 'how are you?' nothing in that vein. "Are you sitting down?"

"It's five am here. I'm in Venice. What's happened?"

"Charlotte's going to sue Dad."

Not the sort of sentence that makes sense when you've just awoken after a heavy party, or think you have. Too much like a continuation of dreamland. "Charlotte's going to sue Dad," I said to myself.

I heard it. It sounded bad.

"She's claiming he abused her," Julia said.

Suddenly, it was as if someone had thrown a bucket of water over me. This was *Charlotte* she was talking about: our sister, two years younger than me, three older than Julia. And this was Dad –

"*Our* Dad?" I said.

"Our Charlotte, our Dad."

"I don't understand. Why? How? Oh my God."

Soraya sat up in bed, nearly knocking the phone out of

my hand. "What's going on? Is everything okay?"

I shushed her.

"That was precisely my view," Julia went on. "I know you're supposed to believe the accuser nowadays. And no one's a bigger supporter of hashtag-me too than I am. And I know the family – apart from the victim, obviously – is always last to admit it, or even realise there's a problem in the first place. I know all that. But this is complete bullshit. And that somehow makes it twenty times worse."

Soraya looked at me. I ran my hand reassuringly across her hair. The last thing I wanted was her contribution to the confusion. She lay down, and to all appearances went straight back to sleep. I threw a sheet over myself, took the phone out onto the balcony, sat on one of the metal chairs.

"What precisely is she saying?" I asked.

"God knows what Mum's going to think," Julia carried on, not answering my question. "Or in fact, how it'll affect all of us. Families implode over less than this."

It's not like Julia to get angry. Or show any emotion at all. I got a sense of the almighty row there'd already been. And the damage it had done.

"What precisely is she saying?" I asked, for a second time.

"I'm glad you asked that," she said. "Because, according to her, you're involved."

"What do you mean? And if you're 'glad' I asked it, why didn't you answer when I asked first time round?"

I should have been worrying about how I was supposedly 'involved', but then we were both of us putting tangential questions, probably because the central thing was so hideous. *She's claiming he abused her.*

"Of course you're not *involved*," Julia said irritably. "Not really. It's just her gormless fantasy. She's stupid, that's the bottom line. Always has been, always will be. You're a world famous mega-millionaire, I'm a prize-winning novelist, Mabel's about to graduate in medicine. Even John's got talent, though why he prefers the life of a travelling salesman baffles all of us. What's *she* got? Her candle so-called business and a truckload of whacky beliefs about the healing power of crystals. And right now, the bottom's dropped right out of the New Age airy-fairy-crap market so, poor thing, she feels an abject failure. That's the trouble with the truth, of course: it will come out. And she needs someone to blame. Anyone that isn't her."

"Please, Julia, just answer my original question: what precisely is she saying? And, while you're on, how the hell am I supposedly 'involved'? Why did you say that, if you're only going to – "

"Okay, hold on to your seat. When you were about thirteen – she would have been eleven – Mum and John and Mabel and I went to see Auntie Jill in the Lake District, leaving you and Charlotte at home with Dad. Do you remember that?"

I took a sharp breath and let out an involuntary, "Oh, God."

Pause.

"Hannah?" she said. "Are you still there?"

"That's what this is about?" I replied feebly.

In some ways, this sudden realisation was a good thing. Now I had the measure of it. Abuse, maybe, yes, according to one definition. Nothing sexual. Nothing violent. Not even any touching. Seriously coercive, though. And way beyond a father's rights. Psychological abuse. I can see how it could conceivably have messed Charlotte up; how she might have buried it her whole life, until one day – sometime recently – she went to whatever passed for a professional psychologist in her world. A shaman? And the shaman must have said, *What happened to you was* wrong, *Charlotte. You need to confront it, stop running away. You need closure.*

Terms like 'abuse' are fluid, up to a point. There's a strong consensus about its central characteristics, but disagreement concerning the periphery. Corporal punishment for kids was the norm when our parents were young. Nowadays, it's grounds for taking a child into care. Is continual criticism abuse? What if it's justified? Who judges? Physical, sexual, psychological, neglect. All this ran through my head at once, like someone reading a textbook aloud to me at speed.

"What actually happened?" Julia said at last. "Charlotte span some yarn about Dad locking you both in the front room for several days, no food, virtually nothing to drink, and then, when he let you *out* of the front room, stopping you leaving the house. Also, alcohol, lots of it. And then – so she says – he swore you both to secrecy before Mum got back. So she still doesn't know. I mean, if that's true… "

The ellipsis was quite deliberate: designed for me to fill in.

"I'm afraid it is," I said quietly.

"Er... what?"

"But it wasn't abuse," I added.

"Just on the basis of the events I've just summarised, I can think of one or two lawyers who might well disagree. So it actually happened? My God. Maybe I'd better ring Charlotte and apologise."

"It was a one-off. And there *was* food: a pizza, I think, and sausage rolls, and a big bottle of lemonade. We weren't *starved*. And he was having a breakdown. Mum and he ... well, you know. She didn't go to Auntie Jill's for no reason."

"Irrelevant."

Suddenly, I was angry. With both women. Asinine, banal, small-minded... Particularly unforgivable in Julia, since she was supposed to be an artist. I had a strong sense she felt the same way about me: idiotic, delusional. We both wanted to hang up.

"I don't know what Charlotte's next move is going to be," she said coldly. "My guess is she intends to cite you in some upcoming legal action as either a witness or an accessory. The latter's probably impossible, since you were only thirteen, but you urgently need to touch base with her. And I mean *urgently*."

It was the first time Julia had ever talked to me like this. Normally, her being much younger, she was vaguely deferential. But obviously, I'd fazed her.

"On second thoughts," she went on, "don't call her. If you do, it'll probably get confrontational. She'll know I've been on the phone to you. We'll have been *conspiring*. I don't want to be tarred with that brush. Not after what I've just heard you say. She told me she'd call you tomorrow.

When you pick up, pretend you don't know why. You need to sort it out between you. It sounds sordid to me."

"Well, it wasn't."

"Good night, Hannah. Pleasant dreams."

She put the phone down to stress her sarcasm. Probably also to stop me getting in some kind of return dig.

She needn't have bothered. Fact is, I could see she had a point.

Maybe I had done wrong, all those years ago. I'd certainly buried it in the meantime.

Perhaps because I'd benefitted.

Victim or accessory? Or both? Anyway, there *had been* food.

Poor, poor Charlotte and her stupid, pathetic candles.

When, an hour later, Soraya came out onto the balcony and put her arms round me, I was still crying.

I Get Mercilessly Grilled

The sun came up suddenly, like it does in that part of the world, and my mood changed. I didn't feel sorry for Charlotte any more. In fact, I wanted to kill her. I couldn't wait to pick up the phone and give her a piece of my mind.

Obviously, the first thing I had to do was concoct a plausible lie for Soraya. This was family stuff, and it was bad. It needed containing, not spreading.

"What's the matter?" she asked, when she'd put her arms round me.

"Charlotte's business has gone down the dip," I said.

Feeble reason to cry, but it had to be something true, and that was all I could think of.

"Your sister?" Soraya said. "You mean her candle shop thingy?"

I nodded.

"Can't you just give her some money?" she asked.

"She won't accept it. Not from me. She's too proud." I had to force out the last three words.

"So what's going to happen to her? Will she lose her house?"

"I don't know."

"You could offer her a loan, couldn't you?"

"She won't take that either."

"You'd be surprised what people'll take when they've got their backs to the wall. She's got a kid, hasn't she?"

"A little boy. Seth."

"What's her husband do again? Is he in the candle business too?"

"Joint ownership, yes. Seventy-thirty hers."

"Why's it gone bust?"

I hadn't expected this kind of interrogation. I didn't actually know the answer, which probably wouldn't have mattered, but for some reason, I felt I had to make something up. "People have stopped buying candles for magical purposes, I think. That should be mag-*ick*-al, with a K. That's her niche. The *Women Who Run with the Wolves* and Harmony Nice set. It's what the Yankee Candle Company can't compete with. Or so she thought. Turns out they don't have to."

"So she's essentially making candles for zonked out

hippy-types, yeah?"

"I'm not sure – "

"No wonder she's gone down the pan. You can't rely on those sorts for a steady income. They're there one day, gone the next. And most of them are middle class. Your sister might think she's making a top-notch product, filling it with the spirit of the moon goddess and all that, but Jeremy and Jocasta only want authenticity when they can flaunt it. How are you going to flaunt a candle?"

"See your point." I hadn't expected her to take it this seriously. She was actually angry. The second time in twenty-four hours I wished I hadn't said anything.

"I should have a word with her," she said. "I could part buy her out and make the whole thing a bit more ruthless. And diversify. Together, we might be able to claw our way back from the brink. The hippies will always let you down in the end. Candles are due a comeback, in my opinion."

"Really."

"I'm serious."

"You've already got a job," I said. "You're a singer."

"I'm not going to be a singer for ever."

"Why not?"

"I'm not stupid. We're stuck in sixth in the US, and we'll probably find out we're stuck in seventh in the UK. Anyway, I'm only where I am because I look like I do."

"Rubbish."

"Ten years time, people will have forgotten me. And don't give me all that *but you can really sing* crap. The world's run by men, for men. There's always another great voice, but your body breaks down. Men want to see a better one."

I sighed. This was all because we were waiting for the UK Singles Chart and Venice had sucked the *joie de vivre* out of us, and Harlinne was probably in there somewhere too. And it was untrue. I couldn't cope with it now.

"There are better ways of diversifying than going into candles," I told her.

"It's not about candles," she said. "It's about you and me. Me stepping into the breach and rescuing your sister, and so indirectly helping you. Why? Because I love you."

I reached for her hand across the table and squeezed it. "I love you too," I said. "But let me try and sort it myself first. She's supposed to be ringing me today."

Womance/Sismance

I should probably explain about me and Soraya. First up, we've never actually had sex, whatever you might be thinking. Yet if it ever came to crunch-time, we'd do literally anything for each other. Routinely, we do a fair amount of touching, kissing, holding hands, and we exchange endearments and mean them. I love you, baby. And when we're on tour, or doing a gig, we sleep together – I mean in the same bed. Like sisters, maybe? 'Womance'? 'Sismance'? Both real words. She says I'm the only person she's ever truly loved.

That's it. That's all there is.

I say 'all' but of course it's a lot. Especially given that I'm married. I'm pretty sure Soraya's a lesbian, but as far as

I know, I'm neither straight nor gay nor bi. I love specific people, that's as much as I can honestly say. I love Tim and I love Soraya, but I'm not attracted to generalities like 'men' or 'women'. And I know how lame that sounds. But it is what it is.

And I don't *know* what it is. Not exactly.

And I don't feel the need to. Because I'm not unhappy. Far from it.

How do I love them? One: totally differently to the way I love (a) my biological family and (b) my friends. Two: in a way that's somehow based on physical and spiritual proximity – on breath and skin contact and smiles – even when we're apart for long periods (as Tim and I often are). Three: in a way that isn't primarily about sexual organs.

Maybe some of this is because I was born in 1981. I won't bore you with the details, but the statistics definitely support the idea that we millennials are having a lot less sex, and are happy with it. If that's so, maybe I'm not so screwy after all.

I'd never leave Tim, but nor would I ever leave Soraya. And they both know that. I'm exclusive to two people, but I can't whittle it down any further. If they ever decided to fight over me, and they got really serious about it, then I'd probably take myself off somewhere like Beachy Head. But I know for a fact that'll never happen. I'll explain later.

Do either of them ever have sex with other people? Soraya, yes, sometimes. I don't know the details, and I don't care. I want her to be happy. Tim: I doubt it. He feels the same way about me as I feel about him. We have sex, yes, but it's sex, that's all. It's not the proverbial be all and end all. It's not art, or great thought, or companionship or affection or even love: it's biology.

Anyway, I hope that clarifies matters.

But it probably doesn't, because that's only about 10% of it.

You'll have to wait for the other 90%. What we writers call a 'cliff hanger'.

Why?

Because I don't want you looking at me in a different way. I'm Hannah Lexingwood. I'm at the top of my game, as the cliché goes: manager of the world's number one rock band, mega-millionaire, world top ten influential person, &c. Strong, healthy, wealthy and wise.

And I definitely don't need looking after.

Time to Think

It seems to be a universal rule of life that you'll only ever get time to think deeply about something when you don't need it and would rather not have it. I waited all that day for Charlotte to ring, and she didn't.

Being in Venice didn't help. With the paparazzi decamped outside our hotel, and a shortage of dry land to hand, we were effectively confined to barracks. Four in the afternoon found us in exactly the same positions as yesterday: me in bed with laptop and earphones, Soraya sprawled on the sofa with headphones. This time, she was reading a novel. I couldn't see what it was, but, going by the cover's colour-scheme not one of Julia's, thank God. That would have been a bitter irony too far.

"I'm bored," she said eventually. "What are we doing tonight?"

"What would you like to do?"

"Haven't we been invited anywhere?"

"Lots of places. Three private parties, one boutique nightclub with VIP passes. Take your pick."

"I don't want to go anywhere people know us," she told me. "What about one of those jazz bars? We could get Ian and Fred, the security guys, to be our partners, just so we look normal, and we could get disguises. No one need know it's us. I'm sick of being the centre of attention all the time. It's okay normally, but here it's claustrophobic."

"We're leaving tomorrow. And depending on where *Top of My Tower* is, we may or may not feel like going out."

"You're right. Let's stay here and either celebrate or commiserate. In any case, I don't want to bump into Harlinne."

I laughed. "She's bang on the nail about climate change, though. A few weeks ago we were lying down on bridges in Central London, trying to stop traffic. Remember that?"

"Yeah, but at least Extinction Rebellion's doing something. Harlinne thinks it's all inevitable."

"She's a very good mover and shaker. She gets things done, so they say."

Soraya put her hand on her bald patch. "Yeah, thanks, Harlinne. Much appreciated."

"The cover of *Harper's* is worth the aggro."

"I doubt it. They need us more than we need them."

"Famous last words. Wait till after the Chart Show."

She scoffed. "You really think we'll have dropped?

Come on, we were seventh. That had to be a miscount. We'll be number one. I know it didn't happen in America, but it will, even there, I'm certain."

"When celebrities start thinking like that, it's usually because they've become complacent. Then they start getting cocky. Then they lose friends and alienate people, and suddenly, they're not so famous any more. To get back to the point, *Harper's Bazaar's* an institution. It's been around since the 1860s. It doesn't need anyone, let alone us."

"Moral of the story: be grateful for Harlinne."

"Exactly."

She laughed and broke into song. "Thank you, Harlinne. Thank you for the hairline. For making me itch like hell. Though you never got one yourself."

"What were you talking to her about, at the party?"

She turned to look suspiciously at me. "Funny time to ask."

"You don't have to say. I just wondered if she was trying to sign you up."

"Jealous?"

"Might be. Was she?"

"No."

"Fine."

"Fine," she echoed.

"Fine," I repeated.

"Happy now?"

"I'm fine."

"Want to know what we *were* talking about?" she asked. "Or are you just interested in what we *weren't?*"

"Since I'm your mother, I demand to know everything. And don't you dare leave anything out, young lady. I *will* find out."

"She used to organise road trips across the USA for tourists." She left a pregnant pause. "Call her, if you like. Ask her."

I laughed. "Bloody hell, I didn't know you were still thinking about that. How did you find out *she* was in that line of work?"

"Online. Then I messaged her and asked her about it. Just casually, while I finished listening to *All of the Stars*. Remember that? I told her not to tell you. When we met on the yacht, she wanted to discuss it. By that time, you'd got cold feet, and I assumed you'd be narked, so I took her off alone. But she's not the kind who takes no for an answer."

"Weird, given that she believes the end of the world's round the corner."

"*So true,* as Donald Trump would say. That's why I don't want to bump into her tonight."

"She's probably gone back to America now. She only came here as part of the *Harper's* thing and probably Marinello's party. Do you really want to go on a USA road trip?"

"One day, maybe. Not now. Let's just focus on worrying about *Top of My Tower* for the time being."

She put her novel to one side and picked up her phone. I went back to what I'd been doing earlier, which was searching for signs of Charlotte on the internet. She was a ferocious blogger as a rule, but, perhaps for obvious reasons, 'Contemplations of a West Country Candle Creator' hadn't been updated for several days.

Four pm. Since the UK was an hour behind us, still sixty minutes till Radio 1 revealed all. Or started to. It was a two-hour show, and God willing, we wouldn't learn our fate till the end, or close to. We'd listen together online, as always, clutching each other ever more tightly from number ten downwards and ... I didn't have a good feeling about this. Usually, we'd celebrate. We weren't used to losing. How would we cope if it really *was* bad news?

I'd been so busy searching for clues about my sister, I hadn't noticed what Soraya was doing. She had a half-empty bottle of Scotch by her side. She took a pull.

Have you drunk all that? would make her angry. It didn't pay to confront her when she was liquoring up, as she obviously was now. Over the years, it had become less and less of a problem. Partly because I'd helped her. But success had also done her good.

Maybe she was making up for being such a goody-goody at the party last night. More ominously, perhaps, underneath, she was as scared about the next two hours as I was.

In any case, I knew how to deal with it. "Are you going to share that?" I asked.

She grinned. "I was wondering when you were going to ask."

Hard & Soft Drugs and Other Animals

I was wondering when you were going to ask. Probably by now, you're thinking, where are all the drugs? Fully

Magic Coal Tar Lounge is a rock 'n' roll band (according to me; you'll get a different assessment from Soraya: more like 'an everything band'), so where are all the drugs? That yacht in the lagoon, for example. Shouldn't we all – Soraya, Harlinne and I – have repaired to the toilet for twenty minutes to do a line or three? Shouldn't our noses be rotting? Shouldn't someone – the hotel manager, perhaps, or one of the paparazzi – have, at some point, found at least one of us face-down in a pool of her own vomit with a needle sticking out of her arm? Shouldn't that person be blue in the face and cold to the touch? *If I hadn't called the ambulance in time ... I can't imagine! ... She/ they can't go on like this ... She's/ they're headed for an early grave!* Hey, that's the music biz. That's the expectation.

It's a lot to live up to. Soraya grew up on a council estate in Rotherham. In her world, you either hung with the druggies, or you avoided them altogether. Largely due to her dad, she took the latter route. Not easily, from what she tells me.

I'm middle-class through and through. I did cannabis in my late teens and early twenties, but I was always conscious that (pathetic though it sounds) *my parents wouldn't really approve.*

So there we are. What it boils down to, once again, dear reader, is that both Soraya and I are millennials. As such, we actually care what our parents think. Long after we 'should'.

Should in inverted commas. Because actually, that's a good thing. As is the fact that we're not sex-obsessed. In most cultures, it'd be seen as a virtue.

But of course, we do fantasise about drugs.
Sometimes.

I remember a conversation Soraya and I had last New Year's Eve.

SORAYA: I'm pissed. Happy pissed.
HANNAH: (Laughs) Me too!
SORAYA: How about taking it to the next level?
HANNAH: Meaning what?
SORAYA: There's an old guy back there selling LSD.
HANNAH: LSD?
SORAYA: You know: as in, *The Beatles*? I can get us two tabs.
HANNAH: Don't bother.
SORAYA: Really?
HANNAH: You don't know how pure it is. Or what it is. It's not like the 1960s, where you had a *bona fide* counterculture, selflessly devoted to turning the world on by any means necessary. You actually had qualified chemists in those days, trying to make it hundred per cent pure. Nowadays, all you have is chancers, out to make a buck. We could easily end up having a bad trip. They say you never recover from that. Ever.

(Long pause)

SORAYA: That was quite articulate for a drunk.
HANNAH: Thank you.

SORAYA: A bit like a university lecture.
HANNAH: Thanks.
SORAYA: (Sighs) Okay then, you win. Fancy another drink?
HANNAH: I'll have half a pint of lager, please.
SORAYA: Oh, come *on*, Hannah!
HANNAH: (Laughs) *What?*
SORAYA: At least make it a *full pint!*
HANNAH: I *can't!*
SORAYA: Compromise then. Two pints between us.
HANNAH: (Shrugs) Yeah, okay.

One day, we'll do LSD. We'll go into a parallel world, and see everything anew.

That's our dream. We're just waiting for another Owsley Stanley.

How We Ended Up Breaking the Law

For some reason, probably because I was so focused on Charlotte, I didn't actually check my own email. Who does email nowadays? For business purposes, okay, but personal stuff?

Answer: a writer. Specifically, a novelist. By this time, I'd stopped caring so much. Soraya had passed me the Scotch and, after a few swigs, I was in *que sera, sera* mode. Alcohol has a way of doing that, of course, depending on the mood you're in when you start.

By the time I spotted the message (title: 'Lottie latest'), the UK countdown was halfway through. We'd just had fifteen, and we were in the middle of Yellow Bob, 'Misty'. So far, so good, but still a way to go.

I haven't a phone signal this end, so I hope this reaches you. I've had another talk with Charlotte. She may have changed her mind. Rethink, therefore: you need to call her. She knows I've spoken to you. She's scared you're going to blow your top. Don't, obviously.

I wasn't in the mood for this. How did Julia get to be such a bossyboots all of a sudden?

To be fair to her, though, this was serious.

Typical Charlotte. Telling Julia she wants to name me as an accessory or a witness, then worrying about me 'blowing my top'.

Mind you, nothing Charlotte ever did made sense. I'm surprised the candle shit hadn't gone bust in the noughties.

Julia had sent this message an hour ago. That's how long it had taken me to do the sensible thing and look at my own inbox.

An hour. Mind you, why *should* I look at my email? Why couldn't she do Facebook Messenger or Twitter or Snapchat, like a normal person?

Because she was bloody Julia, that's why. And she *wasn't* normal. Four years ago, just before she met Knut, her boyfriend died in a fire, and she lost her memory. Bad time. I won't go into the details because they're a matter of public record, but no one in my family's *entirely* right in the head. Maybe Mum, that's all.

Another thirty minutes wouldn't hurt. One thing at a time. I really, really needed to know where *Top of My Tower* was. Once I'd got closure on that, I could cope with anything. In fact, with a bit of Scotch inside me, a conversation with Charlotte would probably be a whole lot easier. I should call her soon as I found out about *Tower*, before the effects wore off. Or before they got worse; before I started getting super grouchy.

It was while I was trying to work out what I needed to say that I became aware of two things: a song I recognised, and Soraya on her feet with a face like thunder.

I'd love to say the truth kicked in like a bad dream, but that would be a cliché. The fact is, I didn't need any sense of being flung over a cliff edge, because Soraya saved me the trouble.

"Thirteen," she said. "We're at thirteen."

Like four hammer blows. Each ramming the central fact home.

Thirteen?

Thirteen?

'Shocked' would be an understatement; but at least I recognised myself. I was Traumatised Hannah, one of the less alluring versions of me. I didn't recognise Soraya at all. She'd actually come out in hives. She stood in her underwear with that horrendous bald patch, head drooping, hair (what remained of it) tangled, mouth open, arms limp, knees trembling, looking like she was about to cry; and that the reason she was about to cry was she'd just been attacked by something with full authority to inflict limitless suffering. Like Radio 1.

"We're at number thirteen," she said.

"I can't believe it," I said. I was talking to myself as much as her. "What's wrong with people? This is our *best song!*"

"*Best song ever!* What's it mean? *What does it mean, Hannah?*"

I could probably have cobbled together an answer, but I could see it was a rhetorical question. She *knew* what it meant. It meant we'd lost the ability to assess our own work.

"WHAT DOES IT MEAN?" Her phone rang, snapping her out of monomania – by which I mean, she turned robotically and picked it up. "Hello?"

Thirteen!

Shit, that was bad.

Before I could ask her who was calling, my own phone rang. I looked at the screen to make sure it wasn't bloody Charlotte. Last thing I needed.

It wasn't. It was Elliot, the songwriter, one of the band. *Four great guys, one stellar woman.* Which sounded so hollow now.

"I assume you've been listening to the radio," he said laconically. "I'd just like to say sorry. I thought it was my best ever song."

"It *is!*"

"The world doesn't seem to think so."

Soraya went into the bathroom, then she apparently changed her mind. She turned and rushed out at speed. She screamed. She kicked a table. She pushed four vases over. She picked up a fifth and threw it at the mirror opposite the bed.

I ducked to avoid the explosion. "I have to go," I told Elliot.

"Is that who I think it is?" he asked. "Has she been drinking again?"

"Just a bit."

She picked up two fistfuls of flowers and hurled them at the dressing table, then knocked four more vases over. She grabbed a bunch of gladioli by the petals and ran onto the balcony and threw them down into the street where the paparazzi were. Distant yells of mingled indignation and appreciation. Someone wolf whistled. She was still in her underwear, and, although she didn't look like anyone's idea of a hot date – more like Gollum in lingerie – it was definitely what some of them had been waiting for. They probably couldn't believe their luck. She rushed back in, grabbed two vases full of flowers and took them out onto the balcony and threw them down into the street, vases and all, and started screaming obscenities.

I ran outside and grabbed her. She tried to kiss my lips. We fell over, smashing something or other, and started wrestling. One of us was bleeding: that was blood on the floor. I laughed. She grabbed my hair and tried to kiss me again. I rammed half an orchid into her mouth.

Ten minutes later, the police arrived.

Just Like the Hellraisers of Yore

You don't get much of that any more: rock stars trashing hotel rooms. I'm not saying I ever approved, but I suppose it's what the public gets when it pays you a zillion dollars a week but imprisons you in a succession of small, identical, and horribly anonymous living spaces. You know you're allowed to go ape-shit because you can pay for whatever damage you cause. And it relieves the tension. Even though you usually feel a bit guilty, the relief always trumps the guilt.

You've probably twigged by now: this isn't the first time something like this has ever happened.

Just not with such a dark backdrop. Never anything like seventh to thirteenth.

I didn't find out till later, but Soraya wasn't just drinking and listening to the radio. She was reading magazine articles on her phone. Music magazine articles. And they all seemed to know what was coming. And they loved it.

Things like: *All Good Things Must Come to an End? It looks as if the mighty Lexingwood-Coal Tar machine might finally be about to come off the rails. According to an unofficial UK chart released yesterday, the band's latest offering,* Top of My Tower, *could be headed for the most spectacular drop of any Fully Magic Coal Tar single since the band formed in 2009, and the first from outside the top five since they appointed Hannah Lexingwood manager in 2012…*

And: *One false step for the world's most 'right on' band. As an outsider, and certainly not a fan, I've always found it difficult to work out just how Soraya Snow and Hannah Lexingwood manage to maintain a chart topping rock career and still find time to virtue-signal at the scores of left-ish protests they seem delighted to attend. On the evidence of* Top of My Tower, *however, their juggling act is becoming increasingly difficult to …*

And: *Soraya Snow and Hannah Lexingwood: Time Up for Britain's Most Prominent Snowflakes? A little bird tells me* Top of My Tower *may be about to go the same way as The Woke Duo's ill-conceived mania for Bitcoin, in which they're rumoured to have lost at least £20 million…*

Of course there were the usual wordplays: *Not so Fully Magic This Time, Has the Full Magic Run Out? Only Slightly Magic, The Coal Tar Magic: Half Full or Half Empty?*

And the customary desperate attempts to get something out of Soraya's surname. *Snow Joke When Your Turkey's Cooked, Snowflake Soraya Heading for a Heavy Fall? Please Don't Let the Snow Fall*, and so on and so on *ad nauseam*.

Snowflake: it used to be a synonym for someone who crumbles easily. Lately, it's morphed to mean anyone with a predilection to liberalism. It means you're into social media, you like cats doing cute things on Instagram (what the hell's wrong with *that?*), you're pro-Europe, you're into human rights, gender politics, Noam Chomsky, you at least *sympathise* with vegans, and you think more or less anything's preferable to war and violence. Yes, you may sometimes get emotional, but bloody hell, let's be fair: thanks to the Establishment, the world *is* a *hell* of a lot crapper than it ought to be.

The police – two male officers with bulky uniforms and grim faces – frogmarched us downstairs and into a boat. I didn't know where they were taking us, but we were a long time aboard, and when we alighted, we were on a quayside somewhere I didn't recognise. It was cloudy and raining, and there were single-storey industrial units and cranes. A new set of police officers handcuffed us and transferred us to a van. Again, the journey took an age. Somewhere far inland.

I noticed that Soraya had a black eye. Had I given her that? It looked pretty cool. It'd probably look even better on the mug shot.

My lip hurt. I touched it. Blood.

Of course, we wouldn't be charged. We had Maxwell Clunes, an expensive public relations firm, to take care of that sort of thing. Someone – Maria or Nora, most likely – would smooth things over with the hotel and, assuming no one had been seriously hurt, with the photographers. They'd offer an exclusive interview in exchange. By now, I was more worried about Charlotte. I'd been supposed to be ringing her.

The last two hours had the taste of a scripted downfall.

Soraya and I spent a night apart in two cells. When we next met, it was on the way to a crisis meeting with our 'people': the four other members of the band, two top executives from the record company, their accountant, an image consultant, our live gig agent, two lawyers, Nora from Maxwell Clunes. By this time – first thing I did when the police receptionist gave me my phone back – I'd called Charlotte.

I'd realised what was coming, you see. I may be a millennial *snowflake* drip, but I didn't get to be one of the world's top music execs for no reason. A sixth sense, you might call it. Foreknowledge. Once armed with it, I move fast. Thought, knowledge, conclusion, action, bang, bang, bang, not a second to lose: every plank nailed in place to my exact specifications, and by the time the sun goes behind a cloud and it starts drizzling, I've built Noah's Ark. Anyone, or anything, I don't like gets left outside.

So what exactly did I foresee?

Firstly, the band was going to split up. The decision had already been taken, and neither Soraya nor I had been consulted. It would probably come as a huge shock to her. If I'd found out yesterday, I'd have been the same. They'd try to tell us nicely, because they were nice guys, and they'd hope we could go on being friends. Soraya would see it as the end of her world. She'd probably be suicidal.

Second, Charlotte had the power to destroy me. She wouldn't even know she'd done it till it was too late. But even with her assurances to Julia, that outcome was still on the cards. She was massively unpredictable.

So my sister had to be taken care of, and the band had to be kept together.

What next then? Easy. I made the decision early, while Soraya and I were still in the police van.

We were going on a road trip across America. And we were taking Charlotte.

PART TWO:

MORE ITALY

O Give Me a Dollop More Strength, Lord

Two women from Maxwell Clunes awaited me in the foyer of the police station while a uniformed receptionist returned my phone sealed in a little transparent bag. They looked to be in their thirties with bobs and designer glasses. As befitted a couple of PR company lawyers representing a rock and roll rebel, they wore brand new leather jackets, jeans and trainers. Like extras from *Grease*. They smiled.

"I'm Judy," the taller one said when I'd finished signing forms and we were on the way outside. "This is Maddie. There'll be no charges, of course. No one was hurt. Nora's set up a meeting for you with the other band members and a few members of your corporate team."

"What sort of meeting?" I asked, trying to sound as if I hadn't expected something of the kind.

"We don't really know," Maddie said.

"We're only mid-level clearance, I'm afraid," Judy quipped. "We've merely been asked to accompany you and answer any questions you might have about the legal side: you and Soraya, that is. Set your minds at rest."

"What if we don't *want* to go to a meeting?" I asked.

It was both a stupid question and a good one.

Stupid because *Top of My Pointless Crappy Tower* had just bombed, everyone had obviously flown over here to be with us, and, given that we were likely only looking at a twenty-minute car journey, why *wouldn't* we want to meet up? *Good* because I'm the manager and I'm the one who calls the shots. People don't usually get to set up meetings and subpoena me.

"I – I don't know," Judy replied. "They're all waiting for you."

I suddenly felt sorry for her. She was doing her best. "It was a hypothetical question," I said. "You've just got me out of jail. I'm in your hands. Could I get some ice for my lip?"

"Absolutely!"

So my presentiments had all been correct. This was Fully Magic Split-Up Lounge. It would happen with or without Soraya and I, and it was fully deducible in the here and now from (a) my being summoned and (b) Maddie and Judy's obvious reluctance to be drawn.

The paparazzi awaited us outside. It was super sunny. Maddie touched my arm gently to indicate that I should stop walking before we reached the police station's threshold. She took out her phone.

"The limo's just by the kerb," she told me. "We've got six guys waiting to escort you. I'll call them now, if that's okay?"

It was about eight yards away. "Where's Soraya?" I asked.

"Upstairs. Down any second. Judy's just texting her."

"I don't want to go outside yet. I need to make a phone call in private. It'll only take a minute. Not in the back of the car. It's delicate."

Maddie considered this. "I'm not sure we can guarantee anywhere completely private in here. There's always a possibility of someone overhearing, and if it's a personal call of some nature, some of the details could easily leak to the press. Why don't you wait till we get to the hotel? I can set you up with a vacant room and you can lock the door. I mean, before you go up to the meeting?"

"That's a really good suggestion," I said. "Thank you. I've had a rough night, and I'm clearly not thinking straight. It's a good job you're here."

She flushed with pleasure. "That's absolutely no problem! Don't mention it!"

The Wonderful Unreasonable Demands of Your Average Rock Star

Soraya and I wore beanies, oversized T-shirts, sweat pants, grey socks and multi-coloured sliders. She had sunglasses to hide her black eye. We made it to the car without incident, although I won't say we weren't yelled at and taunted. Anything to get a reaction, but with six minders in the wings and Maddie and Judy reassuring us like we might panic, things weren't likely to get out of control.

"There'll be more photographers at the hotel," Maddie said. For a moment, I was indignant – I really didn't need to be told how these things worked – then I saw: she wasn't telling me: she was telling Judy.

"They're actually following us!" Judy said. She sounded both gleeful and horrified.

I suddenly realised, as I occasionally did, how weird all this was. Being chased at low speed by a horde of peeping cars, mopeds and scooters. Obviously, I knew ordinary people didn't have to put up with it. But I sometimes forgot: they didn't have to put up with *anything remotely similar*.

"This is crazy!" Maddie said in the same tone of mingled elation and dread.

When we got to The Felicity Inn, we rushed inside like we were re-enacting *A Hard Day's Night*. The hotel security team was on hand to make the reception area a paparazzi-free Green Zone. Maddie had rung ahead to procure a room where I could call Charlotte, but she still had to confirm the details. Lots of staff waited to greet us. We said hello several times, accepted two bunches of flowers and the manager's personal welcome, signed a few autographs for five of the guests and smiled a lot in the way rock stars aren't supposed to. *Hi, I'm Ms Chart Topper, pleased to meet you, hope I've made your day.* When, out of the blue, Soraya asked for a large strawberry gelato with chocolate sprinkles, the manager looked like his dreams had come true. A diva: hopefully, this would be the first of a torrent of demands, each more unreasonable than the last, culminating with, *I want a tinfoil hat, people, now*. Something to entertain his friends and relations with for the rest of his life.

"Where are you going?" Soraya asked me, when Maddie confirmed the room.

"I've got to phone Charlotte. Just stay here. I'll be back."

"Can't I come with you? I won't listen if you don't want me to. I can put some headphones on and listen to music."

I turned to Maddie. "Have they sent over our things from the *Adriatico?*"

"I, er, think so." Her phone hovered, like was it all right for her to call someone and get a more definitive answer?

"Ask the manager to get me a pair of headphones and an MP3 player with a few pre-loaded tracks," I said. "It doesn't matter what."

"Absolutely," Maddie said.

"Come with me," I told Soraya. I couldn't just leave her on her own, sitting on a chair eating her gelato, complete strangers papping her on their phones and talking about her like she couldn't hear them.

She picked up her ice-cream and followed Maddie and I. We walked along two corridors and entered a ground floor room with an *en suite*.

"The headphones will be along in a minute," Maddie said. "Is this room okay, size-wise?"

"It's perfect," I replied.

"I'll go in the shower and lock the door," Soraya told me. "I won't hear anything. Please could you get me some new clothes?" she asked Maddie. "I stink."

"Absolutely," Maddie said. It was the first time Soraya had spoken to her. Never mind that Maddie was probably a highly trained professional with several years at university behind her, Soraya had actually used the word 'please'. "Any preference?" she asked, registering almost too late that clothes were a minefield.

"A dress, tights, shoes, jeans, anything," Soraya said flatly.

"And cancel the headphones," I added. "I'd rather not be disturbed."

Maddie closed herself out with an ingratiating smile. Soraya hurriedly finished her gelato, took off her sunglasses and went into the shower. She locked the door behind her. I took out my phone and pressed 'call'.

It rang three times. I felt a rage coming on at the very thought of it going to voicemail. I hadn't even considered that possibility – till now.

"Hannah?" Charlotte said. "Is that you?"

"Hi," I replied in as even a tone as I could manage. Now I'd actually got through, I realised I didn't have a script. "How're things?"

"I – I know what you're ringing for. I just want to tell you, before you get mad: it's not going to happen. Me suing Dad, I mean. It was just a crazy idea I had. Things haven't been going too well for me and Marcus lately. I mean, in the business sense. Not in the bedroom."

"Slightly too much information at the end there."

She sighed. "Yeah, sorry. To be honest, I'd had a bottle and a half of wine when I rang Julia the other night. I never really had any intention of suing anyone. True, Dad locked us in that room, and he played us all that horrible music more or less non-stop, until I actually cried, insisting that we listen to it and so on, but well, that's Dad."

I laughed. "Bloody hell, Charlotte. Don't make excuses for him. It *was* wrong."

"You're on my side?"

"Up to a point. I'm not sure it's a sue-able wrong. It wasn't very nice, and I can see how it might have been scary – you were younger than me – but I think you'd be hard-pressed to get a judge to recognise it as actual abuse. He just wanted us to like his kind of music, that's all."

"I guess. But why?"

"Parents do stupid things sometimes when they want their kids to turn out a certain way. Look at all the dads who pressure their sons to be good at football. They can be utterly screwy and unpleasant about it. Or parents who want their kids to be great musicians, or get fabulous exam results; who are trying to live vicariously through their children. *You WILL stay there and practise until you get it RIGHT, I don't care HOW long it takes or HOW hard you cry!* Arguably, they're all 'abusers' of a sort."

"Marcus says it's a snowflake's definition of abuse."

That word again. I sighed. But Marcus had a point.

"He says Dad just cared about us," Charlotte continued. "And he wasn't right in the head. That's why he did it."

"I'm sure that's true. And I think he regretted it afterwards. He never tried anything similar again."

"He never said sorry, though."

I nodded. "That's true. I might have a word with him."

"Maybe you should."

"I will."

I think we knew we were entering dangerous territory. The truth is, we'd inherited completely different outlooks on what had happened. At some point during the internment, something in me had clicked: I saw how pathetic he was, but also why he was so desperate for us to like his music. And how it was even better after a glass of bourbon. After the second day, I stopped feeling annoyed or resentful. I actually felt grateful.

There'd been no eureka moment for Charlotte, though. For her, it'd just been cruelty. And that was the essence of the problem, for both of us. What had happened in those few days had in some way *created* me. But it didn't become right by virtue of being 50% successful. Obviously not.

"I *will* have a word with him," I said. "That wasn't the only reason I rang. Soraya and I are going on a road trip across the USA, and we want you to come."

"Oh, wow. I can't."

I hooted. "That was quick! Why not?"

"I'd have to leave little Seth behind. Are you taking baby Lek?"

"Actually, no. Tim's got some time off, and Lek's no longer breast-feeding, and that's why God invented Skype: so my lovely daughter could live in England and I could carry on globe-trotting, and we need never be apart. And I don't feel any guilt about that. Whatsoever. All the time. Anyway, you should try it."

"I don't deserve a holiday."

"You mean because the candles failed?"

I heard her swallow. "Yes."

"In that case, I've got good news. I've been talking to Soraya. She thinks they can be made to pay."

"*Your* Soraya? Soraya *Snow*? I mean, don't get me wrong: fabulous. But just putting my business hat on for a moment, what does she know about candles?"

"It's not a question of that. It's a question of her having an unlimited income and easy access to top business consultants."

"Sounds like selling out to The Man to me. No disrespect to Soraya. I'm not saying she's The Man. But maybe she knows The Man. A bit."

I laughed. "Put it like this: you can either get a little help from The Man and keep the candles, or you can walk away from The Man and say goodbye to the candles for ever. If you choose the latter, The Man wins. Because The Man wants to see you on your knees, totally candle-less. And I can't believe I'm talking like this."

"So what are you proposing? I go on a road trip with you and Soraya, and some top-notch business consultants come in and salvage the candle business, and they show Marcus what to do, and when I get back, everything's back to re-set, and hunky-dory?"

"Has The Man ever let anyone down?"

"So won't Soraya then own it?"

"Soraya may have access to quality business advice, but she's no interest in making a long-term living from candles. She's doing this because she loves me, and she knows you and I need a prolonged opportunity to talk."

"Does she know what about?"

"No, but she knows it's important."

"Why can't we just talk then? Why the 'road trip across America' thing?"

"Because Soraya actually wants a road trip across America. And this way, we all win."

"Do I get free child care?"

"Yep."

I know it's impossible but I actually heard her smile down the phone. "Done."

"Hooray! I'll be in touch. Got to go now. I've an urgent meeting to attend."

I hung up and turned to the bathroom door. *"You can come out now!"*

Musical Differences

Maddie was waiting to escort us to the penthouse suite. When we walked in, the others didn't look particularly pleased to see us. There was a low table with drinks and snacks, and fourteen padded armchairs, all cream, subtly facing it. In any honest business meeting, the table would have been waist-height, and the chairs would have been designed to fit it, and we'd have sat tucked in, straight-backed, in a strict rectangle. But the music business wasn't honest. Let's face it, how can the commodification of creativity ever really be honest? So we'd have to lounge around like we were having some kind of love-in while, one by one, the execs and the other band members stuck their knives into our backs.

It got off to a bad start. "What the hell's going on?" Soraya demanded.

Including us two, there were fourteen people in the room. The two record company guys, Will and Jeremy, our live gig agent, Anwulika, Nora from Maxwell Clunes and Sanjay the accountant, had all donned smiles and advanced to greet us. Soraya's hostility stopped them in their tracks.

"Have a canapé, Soraya," Elliot said, without looking at her. "They're specially designed for 'not-yet vegans' like you. Normal canapés. Have one."

In total, five people had put on false smiles and tried to go through the motions. That left seven who hadn't. Ominously, four of those were band members.

"What's going on, Elliot?" I asked, repeating Soraya's question but without the aggression.

Elliot turned to face me as I took the only remaining chair in the room. "Where do you see us being in ten years' time, Hannah?" he asked.

"Would you like a drink, Hannah?" Kathleen said sweetly, getting up. "Soraya?"

"I'll have a tequila," Soraya said.

Gaz let out a theatrical groan. "Yeah, that's a good answer to a straight question, Soz. Ten years' time, rehab. If you're lucky."

"Don't call me Soz," Soraya said.

"Why not?" Gaz shot back.

"We don't have any spirits, Soraya," Kathleen said, as if she was talking to a child. "You can have a glass of white wine. It's very good. It's Gavi di Gavi La Scolca Bobo."

Soraya looked at her as if she was deranged.

I turned to Elliot. "Bigger and better. That's where I see us in ten years' time. Roughly, where U2 and the Rolling Stones are now. Unassailable."

Gaz laughed. "The Stones have Jagger, obviously, and U2's got Bono, but neither are out front in quite the way Soraya is."

"Talk about me as if I'm not here," Soraya said.

"That's nonsense," I said. "It's 'Fully Magic Coal Tar Lounge', not 'Soraya and the Coal Tars'. We've all got roles. We're equally integral. And if you're going to criticise Soraya because she goes on the occasional bender, you might as well go and join a chamber orchestra. This is rock music. It's part of the lifestyle."

Gaz shrugged. "Believe it or not, I don't want to see her getting hurt. Too many good people have become martyrs to the phoney 'rock and roll lifestyle'. It's a delusion. You're actually being sacrificed on the altar of corporate profit."

I sighed. "Point taken."

"I take it you noticed how *Top of My Tower* bombed," Elliot said.

The record executives let out a string of protests. Will finally got his voice above the others: "I'd hardly describe seventh as bombing!"

Sanjay the accountant looked equally sceptical. "I can't recall the last time U2 or the Rolling Stones got more than that. Seventh is good!"

"Maybe that's because you don't know anything about the charts," Elliot told him. "Sorry," he added, "that's was uncalled for."

"Don't mention it," Sanjay said, helping himself to a mini pizza.

It was the sort of meeting fourteen snowflakes might have. Heading in a fixed direction whilst deeply concerned to be inoffensive.

"I must admit I was worried about dropping from seventh yesterday," I said. "Thirteenth is a long way to fall, and not very lucky. But then I remembered: we don't make our money from records. We make it from live performances."

"I don't care about the money any more," Olly said, from the corner. "I don't want another year like 2015. A hundred and twenty gigs. I know we made five hundred million, but I've got my cut now."

"What *do* you actually want?" I asked. I looked over towards Paul, sitting by the curtains, the only member of the band who hadn't spoken yet. He simply shrugged. Typical Paul.

"Have you seen the music press lately?" Elliot asked. "Have you seen what they're saying about us? It wasn't a freak accident that *Top of My Tower* bombed. Arguably, it was inevitable."

"I'm sure that's an exaggeration, Elliot," Sanjay said. "With respect."

"Maybe that's because you don't know anything about the charts," Elliot told him for the second time. "Sorry," he added again, "that's was uncalled for."

"Don't mention it," Sanjay said again.

Elliot turned to our image consultant. "Colleen?"

"Thank you, Elliot," Colleen said, in the tone of someone about to make a speech at a funeral. "We've done a lot of research lately – "

"At our request," Will said.

"What we've discovered is that Fully Magic Coal Tar Lounge is increasingly coming to be associated with a specific kind of political outlook."

"We've always been that," I shot back.

"Unfortunately, it's an outlook that's becoming less and less fashionable," Colleen said. "We, er, suspect it's beginning to turn young people off a little."

"It's just the music press against us now," Elliot said. "Soon it'll be the tabloids."

"So this is what it's come to," I said bitterly. "We're scared of the bloody tabloids."

"Your fight was never ours," Gaz said. "You and Soraya are the politicos, not us four. We're just ordinary guys."

"For what it's worth," Olly said. "I hate politics."

"You and Soraya are the ones who used to hang out with Chapman Hill," Elliot said. "Not us. It was you who masterminded World War O, not us. You and Soraya went to that press conference in London to expose the Lord Mayor. You were Crunch magazine's Person of the Year, not any of us. You and Soraya joined Extinction Rebellion for that lie-in, not us."

"What we're suggesting is that we have a long break," Gaz said. "Not exactly a split, because we're all friends, always have been, always will be. Just a musical break."

"Sod off," Soraya said.

"We work on solo projects for a few years," Elliot said, ignoring her, "and perhaps we do a reunion in 2024, or some time after that."

"It works," Gaz said, "because it makes the five of us more like independent players. We don't all stand or fall on the strength of one person."

"You mean me," Soraya said emotionally.

"Obviously, yes," Gaz said. "Two, if we count you, Hannah. You're sort of inseparable nowadays."

"It's best for all of us," Elliot said. "Look, put it another way. I asked you, Hannah, when you came in here, where you see us in ten years time. Your answer? The same, only bigger. But the projections suggest that's not possible."

Out of the corner of my eye, I noticed the record executives and the accountant nodding sagely. In fact, everyone – except Soraya.

"Or rather, it *is* possible," Elliot continued. "But only by restoring us to our original form: five different, equally important individuals. Continuing as we are means four of us fading increasingly into the background, and Soraya taking more and more flak on the front line. And all the evidence suggests she doesn't handle that sort of pressure well."

"Agreed," I said. "I've been hoping we're on the same wavelength, and we are. Time we split up. It's long overdue. Soraya and I have been discussing it for a while."

"Er, what?" Paul said, his first words.

Gaz, Elliot and Olly exchanged looks whose meaning was: *She's calling our bluff, trying to make like* she *thought of splitting up first – even though Elliot didn't call it 'splitting up': he called it 'a long break' (which, hey, guys, means she's trying to up the stakes in the hope that we'll backpedal). Stay strong, guys,* stay strong! No backpedalling!

"I didn't say 'split up,'" Elliot said coolly. "I said, 'take a long break.'"

"We still love you two guys," Gaz said.

"And we love you," I replied, "but, well, all good things must come to an end. Maybe it really is time to say goodbye."

The record execs were exchanging alarmed looks of the *for God's sake start backpedalling!* variety. A war between male band members and non-musical advisers was suddenly on the cards. Obviously, the former would win: they might be heavily outnumbered, but they held all the cards. Meanwhile, Soraya and I had drawn a line in the sand. We had no choice but to stay where we were. Net result: the band was fated to break up.

I turned to Elliot. "Before everyone in the room starts fighting, can I just ask you something?"

He met my gaze. "Anything you like."

"When you were young, did your dad do anything to influence your taste in music?"

He frowned. "What kind of a question is that?"

"You said 'anything you like'," I replied.

"He was a music teacher," he said rancorously, as if he knew I was trying to humiliate him, but hadn't yet worked out how.

"My dad used to make me listen to punk rock in the car on the way to school," Gaz volunteered for no apparent reason. "Obviously, I didn't like it, but I got used to it. What's your point?"

"Look, guys," I said, "I realise I've been a shit manager recently, but I really, really want us to stay together, and so does Soraya. Fully Magic Coal Tar Lounge is a marriage of five people, and it's for life. I admit, I haven't had any new ideas for a long time, and you're right: it's time I started delivering again. We started off as a five-person, all-equally-valuable combo, and we need to get back to that. But I need time to think."

"So what are you proposing, Hannah?" Nora, the head PR honcho, said. She was a black Glaswegian, at least twenty years older than everyone else, and her voice carried a mellow authority.

"Soraya and I are going on a road trip across America," I said. "It's going to be cathartic, to do with my dad – I can't be any more specific than that, and I'm trusting you to keep it completely to yourselves – which is why I asked you that question, Elliot. I wasn't being obtuse or snarky. I'm in a bad place at the moment, and I need your understanding. Give me the trip to come up with some new ideas. I'll pitch them to you when Soraya and I get back, and if you don't like them, then we'll all go on your 'long break', as you call it, and re-form in 2024 – or whenever you want. Be warned, though: if you don't want to stay with me and Soraya, I'll cut my present ties with all four of you. I can't manage five separate individuals, however much I might want to. But I pray to God it won't come to that."

A stunned pause. Then the whole room applauded, the music execs first, then the band members. Paul and Kathleen, at different ends of the room, burst into tears.

Elliot stood up with both palms raised for quiet.

One by one, everyone obliged him.

"How long's it going to take," he asked, "this road trip of yours?"

"I don't know," I said. "Could be a month, could be a year."

Everyone simultaneously started Googling. *How long does a road…*

"It says two to three months!" Olly announced a second later, holding his phone up.

He registered the sceptical expressions surrounding him and double-checked. "Sorry, that's for visiting every state," he said. "Maybe you don't want to do that."

"It's not very rock 'n' roll," Gaz said.

"Forty hours, mine says," Colleen announced, once again holding Google aloft as if it was a magic wand, "which, it says here, you could break down into *five days of driving, eight hours apiece, with four overnight stops.* So five days total."

I laughed. "*Five days?* We might as well be on bloody tour if we're going to bloody *race* across! No way! Anyway, what's it got to do with anyone except me and Soraya? Are you giving me an ultimatum? *Five days to come up with a plan to save the band, Hannah, or we're walking?* Is that what you're saying?"

Silence. Then Elliot. "Obviously not. But I don't want to be in limbo for ever."

"So what do you propose?" I asked nicely. There were lots of things worse than the band going on an amicable break. Like me and Elliot having a blazing row, and him telling me to stuff my pathetic play for time. I needed to tone it down a bit.

"Ten weeks," Soraya interposed. "That's an exact figure. I got it from Harlinne."

"Who's 'Harlinne'?" Elliot said.

"She's organising it for us," Soraya replied.

Suddenly, the conversation had been whipped from beneath me. I was still thinking in one direction; it was going the exact opposite way. The wrong way.

Before I could recover sufficiently, Soraya got her next sentence in:

"She's an expert. You can Google her, if you like. Harlinne Vobrosky, The Vobrosky Agency, New York City."

"You mean the same Harlinne that secured us the *Harper's* job?" Nora said approvingly. "I've heard very good things about her. Two of my friends went on one of her excursions. They thoroughly enjoyed themselves." She laughed. "I mean, once they'd got over the shock. I didn't know she did tourism any more. I thought she'd moved on."

"I persuaded her to change her mind," Soraya said, as if this was in the same league as breaking the Enigma code.

Elliot smiled, shrugged and turned to me. "Okay, ten weeks sounds good to me. You've got yourselves a deal."

"What do you mean, 'shock'?" I asked Nora.

"She's a tiny bit crazy," she replied, not explaining anything.

"We knew that," Soraya interrupted. "That's what we want. We need a shake-up if we're going to come up with new ideas. Alcohol, drugs, a few rattlesnakes in the back of the car – "

"We're not doing drugs," I told her.

Nora laughed. "I think you'll find that's up to Harlinne. And I appreciate you were only joking, Soraya, but I wouldn't rule those snakes out, either!"

My mouth opened and stayed open for a second. It closed before it found anything to say.

Truth is, I don't *know* how I'd been planning to put this whole thing together, except that I'd be the one in charge.

I certainly didn't want it organising by some crackpot who might or might not spike your drinks and/ or put a poisonous snake in the glove compartment.

Yet I was trapped. I had a choice.

1. I could call Soraya out now. In that case, it'd look like we were out of synch. Since a united front was all that stood between us and a band break-up, giving that impression probably wasn't advisable.

Or

2. I could let it go for the time being, and challenge Soraya later. But that would mean allowing Harlinne to establish roots in everyone's minds. Subsequently, it would probably inspire *You mean, you're not going with Harlinne after all? Oh, that's such a shame!* – which might be just about bearable – or *Harlinne was a little too hot for you to handle, eh?* – which definitely wouldn't. Because *I* was the crazy one, and Soraya was my nutty second in command. Having a *bona fide* lunatic on board would be a challenge to that. Worse, it risked exposing me as Little Ms Boring. I couldn't do with that kind of self-knowledge, not with all my other problems: viz. having to hide my playlist, manage Charlotte, give Soraya the time of her life, come up with some kind of master plan to save the band.

I suddenly felt like some kind of eighteenth century woman, about to swoon. Thankfully, I was sitting down.

"Could I have a glass of Gavi di Gavi La Scolca Bobo?" I asked Kathleen weakly.

She thought I meant to propose a toast, which is what I'd have wanted her to believe had I been in control. She charged everyone's glasses as if she was *so* pleased it had ended this way, then turned to me.

I raised my wine without getting to my feet. "To the future," I said.

"To the future!" they all replied.

Oh, how the hotel-trashing, guitar-smashing, high-on-booze-'n'-benzedrine hell raisers of yesteryear would have approved. Just like *Downton Abbey*.

When Showdowns Backfire

"This is your room for the next few days," Nora told us, as she picked up her briefcase. "Yours and Soraya's. Be careful with it. Joke. And have a good time in the USA."

She was the last of 'our people' to go. I stood up politely to see her off. She hugged me and kissed my cheek.

Next up: how to deal with Soraya.

She seemed to know what was coming. "Don't be mad with me," she said, when Nora had closed the door behind her. "I had to say something, otherwise they'd have been like, *Oh, they're not going on a road trip at all. They're just playing for time.* I had to make it believable. Anyway, you told them we were going on a road trip. You never thought to run it past me – "

"I thought you *wanted* to go on one!"

"You told me we *couldn't!* Why didn't you tell me beforehand? I *could* have been like, *Wait a minute, Hannah, you never said anything!* But I wasn't. I played ball, and I actually made it super-plausible by adding Harlinne."

"I thought I *had* told you."

She did a double-take. "Er, *no.*"

"I wanted it to be a surprise."

She laughed incredulously. "Get your story straight, Hannah. It can't be both."

"Sorry."

Silence. She shrugged. "Apology accepted."

"But there's worse, I'm afraid."

"Go on."

"We're taking Charlotte."

Her eyes bored into me and she bit her lip. "When was this decided?" she asked eventually.

I'd begun by thinking I was going to scold Soraya. Now I realised the boot was on the other foot, and it was much bigger than I thought.

"I told her you were thinking of taking over her candle business," I said. "You said you were serious."

"Once again: you told me to butt out. You seem to be changing your mind a lot. Or rather, you keep changing mine for me."

"I didn't tell you to 'butt out'."

"'There are better ways of diversifying than going into candles.' That's what you said."

"Sorry."

"I think you and Charlotte should go on this road trip – *our* road trip – on your own. I mean, that's what you were phoning her about downstairs, right? When you made me go into the bathroom? I wonder why you didn't want me to know. Well, could it possibly be, because you weren't actually thinking of including me at all?"

"Like Gaz just said: we're inseparable. How could either of us go on a secret road trip? Anyway, she knows I'm bringing you. I told her."

"Prove it. Text her now. Text: *Soraya's having second thoughts about coming.* Let's see what she pings back. Because I think she'll probably be like: *What are you talking about, who said anything about bringing Soraya?*"

I put on my most derisory face. "Really. What are you prepared to bet? And it's got to be something I actually want. Not like your usual 'ten pounds.'"

"So what do you actually want?"

"The return of your trust in me."

"Aww, how cute. Not."

She shrugged. I got my phone out. With her looking over my shoulder, I texted the second thoughts message, pressed 'send' and put it on the table. We sat in an atmosphere of gradually increasing mistrust for thirty minutes, then there was a little ding. I picked it up, unlocked it, and passed it over.

She read Charlotte's words aloud: *That's a real shame. I was looking forward to meeting her. So do you mean it'll just be the two of us?*

"See, I was telling the truth," I said, trying to sound as humble as possible.

"The fact remains, though: you still didn't tell me."

"When I say, 'I thought I had' and 'I wanted it to be a surprise', that's not entirely a contradiction. I *thought* I *had*, and I also thought that, *before* that, I'd intended it as a surprise."

She rolled her eyes. "Have you ever heard the phrase, 'Time to stop digging'?"

"Okay, sorry, I'm sorry. Don't come then. That's fine. You're right. I should have told you. I didn't."

"Right." She smiled humourlessly. "The problem is, Hannah, everyone's *expecting* us to go now. It's not just a road trip any more. You've turned it into a Save the Band expedition."

"So what do you want me to do? I've apologised, but that's not enough, apparently. Tell me what would make things okay. I'll do whatever I can to make it up to you. Anything. I mean it."

"How about we compromise? Tell your sister she can't come but I'll still bankroll her candle factory."

"Okay, look, I haven't been entirely straight with you so far."

"No kidding. *Really?*"

"No," I said.

"Bloody hell, Hannah. I'm beginning to think splitting Fully Magic Coal Tar Lounge is a good idea. I mean, like splitting it from the manager. Go on. And make it quick. And no more bullshit. I want the truth, the whole truth and nothing but the truth, so help you God."

I cleared my throat. "The other night, when you woke up next to me and I was on the phone, that was my sister, Julia. She'd been talking to Charlotte, and Charlotte was considering suing our father. It's a long story, but when Charlotte and I were young – I was thirteen, she was eleven –

Dad locked us in the house and made us listen to his music. I mean, relentlessly. And he gave us alcohol. Mum had gone off with John and Mabel and Julia to 'visit' Auntie Jill, in the Lake District. I think Mum and Dad had had a major row over something, and he was undergoing a bit of a breakdown. Anyway, Charlotte was traumatised, and she hasn't quite got over it, and she's – she *was* – convinced it was abuse. Julia persuaded her otherwise, at least for now. But the candles really are going down the spout, and there's a history of weird and wonderful behaviour in our family, so I'm not convinced she's entirely on board with the 'don't sue Dad' message."

"Your dad: did he like…? I mean, was there any – ?"

"Nothing like that, no. Nothing sexual, no violence. Just music and imprisonment and booze and maybe a raised voice or three. Literally three."

"But you had food, yeah? You could go to the toilet?"

"Yes, but – "

"What about at night? Was there, like, sleep deprivation?"

"I can't remember. A bit. We stayed up long after our normal bedtimes, listening to Pink Floyd."

"My God. And that's the sort of music it was? Like sixties and seventies stuff?"

"Probably a bit of eighties, too."

"It sounds hilarious. And, what, Charlotte's claiming chronic shell shock?"

"It may sound funny to you, but it's a matter of perspective. Look, I don't want her to turn on Dad – "

"She hasn't got a hope in hell of getting *that* to court. Apart from the Pink Floyd bit maybe."

"Even assuming you're right, it's hardly the point."

"So we're taking her across America so you can iron things out, yeah? All right, count me in."

"What?" I stood up because I just had to. "Really?"

"Like I said first time we talked out this, life's all about you and me. Me stepping into the breach. For you."

I walked over, knelt down and hugged her fiercely. "You're a brilliant girlfriend."

"But don't keep anything back. I'm warning you. No more keeping me in the dark, or we're finished."

"Well, while we're on the subject, there is something I've been meaning to tell you. It's about, er, the kind of *music* I might like to listen to in the car? And how that actually might be a direct or indirect consequence of what happened those few days when my dad locked me and Charlotte in the house?"

She drew back a little and nodded. *Go on.*

I told her how I regularly worshipped at the MP3 player of the Ancients. It emerged in a torrent, and I realised I was probably speaking far too fast and not making much sense. I mentioned Joni Mitchell, Jefferson Airplane, Led Zeppelin, Love, Yes, X-Ray Spex, Deep Purple, Barclay James Harvest and about ten others. I looked at the floor so I could spew it out without faltering. After I'd finished speaking she looked me hard in the eyes.

"God, you're seriously screwy," she said after a while. "I mean, who *cares* what bloody music you like? I mean, if it had been eighteenth century string quartets, I might have thought, 'How did she ever carve a name for herself in the rock business?', but I wouldn't have looked *down* on you. Bloody *hell*, Hannah. You're majorly stupid!"

I hugged her again, then poured myself another glass of wine and resumed my chair. "So we can listen to some of that as we drive across the States?"

She laughed. "You haven't really thought this through, have you?"

"What do you mean?"

"You've just told me that this is the kind of music that your sister claims gave her some sort of post-traumatic stress disorder, and you're actually thinking of *playing* it to her, while we're all in the car? How well do you think that's likely to go down?"

The penny dropped. "Oh, shit, yes." I don't understand why I hadn't seen it before.

"What kind of music does Charlotte like?" she asked.

"New Age."

"Which is?"

"Panpipes, chill out meditation, soothing harmonies, Celtic, Native American, Tibetan chants, sounds of nature: rainfall, birdsong, whales."

"Bloody hell."

"I know."

"I'm sorry I doubted her," Soraya said. "She's obviously damaged. And that's what we're going to have to listen to for *two months?*"

"I'm sure she won't mind listening to your stuff. It's mine that'll make her freak out."

"That settles it," she said firmly. "We're definitely going with Harlinne."

"I'm not sure I see the connection," I said, in as placating a tone as I could manage. By this time, I'd reconciled myself to Harlinne as a possible price for keeping Soraya sweet, but –

"Has it occurred to you yet that there are going to be precisely *three* of us on this trip?" Soraya asked.

"I can count that far, so yes. You, me and Charlotte." I held my fingers up between us. "Not four, not two, but something in between."

"Stop being facetious for a moment, Hannah. I've got a massive hangover and my eye's hurting. I'm just saying, three's a crowd. It's a well known saying. We probably need someone else."

"Can we just go back a bit? I told you the sort of thing Charlotte listens to. You said, 'That settles it, we're going with Harlinne.' I still don't know what connection you made."

"We need someone to inject a bit of unpredictability. Shake things up a bit. Don't take this the wrong way, but this little sister of yours doesn't sound very interesting. She's into Tibetan chill-out, she's got PTSD because your dad made her listen to a bit of prog rock twentysomething years ago, and she makes candles for a living. What kind of a resume is that? Maybe we should bring John."

"My brother?"

"A man might help keep us from killing each other. He'd probably carry our bags too. We could use him as a slave."

"I could try asking him, but he'd probably run a mile. I know I would."

"Yeah, me too."

We sat around with depressed limbs and faces for about half an hour, trying to think round the impasse. The obvious choice was Harlinne: she might agree to accompany us, at the right price. But then, so might anyone. Who did we *want* to come? No one.

We were close to falling off our chairs with sheer misery when my phone rang. *Julia.*

How I'm Always Having to Explain Myself to Someone

"Hi, Julia," I said making no attempt to disguise my total lack of enthusiasm for talking to her or anyone at all.

"I hear you're planning a road trip across America," she said in the same tone.

"Yep."

"You realise that's not a normal way of dealing with something like this? The customary response is to go to some sort of clinical psychotherapist, a qualified professional. Talk the experience through in his or her presence. And get dad involved, by force if need be."

"You know as well as I do that Charlotte wouldn't go for that. She's one hundred per cent alternative medicine, always has been. Anyway, it sounds a lot like legitimising her interpretation of events back then, which I'm not happy to do."

"It's your word against hers. I'm not necessarily doubting you. I'm just saying – "

"The most passive-aggressive clause in the English language."

"This is serious, and I may have spoken over-harshly to you last time I called – I'm sorry about that: I regretted it as soon as I put the phone down – but I'm just trying to help. If the family implodes, it affects me too."

"Yes, fair point."

"I understand Soraya was going originally – on this road trip of yours – but now she's cried off?"

"She's cried back on again at my insistence. I can't do three thousand miles alone with Charlotte."

"You're travelling by car, right? I mean, that's how road trips usually work. I'm only asking because it's not been five minutes since you were lying down on that bridge in London protesting about exhaust fumes. I realise I'm not putting this very well, or tactfully. I'm just trying to ask a question. Re-set. Hannah, are you going by car?"

"I believe so," I replied. "But I'm not organising it."

"Who's your coordinator then?"

"Harlinne Vobrosky. New York."

"A travel agent, right? I mean, not someone who's coming with you."

I suddenly saw where this was leading. And that it wasn't necessarily bad news. "Would you like to come?" I asked.

"Strictly speaking, no. But you've already admitted you and Charlotte alone's out of the question. I agree. Yet adding Soraya into the mix may not be in anyone's interests. I'm not judging. I know it goes with the territory you've both chosen, and she's no 'worse' than anyone else in the business – in inverted commas, notice. But Charlotte's not like that."

I sighed. On the one hand, it showed what a brilliant job our PR guys were doing. *That time you both dangled from a tenth floor balcony in Shanghai, and Soraya's left shoe landed on a police car, and you were taken to ...* Mountains from molehills, most of it. Truth is, three-quarters of a bottle of Scotch, a few broken vases, a black eye and a cut lip was about as wild as it ever got. I'd explained all this to mum and dad years ago, but Julia hadn't been there. For obvious reasons, I'd wanted to limit the Clued Up to as few individuals as possible. Need to know basis only.

"And three's a crowd," Julia added, as if she could hear me thinking. "I'm not asking you if I can come. I'm suggesting that four might be better than three. And that your fourth needs to be someone neutral, halfway between you and Charlotte. And not a – how can I put this? – *party animal?* Am I making sense? I'm offering myself. But only if you're in a quandary such that – "

"I'll have to ask Soraya," I said. "This was meant to be her road trip. Or rather, ours. Then I invited Charlotte without asking, and she was seriously pissed off."

"How long will I – ?"

"She's just here. Hang on." I put my finger over the receiver and turned to Soraya. "Julia wants to come."

"Yeah, okay," Soraya said.

"Really?"

"Who else are we going to get?"

"Welcome aboard," I told Julia.

"That didn't take long!" Julia said. "Okay, look, I'm not asking for charity: I'll pay my own way."

"I've *got* money, Julia. I can afford to pay for you a zillion times over. Don't do a Mum and Dad on me. There are more important things."

"Anyway, I believe I can start helping out now. I'll call Charlotte and tell her to stop adding to her USA itinerary. In fact, I can tell her to scrap it altogether. I mean, that's Harlinne Vobrosky's job, isn't it?"

"She's making an *itinerary?* Bloody hell, she doesn't waste time! It's only about two hours since I was on the phone to her! What's on – ? Wait, no, let me guess. Native American reservations and sacred sites?"

"Check. I suppose we'll have to visit *some*, though."

"I'll ask Harlinne. *Where are Native Americans most likely to indulge a tourist?*"

"She's just excited," Julia said. "At least she's throwing herself into the spirit of the thing. You must have some places you want to go?"

"Not really. It's supposed to be a road trip. I don't suppose Jack Kerouac was like, *I'll make a list of my top twenty places to visit, then I'll buy a map, and I'll spend Sunday afternoon at the kitchen table with a ball of string and a few drawing pins, calculating routes.* You're supposed to start on the East Coast and head westwards until you reach the Pacific. That's it. You let the road lead you. The only obligatory stops are for petrol-stroke-gas."

"Maybe in that case, we should dispense with Harlinne altogether. I don't mean that to sound critical; the opposite: that you're absolutely right."

"Harlinne's non-negotiable. She and Soraya have already come to an arrangement."

Soraya looked at me and nodded slowly. *I've made enough compromises.*

"That's also fine," Julia said. "It's an exercise in psychogeography then. Guy Debord, Situationism, that sort of thing, but tailored for the USA."

As so often, when Julia got excited, she talked about things she knew but no one else did.

"Exactly," I said.

"How long do you anticipate it taking?"

"Harlinne says ten weeks, but that's not written in stone."

"Sounds about right," she said.

"Can Knut put up with you being away from home for that long? I mean, isn't the farm busy?"

"We already discussed it. Just as a hypothetical, you understand. He's fully on board."

"Just one rule," I said. "No one's allowed to mention Brexit or Donald Trump."

"Suits me."

I hadn't noticed, but Soraya was on her phone, and she was passing it to me. "It's Harlinne," she told me. "Says she wants to speak to the organ grinder."

"I've got to go," I told Julia. "I'll get back to you with the details. Start packing, but not too much."

Begin With Harlinne

"Hello, Hannah," Harlinne said, when I accepted the phone. I felt like someone's PA, definitely not my own. Since Soraya had put it on speaker, I put it on the table. "Soraya tells me you've both decided to go ahead with your

American road trip, and that you'd like me to organise things. I charge ten thousand dollars per person. For that you get a car, insurance, an itinerary if you want it, and I'm personally on call for you day and night. I definitely didn't call you 'the organ grinder', by the way. That's just Soraya's quaint British sense of humour."

"There are going to be four of us."

"Ideal. Any special requirements?"

"We'd like an eco-friendly car. As green as possible. A hybrid, at least. And nothing huge: we won't be carrying a lot of luggage."

"You'll want a big trunk, though?"

"Reasonable, that's all. We expect to have to visit laundrettes, and so on. We can travel light. A few changes of clothing."

"Do you want it to be a real road trip?" she asked sweetly.

"I'm not sure what you mean," I said.

"Well, let me put it like this, and I'm not criticising *anyone*, dear, but some of my clients, well, they *say* they want a road trip, but what they *really* want is to visit the tourist traps: Statue of Liberty, Mount Rushmore, Niagara Falls, The Grand Canyon. You know what I mean?"

"They want to learn about America."

"Pree-cise-ley. And they want to do it by car. Now that's more than fine by me. I love my country, and it makes me proud that people want to find out about it. But it's not what I'd call a real USA road trip."

"Weirdly, I've just been talking to my sister about this exact same thing."

"Really? And what did you say? Sorry if that sounds a little direct, Sweetheart, but it's my job to find out exactly what you want and provide it. Any insight you'd be willing to give me would be more than welcome."

"I was saying that you begin on the East coast and head for the Pacific. How you get there's irrelevant, and not something you plan. We're really going on this trip so we can find out about ourselves. Specifically – without giving too much away – I need to have a series of heart-to-hearts with my younger sister."

"It's about *you yourselves becoming the US frontier*, in other words! Just following the setting sun!"

I wasn't sure what 'becoming the US frontier' meant, but it sounded innocuous. "That's the idea, yes."

"I love it! And for that reason, it doesn't matter where on the East coast you begin? It doesn't have to be New York City, say, or Boston?"

"It can be in the middle of nowhere for all I care. We just want a car, a set of keys, and a road to drive away from the ocean on."

"Oh, my! You're my ideal customer!"

She sounded genuinely excited, like I'd made her day, and if only everyone could resemble me and Soraya.

"Thanks," I said. I didn't want her to stray too far from a strictly professional approach. I remembered what Nora had said about 'shock', and that she hadn't seen Soraya's quips about drugs and snakes as totally outlandish.

"Here's what we're going to do," Harlinne said, "and I do the same thing with all my best clients. By 'best', I don't mean 'highest paying': I mean most adventurous. The genuine ones. I want you to leave all your credit cards with me before you set off. I'll put them in a safe deposit in my bank. I'll send someone to meet you all at the airport, then we'll transfer you all to a car with blacked-out windows. I mean, the police kind, so you can't see anything outside. I want your destination – your road trip's starting-point, because that's where it'll take you – to be a complete surprise. This won't be the car you're doing your road trip in, by the way. It'll be a chauffeur-driven limo. A kind of Say Farewell to Luxury ride. You could be travelling for a few hours, or you could be travelling for a few minutes. I won't be accompanying you at that point. But I will be there at your destination-stroke-starting point. When the limo pulls to a halt, the chauffeur will politely ask you to exit the vehicle. I'll be waiting on the roadside to greet you. A little bit of ritual enters the equation here, designed to signify your readiness to engage directly with the sacred universe that is America. One: you all give me your passports for safe-keeping, and two: you give me your phones to look after for the duration of your trip. Jack Kerouac never had a mobile phone, and do you know what he'd have done with one if anyone had ever given him one? He'd have tossed it out of the window on the New Jersey Turnpike. The Merry Pranksters never had mobile phones, and do you know how they'd have reacted if anyone had ever given them some? They'd have put them under the front tyres of that big yellow Furthur bus, and run them over."

"Okay," I said, trying to get my head round all this. "So we give you our passports and our phones and credit cards. What if there's an emergency?"

"You'll have my number and a pay-as-you-go. I'll also provide you with a daily food, accommodation and clothing allowance and a list of places you can draw the money. But it won't be unlimited. Not what you're used to, probably."

"Sounds fair enough. Except I'll definitely need to Skype my daughter and husband at some point. Frequently, if I'm honest."

"That's what internet cafés are for, honey. And libraries. I know it sounds brutal, but phones are phones, and they stop you interacting with the people sitting right next to you. The horrible irony of modern communication. Anyway, the world's absolutely full of phones. You can always get another if you absolutely have to."

"What if one of us brings a credit card? I mean, mistakenly?"

"That would be cheating. If you were to do that, it'd be a mighty, mighty shame. And you'd be the losers."

It was all beginning to sound a bit creepy, to be honest. I looked over at Soraya. She gave me a 'go with it' shrug. I think she was past caring.

Above all, at this point, I wanted to make things right between me and Soraya. Nothing else seemed to matter. I pictured Harlinne in her New York office, worsted skirt-suit, stubbing out her cheroot in a cut-glass ashtray.

"It's a deal," I said.

"Oh, I'm *so* pleased! I'll send you an invoice, and we'll thrash out a few more details, and then we're set to go!"

"We're looking for asap," I said. Quite frankly, I'd gone right off the idea of a road trip. I wish I'd never mentioned it back in Venice. I felt sick to the pit of my stomach.

What We Never Mention

Very few people know the whole story: six or seven medical professionals, my parents, plus Tim and Soraya. Not my siblings, and definitely none of my friends. The band's supposed to have gathered bits of it from hearsay. Probably Elliot picked up the most, but not even he knows that much.

Short bit of history. Tim and I married in 2010. I became FMCTL's manager in 2012, three years after the group formed, and the same day I met Soraya. For twelve months, things went smoothly. Elliot wrote Coal Tar Stomp, we did a twelve-stop US tour, we released an album the critics loved. Yet throughout that whole amazing year, something felt subtly wrong.

The truth took a while to emerge, as they say it often does in these sorts of cases. I was tired all the time (but then I worked 24/7), I bruised a lot (but I often helped the roadies lug equipment), and I kept getting ill (but I met people from all over the world, you'd no idea what they'd been in contact with). In short, I never seemed in great shape, but I didn't dwell on it, just put it down to the lifestyle. At the same time, I thought everyone who'd ever been in the business must have been making it up: *this* was living it to the max, and, hey, keep it a closely guarded secret that it's not half as riotous as it's usually depicted.

It was 2013 when I finally got a blood test. I was feeling crappy almost continually by then, which is why I went to the doctor at all, of course. Usually, I'm far too busy for all the be-careful-look-after-yourself shit. I was thirty-two years old. The GP called me back the same day. He'd booked an appointment with a haematologist at Maidstone Hospital. *We'll tell you why when you get there.* Soraya and I were more or less joined at the hip even in those days, so she was with me when the call came through. And she's as good at reading between the lines as any normal person. Mysteriously, though, she decided not to come with me. "You need Tim," was all she said.

To cut a long story short, I had acute myeloid leukaemia and a serious dose of pneumonia. Pathetically, I told Tim not to let Mum and Dad know, but of course, I was pretty disoriented (they were wheeling me fast along a never-ending corridor on a gurney as I gave him my solemn instructions), and deep down I must have known it'd get back to them anyway. I was going to need a bone marrow transplant, and your best chance of a match is with a sibling. As luck would have it, I'm one of five children. Bad news always spreads like wildfire in any family.

The doctors put me on oxygen support and, over the course of roughly a week, brought the pneumonia under control, then started chemotherapy. Of course, Tim *had* to tell my parents, but to be fair he did persuade them not to tell my brother and sisters. That was made easier/possible at all by the fact that the perfect bone marrow match had already been found. Because he'd also told Soraya (I don't know how much she had to twist his arm: history hasn't preserved the details). And by some miracle of fate, it turned out I'd actually teamed up with my ideal donor twelve months beforehand.

I don't know whether any of my siblings would have been compatible. It never became an issue. Tim wasn't a match. My parents weren't. Soraya didn't even wait to be asked. She got herself tested in a private clinic in London and had a courier deliver the results to the oncologists. Thirty minutes after receiving the (incredulous, by all accounts) call-up, she presented herself in Maidstone, complete with an overnight-stay bag. Astonishing maturity: she was only twenty-two years old.

For me, it was a long, painful ordeal – nearly a year till I was back with the band, and even then on a strictly limited basis. I learned to pray. Each evening, I'd say something like, *God, I know not everything I've done today has been good or had any point, but look after those I love and please don't let go of me*. And I'd always end with, *Your servant, Hannah*, like signing a letter. I don't know whether it had any effect, but it became a habit. I still do it every night before I go to sleep. *Yours faithfully, Hannah Lexingwood. PS...* Anyway, I'm here now, and back to where I ought to be... touch wood.

But that's not the end of this particular story. Because Tim and I had always wanted a family, and the treatment had left me with a serious case of female infertility. IVF came galloping to the rescue. Soraya's egg, Tim's sperm, brought together in some kind of petri dish and implanted into my body. Twelve months later, by the magic of caesarean, a beautiful baby girl, name of Lek.

The weird thing is, Soraya doesn't actually think she's done much. We hardly ever talk about it. She definitely doesn't lean on what she achieved to probe areas of my life I'd rather keep private. We still have secrets from each other, and she can still come out with things like, "This little sister of yours..." reminding me, with a bit of a jolt, that although she's an utterly integral part of my family (how could she *not* be?) there are still members of my wider family she knows little or nothing about.

As I said earlier, hardly anyone knows any of this. I guess they just look at me and her – *The Not Quite Lesbian Couple* as Rock Hoedown called us – and think we're anomalous.

We are.

Loganberries and Folk

The hotel manager kept ringing up to find out if we needed anything. Soraya asked if anyone local had a dog, and would they mind bringing it upstairs to play with us? Twenty minutes later, an eighteen year-old local student called Yolande turned up at our door – frizzy yellow hair, Vans, big smile – restraining a pair of Affenpinscher puppies on long leads. We played fetch with them for over an hour while Yolande helped herself to wine and canapés. We put the TV news on: a short bit at the end about how the famous rock band had spent part of the day at the Grand in Verona, a clip of the four guys leaving and getting in a car. Suddenly Soraya declared that the dogs were getting tired and needed to go home. She gave Yolande two hundred euros for dog food, and an unopened bottle of Pinot Gris for herself. Yolande reacted the way people always do when time's up: she asked for a selfie. Afterwards, Soraya sent down for two bottles of twelve-year-old malt whisky and, when they arrived, took a swig from one, then poured both down the sink simultaneously as if there was no time to lose. An hour later, we ate in the hotel restaurant while too many staff stood on the side lines looking nervous, as if they'd been told (and this is no exaggeration: I've seen it before), *no one gets overly close to them or you're fired*. We ate prawn linguine and drank vermouth. The restaurant was huge and carpeted, with circular tables, white walls, a high ceiling and chandeliers. The other guests were mostly middle aged and elderly, well dressed. They didn't avoid eye-contact, but neither did they seek it. Probably past the age at which Fully Magic Coal Tar Lounge is anything other than a string of words. We made up harmless stories about them. When we got back to our room, the lack of Affenpinschers made it feel empty. We called down and asked the manager if he could arrange disguises and get some security guys to accompany us to a club. He'd be *delighted*, he said, without a scintilla of irony. There was a crowd at the front of the hotel, but we left by a half-concealed exit that ran through the basement to the hotel's rear, where a tiny car awaited us, the kind of thing a *normal person* would drive. Half an hour later, we were somewhere on the outskirts of town, down a rickety flight of stairs, nothing like London, rather low multi-coloured lights resembling an old-fashioned disco; but a good DJ. We danced for an hour, then four guys started getting overfamiliar (sadly, all too predictable), and we left.

When we rolled up back at the hotel, we got in bed, switched off the lights and lay in silence for a long time. I fell into one of those obsessive half-dreams everyone sometimes has, in which you're never quite sure whether you're awake or asleep. It focussed on our arrival at the hotel that morning when Soraya asked for a strawberry gelato. She'd made it too easy for them. Anyone could unearth strawberry ice-cream anytime, anywhere in the world. Much better to ask for something almost, but not quite, impossible to procure. Loganberry would have worked, so might guavaberry or even gooseberry. And *chocolate sprinkles?* How amateurish was *that?* I needed to have a word with her tomorrow morning.

Mind you, asking for those dogs had been a stylish touch.

Outside, the crowd hadn't dispersed. At irregular intervals, someone would shout 'Soraya!'

"Are you awake?" she whispered.

I hesitated. What was the likelihood this was a conversation I'd want? "Yeah," I said eventually.

"If the band splits, we could go into folk music. Just you and me. No singles, just touring. You still play a pretty mean guitar."

"I wouldn't go that far. I keep my hand in."

"Guerrilla musicians. Just popping up anywhere, singing a song or two, then disappearing – until the next gig."

"It's… an idea."

"We'd need to do something as different to the Coal Tars as possible. And it would need to be edgy."

I hmm-ed. "Pop-up singers has been done before."

"Not by us."

"I'll think about it, okay?"

"It's about where and when we appear – timing's everything: I'm not talking about some lame 'flash mob-y' crap – and how disruptive we make it, and whether the police can be arsed to come after us, and how long we can keep evading them. It's about breaking and entering places, and filming ourselves and putting it on YouTube. You need to write some songs."

"Me? What makes you think I've got any talent in that direction?"

"You've got a heart, right? You just write from that. That's where good songs come from. Not, like Elliot probably thinks, from sitting down with a big glass of mineral water, a miniature keyboard and a copy of *Music Theory in Practice*. Anyone can write songs, but only as good as their muse'll let them."

"Right."

"When we get to America, that's the first thing we're going to do. I'm going to buy you a new guitar, and we're going to write twenty songs together. Sod the band. Sod your sisters. This is about us."

"You should have asked for a loganberry gelato."

"What?"

"This morning. Loganberry, not strawberry. It's about preserving the mystique."

"What the hell are you *talking* about?" She frowned. "What *is* loganberry, anyway?"

"It's an actual berry. Halfway between a blackberry and a raspberry."

"I didn't want a logan-bloody-berry gelato. I wanted a

strawberry one. Are you half asleep or something? You're talking rubbish."

"I wouldn't mind a strawberry gelato myself," I said.

"Call downstairs. I'm not stopping you."

"But if I did, I'd ask for a loganberry gelato."

"And they'd be like, 'I'm really sorry, Mrs Lexingwood, but we've only got access to strawberry at this late hour – '"

"And I'd be like, *Get me my loganberry gelato, NOW!*"

"Imagine if we broke into the Bank of England and recorded a session there."

"Why don't we break into Fort Knox while we're on?" I said. "We're going to America. We might as well."

"*How did they get into two of the most secure buildings in the world? This is Huw Edwards reporting live from Threadneedle Street.*"

"*Both suspects are still at large.*"

"*Members of the public have been warned not to approach them.*"

I sighed. "*The duo can be recognised by the fact that they have world famous faces and one of them is carrying a large acoustic guitar.*"

"Anyway, that's what you're doing when we get to America. Writing songs."

It seemed like a good place to end a meaningless conversation. When I don't reply for two minutes, Soraya usually thinks she's won.

Then she forgets we ever had a conversation.

God, I know not everything I've done today has been good or had any point, but look after those I love and please don't let go of me. Your servant, Hannah.

PART THREE:

LONDON TO NEW JERSEY

Trying to Raise the Enthusiasm

A WEEK AT HOME IN LONDON. WE TOOK LEK OUT IN the pushchair, shopped, napped, played computer games, practised yoga, picnicked on Hampstead Heath. The sun shone in a pale sky and a cold wind blustered and we wore jumpers indoors. Tim left the house each morning at eight and got back around six, so we didn't see much of him. In preparation for America, we got grade one haircuts and experimented with wigs and sunglasses. Each evening, the three of us ate dinner (something I made: I'm not a bad cook), then talked and watched TV in the living room till Lek fell asleep. We turned in around ten. Soraya has a bed here. She doesn't stay with us much normally – once or twice a year, a few days at a time – but she knows the 'our' in 'our house' includes her. Literally: she's in the title deeds.

Throughout, I had the sense of counting down to something I wasn't looking forward to. I hadn't properly researched Harlinne, I realised that much. I'd simply fallen in with Soraya's assumption that, since she'd got us the cover of a major glossy, her expertise must know no bounds. Long after I should have, I sought reassurance by going to her website. Yellow font on a blue background, two pages long, and not even a proper menu: the sort of thing your ten year-old nephew cobbles together, unasked, one rainy Sunday afternoon, and you keep it partly for sentimental reasons and partly because, oh, well, *everyone* needs an 'internet presence' nowadays, don't they? But you never look at it, and you don't honestly expect anyone else to. It had a single sentence about her past – "Harlinne Vobrosky used to work in tourism, and specialised in self-drive USA car journeys tailored to adventurous vacationers" – plus her email address. Not even a photo of her. I couldn't mention any of this to Soraya, of course. I knew exactly what she'd say. *Why do you always have to be so bloody neurotic all the time, Hannah? Why can't you just enjoy life?* Well, that's the difference between a star and a star's manager.

Charlotte arrived the day before we were due to set off for New York. I met her at Paddington while Soraya and Eva, our au pair, took Lek to the park. A feeling of awkwardness prevailed, due to the Dad business. We ate bagels in McDonald's and made small talk about the train journey from Devon. Her pink-framed glasses and hennaed hair were completely unchanged from last time we'd met, two months ago, but also, depressingly, were her black zip hoodie and plain below-the-knee skirt that didn't look as if it had ever seen an iron. She's eight inches shorter than me and three stone heavier, but I wish to God she'd make more of herself. She looks like a cross between a Goth and Didi Pickles from *Rugrats*.

The plan was to meet Julia in America. The flight from Oslo to New York isn't that much longer than from Heathrow, and coming to England first would add an extra two hours.

The next day, Tim and Lek accompanied us to Heathrow and we said an emotional goodbye at Departures. As usual, we all cried a bit.

Arrivals and Beyond

Soraya and I wore mini-skirts, sunglasses and our new hyper-real wigs – hers, black, curly long; mine strawberry blonde, frizzy, high as a halo – and Charlotte wore a pale blue wrap-around dress and black leggings. We had to remove the hairpieces to get through customs, but there was no aggro. Presumably, our faces matched our passports, even though our scalps didn't. I was impressed. The mark of a free country in my opinion: you don't have to cover your head, and your hair can be any way you like.

Julia wasn't hard to spot, even in the megalopolis that is JFK. She never seems to age. Hollow cheeks, small nose and wide apart, intense blue eyes. It's partly the seriousness that makes her stand out, but also that, since she's tall and attractive ('striking', men sometimes call her), she draws gazes. You simply follow them to their point of intersection. She wore a yellow dress, canvas baseball trainers, a stars and stripes newsboy cap, and had her long hair in a ponytail. Like us, she trailed a satisfying small travel bag on a wheelie frame. Unlike us, she carried a paperback.

"My God, is that you?" she exclaimed when we took off our sunglasses. "I recognised you, Lottie, but – is that – hair – ?"

Soraya and I removed our wigs.

"Wow," Julia said. She laughed nervously, looking quickly from one of us to the other and back again. "Have you, er, joined the US marines?"

"We wish," Soraya said. "We were in Venice for the Biennale."

"Ah," she said.

"Look out for us on the magazine stands," I said.

We all hugged. She seemed pleased to see us, but you could never really tell with Julia: novelists everywhere probably prefer to be indoors typing. We exchanged anecdotes about the plane journey, then went to find Harlinne's limo. Not one of us said how excited we were. I didn't begin to relax: no sense of *thank goodness it's finally begun*. In fact, I think arriving in America actually put me more on edge.

"What do you think of my cap?" Julia said.

"Sexy," Soraya replied.

"What are you reading?" I asked.

Julia held it up. *Ralph Waldo Emerson: Selected Essays*. "Thought I'd immerse myself as fully as possible," she said.

When we got to the meeting point, there was no mistaking our driver: an elderly black man in a suit and a peaked cap of the sort chauffeurs used to wear in the 1930s, holding an A3 banner at chest height: HANNAH, JULIA, SORAYA, CHARLOTTE. He seemed to know he'd located us the moment we made eye-contact. He lowered the sign, relaxed a little and grinned.

"Harlinne's ladies?" he said before any of us could ask anything. "I'm Rudolph Williams, but you can just call me Rudolph. Follow me, please."

The limo was exactly that: a luxury car with an opaque partition between ourselves and the driver. Bright red bodywork, long bonnet, spacious trunk. Roughly as we'd been warned, its windows were whitewashed from the inside. We put our bags in the back and got in facing each other, Julia and Charlotte on one side, me and Soraya on the other.

Soraya and I removed our wigs. Rudolph – about to close the door on us – let out an involuntary 'whoa'. When he shut us in, it was dark.

"Well, this is cosy," Julia said.

"I expected it to be longer," Charlotte said. "The car, I mean. Not that it matters. Like one of those they have at proms."

"That's a stretch limo, dear," Julia told her.

Rudolph got in the front – we felt the car bounce slightly. He slid open the glass compartment that separated us from him, letting a shaft of light in. "You all got your passports, credit cards and phones? Ms Vobrosky particularly asked me to check."

We nodded. Then, realising he probably couldn't see us, we grunted our assent.

"Reach above you," he said. "There's a light. Switch it on if you want to see anything."

"Why would we?" Soraya asked drily.

"How long will it be till we reach our destination?" Charlotte said.

"That would be telling," Rudolph replied jocosely.

"It's just," she continued, "if it's more than an hour, I may need to use the toilet. Shouldn't we *all* go to the toilet, just to be on the safe side, before we set off?"

"The bathroom?" he said.

"That's right," she replied.

He looked hugely disappointed, as if this somehow confirmed his worst fears. "Anyone *else* want to use the bathroom?"

Julia switched the light on. We all tentatively raised our hands.

"Better safe than sorry," Soraya explained.

He sighed irritably. "Well, why didn't any of you *say* anything? Why not go when you were in the airport? Why wait till you're in the *car*?"

"We're not saying we need to use the bathroom *now*," Julia told him tetchily. "But it depends how long it'll take to get wherever we're going. And, as I understand it, you're not allowed to tell us."

"There's a diner in about ten minutes' time," he said. "I won't be giving anything away if we stop there. It's got a bathroom. Straight in and out, though. Don't want to keep Ms Vobrosky waiting."

He closed the partition. We felt the car pull away and heard the gears ascend and descend and ascend again.

Soraya took her phone out, went to Google Maps, and saw we were leaving the airport. We turned south, then her screen went white with three words in the centre: *No internet connection.*

"It might just be the area," I told her. "Try again in ten minutes."

"I hate this kind of thing," Julia said.

"What do you mean?" I asked.

"All the theatre," she replied. "*Now, children, you've decided to go on a road trip across my country, but since you're British, you probably won't be able to just get in a car and drive it –* "

"I'm sure it's not meant that way," Charlotte said. "Harlinne probably just wants to give us a few hints and tips. Things like, drive on the right."

"Why can't she give us *written* instructions?" Julia said.

I felt like saying, 'because she's not a prize-winning novelist', but I bit my tongue. Even so, I couldn't do anything about the awkward silence.

"Sorry, I'm ruining it for everyone," Julia said. "We've only just left the airport and I'm already moaning. Ignore me."

Julia had insisted on paying her own way, despite everything I'd done to dissuade her, so maybe she was entitled to complain. A bit. I mean, the blacked-out windows ... Yes, I'd known in advance, but actually experiencing it was another matter. And Rudolph wasn't exactly the friendliest of guys.

At this point, I realised exactly what had been bugging me about this trip, right from the outset. It wasn't Harlinne. At least, not particularly.

It was everything.

Horror Squared

Julia's 'I hate this kind of thing' had suddenly crystallised the problem. Looking back, I can see it – the problem, I mean – was like a tiny, overheated, oxygen-depleted room containing six interrelated elephants.

1. Julia and Charlotte and I had a shared history going back thirty-two years. Soraya hadn't played any part in that. Soraya hardly knew my sisters.
2. Worse, personality-wise, Julia and Charlotte were nothing like Soraya. I couldn't even imagine them being friends.
3. Julia and Charlotte didn't know anything about my Soraya-assisted triumph over cancer. I had no idea how to tell them.
4. Nor did they know Soraya was Lek's biological mother. Again, probably too late to start making revelations.
5. Depending on how she chose to look at it, Soraya was outnumbered either three, or two to one. She didn't react well to that sort of thing.
6. Even without all the above, there was a good chance we'd end up hating each other. We were just too different.

It was mainly a knowledge gulf, in other words. On one side: what Julia and Charlotte knew about themselves and me; on the other: what Soraya and I knew about ourselves. I was like the bridge between the two sides. But a bridge that explodes when anyone tries to cross it.

"So, Soraya, how are things?" Julia asked.

"Fine, Julia," Soraya said indifferently. "How are things with you?"

"Er, fine, Soraya," Julia said.

"The band may be splitting up," I put in, by way of assisting the exchange. "Soraya and I are here to think of a way to inject new life into it."

"Fully Magic Coal Tar Lounge are *splitting up?*" Charlotte said.

"Ssh!" I swept my eyes at the partition. "Strictly between us four."

"I'm sorry to hear that, Soraya," Julia said.

"That's okay, Julia," Soraya replied.

I frowned. "Okay, why don't you two stop using each other's first names in that slightly creepy, passive-aggressive way?"

"I'm not sure what you mean, Hannah," Julia said.

"Bloody hell, Julia," I said, "yes you do. You talk to someone sitting across from you, and you use their first name, that comes across as a little patronising."

Julia flicked her eyebrows and looked away as if to say, *Thanks, Mum.*

Soraya ignored me. She scratched at the whitewash on the window. She made a hole big enough to see through. She looked out, sighed wearily, and checked her phone again. *No internet connection.*

Five minutes later, the car drew to a gentle halt. It bobbed gently as Rudolph got out. He pulled open the door from outside and apparently registered the hole in the whitewash.

"How did that happen?" he asked.

"It was there when we got in," Soraya said.

"No, it wasn't," he replied.

"Okay, I did it," she said. "I suffer from claustrophobia."

"That true?" he asked.

She rolled her eyes. "Okay, no. But I might have done."

"Get out and go to the bathroom," he commanded. "And be quick about it."

"Can I just ask you a question?" she said, not moving. "Were we actually locked in, just now?"

"The car's got central locking, yes, and I applied it for your own safety."

"So what if we, say, go over a ravine?" she asked, "and you get killed? How are we going to get out?"

"There aren't any ravines on the way," he said. He seemed to relinquish something of the will to live. "But I take your point. It's a fair question. There's an emergency release button by the light. And thanks for your concern about me, by the way. Maybe I haven't actually been killed. Maybe I'm just stunned. Try ringing 911."

She looked for the emergency release. "I can't see anything."

"Maybe it ain't *exactly* there, I can't remember. But it's somewhere. You've just got to look for it a bit harder. I'll find it while you're in the bathroom. Now go."

We got out. Soraya clearly wanted to continue the argument, but I linked arms with her and marched her towards the diner.

McFadyens was a low red-brick building with large windows and a terracotta roof. It had an expanse of grass in front, then the freeway. Behind it, a row of pine trees, and on both sides, tarmac. The sun shone and the passing traffic roared. We could have been in England on any major motorway.

"I'm sorry if I offended you," Julia told Soraya as we walked inside the building. "I mean it. I apologise."

"It was my fault," Soraya said. "I was only messing around, and Hannah took it the wrong way. Sorry she had a pop at you. Incidentally, there's something you should know about me and Hannah."

"You'll, er, be sharing a room?" Charlotte said. "It's okay. We know. We read *Hello!*"

"*I* don't," Julia said. "Just for the record."

Charlotte shrugged. "It was just a figure of speech. Neither do I."

"Neither of you reads *Hello*?" Soraya asked as if it was incredible.

Julia ignored her. "Does Tim know? I know it's none of my business, and I'm not remotely judging. I'm just curious."

"He knows," I said.

I noticed Soraya's expression change. She didn't like people questioning her relationship with Tim. I'd done it in Venice. I'd got away with it because I'd backtracked and claimed to be joking. But Julia wasn't joking.

"Anyhow, it wasn't that," Soraya said, more breezily than I knew she felt. "We don't actually have sex, by the way. We just pretend to, for *Hello*. Although, frankly, I wouldn't say no," she added, looking me up and down.

"Like Morecambe and Wise?" Charlotte asked. "You just, um, literally sleep together? Like in a big double bed?"

"Sometimes, we read our phones or talk a bit beforehand," I said trying not to blush.

"What were you talking about a moment ago?" Julia asked Soraya. "You said: 'there's something you should know about me and Hannah.'"

Even I didn't know what was coming. I think it had changed, the original jettisoned by Julia's remark about Tim. We'd all stopped at the entrance to the bathroom.

Soraya took a step back. "A few years ago, Hannah had leukaemia. I gave her some of my bone marrow, and when, later, she couldn't have children, I donated an egg. Lek's partly my daughter."

If, in the car, someone had said, 'In ten minutes' time, Soraya will blurt out your biggest secret and there's nothing you can do about it', I'd have gnashed my teeth, screamed and tried to get the door open; even if that meant throwing myself into the middle of a busy freeway. But when it happened, it was a bit like an unexpected vomiting attack. Shocking, physically jarring, horrible to behold, but also accompanied by a background sense of relief. As if I knew that this, and only this, could offer a possible cure.

"Er, *pardon?*" Julia said.

"Was that a *joke?*" Charlotte asked. "Is… er, Hannah?"

I've no idea where it came from, but Soraya passed me a half bottle of vodka. She'd already unscrewed the cap. I can't remember whether I took a pull.

Probably, yes.

Road Trip: The End

According to quantum physics, the universe is literally always splitting in half. At this point, there were precisely two parallel worlds.

In the first, Charlotte and Julia expressed incredulity, then sympathy, then they laughed, then cried a little, and we all hugged over and over and they said things like, *I can't believe you didn't tell us, thank God you're all right, don't ever do that again, we love you so much, let's get back in the car and make the most of the little time we've all got left, as for man, his days are as grass, as a flower of the field, so he flourisheth, for the wind passeth over it, and it is gone, and the place thereof shall know it no more,* etc. etc.

In the second world, they expressed incredulity, then jealousy, then indignation, then anger, then more anger, then cried a little, then they said things like, *we've had enough of this bloody stupid road trip, I can't believe you didn't tell us, don't you think it's important for families to share the bad along with the good, shouldn't you have come to us for bone marrow/ eggs, do you really think you're capable of an actual road trip across America, it's not going to be a stroll in the park, anything could happen, what if you take a knock, yes you may think you've got over it, but these things have a habit of coming back, I can't believe you're thirty-eight years old, you're like a teenager, if you're determined to go ahead with this crazy venture, you can count us out, we don't want that on our consciences, not after you didn't even think to inform us, behold, I am coming soon, bringing my recompense with me to repay everyone for what he has done, and the gates of Hades shall be opened for you,* etc. etc.

Naturally, I was in the second world. After about a minute, the *McFadyens* manager – 'Marvin', his badge said: a pale, ginger-bearded man in his late twenties – came and politely asked us to take our fight outside: we were upsetting the customers. We went and stood on the grass. I should mention that Soraya had completely deserted me, taking her vodka with her. She was sitting on the ground, back propped up against the limo, motionless. Next to her stood Rudolph, apparently serenading her with an acoustic guitar. Neither of them registered our reappearance. As far as I knew, none of us had actually been to the 'bathroom'.

"I assume you told Mum and Dad?" Julia asked. "I mean, you must have done, right?"

"Tim told them," I said. "I asked him not to."

"*Why?*" Charlotte let out.

I could feel myself welling up now. "Because I don't want you to *look at me in a different way!* I'm Hannah Lexingwood née Mordred, your big sister. I don't want to be Hannah Lexingwood Cancer Survivor, oh, look out, be gentle with her, keep an eye on her, don't let her climb the scaffolding to help rig up the mic, it'll be your fault if she has a fainting spell, she's so fragile – "

"Does John know?" Julia asked.

"No."

"What about Mabel?"

"I don't even *know* Mabel, not really. Not to talk to. I mean, she's my – our – sister, but she's twelve years younger than me. She always treats me like I'm a cross between a fragile maiden aunt and some kind of crazy Borgia woman."

"Wonder why. What about the haircut? How recent was all this? You must have had chemo, right? That story about the Biennale: that was complete bullshit, yes?"

"No! This is nothing to do with chemo!"

Julia put her hands on her hips. "Come on, Hannah, please. Give us *some* credit, for God's sake! We're not *completely* stupid!"

"I can show you – my phone – " I fumbled in my bag for it. My hand shook as I accessed it.

To be fair to Julia, she was at least concerned enough to let me show her Soraya and I in San Marco getting sheared. She scrutinised each photo carefully, then took my phone away and checked the files' dates. I realised she wasn't just point-scoring; she cared. I felt wretched.

Charlotte was still crying. I didn't have enough information to assess whether it was because – as often happens in these sorts of cases – she wanted to make herself the centre of attention, or because she was genuinely upset about me. Part of me wanted to put my arm round her and repeatedly apologise. Another part didn't.

The annoying thing was, it was Julia who was sowing the seeds of dissent. She was the calm, controlled one with the aggressive list of questions waiting to be answered.

On the other hand, she was probably saying things Charlotte would have said had she been capable of talking.

"This is over," Julia said. "We're going home." Charlotte nodded. Julia put her arm round her and said, "Come on, let's get this farce done with."

We got in the car. Soraya climbed in next to me with the acoustic guitar.

"Where did you get that?" I asked miserably, trying to sound like I cared.

"I bought it from a guy in the café," she said.

"Diner," Julia corrected her coldly.

"I gave him two hundred dollars," she said. "It's probably only worth fifty, tops. I mean, it *would* be worth that, new. But it plays a good tune." She strummed a chord and tried to pass it to me. "Here."

"No, thanks," I said.

"Look, I know you all probably hate me now," she said arranging the guitar on her thigh and taking out a plectrum. "But this is for the long-term best."

She leaned forward and knocked on the partition.

Rudolph opened it. "Yeah?"

"Let's roll," she told him.

Since no one had bothered to switch on the light, we sat in darkness. Soraya strummed another chord then played *Gates of Eden*. She sang at the top of her voice. Because the guitar was steel stringed, the volume was overwhelming, but no one complained, or, if they did, I didn't hear, and neither did Soraya. None of us could see each other: during the (non-) toilet break, Rudolph had whitewashed over the hole Soraya had scraped. Total dedication; you had to admire him.

Soraya's voice isn't what's usually described as 'melodious'. One critic memorably described her as a cross between Janis Joplin and George Formby. There's a lot of suppressed anger in there, but she can also do sensitivity, thoughtfulness, melancholy. In short, she knows twenty ways to hit a note, but not on any instrument you've ever heard before. You can invariably tell it's her before the end of the second bar. And the power. Her voice can literally break glass. That doesn't make much difference in the studio, of course, but live, it's mind-blowing.

After *Gates of Eden* – to which she added at least ten verses of her own – she segued to *Communist Daughter*, then *Flying Fishes*, then *Poker Face*, then *Goodbye England*. I could feel a blinding headache coming on. I guessed Charlotte and Julia weren't faring much better. They texted each other for a while then stopped. In between verses, I thought I heard them sniffling.

The journey seemed to take forever. At some point – maybe it was the music – I realised Julia and Charlotte were right. I finally started weeping too. I remembered when we were all kids, and it hit me that this might be the end. Hadrian's Wall, sunset. Above us, the first evening stars. Surrounded by fields of sheep, pretending to be Roman gods. Who was I? Minerva, that's right. Julia, beautiful even as a child, and smug with it, had to be Venus (I can't remember whether that was something she chose, or whether we'd forced it on her); Charlotte, Diana; John, Heracles. Something real about it, too, like we'd actually collapsed the gap between the third century and the twentieth.

We'd all been different to one another in those days too: every bit as much as now. But that hadn't stopped us being friends.

So what had gone wrong? How did we get *here*?

Adulthood, that's what. It strips away the magic, and that spoils everything.

Maybe I couldn't salvage my relationship with them any more. I'd asked for their forgiveness and it hadn't been forthcoming. I should have told them years ago, at the outset. Too, too late now.

I was suddenly filled with a sense of injustice, but directed elsewhere. The band – why the hell was the *band* splitting up? Hadn't I suffered enough? How the *bloody hell dare* Elliot and Gaz and Paul and Olly talk about leaving? They'd be *nothing* without Soraya! They might be talented, but talent's as common as grass in the music business. You need something above and beyond. She had ten times more than the four of them put together.

I took out my phone, went to contacts and called Elliot. It rang three times before he picked up. "Hannah?"

"I just want you to hear what you'll be missing," I said. I pointed the phone at Soraya. Its light dimly illuminated my sisters' faces. They looked like they'd had enough sound-torture: they were close to breaking. Soraya finished *Goodbye England* and went straight into *South London Forever*.

"What the hell *is* it?" Elliot said when I put the phone back on my ear. He sounded genuinely nonplussed.

I hung up, returning us all to darkness. I fell into a reverie. Yes, I may have been dehydrated, in desperate need of a toilet break and suffering from a pounding headache, and Soraya was singing at 120 decibels, but I could actually feel myself falling asleep. It was hot in here. I went back in time to the preparations for Coal Tar's first stadium concert, in 2012. Monday, the crew laid the floor for the cranes to drive on, Wednesday they built the steel system to hang the PA, sound, lighting, thirty-two trucks, Thursday, they attached those hundreds of metres of wiring -

"Stop playing that BLOODY GUITAR!" Julia screamed.

I almost hit my head on the ceiling. Soraya froze. Total silence.

Or that's what it felt like. In reality, the car must have been making some kind of noise, and there must have been traffic outside. Yet it seemed so quiet, it actually hurt.

"Switch the light on," Julia ordered. "We've something to say."

"I'm not your servant," Soraya said.

Julia fiddled about with the ceiling for a few moments and the light came on. "Sorry, I didn't mean to disrespect your singing or playing," she said desolately. She wiped her eyes. "It's just a bit loud."

"Apology accepted," Soraya said.

Actually, we were all dripping with sweat. We looked like someone had just rescued us from a pond.

"I think we should go ahead with the road trip," Charlotte said quietly.

"I'm prepared to support Charlotte," Julia said frostily. "And therefore I too agree to continue as originally planned."

Before I could express my gratitude and repeat how sorry I was, Soraya held her hand up and laughed.

"*You* want to come with *us?*" she said. "Well, that's kind of you. Thank you humbly. I mean, really. Only, what makes you think either of *us* wants to go anywhere at all with *you* two?"

I turned to her. "Soraya – "

"She's had bloody *cancer*," Soraya went on, "and all she did was not bother you because she didn't need to, and now it gets out, and what do you two do? You *judge* her. How totally self-centred – "

"Hang on, *no*," Julia said, raising her voice. "That's utterly unfair. We were shocked and offended at being kept in the dark. Do you realise how patronising that is? *Oh, let's just not tell them, we don't want them to get upset, let's just let them get on with their little lives, after all –* "

"It wasn't like that," I said weakly.

"Well done for really upsetting her," Soraya said, going on the offensive again.

Silence. Like the deathly hush at the eye of some kind of explosion.

"Can I ask you something, Soraya?" Julia said calmly.

"Anything you like, Julia," Soraya replied. We were back to that again.

"You've got a thing for my sister, yes?"

"I love her, yes," Soraya said. She scoffed. "Twice as much as you two put together, apparently."

"Okay; well then, imagine the boot had been on the other foot. Hannah gets cancer, she goes off for however long it was – whatever: you don't see her in all that time – and when she finally reappears, she makes as if nothing's ever happened. But later on it turns out that, during the time she was away, she had a condition that nearly killed her. And the only way you ever find out is because one of her friends – someone who was, and is, *actually in the loop* – reveals it in a totally random way in a diner somewhere at the start of a holiday you're all supposed to be going on. How do you *feel* about that, Soraya? Does it make you feel *good* about yourself? Are you all pure sympathy: *oh, you poor thing, I do hope you're all right now?* Or do you start questioning your relationship with her? Do you actually, at any point at all, get *angry?*"

More silence. Soraya looked at me.

"Julia's got a point," I told her.

Soraya shrugged. "I thought I was doing everyone a favour. I actually was. You should probably have told them at the start."

She was talking exclusively to me, as if my sisters had simply vanished into thin air.

"I know," I told her.

"Look, Soraya," Julia went on, breaking the spell, "I'm not angry with you. You're right. It had to emerge, and, after all this time – I'm assuming it happened well before Lek was born – it could probably only surface in the 'wrong' way. You've done us all a favour. But it's simply not *fair* to accuse us of not loving Hannah. We *do*."

Soraya swallowed emotionally. More silence. "I'm sorry," she said eventually. "And I'm sorry for saying we don't want to go on holiday with you. We do."

She took my hand. I squeezed back hard.

"Back to you, Hannah," Julia said, obviously not finished. "You probably won't get this, but we're not just mad about being kept in the dark. That's bad enough, but – I'll be honest with you here – we both feel – felt?

feel? I don't know the right term… *jealous*. I admit that's irrational, as envy always is. But sometimes it's also natural. *I'd* have liked to save you from cancer! *I'd* have liked to give you an egg! Ditto Charlotte. We never got the chance because we were never asked!"

We'd reached the knife-edge moment. I had to say the exact words they needed to hear, and that probably meant rehearsing each sentence in my head before uttering it. Only there wasn't time. I sat paralysed.

Soraya suddenly cut the silence. "Okay, here's the deal, Ladies. She *would* have come to you for bone marrow if I hadn't got myself tested the minute I found out. For what it's worth, I didn't expect a match: the odds are totally against it. She was going to die; I love her like crazy; I just needed to feel I was doing something. When the doctors gave me the green light, I couldn't believe it. But then I saw: it was meant to be. Fate loved me. It had given me a way of tying my one true love and me together forever. The egg thing was a kind of natural follow-on from that, later. It couldn't really have been anything else, given how much I was in your sister's good books at that point. I got first dibs, and I pounced on it. Never look a gift horse etcetera. In the end, nobody got hurt," she went on. "The opposite. Hannah's alive; Lek's healthy and beautiful; you've even got a step-sister-y thing of sorts, and if you're ever in any trouble, I'll shift heaven and earth to help you. Okay, jealousy is natural. I understand you feeling pissed off. But you're not stupid. You'll get over it. I'm not hard-hearted and I'm not selfish. Ideally, I want you both to like me, but I can't make you."

Julia and Charlotte exchanged bemused looks. Then sighs. They didn't say anything.

Bloody hell, it looked – like they might have been won over?

"Jealousy *is* stupid," Charlotte said eventually. "It may be natural – occasionally – but so are lots of hateful things. It's how you deal with those things that matters."

"You're right," Julia agreed. "It's about where we are now."

Bloody hell. Consensus achieved.

Charlotte turned to Soraya. "Who knows? Our bone marrow might not have been as good as yours, nor might our eggs. I'm not putting Julia and I down, obviously, but things have definitely worked out, and, thinking about it properly, I wouldn't want to go back in time, just so we could do things 'our' way. I can't imagine anything more arrogant. And I do like you."

We sat in silence for a full second, grinning apprehensively at each other.

"Then it's settled," Julia pronounced finally, in an exhausted voice. "America, look out. Here we come."

Or Here We Don't Come

From one extreme to the other. Suddenly, we were four best friends. It started slowly, of course, but it was like we'd all separately spotted the Celestial City, and we knew there was still a long way before we reached it, but we were pilgrims and so we took pleasure in encouraging each other. Obviously, it began with a long discussion of my cancer and Lek's parentage. It went from there into what I needed to do now.

"Obviously, you need to tell John and Mabel," Julia said, "at the earliest possible opportunity. However healthy you might think you are, there is always the possibility of a relapse. If, God forbid, that occurs, they'll probably find out it's not the first time, then they're going to feel like we did; only worse, because when the circle of people who knew widened, like it just has, they *still* weren't allowed in. And it'll look as if Lottie and I were complicit in that."

I didn't argue. Now I'd got through the trauma of telling Julia and Charlotte, informing my remaining siblings was the obvious next step. And it felt like it'd be relatively easy.

An hour later, Julia began suggesting ideas for the road trip.

"We could make this a rock and roll themed trip," she said. "We should begin at the Hitchcock Estate. It's where Timothy Leary lived. You know: *turn on, tune in, drop out*, or words to that effect. Visit hallowed ground, like where Woodstock was held. There's a museum there now, I think."

"And we could do writers' places," I said. "I don't know where Edith Wharton lived, or Toni Morrison or *I Know Why the Caged Bird* – "

"Maya Angelou," Julia said.

"I mean, I'm pretty sure Ernest Hemingway lived in Florida for a while – "

"I'd love to go to Maine," Charlotte said. "There's a real spiritual culture up there. Actual witches. Like Wicca, but American."

"Are you into Wicca?" Soraya asked.

"Where would *you* like to go, Soraya?" Charlotte said. "We've got the whole of America."

"Maybe where Adam Richman goes?" Soraya said. "*Man v Food?* I'm not bothered about famous dead people. I'd like to go to see some baseball, or a football game. Maybe the *Friends* café, or Seattle to see where *Grey's Anatomy* was filmed."

"Seriously?" Julia said. "You're into *Grey's Anatomy?*"

"I've only seen series one," Soraya said.

"It goes radically downhill after that," Julia told her. "All the 'soul mate' baloney? No thanks. Maybe it's because I'm British and cynical – "

Charlotte hooted. "It definitely *is!* I *love Grey's Anatomy!* Don't listen to her, Soraya. I've seen to the end of series five – "

"It's bullshit," Julia said.

We laughed. We got excited. We talked at and to each other and flapped our hands and touched each other's arms and knees for redoubled emphasis and said 'Oh my God!' We talked about Montgomery Alabama, Mount Rushmore, Wounded Knee, the Rockies, Thelma and Louise, Taos Pueblo, Donald Trump, Naomi Wolf, The Cherokee Heritage Centre, surfing in California, Little Bighorn, Ken Kesey, Donna Tartt, Sand Creek, Sara Davidson, Sitting Bull, The Statue of Liberty, Alexandria Ocasio-Cortez, *True Detective*, Crazy Horse, The Golden Gate Bridge.

Yes, we'd fall out again. Over the course of three thousand miles, of course we would. But Soraya's revelation had changed us. We were four now, a team, instead of three plus one, or two plus two. All things considered, it boded excellently. Yes, we would go to the Hitchcock Estate, to a baseball game, to watch some football, to Salem, to a *Man v Food* joint, to wherever the hell Edith Wharton used to live. It'd be a proper road trip and we'd not only do it, and enjoy it: we'd use it to live life to the max. We'd fall in love with America so deeply, we'd never, ever want to leave, or be apart from each other again.

"I'm sorry," Julia said suddenly. "But I'm actually desperate to go to the toilet."

"Me too," Charlotte and I said together.

"I've been holding on to it for as long as possible," Charlotte said. "But I actually forgot to go when we stopped at that diner. You know, with all the, er … surprise, and everything. I'm going to wet myself if we don't stop again soon."

"We've been driving for long enough," Julia said. "We must be nearly in the Florida Keys now."

Soraya knocked on the partition. "Rudy?"

It flew open. "Yes?"

"Could we stop for another bathroom break, please?" she asked. "Unless you want us to wet the upholstery."

He laughed. "Gimme five minutes." The partition closed again.

As always, once you realise you actually need to go to the toilet, the urge seems to multiply ten times over. Five minutes became six, then seven, then eight. When the car pulled to a halt, we'd crossed our legs twice over: thigh over thigh, foot behind calf, toes desperately trying for something more. I wasn't sure I'd actually be able to walk, assuming I could even get out.

Rudolph opened the door for us. He grimaced slightly, as what was presumably the gross odour of four women who'd been sweating for several hours hit him full on.

We didn't exactly pile out, more like edged our way to the threshold, lowered ourselves painstakingly onto the tarmac and began to hobble. Julia was actually doubled over.

It suddenly struck me that we'd been here before. I had other things on my mind, so it began vaguely, as a sense of déjà vu, and only slowly became more concrete. The low red-brick building, the large windows, the terracotta roof…

We were back at *McFadyens*.

Toilet Break/ Conference

None of us thought to query the fact. We had other things to think about. Luckily, the Women's had four separate cubicles. I went into the one closest to the door. The experience of expelling half my body weight made me flush with euphoria and exhaustion, as if I'd crossed an impossible finish line, and my body could finally admit the colossal sacrifices it had made. I put my elbows on my knees and rubbed my face to reanimate it.

When I came out, Julia was standing in front of the line of washbasins, half-undressed to the waist. She smelt her armpits.

"I badly need two aspirin, a litre of mineral water and a hot bath," she said miserably. She examined her makeup in the mirror, and the more important reality seemed to hit her. "This place looks very like where we were earlier."

Soraya emerged from her cubicle. She too appraised her face in the mirror. "It *is* where we were earlier," she said. "You're probably going to hate me again, but I gave Rudy a big wad of cash to drive round in a circle for however long it took for us all to iron out our differences. It was my fault it all kicked off. I had to make it right again."

"We never hated you," Julia said. "Hannah, maybe. And that was a joke, by the way."

I chuckled. "Not a very good one."

"You deserved it," Julia replied, "and it's all in the past now."

Charlotte came out. "So how far are we from JFK?"

Soraya shrugged. "Maybe five minutes?"

I turned to her. "So we've been driving for – what? – four, five hours? And we're only just round the corner from where we started?"

"For the answer to that question," Julia said, "look around you. Do you actually know where we're *going* on this journey from hell, Soraya? To obviate any misunderstanding, by 'hell', I don't mean the company; I mean being cooped up like four refugees in a shipping container."

"Somewhere in New Jersey," Soraya said. "It's only about an hour and a half from the airport. Or it would have been."

"It still is, apparently," I said. "Frankly, now that I've had the mother of all wees, my life's complete, so I don't care what else happens. How did you get that out of him? I thought it was supposed to be a closely guarded secret."

"Cash for cooperation," Soraya said. "It was part of our sordid deal."

I filled a basin and began to wash my face and neck. "Does Harlinne know we're going to be late?"

Soraya nodded. "He's going to give her an estimated time of arrival when I give him the nod. Which will be in about an hour's time."

"What do you mean?" Charlotte asked. "What else are we going to be doing?"

Soraya turned to her. "We're going to be showering and having something to eat and drink. By drink, I don't just mean water. I mean, a few Kentucky bourbons to celebrate the fact that we're now friends and that, between us, we've just produced enough high quality urine to flood the Hudson River. I've got a huge billfold in my bag. Harlinne's going to confiscate our credit cards, so it makes sense to cheat, right? Anyway, this may be just a diner, but I'm pretty sure they can get us a decent shower if I actually make it worth their while. Even if they have to drive us someplace. I'm not getting back in that limo again like this. Depending on how the upholstery smells, I may not be getting back in at all. Thinking about it, I might pay Rudy to go and get it valeted somewhere while we eat. He's a nice guy, and he's one hell of a good guitarist. You need to hear him, Hannah. He's even better than you."

"I'm crap," I said. "Does he play the harmonica at all? Because that's what we most need. It sounds old-fashioned, but it's a brilliant combination. Rock music never made the most of it. It's ripe for a major, major comeback."

Julia cleared her throat. "I'm starving."

A Wash and a Drink

Marvin, the diner manager, didn't look pleased to see us again. On our last encounter, four or five hours ago, he'd thrown us out, and we'd gone radically downhill since then. But Soraya's billfold changed his mind; in exchange for a mere $500, he started being nice to us. There was a holiday apartment behind the pine trees, he said, where we could shower, and it had a washbasin and a tumble dryer. He brought us aspirin. He took our meal order, and when we were all ready, he brought us a bottle of Knob Creek disguised as orange-juice. To prove its provenance, she showed us the original empty under the table, partly wrapped in a towel, again to hide it. Like a secret agent thing.

When he'd gone we all looked at it. And at our four empty wine glasses. We'd already consumed enough water to more than compensate for the urine depletion.

"I've still got a headache," Julia said. "And we're meeting this 'Harlinne' of yours in ninety minutes' time. Presumably, she'll give us a set of car keys. One of us needs to be fit to drive. Save me some and I'll join you once we've found a motel. I'm just trying to think ahead, not being a killjoy."

"To hell with Harlinne," Soraya said. "You were right, Julia."

Julia laughed. "About what?"

"You said you hate the theatre of it all," Soraya said. "Let's show her who's boss. It's our road trip, right? She's got us a car. I can get Rudy to ring ahead, tell her we've all had a drink. She can take it to a motel somewhere."

"That might sound a bit rude?" Charlotte said.

"No, but I'd *pay* her," Soraya said. "She's a businesswoman. I agree, we can't expect her to do it for no money, but hey, let's just allow her to name her price."

Julia shook her head. "You're doing a lot of spending, Soraya. Let me at least go halves with you."

"Done," Soraya said. She opened the bottle and poured everyone what I'd guesstimate was a triple.

And Behold, Harlinne Again

I'd like to say this is where things began to go wrong, but of course, the credit for that can probably go to Venice. Rudolph drove somewhere to get the car valeted, then Soraya made him come and eat with us. I say *with*: by this time, we'd all finished. He had a small burger, fries, and a glass of milk. He ate daintily. He didn't look at us. We hid what remained of the bourbon in Soraya's bag, where it probably joined what remained of the vodka. Quite a minibar.

"What did Harlinne say?" I asked.

"Couldn't get through to her," he replied. "I texted to let her know we're on our way, but I don't know whether she got it. Pretty sure she won't let you guys down. She's never disappointed anyone before."

"What about the car?" Soraya asked. "Did you put my offer to her?"

"Five hundred dollars to take it to a motel, and then me drive you there? Yeah, but again, no reply. How much money you actually *got*, if you don't mind me asking? You could probably have persuaded her to do that for much less. I'm just saying, don't go throwing your cash around in this country, or pretty soon you won't have any."

"Thanks," Soraya said. She winked at me. He had no idea who we were. The wigs may not have worked – we'd taken them off too often – but the baldness had. And the fact that we'd washed off all our makeup.

When we got in the car, it smelt of lavender. Apart from that, nothing had changed. Rudolph's deal with Soraya may have made him at least two thousand dollars better off, but it hadn't persuaded him to strip the whitewash. We still didn't know where the emergency release button was for the central locking. Not that we cared. We'd all eaten and had a drink and we fell asleep.

Next thing I was aware of, the car door was open and Rudolph was standing to attention in what looked like bright sunshine. For a weird moment, I had no idea what was going on, or even exactly where I was. Then it came flooding back. Bloody hell, the road trip. I just wanted to curl up in bed somewhere.

The others looked equally fed up. We got out grudgingly, Soraya and I pulling on our wigs, and Rudolph made us line up on the pavement. We didn't speak. I guess we were all in the same frame of mind: let's get this over with, find somewhere to crash, and have a fourteen-hour sleep. Soraya clutched the guitar like it was a giant teddy bear. She looked miserable.

We were on a short, fat bridge across a fairly wide river that, about five hundred yards away, emptied into the sea. The weather was fabulous: a cloudless sky and a gentle ocean-bound breeze. Cars passed slowly on both sides. There were white balustrades, and a pair of squat towers, one at either end. Beneath the side where we stood, a pair of what looked to be sea defensive walls extending into the ocean; opposite, inexpensive grey-brick houses and grass. Later on, I discovered this was Ocean Avenue, Avon-by-the-Sea, New Jersey. At the time, I could have been anywhere.

Further up the road, parked partly on the pavement, and also over what looked suspiciously like a single yellow line, stood a small blue hatchback. I don't know anything about cars, so don't ask me to be more specific. It didn't look like any kind of convertible, or even particularly American, but, as far as I could tell, its windows weren't whitewashed. I kind of felt that it was our car, but I could have been wrong.

Rudolph had driven off. But then we saw him coming back again. He slowed down in front of us and Harlinne got out from the rear, where, a couple of minutes earlier, we'd been sitting. In her worsted skirt-suit, court shoes, designer sunglasses and bouffant, she would have looked like the queen of something, had it not been for the *Make America Great Again* baseball cap perched on her hair and the little Stars and Stripes flag on a stick she held.

As soon as she was on the pavement, Rudolph drove off again. Julia was right: this was classic theatre of the ludicrous.

"Hello, ladies, and welcome to America," Harlinne said.

We all murmured polite thank yous.

She gave me a small plastic bag. "Very important: don't open this until after I've gone. Now, I'm going to need your phones, credit cards and passports for safe-keeping, ladies."

We were too tired to argue, and to be honest, we did see the necessity. We didn't want our passports getting stolen and we knew that, to fully immerse ourselves in the Sea to Shining Sea experience, our credit cards and phones would also have to go. And we'd been warned in advance. She collected them from us in a small wooden box.

"A road trip across America is a glorious thing," she said, when the transference was complete, "but only to the extent that it opens up the possibility of greater self-knowledge. You're not traversing the continental land-mass, in other words. You're traversing your *own* individual potentials and your own limitations. Think you're up to it? To do it, you have to be completely at the mercy of the open road. Do you think Jack Kerouac had a mobile phone?"

I inwardly rolled my eyes. Not again. Why was she so determined to point out that Jack bloody Kerouac hadn't owned a phone?

"It was 1947," Julia said. "He'd have needed a very long wire. Sorry," she went on, "I'm a novelist by profession."

Harlinne ignored her. "Do you think Ken Kesey had a phone?"

Please, God: no one ask who Ken Kesey is/ was.

Julia frowned. "The author of *One Flew Over the Cuckoo's Nest?*"

"That's right," Harlinne said tetchily.

"He died in 2001," Julia said. "So possibly he did have a phone, yes."

"I meant, in the 1960s," Harlinne replied.

Julia sighed. "In that case, no. Look, it's an established fact that the first mobile phone call was made by a Motorola executive on April the third, 1973. We can therefore safely assume that anything before that date didn't involve mobile phones."

"Julia, please," I said. She'd been on *University Challenge* in 2006, so I'd grown used to this sort of thing.

"Sorry," she replied. "I just thought the car was going to be at a motel, that's all. That is our car, I assume?" she said, looking at the blue hatchback.

"It's about baring your souls," Harlinne said, without answering the question. "Has anyone got any more questions?"

"Is that blue thing our car?" Soraya said.

"It *is*," Harlinne replied, as if to confirm how lucky we were. "The keys are under the visor. Rudolph loaded your luggage into the trunk while you were asleep. Any further questions?"

If Harlinne had been a routine kind of tour operator, and we'd been in a normal frame of mind, we'd probably have grilled her for at least ten minutes, just for politeness' sake, but we were tired and depressed. We muttered four polite nos.

"In that case, I hereby declare this road trip *open!*" she declared.

At that point, two unbelievable things occurred, and I'm just going to set them down as they happened, without recording my feelings, since I imagine they'll probably be obvious to anyone with an ounce of human sympathy. Firstly, she took the wooden box with our phones, cards and passports in and tipped it into the river. The gap between the upturned box and the balustrade was roughly six inches, so all I saw was a falling blur. Secondly, Rudolph pulled up in the limo. She got in, slammed the door shut, and engaged the central locking.

She wound the window down. She took off her sunglasses. She smiled. "Don't worry, you'll find everything you need in that bag. And there's a thousand dollars in unused banknotes in the car. I'll wire you more in five days. Details of how to receive it are in the glovebox."

The limo pulled away.

I admit, I felt a huge sense of relief, though not entirely pure. I thought she'd done some kind of a Derren Brown stunt: only *appeared* to throw our phones, cards and passports into the river. When we opened the plastic bag, there they'd be, good as new, and we'd be shocked and delighted and, yes, it really *would* be high quality theatre. We'd ask each other how she'd done it, and we'd be like *phew* and *thank God*. We'd laugh a bit, roll our eyes, shake our heads, then we'd get on with the serious business of trying to find a way of getting the car to some kind of motel.

"Er, did you see what she just did?" Charlotte said. "She threw our passports and things off the bridge into the sea."

"No, no, that's not possible," Julia said. I could tell she was having the same thought as me. "Look in the bag, Hannah. They'll be in the bag."

"How the hell could they be in the BAG?" Soraya burst out. As so often in the past, her extreme pessimism about human nature became a short cut to the truth. *"Oh my GOD, she's thrown our PHONES into the freaking RIVER!"*

We could have just opened the bag, but we didn't. We fell on it like hungry werewolves on a sack of meat. We literally tore it to shreds.

What we found: firstly, four passports.

But not ours.

Or rather – yes, *ours*. They had our names and photos inside.

But – no, *not* ours! These were black. They were US passports: they had an eagle in the middle and the words, 'United States of America' at the bottom.

Also, four US driving licences. Not international ones like we were supposed to have, but with NEW JERSEY in red, above our photos.

There was a handwritten note accompanying all this.

Congratulations on throwing yourself on the mercy of the open road. It will be kind to you only if you have complete faith in your ability to cope with anything it may throw at you. From now until the end of the trip, I want you to consider yourselves honorary Americans, so please find enclosed your tickets to a magical journey. Whatever you might think you saw, by the way, I've got your actual driving licences, credit cards, and your passports, and your phones. Or maybe I haven't! Maybe they're at the bottom of Shark River! Maybe they've reached the Atlantic by now! Who knows? And hey, who cares? Have fun! Call me if you need anything. But try not to. Lots of love, Harlinne.

Julia was still freaking out over the new documentation. "Oh, shit," she said. "Shit, shit, shit. She's – she's – Do you realise how much trouble we could be in if we're found with these?"

My stomach also turned over. "I – I know."

"There's a police car coming," Charlotte said.

We all turned simultaneously, like four meerkats. No doubt about it: the way the driver eyeballed us: he was coming for us. He gave us a little whoo on his siren by way of saying *hi* and *freeze*.

Julia grabbed the passports and the licences and what remained of the plastic bag and hurled them over the balustrade. The wind had picked up, so they flew for quite a distance.

God, please don't let them float.

Sorry, America

The police car pulled up on the 'sidewalk', as we might as well call it from now. It dispensed an officer in a short-sleeve black tunic and trousers with a yellow stripe down the side; about twenty-nine, crew cut, stocky, grim. I'd seen that expression in policemen before, most recently in Venice. Not *whether* you were going to be charged, but *what with*. He pulled on his hat with both hands to make himself doubly sombre. We lined up in roughly the same way we had earlier with Harlinne. "Be apologetic," Julia whispered.

"What were you just doing, ma'am?" he asked Julia, coming to a stop in front of her. "I mean, what did you just throw over the bridge?"

Julia shrugged. "Oh, you know, only litter."

"'Only litter.'" He walked along the line like he was inspecting us. "That your car?" he asked.

"We were just about to move it, officer," I said sweetly.

"It's parked illegally," he said. "And for your information, littering's also against the law. I need whoever's the driver here to go get her licence."

We looked at each other as discreetly as we could, which probably wasn't very discreetly. We were all thinking the same thing. Harlinne's *I've got your actual driving licences, credit cards, and your passports, and your phones.*

"Oh, I *hope* you didn't throw our licences over the side by mistake, Julia," I said.

"Damn," Julia said unconvincingly. "I thought it was litter."

"I should have stopped you," I said. "I wasn't thinking."

"You ladies trying to be funny?" the policeman asked.

"No," we said together.

Charlotte burped. She put her hand over her mouth a second too late.

"Have you been *drinking*, ma'am?" the policeman asked her. As if he hadn't expected the problem to be this big.

No answer. The wind howled slightly, as in a horror film. He took a step back and addressed the same question to all of us. We looked uncertainly at each other.

"I'm going to need you all to take a breathalyser test," he said.

Soraya's wig blew off.

PART FOUR:

NEW JERSEY TO NEW YORK

Bad Start

WE DIDN'T DECLINE THE BREATHALYSER OR RESIST arrest, so Officer Whatever didn't feel the need to cuff us. As we got into the car, a small crowd gathered to watch. He drove us to the police station, a two storey red brick building with lots of aerials and square, unforgiving windows. We checked in at reception, then we were taken to some kind of custody suite to give our details.

Probably only Julia could be charged with anything specific, but the car was going to be a problem. With no documentation, there was nothing official to tie us to it; yet it contained our luggage, which would raise the possibility that we'd stolen it.

And then there was the lack of documentation itself. From their point of view, who exactly *were* we? What had we been so eager to dump? Why were Soraya and I wearing wigs?

It quickly became clear that we had an extra problem, of which I wasn't aware until, about an hour after our arrival, a middle aged female detective, called Hernandez, sat me at a desk. A small man in a suit sat to one side, apparently taking notes. She switched a cassette recorder on.

"It says here you're Hannah Lexingwood," she said. "The world famous music executive. That right?"

"That's correct," I replied.

"And your bald friend out there is Soraya Snow, of whom even I've heard. Lead singer of The Fully Magic Coal Tar Lounge."

"Er, yes. There's no 'The'."

"Pardon me?"

"No 'The'. It's just 'Fully Magic Coal Tar Lounge'."

"And *this* woman" – she slid Julia's mugshot across at me – "is Julia Mordred, a prize-winning British novelist."

"And Charlotte owns a candle shop in Devon," I said.

"In Britain."

"That's right. We're all British. We've got British accents."

She chuckled derisively. "*Anyone* can do a British accent, honey. Look, can I let you into a little secret? We're not going to start helping you till you start levelling with us. What were you throwing over the side of that bridge? Where are your papers, if you're British? Because you surely didn't just drop out of the sky. Why did your friend have two bottles of liquor and a ten thousand dollar billfold in her bag?"

"Soraya had *ten thousand dollars?*"

"Stop calling her 'Soraya'. What's her real name?"

"Really. It's Soraya. Soraya Snow."

She sighed. "Okay, let's talk about the car again. Where did you get it?"

"I've told you, we booked a tour with Harlinne Vobrosky, the New York talent agent. She got us – "

"This is the woman with the yellow-on-blue website, yes? Because I've got to say, that doesn't look real. And before you say, 'call her', we've tried."

"Keep trying. Please."

"Was it drugs?"

"What?"

"Someone sees a police car coming, they're holding a large package of some controlled substance; they might very well throw it in the river."

"It was litter."

She chuckled again. "Let's just think about that, shall we? According to you, you're holding a pile of litter. You probably know littering's illegal. It is in Britain, right? At the very least, it's anti-social. Then you spot a police car. Now if that was me, and I'd been disposed to drop litter, which I'm not, the sight of a police car would've made me think twice. I'd be like, 'Hey, I *was* going to throw this stuff over the bridge, but now I'd better *not* since I don't want to get in trouble.' But that was the exact opposite of what your friend did. And by the way, I read a lot of novels and I don't know *any* famous novelist who takes delight in littering. Most novelists I know actually *care* about the environment."

"Okay, look, put it this way: if we're pretending to be someone we're not, why don't we pretend to be 'ordinary Joes'? Why am I pretending to be a top music executive and my friend's pretending to be – "

"Because you're brazen, that's why. Your kind likes to make fun of the police. You think you can snub your nose at us and get away with it. *My name's Nancy Pelosi, and there ain't a damn thing you can do about it, Pig.* Either that, or you're delusional. And of course you don't want us to find out who you really are, because that would mean us discovering you've got a criminal record a mile long. With that haircut of yours, honey, I'm pretty damn sure you're on the run. Because that would definitely fit."

"Look, I think I can – "

"I notice you still haven't asked for a lawyer."

"I don't like lawyers. Besides, I thought we could sort this out amicably."

"Well, we can't. You'd better start praying we don't get no reported robberies yesterday or today or the day before, because you might start fitting the bill."

"I can prove I'm Hannah Lexingwood. I was arrested in Venice just over a week ago. *They* took my fingerprints. *You've* got my fingerprints – "

She narrowed her eyes like we might be getting somewhere. "Venice in Los Angeles or Venice, Florida?"

"Venice Italy. Soraya and I were there for the Biennale."

"The BN *what?*"

"It's a – "

"Look, this is what's going to happen now. We're going to put you in a quiet room on your own, to think through everything you've said here today. If you decide you want a lawyer at any stage, just shout. But, attorney or not, you probably won't be leaving any time soon. We're all going to sit tight and see what turns up. My guess is, something *will*, something unpleasant – a person's been robbed or mugged or some badass guy's looking high and low for his delivery – and you'll have a lot more explaining to do. And that won't be long coming."

"If we'd thrown a package of drugs into the river, it'd just have gone straight down. Like a brick. This flew off in the air."

"Some of it did. We can't vouch for all of it."

"Haven't you got CCTV?"

"We're still retrieving it. But it's not going to cover every possible angle."

Interview over, 5.55pm. As promised, I was taken to a 'room' – obviously, a cell – on my own to think through what I'd said. Square, pale yellow walls, a hard bench, a stainless steel toilet/ 'bathroom'.

At this point, you're probably wondering why I didn't simply shop Harlinne. I mean, yes, I'd mentioned her. She was our 'tour operator'. But I hadn't said anything that could get her into serious trouble. It wasn't just that the truth required a long explanation – *she took our passports, driving licences and phones, dumped them in the river and replaced them with US forgeries* – which they probably wouldn't believe; more that her handwritten note had somehow 'got' to me. She was definitely crazy and possibly malicious – as Soraya later said, *Remember that feeling when you finally realised your grandma was evil?* – but she was also rock 'n' roll in the completely-off-the-freakin'-wall,-man sense, and her appeals to Jack Kerouac and Ken Kesey had undoubtedly worked on Julia, because she didn't say anything either. Nor did Charlotte or Soraya. Honour among thieves perhaps.

I could see what was coming. The police would get hold of the CCTV. They'd spot a short, well-dressed woman in a limo pulling up next to us, then taking something from us, tipping it into the river, then giving us something ... It *could* look like a drugs exchange, just about, yes. Especially the way we'd all descended on the bag like we were ravenous for a fix.

But then they'd go back in time, maybe. Rudolph loading our car, what would they make of that?

It didn't matter. If the truth is sufficiently incredible, it has a sell-by date, by which I mean, there comes a point at which no one will even entertain it any more. I guess that's fair. When people are caught in a wrongdoing and they start explaining with a lie, then once that's uncovered, their next lie will usually be less credible. And so on: they gradually lose any right to be taken seriously. If the truth's completely bonkers and you put it right at the end of the process, it's got no chance whatsoever.

All of which would be a complete waste of everyone's time. I wasn't scared. I knew we'd get out eventually. I'd been arrested dozens of times before, so had Soraya. Forget about Venice; sooner or later, someone would check the zillions of fingerprints on IDENT1, and they'd find an indisputable match. And since the New Jersey Police Department didn't actually have anything on us except 'littering', and because we'd been telling the (qualified) truth all along, they'd probably feel obliged to release us with a warning.

I knew how to be 'brazen' as Hernandez put it. I was being nice to her not because I was afraid, but because I could see she was one of the good ones.

Besides, it rarely pays to be a smart arse.

I was completely shattered now. I knew the NJPD probably wouldn't like it – I was supposed to be 'thinking' – but I lay down on the bench, turned on my side and put my hands flat together under my left temple.

Five minutes later, I was asleep.

'The Road Will be Kind to You'

I awoke to the sound of a key being turned in the lock. I sat up and remembered where I was. I'd no idea how much time had passed. I swung my legs over the side of the bench, rubbed my eyes, slipped on my shoes and yawned.

Detective Hernandez carried a clipboard. She grinned. "Had a good sleep, *Ms Lexingwood?*"

I wasn't sure whether she was being sarcastic. Probably.

"It was a long day," I said.

"Okay," she said. "We just need to ask you some more questions, then you're free to go. Your lawyer's outside."

"I didn't ask for one," I said. "I'm sorry about what happened, but it was nothing really. We littered. We lost our passports and driving licences. That's it."

"You mean Harlinne Vobrosky *took* your driving licences and passports and threw them into the river. Apparently."

"Er…"

"And replaced them with forged US documents. That *was* what you were throwing in the river, right?"

I sighed.

"Why didn't you tell us?" she asked.

"Would you have believed me? Would anyone?"

"You could at least have *tried* us." She stood over me. "The truth's always better than a lie."

"I just didn't tell you everything, that's all." I was still at least a quarter asleep and it felt like I was talking to some kind of counsellor. "I didn't want to get Harlinne into trouble, if I'm totally honest."

"How well do you know her?"

"She got us a gig – a photo-shoot – in Venice. She organised our road trip, such as it was."

She chortled. "We've confirmed what you said about you getting arrested in Italy. You and your friend are quite the live wires, if you don't mind me saying."

"How did you find out about Harlinne? Did one of the others tell you?"

She shook her head. "In terms of what *not* to tell us, you all did an excellent job of getting your stories straight in advance."

"We didn't even discuss it, honestly."

"Maybe you've got a psychic link then. In any case, we traced that little blue vehicle of hers to a car-hire firm in Wisconsin. No easy feat: to say it's a small fry outfit would be a major understatement. Anyhow, the owner knew where to find her. It may interest you to know that Harlinne Vobrosky's got a string of criminal convictions stretching all the way back to the late nineteen-fifties."

I sat up. "The *nineteen fifties?* How *old* is she then?"

"Let me see. She was born in nineteen thirty. That would make her eighty-nine."

"*Eighty-nine?* I thought she was in her sixties!"

"She most recently served time for fraud in a local correctional centre for women. We retrieved your passports and driver's licences from her New York 'office' – her tipping them in the river was pure David Blaine – but we also discovered lots of other stuff. Long story short, there's a warrant out for her arrest."

"Wow. What sort of 'other stuff'?"

"Forged documents. The sort we picked up from the river with your faces on."

It made me wonder, just fleetingly, whether the Venice photo shoot had been genuine. But then, I *knew* it was. I knew the photographers. I'd had it from Maxwell Clunes. I'd had it from *Harper's Bazaar* itself. So how the hell had an eighty-nine-year-old woman from a correctional facility ingratiated themselves with a world-class magazine?

Answer: I don't know.

I'd like to say I admired her even more, but that would be a lie. *Fraud.* Cheating people.

I sighed. It's at times like this that I realise how hollow I actually am. Then a black cloud descends and my whole life seems like one long sham. The me I suppose I'd like to be worships the whole rock 'n' roll thing: its contempt for ordinariness, its reckless transgression of moral and legal boundaries. But the real me just wants people to be decent. I guess I'm a *snowflake* at heart. And I despise myself for it.

It's one of the reasons I need Soraya. But sometimes, I feel such self-disdain, I can't even face her. Then I need to be alone. She knows I'm a phoney, of course. It's one of the reasons behind *You're so bloody prissy and middle-class, Hannah*. Harsh. But I put up with it because it's true.

I didn't want any more road tripping. I wanted another shower, then New York and a five star hotel. I didn't care how similar it was to other hotels. The band was finished, but Soraya's revelations to my sisters *en route* from JFK had probably stymied whatever remained of Charlotte's desire to sue Dad. I was a *cancer victim* now. Anything remotely upsetting might cause me to relapse. And she knew enough to realise I really didn't want her splitting the family down the middle.

On the other hand, that wasn't entirely the point. Not morally. We still needed to talk.

But I couldn't be bothered. I'd had enough.

So what did that make me? No bloody wonder I despised myself.

Hernandez was still standing over me. "You all right, honey?" she asked.

Odd to hear a detective call you 'honey'. But also, strangely comforting.

"Could I just stay here for a while?" I asked.

She laughed. "This isn't a hotel, Ms Lexingwood. We need it. Now come on, get up."

I Want Out!

Maybe it's time start my life anew? I didn't actually need to be the manager of a rock band any more. The Coal Tars had played as big as we were ever likely to get, won all the awards worth having, made too much money. Elliot was right: where now? The Beatles had split up in 1970; that, then never re-forming, was their best ever move. We weren't them, but who the hell could be any more? It didn't mean we couldn't imitate them in that respect and reap the dividends.

I badly needed to get to New York and that hotel and that hot shower and that bed with a soft mattress and big duvet. First step on The Highway to The Rest of My Life. JFK to New Jersey was as much epiphany as anyone could cope with. Since epiphany was what road trips were all about, it had served its purpose. Henceforth, I needed to settle down in London NW3, look after Tim and Lek, Skype Soraya every night, wait on her hand and foot when she came to visit (or less likely, to live with us), start scouting for primary schools.

Because rock 'n' roll didn't really mean anything, hadn't for decades. Nowadays, all the world's rule breakers, drug users and alcoholics were mean-spirited nonentities. They lived in big houses and drove big cars and pinched pennies.

So maybe I ought to pride myself on being a snowflake.

What it was really all about, maybe: turning a denigrating label on its head. A *yes, that's me, so up yours* to the whole stupid planet.

I could feel myself slipping into a black depression. It had happened before. Four years ago, I'd taken myself off to a hotel in Prague. Which mightn't have been so bad, except we were touring in Denmark at the time. I don't even know how Tim and Soraya found me. I guess I'm at least slightly transparent.

Me, me, me – how it always starts. I needed to find Soraya.

No such luck. Hernandez led me along a narrow corridor. We passed seven or eight police officers and clerical workers. They looked at me with that faint should-I-smile-or-not-and-is-it-even-allowed expression I'd grown used to over the years, their pace slowing infinitesimally to get a better look at my face, assess the precise degree of my ugliness so they could tell all their friends that evening. They knew exactly who I was, all about me. Anything they hadn't known when I'd arrived here, they'd found out.

Hernandez opened the door to an office with a single besuited man inside. "Your lawyer," she said. "We don't do this for everyone, but there's press folk outside, and you need a bit of privacy. I'll be back in three minutes, then you can answer one or two questions about Vobrosky. In the meantime, we'll try and figure a way of getting you out of here without too much fuss. I'm not promising anything, mind. This is relatively new territory for us, and whatever your attorney may be about to tell you, the press are your problem, not ours."

She closed herself out.

Simon Parker was a tall, quince-shaped man of about fifty in a grey suit, carrying a briefcase. He smiled, introduced himself and shook my hand.

"Since you're no longer in trouble, you may not need me any more," he said, "but I'll let you be the judge of that. I'm completely at your disposal."

At this point, I could have said, *I need you to get me out of here as quickly and efficiently as possible. I want a reservation for tonight at a hotel somewhere in Central Manhattan.*

But I didn't. "Where's Soraya?" I asked.

"One of the junior partners is looking after her. Maddie."

"From Verona?"

"And we've put Judy with your youngest sister. Judy with Julia," he added, as if the slight aural resemblance was funny. He was nervous.

"Who's with Charlotte?" I asked.

"That'd be Ian. Don't worry. It's all in hand. All bases covered."

I nodded. I was falling back into generalship mode, the manner of relating to the world a lot of people assumed I inhabited most naturally. "Let's get these questions with the police out of the way as quickly and painlessly as possible," I said. "Then we need to shake off the paparazzi and find somewhere to stay the night."

"We've booked you two adjoining double rooms at a hotel in New York City. West 63rd Street, five stars. We figured you might be having second thoughts about this *road trip* of yours. Otherwise, it's a great place to regroup and make new arrangements."

"How far?"

"Just over an hour, traffic permitting. There's a car nearby waiting to transport you."

"Excellent work, Simon," I said.

Carry On Road Tripping

We spent two days in New York. We'd all thought about jacking it in and going back to Europe, but it seemed cowardly, and worse: something we'd maybe regret the rest of our lives. What we needed was a plan. Maxwell Clunes would organise the car: something electric, we didn't care what it looked like. We bought an A1 size map of the USA and spread it on the table in my and Soraya's room: four armchairs, a sofa, a huge bed, three wardrobes, a table to eat at, and a spacious balcony with a view of Central Park. Julia and Charlotte's room was the same, and was linked to ours by an adjoining door. We got three bottles of red wine in and put Miles Davis on. Charlotte and I Skyped Marcus and Tim, Julia Skyped Knut and we waited till we'd drunk bottle number two to get started planning.

We wouldn't rush across America, but neither would we get diverted. The only two necessaries were Monument Valley and virtually everywhere in California. The former because, we agreed, you couldn't really say you'd been to America if you hadn't seen it. Also, there were Native Americans there (Charlotte). California because of San Francisco (Soraya and me), the beaches (Soraya), *Loose Change* (Julia and me) and *California Dreamin'* (me).

"What's *Loose Change*?" Soraya asked.

"A novel about three women," Julia said. "Should be a classic, but isn't. Incidentally, you'll find everything you'd ever want to know about Jack Kerouac *et al.* in Joyce Johnson's *Minor Characters*. They're no sort of role models for us."

"So where are we going from New York?" I asked. "And who's going to be our main driver?"

"Not me," Soraya said.

"We'll take it in turns," Julia said. She drank some wine then ran her finger over the map. "Pennsylvania – yes? – West Virginia, Kentucky, Tennessee, Mississippi,

Louisiana, Texas, New Mexico, up into Utah, dip into Arizona for Monument Valley and the Grand Canyon, then over to California."

"Down and along," Charlotte said. "Wouldn't it be better to go straight across? Pennsylvania, Ohio, Indiana, Illinois, Missouri, Kansas, Colorado, Utah, Arizona, California?"

"That way we could have an early stop in Chicago," Soraya said.

"What's in Chicago?" Julia said. "I mean, specifically?"

Soraya shrugged. "You can't really say you've been across the USA if you haven't called in at Chicago."

"Maybe if Chicago stretched from the Canadian border to the Gulf of Mexico," Julia said. "But it doesn't."

"I think you know what we mean," I told her.

"Even with Charlotte's 'straight line', we'd have to make a detour," she replied. Then, just when we thought she was about to become *University Challenge* Julia again, she added, "but I take your point, yes."

"It *is* out of our way, though," I said compromisingly.

"Let's get another bottle of wine up," she said. "I'm paying."

I laughed. "Julia, will you stop saying 'I'm paying' all the time? I'm making more money than I can ever spend just by sitting here. I don't even deserve it. I'm earning gazillions thanks to royalties and astute investments by people – not me – who know what to invest in."

"Sorry to pry," Julia said. "But I heard you lost your shirt on Bitcoin."

"I love being in America," Charlotte said emotionally. "I really *love* it here."

We all looked at her, then at each other. It was left to me to put my arm round her, in the conventional way, and say, 'Awww'. I had no real idea what had set her off, but I felt the sisterly connection.

"I might try and get citizenship," she said, "when this is over. Seth and Marcus and me. We could begin again in the land of opportunity."

"It's not that easy," Julia said.

"Maybe best not to get carried away," Soraya said. "What have we seen? The interior of a blacked-out limo, then *McFadyen's*, then Shark River – lot of fun *that* was – then a police station, and now the inside of a five star hotel. Not representative. Probably. Be weird if it was."

"I didn't lose my shirt on Bitcoin," I told Julia. "I lost spare change. Besides, Bitcoin's not dead."

"It's doing a very good imitation of not being alive," Julia replied.

"I actually mined Bitcoins," Soraya said. "I've given up now because of the environment. I'm a Bitcoin zillionaire, though. So is Hannah. When the world financial system crashes, me and her'll be the only ones left with any buying power. Let's see who's laughing then."

"None of us," Julia said. "It's an event that lies so far in the future, we'll all be dead."

Charlotte had gone out onto the balcony. Julia gave me a look and swept her eyes. *Follow her*. Soraya smiled knowingly.

I nodded. Julia and Soraya looked at each other, Julia in a *So you do know about this?* kind of way. Soraya with a *Why the hell wouldn't I?* Julia: *Hey, sorry for asking*. Soraya: *That's okay*. Julia: *Truce?* Soraya: *Sure*.

I pushed the curtains aside, opened the balcony door, and stepped into the semi-dark 900 feet above sea level. The city lights flickered like hungry ghosts; the grumble of traffic and the sky's nothingness resembled every Big Apple sitcom/ film ever made. *Friends, Breakfast at Tiffany's, Taxi Driver, New York, I Love You, The Devil Wears Prada.*

"Hi," I said.

"This is just fabulous," she said. "I can't believe it. I can't believe I'm here."

"You'd probably miss Devon if you made it permanent."

"There's only so much clotted cream you can eat." She laughed. "Although you wouldn't think it from looking at me."

"You're absolutely fine."

"I need to lose weight."

"Even if you did – and you don't – most thin people are miserable."

"*You're* not."

I smiled. Boring conversation, and probably not what either of us wanted. We leaned over the railings to look down into the street. I linked arms with her, partly for warmth. "I have my moments."

"I've had an idea about Dad," she said. "We could go and see him when all this is over."

"In Hexham?"

"Just for closure. I was stupid to say I was going to sue him. I love him. But I do want to talk about it. And I'm sure he must remember."

"You don't forget something like that. I've a better idea. We should invite him and Mum over here. I mean, to meet us when we're in California."

"You mean, like, ambush him?"

I hooted. "We'd be ambushing him *wherever* we raised it."

"True. Do you think they'd come?"

"Three quarters of their daughters are over here. We might even be able to persuade Mabel to come, whoever *she* is. And John and Phyllis."

"And you can tell them about your cancer scare. Kill two birds with one stone, if that doesn't sound too insensitive."

"Done. And Tim and Lek and Marcus and Seth and Knut. Mum's part-time at work now, and Dad's retired. It'd be a family one-off. They wouldn't want to miss that."

"We'd need to let them know now. It's something like a twelve-hour flight. They couldn't just drop in and fly out again – "

"And we'd need to raise the question of My Big Fat Musical Lock-In discreetly. Mum probably doesn't know a thing about it. She might go ballistic with him, even after all these years. You know how she is: slow to anger…"

"But spectacular when she's on the boil."

"I'll call them tomorrow," I said. "Hexham's five hours ahead of New York. It'll be the middle of the night there now."

She took another look at the city and shivered. "Maybe we should let bygones be bygones. I'm not even sure me being upset that day when I called Julia was about Dad."

"So you've said. You'd had a bottle and a half of wine, and your candle shop was sinking. How's Marcus getting on with the business consultants, by the way?"

"Probably okay. I didn't mean that."

"You've lost me then," I said.

"I'm a bit psychic. We probably all are, really: I mean, all people. There's nothing special about Charlotte Pattinson, except that I'm open to my own potential. When you told me you had cancer – "

"I can't take the credit for that. It was Soraya."

"Once I'd come to terms with it, I realised that what I'd been feeling was that something was *dividing* us. You and me. Something big. In reality, it was your cancer, but I didn't know about it, but I tried to work out what it might be. And that was all I could think of. The Big Musical Lock-In." She laughed. "It sounds like something Mum and Dad would go on a coach trip to London for. *Now showing in the West End!*"

"Why would what Dad did divide us? We were both 'victims.'"

She laughed again. "Because you *enjoyed* it, Hannah! Let's be honest. You got something *out* of it, at least. I'm not blaming you. I haven't said this before, but I know full well it wasn't *all* bad. When you said that thing on the phone about parents being hard on their children to make them learn some kind of skill and become talented, I realised that's what had happened to you. It didn't happen to me, but when I think about it, I'm actually pleased it happened at all. If it hadn't, we might *both* have been mediocre."

I don't often cry, I know I've said that before, but this made me well up. I put my hand lightly over the lower part of my face, then I hugged her. "You're not mediocre," I told her. "And I'm not even saying you're right about the other stuff. Come on, let's go inside. I'm freezing."

She laughed. "Because you're thin. Try putting on a few stone."

We went back indoors. It took me a moment to realise that Julia and Soraya weren't where we'd left them. To cut a long story short – there have been enough shocks on this trip – they lay in bed beneath the sheets. As small mercies go, the fact that they weren't actually having sex wasn't to be sniffed at. But their clothes were on the floor, so they had to be naked. Julia sat up against the headboard with a half empty bottle of wine. Soraya lay on Julia's shoulder with her arms round her.

"We haven't done anything we shouldn't," Julia said nonchalantly. "Soraya thinks I'm 'hot', that's all."

"You are," Soraya said.

"We were just experimenting," Julia went on. "And I'm pleased to say I'm still fully heterosexual. However politically incorrect the word 'pleased' may sound. I'm pleased for Knut's sake. That other bottle of wine arrived, by the way."

"We drank it," Soraya said. "Or she did. Sorry."

"We're on holiday," Julia said. "You've got to try new things."

"Get in, if you like," Soraya told Charlotte and I. She laughed. "It's purely physical, Hannah. I could never love Julia like I love you. Seriously."

Julia got out of bed. "Incidentally," she said, as if it was crucial, "we decided we'd go to California by *my* route, then get a *plane* to Chicago. I mean, if that's okay with you two. Didn't we, Soraya? I'm paying." She picked up her clothes and draped them across her forearm. She took another pull and staggered towards the door that linked our two rooms. "Boy, I'm going to have such a headache in the morning. On the plus side, hopefully I won't remember any of this."

"I'll keep reminding you," Soraya told her. "It takes a hell of a lot more than four bottles of wine to make me start losing my memory." She looked at me and patted the empty space Julia had just left. "Come on, baby. Time for bed."

"I'll, er, see you both in the morning," Charlotte said. She followed Julia into the adjoining room and closed the door behind her.

I took off my clothes, put my nightie on – I was still cold – and got in next to Soraya. Whatever you might think, I couldn't have cared less about her and Julia. It was just nice to see everyone finally getting along so well.

"Fancy another bottle of wine?" Soraya whispered.

"I'm good, thanks."

We held hands, said I love you, just like always, turned towards each other and went to sleep.

I don't know how long I'd been lying there when the phone on my bedside table started ringing. I heard Soraya groan. I sat up, switched on my little lamp and picked up the receiver.

"I'm awfully sorry to bother you at this late time, Ms Lexingwood," the hotel receptionist said in his clipped New England accent. "But I've a man here who claims to be an acquaintance of yours. I've had hotel security throw him out twice, but he keeps coming back. He doesn't look like anyone from the press. And he's very insistent."

"Maybe describe him to me," I said irritably. This happens a lot. The receptionists in any hotel can usually only bring themselves to be so ruthless. "Does he have a name?"

"Yes, of course, apologies, I should have mentioned that. An elderly black man in a suit, name of Rudolph Williams."

I took a deep breath. "Okay, put him somewhere we can talk privately. I'll be down in five minutes."

The Return of the Native

The crucial thing was not to wake Soraya, but that wasn't usually a problem. I slipped out of bed and dressed by the light of the bedside lamp – white leggings, rib-knit midi dress, green cardie, pumps – and slipped out of the room.

The receptionist – male, twenties, with blond hair in a side-parting – met me from the lift. He preceded me along a corridor, then down some steps, and opened the door to a room almost entirely occupied by ping-pong tables. Rudolph sat alone on a chair against the wall. He stood as we entered. I still didn't know what to make of his sudden reappearance. I guess curiosity had brought me downstairs.

I gave the receptionist a hundred dollar bill. He said 'thank you' as if it wasn't a cent less than he expected, and closed us in.

"What can I do for you?" I asked. I pulled up a chair and sat opposite him. He seemed to relax a little and sat down. He looked at the floor.

"You still planning on making this road trip across the USA?" he asked eventually.

"We had second thoughts for a few hours, but we're determined to see it through." I suddenly saw what was coming. It should have been obvious all along.

"Need a driver?" he asked.

I shrugged. "Okay."

"Er, what?"

"By 'need a driver', you mean, you?"

"Me, that's right. Did you just say, 'Okay'?"

"I mean, providing you're legally entitled to drive; that your documents are kosher. I learned a few things about Harlinne when the New Jersey police took me into custody."

"Yeah, sorry about that." He grimaced slightly. "She meant well. She's probably certifiable. I don't know whether she's ever let anyone examine her head. Most likely pleaded the fifth amendment."

"Did the police speak to you?"

"I'm a black guy." He chuckled. "So innocent as a matter of policy."

I sighed. "I'll need to see your driving licence, and possibly your passport, and I'll have to run them past someone who knows how to spot a fake. No offence."

"Fine by me. How long will that take?"

"As it happens, I met a very nice woman in that New Jersey police station, name of Detective Hernandez. I'm pretty sure she'll be happy to help me out. The question is, how long will it take you to get me your licence and passport?"

He reached into the inside pocket of his jacket and handed me an envelope. "In there. Let me have them back when you've shown them to the police."

"What kind of a car do you have?"

"You've seen it. I've scraped the whitewash off the windows now."

"That's *your* car? I thought it was Harlinne's."

"Used to be. Then she gave it to me. She's been in and out of rich, see. When she's doing well, she's bighearted. But watch out for her when she's down and out. She tried to get it back, but I wasn't agreeable. She'd signed it over, fair and square. Trouble is, a car without a job isn't a viable thing. That's why I need you. How much do you pay, just out of interest?"

I didn't hear the question. I was looking at his driving licence. "It says here you're *ninety-six*."

"That a problem?" he said half-indignantly. "I've got twenty-twenty vision."

"No. No, not a problem. It's just … well, you only look about seventy, max. And I only had Harlinne down as being in her sixties. It turned out she was – is – *eighty-nine*."

He laughed. "You thought she was in her *sixties?*"

"We all did!"

"Sheesh, it's a good job you've got me! I wouldn't trust any of you ladies driving with eyesight like that, no disrespect."

"Okay, I'll get your documents checked. Come back tomorrow evening. One condition, though. Despite what you've just said, this is a road trip, not a limousine excursion. We really *are* going to want to drive ourselves a fair bit of the way. That'll mean you sitting in the passenger seat, or the rear, no questions asked. And you'd better not be any species of backseat driver."

"I still get paid, though, even when it's not me at the wheel?"

"Obviously."

"Being driven in a limousine in company with four beautiful women: naturally, I'm going to whine my ass off about that. Sorry."

"What for?"

"'Ass'. Not becoming in a driver."

"I forgive you."

We exchanged phone numbers then stood up and shook hands.

"I can see myself out," he said. "Sorry for waking you up in the middle of the night. I tried earlier, but they wouldn't let me in. One last word, however."

"Go on."

"I don't want to alarm you, but I've got a feeling you may not have seen the last of Harlinne."

"How so?"

"I'll be upfront with you. Me and her have known each other since she was seventeen. We've been married four times. I was working for her when you met me, but many's the time the boot's been on the other foot." He sighed. "Times change, positions reverse, then it all swings back again. Anyhow, all the years I've known her, she's forged documents. She was doing it in '47 when we first met, and she was pretty good at it even then. It's all she's ever been to prison for. Probably this time, if they catch her, she won't be coming out."

"Well, let's hope they don't."

"I've known her over seventy years, been married to her four times, but I still don't know who she is, not really. I'm not even sure she'd get into this country today. That's assuming she came from outside, which I'm pretty certain she did. Depending on which Harlinne you believe, and what day you ask her, she's either Jewish, Irish, Mexican, Korean, Italian, Sioux or even Jamaican. Is she black? Look closely. You didn't even know how old she is. You were out by thirty years."

"Maybe we could find her."

He chuckled. "*Find* her? Given there's a warrant out for her arrest, I'm not sure how she feels about you right now, but there's a good chance she isn't pleased. On the other hand, she might see it all as part of life's rich tapestry. I'm serious. She's unreadable, and she's got more so as she's got older. Part of me thinks she may even have expected all this. As she once said, where's the fun when you ain't on the run?"

I laughed. "Wise words. Not."

Mum Talk

Maxwell Clunes wasn't happy that we were going with Rudolph. They'd already bailed us out once – twice, if you counted Venice – and they weren't optimistic about the same level of success next time round. Sooner or later, these sorts of things, your luck runs out and you find yourself breaking rocks in the hot sun.

However, his documents checked out and the others were on board, so that was that. The next day, 1pm, I sat in the bathroom and rang Mum.

"Hello, stranger," she said. "Lovely to hear from you. What's the occasion?"

"Come on, I'm not that bad. I called you last week, when Soraya and I were in London. And lovely to speak to you too, by the way."

"How is she? How are Tim and Lek?"

"Everyone's fine. How are you and Dad?"

"I spent most of the day at the Hospice shop, sorting and labelling items for sale. Your father took a car full of hedge trimmings to the tip. We're having beef stew for dinner. Later on, we'll probably watch something on iPlayer. We haven't decided what yet, such is the depth of our spontaneity. Any recommendations?"

"I'm in New York. I haven't tested the TV yet, but I'm pretty sure it won't do BBC catch-up."

"The Big Apple, eh? That sounds exciting. With the band?"

"With Soraya and Julia and Charlotte."

"Really? No one told me! Why wasn't I invited? That's a joke, by the way. What are you all doing in New York?"

"Going on a road trip. We've hired a car and a driver and we're all going to California."

"Okay, I can't tell whether you're being serious now."

"It's the truth."

"Where are Julia and Charlotte? Are you going to put them on?"

"They don't know I'm calling you."

Her tone changed. "Why, is something wrong?"

"I'm fine."

"Are you sure? Look, I know you don't like me going on about this, but you've got to look after yourself, Hannah. The least sign, get yourself checked out."

"We've been through this before. I know what to do."

"So why are you ringing? And don't take that the wrong way. Incidentally, are you coming here after you've been to New York?"

"You mean, Hexham? Probably, at some stage. But this is a long project. Ten weeks."

"*Ten weeks?*" She laughed. "Well, yes, I suppose that's right. You've got to do it properly. Anyway, don't overdo it. And don't worry about the others, what they think. They haven't had what you have. Are you eating properly?"

"Stop fussing. I'm in a five star hotel."

"Keep it that way."

I scoffed. "What, stay here for the next two months, or go five star hotel-hopping?"

"I hope you *all* have a very good time. Would you like to speak to your dad for a few minutes?"

I laughed. "Sorry, I didn't mean to be sarky. I love you, Mum. But you know I don't like people talking about me having cancer. It's not that I'm in denial or anything. I just prefer to be thought of as the woman who climbs mountains, stops tanks, and generally gives Eddie Hall a run for his money. The World's Strongest Man, before you ask. Or was. I'm not a victim. I'm not even a survivor, not if it means we have to keep talking about it. *You* survived five lots of childbirth. Well done. Really. But 'survivor' isn't who you are."

"You're not going to stop me checking, you know that? I'm your mother. You can be Eddie Hall to everyone else."

"I don't want to *be* him – "

"But I *know* who you are. And worrying's what mums do. What, you think I never ask *the others* whether they're eating properly or looking after themselves?"

"Fair enough, I suppose."

"Shall I put your dad on? And that's not a hostile question."

"Not yet," I said. "I need to talk to the family decision-maker."

Dad's voice from the background: "I heard that!"

"I've got it on speakerphone," Mum said.

"*Hi, Dad!*" I called. "*Love you!*"

"What 'decision' are you talking about?" Mum asked.

"We're – Julia, Charlotte, me and Soraya – going to be in California in eight or nine weeks' time. We're hoping to have a family get-together there. A week, or ten days or so. All expenses paid by me. And yes, I *can* afford that tiny little atom of an expense in my huge universe of earnings. We're inviting Mabel and John and Phyllis, and obviously we'd like you to be there."

"We couldn't let *you* pay."

I sighed. "Why was 'I'm paying' the only thing you just heard? Look, you either let me pay, or you're not coming. And I mean *all* expenses."

"You're a bit of a bully, you know that? And you're working on the assumption that your dad and I can't afford it."

"Rubbish. You don't *have* to, that's all. And however rich you might think you are, there's a limit to your wealth. Whereas I'm literally King Croesus."

"Don't let Julia hear you use 'literally' like that."

"Julia's chilled. So far, I've only seen one *University Challenge* Julia, and I haven't seen Dictionary Julia at all."

"I'll have to find out what we're doing. Call me tomorrow. But provisionally, count us in. Only don't make a habit. It's not good for anyone to get used to being 'looked after', and your father and I are no exception. I love you, but I want to sustain the illusion that I'm also the kind of woman who can stop tanks. *On her own.*"

"You don't need money for that."

"It helps."

"Point taken. It's a one off. Until the next time. I'm not trying to lure you into a culture of dependency, but family reunions at my age are priceless. I've got lots of money and very few things I'd like to spend it on. This is absolute top of my list. So let me. If it helps: you win, I'm a cancer survivor. So I might not be around for much longer. Think how you'll feel if you say no. But you've got to do it on my terms."

"I'm a socialist," she replied. "I don't like being dictated to, even by my own daughter. It tends to put my back up."

I suddenly became teary. "Please, Mum. I'm asking nicely. Just this one time."

A longer than comfortable pause. I realised I'd put her in the same emotional state as me. "Of course we'll be there," she said. "Sorry, I was being facetious. I love you, Beauty. Your father and I love you, and your brother and sisters, more than anything in the world. You know that, don't you?"

I swallowed and tried to make like I wasn't upset. "And obviously. I'm not dying. That's not what this is about."

We exchanged a few more words – literally single words – and hung up.

That one phone call cost me four further calls home: (1) I know the impression I probably gave last night, but I swear to God there's nothing wrong; (2) I realise you're still unconvinced but I swear to God there's nothing wrong; (3) Yes, I *know* I 'like to keep things to myself sometimes' but I swear on *Lek's life* there's nothing wrong; (4) Yes, I'll speak to Dad, if he's there.

The Stolen Limo

Julia was 'ill' the day after she got into bed with Soraya. In other words, she felt bad about what she'd done, and had a serious hangover. She slept most of the morning. When she finally got up, at about eleven, she drank a pint of water and took a paperback into Central Park where she apparently sat alone on a bench for five hours. We didn't see her again till six. She ate frugally in the hotel restaurant with us, still pouring herself water and not saying much. I suspected she was on the brink of announcing her imminent return to Norway. By this time, I'd got Rudolph's documents checked out in my usual super-efficient way and we were ready to roll. With or without Julia, we were going ahead roughly as planned. I called and told him to pick up his licence and passport from reception tonight.

"There's a problem," he said. "More than that, actually. I'm going to have to withdraw. Much against my will, believe me, but such are the vagaries of life. I was just about to call you."

"What do you mean? What's happened?"

"Limo's been stolen. I don't expect to see it again."

"Oh my God! So what are you going to do now?"

"I'm ninety-six. Probably sit down somewhere and switch the TV on. I haven't got a family to speak of, not any more. And I'm tired."

"But, I mean, you *would* be okay driving us, wouldn't you?"

He laughed darkly. "I don't know whether you just heard me – "

"You'd *hire* us a car, you'd occasionally drive us, simple as that. We pay for the vehicle hire and for you to come with us. Accommodation and food thrown in. All expenses paid."

He laughed. "Why would you do that? It's not like we're friends or anything. We've only just met. You don't know anything about me."

"I can't just leave you in New York. You're part of the trip now, like it or not." I didn't say it – I thought it might sound patronising – but I couldn't bear to think of him sitting alone in some sort of old folks' flat, not at ninety-six.

"Come on," I continued, speaking into the silence. "We may not be 'friends', as you put it, but we could be. You could tell us about your life. What's the point of coming to America if we're never going to meet anyone? And the best people to meet, when you're trying to get a hold on a place, are always the old people. But you're not just old, you're *ancient*. And I mean that in a majorly respectful way."

"Thanks."

"Please. Come and get your documents, go and hire us a car, call me with the details, I'll arrange the payment. You pick us up, as arranged, at midday tomorrow."

"I don't know…"

"Put it another way. You came to see me last night, asking for a favour. I didn't quibble, I just said yes. I had faith. I took a leap in the dark. Now I'm asking *you* for a favour, and you actually owe me one. Or look at it from a third angle. If, as a nonagenarian, you're not prepared to 'throw yourself on the mercy of the open road', as Harlinne put it, then when will you ever be? If a person's not prepared to surrender themselves to fate at your age, when will they ever be?"

"Why should they 'ever be'?"

"Because statistically, Rudolph, you're about to die. You don't know what that's going to involve, whether it'll be a transition to a new place or not. No one does. You need to build up your courage. And right now, that means saying yes to whatever opportunities and invitations the universe presents you with."

Long pause. I knew what was coming.

"Can I ask you something personal?" he said.

"Yes, I have," I replied, before he could get the question in. "I had cancer. I had an operation. I beat it. But I was ready to die. I still am."

"Geez. Sorry. And congratulations on your recovery. Really."

"Now let me ask you something. You mentioned Harlinne. Bearing in mind what you said about her last time we met, do you think it's possible that she's the one who stole your limo?"

He laughed as if he hadn't expected me to put him on the ropes this fast. "I think it's entirely likely. Look, Miss… "

"Hannah. Just Hannah."

"This is the other reason I'm crying off. Harlinne may not be around now, but she will be. She'll find me. Doesn't matter how far I run, she always locates me. She's like Lord Baltimore. You ever heard of Lord Baltimore? *Butch Cassidy and the Sundance Kid?* Indian tracker. Genius. In the end, they only escape him by jumping off a five mile high canyon into a raging river. I can't be doing that. Not with my back the way it's been."

"She's far more likely to find you if you're sitting at home watching *Oprah*."

"I don't want *you* to be around when she finds me, that's all. Like I said when we met in that pool room, she may be out for revenge."

"So when you say you don't want to come with us, it's because you're actually thinking of us?"

"Maybe partly, yeah."

"So you're a nice guy."

"Some people say so. Can't speak for it myself."

"*I* say so. Which means I *definitely* want you to come with us. After all, you didn't say she was *certain* to be after vengeance. As I recall, you suggested she could even be up for a spot of forgiveness. 'Might see it all as part of life's rich tapestry', were, I think, your words. The truth is, I actually *want* to see her again, and if being with you gives us the best chance of that, then you're quadruply invited. In fact, I refuse to leave this city without you."

"You want to see her again? Why?"

"I don't know. I honestly don't know. But I do."

He laughed again. "I've done my best to warn you. You won't listen. Okay, count me in."

"Hooray!"

"Spoken like a true English dame. So what's your ideal car?"

"No idea. A self-driving Jacuzzi on wheels. I don't know anything about cars."

"That's not good enough. I need a proper idea."

"Okay, not a gas guzzler. Something green. A car in which we can all talk to each other without being separated by a partition. No whitewashed windows." I suddenly knew. "Something with a good sound system. It needs to be able to play radio, MP3, CDs, and it's got to have Bluetooth. Like I said, come and get your licence tonight and pick us up from the hotel entrance midday tomorrow."

"Let me just get a pen, take down that list."

Soraya's Brilliant Crap Idea and My Brilliant Brilliant One

Back in time a few hours. Charlotte and Soraya went sightseeing and shopping and I stayed in with a bunch of emails five miles long. BBC Radio 6 wanted Soraya and I to host a regular late-night slot, Nora wanted my thoughts: would our fans interpret it as a step down? Yet another offer from *The Voice*, begging Soraya to come back (even after all *this* time?). The usual raft of offers/ pleas for one of the band to appear on some ludicrous reality show. Requests from charities for us to play/ attend/ sign/ speak/ donate. Forwarded fan mail.

I was supposed to be on a holiday of sorts, so I shouldn't even have been looking at all this. And I didn't actually need to. I had 'people' to do the filtering for me. But with the breakup of the band still on the cards, perhaps I needed to remind myself that the world still valued me. Or maybe I was looking for ideas.

In any case, I found one. Julia, of course, had gone to bed early. I Skyped Tim and Lek. Then made a phone call to Rudolph (see above). Afterwards, Soraya, Charlotte and I went to Groove NYC to see Ny-O-Dae. We got back at eleven and had Havana Clubs in the hotel bar. There weren't many people about. We all turned in about 11.45. Charlotte crept into Julia's room, closing the door quietly so as not to wake her. Soraya and I undressed in silence, got into bed and fell asleep quickly.

I can't remember whether I had any sort of dream, but I do remember being suddenly wide awake, as if someone had sounded a klaxon in my ear. I sat up, swung my legs out of bed and planted my feet on the floor. 2am the clock said. I'd had a brainwave – or that's how it seemed: given the time of day, these sorts of things often do: only the harsh light of morning reveals their essential un-doability.

"What's up?" Soraya said.

I switched on my bedside lamp. "You're awake."

"No, I'm fast asleep. I've just been out onto the balcony and you didn't notice. What are you sitting up for?"

"We need to write a song," I said.

"Now?"

"Sometime this trip."

Soraya scoffed. "You've had *my* idea, in other words. Guerrilla musicians? Wondered how long it'd take you to catch up."

"Why are you still awake?"

"I'm thinking about Julia."

I let out a weary breath. "Well, you can't have her. She's my sister, so I've got all the rights to her. And she's married."

She came to sit next to me on the edge of the bed. "It was more like what an attractive couple we'd make. And how brilliant it'd be for both our careers. Because people love that combination of earthy-sexy-gorgeous – that's me, obviously – and spiritual-intellectual-gorgeous. If you can't picture it, then imagine JK Rowling hooking up with Madonna. They're seen out together, but they never tell anyone what they do behind closed doors. And the beauty of it is they needn't even be doing a thing. Bloody hell, can you imagine the appeal? It'd be like the biggest news ever! Like Shakespeare getting it on with Henry the Eighth! And don't give me a history lesson."

"Okay, I'll leave aside the parallels between Julia and JK Rowling, and you and Madonna. *This* is how you see your future?"

"Just for a while. Look, I'm sure we could persuade her. Writers aren't completely indifferent to that sort of thing; they just pretend to be. Partly because they're deluded. They think unflappability's the way to win prizes and get their books onto reading lists in posh universities. I'm sure she'd love to appear in public as my girlfriend. You could manage us."

"What, like you're an act?"

She shrugged. "That's what it would *be*. Nobody would even *mind*. People *want* to believe in fairy tales. If it sells stuff, everyone benefits."

"What sort of stuff? 'Julia and Soraya forever' baseball caps?"

"Magazines, advertising, I don't know. Look, I may not be Madonna and Julia may not be JK Rowling – I'm not saying we're *definitely* not, by the way – but we all know those two aren't *actually* going to hook up. Not ever. In the absence of *them* as a couple, people will be more than happy to settle for us two."

"Tragically, I can see you've thought about this in some detail."

"We could get Knut on board. Because it would have to be scandalous. *Beautiful novelist leaves distraught husband for hot singer. Both at the top of their games.*"

"I wouldn't say Julia's at the 'top of her game.'"

"She *almost* is. If it wasn't for that miserable cow with the fez and the golden armlet, she'd probably have swept the board, prize-wise."

"We don't call other women cows. Besides, she's a nice person, from the little I know about her."

"Her books are un-bloody-readable."

"So what you're proposing is that you, Julia, Knut and I get together and collude in deceiving the public, so we can all make money."

"Forget the money. Think of how *cool* we'd both look. People would talk about us for decades. 'How much of an influence did Soraya Snow have on the writing of Julia Mordred?' They'd make films about us. They'd write books about us. *Important* books, not like *Electrifying Rhythm: The Unofficial Story of Fully Magic Coal Tar Lounge* or any of that shit. We'd be icons."

"You are now."

"We'd be more."

"Even so, it's basically deception."

"Yes, but people *want* to be deceived. In certain areas they *do*," she continued, before I could interrupt. "If you really think about it, the whole celebrity thing's one big fib from top to bottom. Even politics is, nowadays."

"Well, I'm afraid you're going to have to choose between Julia and me."

She frowned. "So what's *your* idea for our future then, Brains? Us writing a song? That's what you said, wasn't it? Basically, *my* idea? I wonder how long it'll take you to claim my 'Julia and Soraya forever' idea."

"If you're going to be like that, I'm not even going to tell you. Look, if you want to get together with Julia, why don't you go next door now and get in bed with her? I'm sure she'll be delighted to see you."

"She hates me, we both know that. She hasn't even talked to me today. I shouldn't have pulled that stunt yesterday. I misread the signals and I was trying to be funny."

"So what you really want me to do is act as an arbitrator, is that it? Because, much as I love you, that's not going to happen."

She laughed. "I don't love Julia. I love you. I don't get much back, physically, but it's enough, given that it's actually true love. I'm sorry. Sorry I talked about your sister like that. Sorry I talked about deceiving the public. Sorry I'm alive."

We went back to bed and lay on our backs for five minutes. Eventually Soraya said: "Your idea. What was it? 'Writing a song.' *A* song. Not several, just one. Come on, tell me. You know you'll have to eventually."

"You'll only laugh. Plan-wise, it was even more kooky than yours."

"But it didn't involve conning people, I assume."

"Correct. It was more virtuous than yours. Which was probably its greatest weakness."

I got up and resumed my former position sitting on the side of the bed. She re-joined me.

"You know the term 'snowflake'?" I asked.

"As in, 'According to the *Daily Moron*, Snowflake Soraya has fallen on her drunken arse again'? I'm familiar with it, yeah."

"Okay, here's my idea. We write a song about *us being* snowflakes. Don't interrupt, just hear me out. Snowflake's a derogatory term, right? No one wants to be called one. But what if we turn it on its head and embrace it? After all, what are you if you're a snowflake? You may not be right about everything, but you mean well. Maybe the world could do with a whole lot more snowflakes. The thing about snowflakes, they melt fast. But not always. Sometimes they turn into a snowstorm. Then you've got to run away and hide."

Soraya stood up. She walked over to the balcony doors and turned round with a pensive expression. "Actually, that's sort of a very good idea."

I suddenly remembered: this was the person who, of everyone in the world, *most got me*. Of *course* she could see what I meant!

"It'd be a hell of a difficult thing," she continued, half talking to herself; she wasn't even looking at me: she was pacing up and down like she'd popped something. "I mean, to overcome that much prejudice. It's an invented term. And the people who coined it have their own agenda. We'd have our work cut out turning it back on them. But everything original's difficult. It's meant to be." She put her hand over her mouth and giggled manically. "You've done it! *Oh my God, you've actually done it!* You came out here looking for an idea, and you've *actually found it,* and we haven't even left New York! The fascists'll be completely blindsided! If we get it right, they'll be KO-ed before they even see it coming! Where's that guitar? Shit, I left it in the police station. We've got to get started. I'm never going to sleep now!"

"I'm not sure we can do this alone," I said. "Like you pointed out, it's a difficult task. And risky. We can't afford to get it even slightly wrong. Mood, lyrics, tune, delivery, everything's got to be perfect. A millimetre out, it'll rebound on us, then we'll be finished, kaput. Luckily, we've got a literary prodigy to hand."

"You mean Julia?"

"She's written poetry. She knows how language works. We're going to need someone like that. Besides, if I don't dangle something like this in front of her, I think there's a strong possibility she'll be on the plane back to Norway tomorrow."

"Let's wake her up!"

"I don't think that's a good idea. It's 2.45 in the morning."

The door to the adjoining room opened. We started.

Julia poked her head into our room. "What's going on?" she asked blearily.

"Get Charlotte," I told her. "I'm ordering drinks and snacks up, and some of the staff and other guests along, and we're going out onto the balcony for a disco. I don't care how cold it is. And don't give me any of that crap about being ill. You feel bad about getting into bed with my soul mate, and you've got a hangover, that's all. *Embrace life, Julia.* Don't go back to Norway. We need you. Knut'll never know, and if you abandon us now, you'll spend the rest of your life wishing you hadn't."

She looked at me like I was insane. Then something within her seemed to light up. She beamed.

"I'll go and wake Lottie," she said.

The next day, at midday precisely, Rudolph pulled up in front of the hotel in a wide, flat, spacious, royal blue car with a retractable hood and a state-of-the-art sound system. We were waiting for him, ready to roll. The porter loaded our bags into the trunk and we got in.

"Where to?" Rudolph asked.

"Pennsylvania then West Virginia," I told him. "Anywhere in either of those states. We'll tell you when to stop. Get as far as you can before the sun sets."

He grinned. "Yes, ma'am."

"And don't call me 'ma'am.'"

PART FIVE:

NEW YORK TO WEST VIRGINIA

Looking for America

AND SO IT COMMENCED, AS ERNEST HEMINGWAY would have said. Rudolph drove out of NYC, then Julia took the wheel while he sat shotgun and told her where to turn. Much of the first part was weirdly like driving along the M1: unimpressive half-grown trees, low central barriers, the occasional pug-ugly bridge overhead. Even the clouds were the same: dense, grey and suspiciously English. The only major difference was that every so often you'd catch sight of something closing fast from the right: a hurtling lorry or a row of cars. And the roadside signs. Something American about the fonts maybe, I don't know. After ten minutes, it started to rain. We slowed for a traffic jam then crawled ten miles.

In the meantime, something happened that I should probably have foreseen. Soraya donned her earphones and listened to music. Charlotte the same. Then, being lonely, I got mine out. We had the greatest sound-system ever out front, but, to be honest, I don't know why I'd ever imagined it'd be useful, given that listening to tunes in a car together was something that last happened a million years ago before iPods were invented. Today 'sharing tunes' meant sending your Facebook friend an attachment. Another of my hopes, smashed, as usual, on the shitty rocks of reality.

The road went on and on. After a while, it wasn't even as exciting as the M1. More like the B679 or the C483.

After three hours, we left the main road. I had no idea why until we pulled up in front of something that looked a bit like a brown aircraft hangar.

Walmart. Acres of parking, lots of couples pushing shopping carts, dozens of grim expressions on faces slouching to or from the entrance.

Every supermarket in the entire world, really. I looked at Google Maps. *Lancaster, PA*. Julia cut the engine.

"Really?" I said. "This is where we're stopping?"

"Why not?" Soraya replied. "They've got everything you want in there."

I ran my hands through what was left of my hair. "Can't we go to some sort of restaurant? I mean, why a supermarket?"

"We're not going to *stay* here," Julia said. "We're just stocking up on provisions."

"You can't get eye-liner in a diner," Soraya said.

"Hold onto those exact words," I told her. "We can use them in our song."

We still hadn't told Julia about the song. She looked interested but like she'd wait till she was asked, and didn't mind if that was never.

"Are we going round as a group?" Charlotte asked. "Or splitting up?"

"It'd be quicker if we each went round alone," Julia said. "So, say back at the car in an hour?"

We all looked at our phones and nodded.

Bloody hell. Like shopping with your parents on a gloomy Sunday afternoon in mid-January, nothing to look forward to because your birthday's miles away and Christmas has gone and school's tomorrow and you still haven't done your homework and it's baked beans for dinner and *Songs of Praise* on the TV. The horrible thing was, we could cross the entire country like this. Drive along a boring road, call in at a supermarket, another boring road, supermarket, road, supermarket, road, until we reached California. Easily possible. The idea that if you just started on the west coast and drove perpetually east you'd get to the heart of America was probably mistaken.

Or maybe this *was* the heart of America.

God, I didn't want to think about that. It was one of those *faux* philosophical thoughts that seemed to contain some deep insight, but was really a short cut to depression.

I realised I'd been left standing. Everyone else was on their way into Walmart, even Rudolph. Ideally, I've have gone back into the car, but Julia had the keys. I followed them, knowing already that I was condemned to wander the never-ending aisles alone, a lost soul desperately looking for something to buy.

Ten minutes later, I stood with an empty shopping basket in front of a rack of bikes. I don't even know what in particular I was looking at, or what I was thinking. Something like *fifty more minutes before I get back in the car, but what's in the car? Nothing.* Something like that.

Suddenly, I felt an arm slip through mine. Soraya. With a basketful of cakes.

"What are you doing?" she said. "You look like a zombie."

"Thanks."

"At least put your wig on, girl."

"It's in the car."

"Let's get you another one, then. Like I said, they do everything here. It's brilliant. I've got you a present, by the way."

"That's nice. What is it?"

"Close your eyes and hold out your hand."

We'd had the *do I have to* argument a million times before. She was always buying me presents. She always gave me the same instructions. Given that she had nothing but cakes in her basket, I didn't expect much of a surprise. Maybe a Krispy Kreme Donut with 'Cheer Up or Else' in piping gel.

Not at all. It was some kind of collection of short white wires. What the – ?

It registered. "Bloody hell," I said. "These are – were – yours?"

"Yep."

"What about the expensive ones?"

"They're in the boot. Trunk. Whatever. I won't be using them again."

I hugged her. "Thank you. You're quite sensitive when you're not badmouthing me."

"And, er, I took yours while you weren't looking, and put them in the bin. And Charlotte's."

"Ever the criminal. I'll live."

Julia and Charlotte came up behind us with half-full baskets. Mainly snacks and beauty products. For some reason, Julia had a lettuce.

"Thinking of making an acquisition?" Julia asked, indicating the bikes. "Maybe we should all get one. Pay Rudolph off – I'm sure he wouldn't mind – and do the rest of the journey that way? We could take them on a train whenever we didn't seem to be covering enough ground. We could go as slow or fast as we liked. Take time out at specific railway stations, depending on what looked interesting."

"Better than what we're doing now," Charlotte said. "I've just been saying to Julia: I'm bored rigid. I keep expecting to pull off at Watford Gap for a tankful of petrol and a Mars bar."

"It'll get better," I told her.

"And I've lost my headphones," she said.

I made a *Such is life* face. "You don't need them. We'll have conversations."

"Four bikes," Julia said. "I wonder how much that'd set us back."

"We could hardly get our four suitcases in the trunk of the *car*," Soraya said. "Imagine trying to pedal with them on the back of one of those."

"I hadn't considered that," Julia told her. "You're right. But we *seriously* need to get off the beaten track."

"Where's Rudolph?" I asked.

"Said he was going back to the car," Charlotte said. "Look, why don't we let him take over the planning? He must know this country better than us. Which isn't saying much, since we don't know anything about it at all. Just tell him roughly what we want: Native Americans, football, *Man vs. Food*, literature, baseball, scenery. Let him choose the route. That doesn't mean he'd have to drive. We'd need to pay him more, obviously, but it'd be a much better experience. I mean, it couldn't be worse. I'd pay my share. Marcus says he's learning a lot about business practices. Which is never what either of us wanted when we were younger – *stay away from The Man*, we always said – but you've got to be realistic when there's a toddler in the mix and Brexit and everything – "

"Let's pay for our shopping and get out of here," Julia said. She looked down into Soraya's basket. "I take it you're fond of cake."

"I take it you're fond of lettuce," Soraya replied.

Julia laughed. "I'll give you one of my leaves if you give me a cake."

"No," Soraya said.

We went through the tills and walked to the car. Rudolph stood against the hood with his hands in his pockets. He raised his head to face us when we were in hailing distance. He didn't look happy.

"Is something the matter?" I asked. "We're not late, are we?"

He nodded across the car park. *Look over there.*

We all followed his sight-line.

One by one, we saw it.

His limo, the one we'd been to New Jersey in, no one inside, parked with its headlights pointed our way.

"Oh my God," Julia said. "Is that …?"

"I knew she'd find me," he said sullenly.

"Have you called the police?" I asked.

"No point," he replied. "Too much explaining to do. Plus, they'd take forever to get here. We couldn't keep watching it that long. And what would we do with it when – or if – we got it back? She'd only steal it again. It's hers now. Get in, quick. We've got to get out of here."

A Definite Sighting of a High-Level Novelist

Obviously, after something like that, he wasn't going to let any one of us drive. He knew this country, we didn't. I don't know whether he was scared, and, if he was, whether it was on our behalves or for himself. We all sat in the back – actually, he'd chosen well: it was big enough for us to spread out in comfortably. We could even face each other a bit.

"Press 'aux'," Soraya told him.

"What?" he returned.

"*AUX!*" she shouted. "On the music player CD thing!"

He took his eyes from the road for a split second, located the button and pressed it. Radiohead: *True Love Waits*.

Soraya's phone. She switched it up.

So much for conversations. *True Love Waits* ran its course, and *Daydreaming* came on. Soraya turned it down a notch. "What shall we talk about?" she asked.

We all looked at each other. Harlinne was probably everyone's first choice, but we didn't want to spook Rudolph any more.

"I saw Paul Auster in Central Park yesterday," Julia said.

"Who?" Soraya asked.

Julia looked at her. "A famous novelist. *The New York Trilogy* and *In the Country of Last Things*. One of my earliest literary obsessions, when I was a teenager. He was so handsome in those days too. He's an old man now, of course."

"Did you go up and say hello?" Soraya asked.

Julia laughed. "No, of course not!"

"Why not?" she said. "It's not like he wouldn't know who you are. He's probably got photos of you on his phone, hopes to meet you at some conference or other, etcetera. I admit, I'm assuming he's hetero."

"He's happily married," Julia said.

"To another novelist?" Soraya asked. She found him on her phone. "Yeah, he *was* pretty good looking once, you're right. For a writer. I mean, he's no Zayn Malik or you-equivalent."

Julia smiled. "When I caught sight of him, it was just like my whole past and present had come together in one moment. But not in any profound way. An 'Oh, that's interesting, who'd have thought it?' kind of feeling. I inhabited the same bit of space as him and, even if he didn't know I was there, I *was*, and the whole universe was witness to our crossing paths, and that somehow made the whole thing eternal. Yep, I know that sounds zany."

"It makes a lot of sense to me," Charlotte said. "I have those sorts of sensations all the time. I've learned not to talk about them in certain sorts of company. I don't mean yours. Most people don't believe in anything nowadays. They think this life is all there is and science has all the answers and future science will be just more of what we've already got; it'll never discover anything about us that isn't sort of known already."

There wasn't much you could say to something like that. You either argued, or uttered some variant of 'hear, hear', or you vacillated and time passed and you ended up saying nothing.

Yet… I don't know. Ever since setting foot in the US, I'd had the increasing sense that Charlotte wasn't the woman I remembered; from meetings stretching back – what? – fifteen years? Perhaps thirty or forty get-togethers in total: days out in London or Torquay, family meals, weddings, baptisms, Christmases, birthdays, Skypes. All along, I'd seen her through the corner of my eye, never directly. As if, sometime during our teenage years, I'd decided she was the family dork, and I'd put on spectacles through which that's how she looked, and not removed them till now.

Along the line, completely unnoticed by me, she'd picked up a kind of quiet dignity. I say this despite knowing that she probably had at least three crystals in her luggage, one for me, one for her and one for Julia. Yes, okay, perhaps she was batshit crazy. But the opposite of strident. She sat and listened most of the time. Too much of the talking on this trip had been me and Soraya and Julia.

"We must have a conversation," Julia told her. "It's a hackneyed way to put it, but I'm actually on a spiritual journey. Partly why I'm here. Like I told Hannah, this trip's an exercise in psychogeography as far as I'm concerned."

Dictionary Julia had finally made an appearance. I'd let one of the other two deal with her. I'd already heard as much as I wanted to about 'psychogeography'.

"I thought you were a Christian," Charlotte said.

Julia smiled wearily. "Used to be. Until I read Robin Lane Fox's *The Unauthorized Version* about a year ago. Afterwards, I realised I hadn't really believed for some time."

"So what are you now?" I asked. "Atheist? Agnostic?"

"After I finished reading that book," she replied, "I had another to hand. One that, in the event, more or less saved my sanity. I'm like Nietzsche in that regard. I mean, I'm not suggesting I've an ounce of his depth or intelligence, but I can't live with just nothing. I can't just *get down with the Instagram crowd and go shopping*."

"What book?" Charlotte said.

Julia smiled. "I don't want to bore everyone. Ask me later if you're really interested."

We looked out of the window at scenery that was becoming steadily more rural. I'm an urbanite by disposition, so I wasn't enthralled, but I could see it was nice. Nicer than the M1 for sure. Ideally, though, I'd have preferred to cross America city by city. I really, *really* wanted to see Philadelphia, for example, but that was probably out of the question now.

Mind you, I suppose whenever you go to America, you probably always fret over things you haven't seen. You can't see everything.

"Does anyone know where we're actually going?" Soraya said. "Rudolph, where are we going? We *are* travelling east, aren't we?"

"A place I know in the mountains!" he called back. "Quiet! It's nice! You'll like it! And yeah, east!"

Beth Orton, George Michael, Solange, Alicia Keys. Pause for Soraya to connect her portable power bank. *Robyn, Dizzee Rascal, Connie Glaser, Dua Lipa, Adele, Lady Leshurr.*

An hour later, we crossed the state line into West Virginia. Julia discreetly ate her lettuce. It got dark. Soon we were deep in the Appalachian Mountains.

The Slightly Sinister Log Cabin

I could have got someone to book our stops in advance – plot a route, choose hotels, call ahead, reserve rooms – or organised the whole thing myself; but that wasn't how I wanted it. If I'm totally honest, I wanted the car to get lost (only, not in a scary way) and for us to pull up after nine hours trying to get our bearings, confronted by a seedy motel with a blinking neon sign, eleven pm, middle of nowhere, the proprietor – forty-five, unshaven, seriously overweight, vest, gym trousers, army boots – sitting behind a desk watching TV and nursing a bottle of Bud, and he'd treat us like, frankly, he couldn't give a damn whether we stayed or fell down a hole. Then he'd leer at Julia or Soraya in a disturbing way… and the whole mental picture went sour.

In practice, thanks to 4G, it's not easy to get lost any more, but this little dream smashed on the shitty rocks of reality largely because of Harlinne. Rudolph was in charge now, and he was taking us where that limo couldn't find us. As we climbed ever higher above sea level, our phones stopped working and it got cold. Bluetooth evaporated. Soraya asked Rudolph to put something on. He said, Jazz okay? she said, Suppose, and we listened to Charlie Parker, Bessie Smith and King Oliver. After an hour spent circumnavigating every mountain in the entire range at least five times, we left the main road for a dirt track and stopped before a large log cabin with no lights on. Low arched roof, square windows lengthwise at irregular intervals, it was surrounded by grass and pine trees, and stood on evenly spaced stacks of rocks. Wooden steps led up to the front door. At one end, we could just see the top of a chimney.

"We should be safe here," Rudolph said.

"Where are we?" Soraya said. "Apart from 'in the hills', obviously."

"Monongahela National Forest," he replied. "And they're mountains."

"Who owns the log cabin?" Julia asked.

"Friend of mine," he replied. "I've got the unlimited use. Now, I know what you're probably thinking. He's a ninety-six-year-old black guy who works as a hired driver. Where'd he get the loan of a nice little place like this?"

"We weren't thinking that at all," Charlotte said.

"I was," Soraya said. "Without the 'black' bit, though. Elderly chauffeur would have been enough."

"You're going to have to trust me," he said.

We got out, weary and stiff, and began to get our luggage from the trunk.

"Is there a Walmart nearby?" Soraya asked.

"You've *been* to Walmart," he said. "This afternoon, remember?"

"Yeah, but I never realised we'd be staying in the mountains," she replied. "I only bought cakes, and I've already had half of them. Julia's eaten her lettuce. How long are we going to be here?"

"Up to you," he said. "A day, a week, a month? You're in charge."

"I don't think I can do another ten-hour stint in the back of that car," Charlotte said, rubbing the small of her back. "Even being driven. It's too much."

"Has it got electricity?" Soraya asked.

He nodded. "There's a generator."

"What about hot running water?" she asked.

"Sure."

"Locks on the doors?"

"Yep."

"Stove? Landline? TV? Washing machine? Tumble dryer? Socket to recharge my recharger? Towels? Clean sheets? What are the beds like?"

"They're hammocks," he said, "and you've got to hang them up yourselves. Boy, you sure ask a lot of questions. Is everyone in Britain like this?"

"Much worse," Julia said.

"Could we go to Walmart tomorrow morning?" Soraya asked.

"Not sure where the closest one is," he said. "But we do have other stores in this country. By the way, that was a joke about the hammocks. There's three bunk beds, one in each bedroom."

"So six beds in total, yeah?" Soraya said.

Julia picked up her travel bag. "How about we switch things around a bit tonight? I mean, maybe Hannah and I in one room, you and Lottie in the other? Just so we can get to know each other a bit more? If you don't agree, just say."

Soraya eyed her suspiciously.

"I'm not going to talk about you," Julia said. "If I was going to raise any kind of issue, I'd do it to your face. But you've given me no cause to. I actually like you a lot."

Even though it was dark, I could see Soraya blush. Or maybe I just felt it. An unexpected burst of heat.

"It's just that you and Lottie don't know each other that well yet," Julia continued. "Tomorrow, or the day after, we'll arrange it so it's me and you in a room, and Lottie and Hannah in another."

"But we're going to go straight to sleep, aren't we?" Soraya said. "I mean, we're not going to be having a conversation at all."

"You'd think so," Julia said. "But we'll all be in strange beds. Your first night in a new place is usually difficult, no matter how tired you may feel. We'll probably try hard to drop off, then realise we can't, then talk."

Soraya shrugged. "What are we going to have for breakfast?"

"I've got bread and butter and strawberry jam," Charlotte said. "I also bought a packet of teabags and a jar of instant coffee. Just in case. I thought something like this might happen."

We all turned to her.

"That's pretty impressive foresight," I said.

Rudolph took something long from the trunk. A rifle. He opened its bolt, checked the breech, and gave a grunt of satisfaction.

Then registered our expressions and the fact that we'd all stopped in our tracks.

"She got together with a group of bikers in '68," he said defensively. "Burned down an entire town. I had to hightail it before she torched me in person. Good example of what she's capable of, and she's not got better over the years. I don't sleep much nowadays. Like I said, I hope we'll be safe here, but I'm sure not taking any chances."

Disturbingly, it was obvious who 'she' was.

"We probably need to talk," I told him.

"In the morning," he replied. "Right now, you need to get some sleep."

Rudolph's Backwards and Forwards Story

The idea that we'd be able to sleep through the possibility of arsonists on motorbikes was optimistic. We entered the log cabin in silence. It had a large living room, with a long recliner sofa, two matching armchairs, a large oblong kitchen table for eight, and a TV. Straight ahead there was a bathroom with a shower and a toilet, then there were three bedrooms, two at opposite ends of the cabin, and one in the middle just behind the living room and next to the kitchen. The latter had a working gas stove, a sink, and a washer dryer. Julia and I chose the end bedroom on the right.

But no one was going to bed yet. Rudolph put his gun in his room and sat at the kitchen table. He seemed to sense an interrogation was on the cards. The best place for it was somewhere we could sit formally. We lit two oil lamps, because the generator needed refuelling and we all agreed that could wait. We put our bags in our rooms without talking, and, one by one, came to sit with him at the table.

Julia started the ball rolling. "Exactly how much danger are we in?"

"I'm pretty sure she won't try to kill *me*," he said. "Thing is, she's tried, more than once, and she's never succeeded. Would seem pointless now. And I doubt she's got that much interest in *you*. Yeah, you sent her on the run again, but like I already said, that's pretty much a way of life, far as she's concerned."

"I don't remember you saying that," Soraya said.

"Nor me," Julia put in.

I put my hand up. "Okay, yes, that would be *me* he told. He said, 'you've got nothing to worry about', so I thought, 'That's okay then'. If he'd said the opposite, then *obviously* I'd have told you. We might not even *be* here."

"*Might* not?" Julia said.

I sighed. "He specifically asked me for a job, I mean, cap in hand, and he's ninety-seven."

"Ninety-*six*," he said.

We all looked at him.

"I can see that's not entirely the point at issue," he said sheepishly.

"We're missing the most important thing here," Charlotte said. She turned to Rudolph. "You just said she's tried to kill you 'more than once'. Were you… ? Surely you weren't serious?"

"Deadly," he said. "You saw that gun of mine just now, right?"

"Er, that's mainly why we're all sitting here," I said.

"Maybe you should start at the beginning," Julia told him. "I'd like to think it's none of my business, but unfortunately, I don't think I've got that luxury any more. Just how bad is the feeling between you and her?"

"I'm warning you," he said, "it's a long tale."

"Better get started then," Charlotte said.

He shrugged and looked at the table. "I was in the US Marine Corps during the war, fought in Okinawa. Could write a whole volume about that, but it's beside the point now. After I was discharged, I played clarinet in a jazz quartet for a while, made a bit of cash, and got myself a car. I first met Harlinne in Texas in the summer of '47. I was driving from Fort Worth to Comanche when I passed this girl with a suitcase, obviously down on her luck. Thin, brown hair down to her shoulders, cheap cotton dress, mean face – kind of attractive too, if you know what I'm saying – flat shoes, ankle socks. The case looked bigger than she did and she was having problems carrying it. I got about five hundred yards ahead, looked in the rear view, and for some reason, thought, Is she *crying?* I don't usually pick up hitchhikers, but I could see she was no regular case. I reversed and asked her where she was headed. The way she replied, it seemed like she'd been waiting for me. I mean, for hours. I even remember a 'Where the hell you been?' in there. Gave me a real hard time explaining I wasn't someone she'd ever met before. In short, she struck me as mighty crazy, but I sure didn't have to persuade her to get in the car. Naturally, we got talking, and after a while I got the weird impression I knew her too. Not just *knew* her, but we'd been together a long time, and I'd somehow forgotten… and now I'd just remembered.

"You know what that's called, don't you? It's called: love at first sight.

"I never did find out what she was running away from on that road from Fort Worth. Me, maybe. After all, she'd claimed to be waiting for me. Truly disturbing thought. Like something from *The Outer Limits*, perhaps. Sorry, you girls won't remember that, way before your time. Anyway, within months of knowing each other, we got engaged, then hitched, and moved up north. Found ourselves a little place in New York City, one of those Harlem River Houses. Mind you, we couldn't have tied the knot if she hadn't had all the documents: she was *Harlinne Vobrosky, born in Ripon, Wisconsin, 20 March 1930, daughter of Stanley and Imelda*. Didn't find out till later that was her speciality, counterfeiting. God knows who she is, really. She's eighty-nine. It's history now. Don't suppose even she knows any more.

"Anywise, that was our first marriage. Very cosy, very traditional. I got a job in the Brooklyn shipyards and went out to work every day while she stayed home cooking and cleaning, like wives were supposed to in those days. For a time, everything was near perfect, then we started arguing. Money, mainly. November of '52 it was, I got home to find she'd cleaned the place out, or rather her lover had. Left me no money, no clothes, no nothing. I was in pretty bad shape afterwards – shock, maybe – and that same month, some of the workforce got laid off and I was among them.

"Don't know how, but I scraped some money together and went back to Texas. Hardly knew why at the time. Nothing more there for me than up north, but I guess I wanted to get away from the memories. To think that, one time, I'd actually owned a car!

"I spent eight years moving from job to job, gradually saving money. But I was soon made aware that *she didn't actually consider herself to have left me.* She kept on discovering where I was, and every so often, she'd send me a billfold, occasionally even more than enough to keep me going. I put some of it away and got a roof over my head ten miles outside Austin. And that's when the letters started arriving. Letters about how she missed me but if we were to get together again, it'd have to be on her terms. She never said anything specific about what she was doing now, but I got the impression she'd more than fallen on her feet.

"Then something miraculous happened. Turns out I had an uncle in Washington DC, where I was born, and he'd left me a whole pile of money. Doctor, he was. I won't go into the details, lots of wrangling by relations closer to him who thought they had more inheritance rights, all smoothed out in the end. Anyway, first off, I bought myself another automobile. Drove it out of the dealership, tankful of gas, thought I'd just go for a long cruise nowhere in particular, simply appreciate the scenery. Hot damn it if, twenty miles out of Austin, night falling fast, I didn't come across Harlinne again, walking along the roadside, suitcase in hand, exactly like before.

"Could have kept on driving. Maybe should have. But I've a feeling I wouldn't have got far. Things had gone seriously wrong for her in NYC or wherever she'd been those last eight years and she'd finally come home to me. And I loved her. God help me, I loved her. And she loved me, or said she did. Hadn't ever stopped loving me.

"We ended up not too different to how we'd been first time round. 'Fresh start'. Way out west in Oregon this time. Her choice. But of course the nineteen sixties, that was an odd decade, and she wasn't the most stable character God ever made. More arguments, more misery. She got into the whole counterculture thing, and not with those fluffy hippy types, either: no, she took up with the Clackamas chapter of the Hell Angels. The night she finally left, they came for me. Torched the place I was living. I got away, or thought I did. But she'd decided to go for the KO, and what Harlinne wants, Harlinne gets. She couldn't kill me so she framed me. Long and short, I ended up doing eight years in a federal prison for a crime I didn't commit. We divorced while I was inside.

"Nineteen seventy-six was when I finally got released, and guess who was waiting for me at the prison gates. Dying, she said she was, there to say goodbye, sorry for everything she'd done but she probably needed looking after, and if I could just see my way to etcetera. We re-married. Don't know whether we still loved each other, or if that had just segued into the fair certainty that we couldn't live without each other. Anyhow, this was when she finally let me in on her little forgery secret, and with her making official papers, me getting a decent job with good pay wasn't a problem.

"Looking back, I believe she really *did* think she was finished with this life, but she 'got better' in '80. Same old pattern. She took all my stuff, ratted me out, left me destitute while she went on to better and finer things. Oh, yeah, and divorced me. It was '92 before the authorities finally caught up with her. Cleverly, she'd pinned the blame on her 'business associates', and, although she did time, it was for something minor.

"She was back on the block in the first year of the new millennium. I can't remember what I was doing then – not much, only, life felt good – but she found me and offered me a job with more pay than I could sensibly turn down. Yeah, and we got married again. I worked for her for eight years, kind of a husband-gofer. Meanwhile, she'd made a lot of friends in shady places over the years, and she had the ability to fabricate just about anything official. That was her ticket to high society. She'd worked out that rich folk can get away with a hell of a lot more than poor folk.

"Even so, there are limits. She was arrested again in '08. If she hadn't reinvented herself as a big shot socialite by then she might have been looking at twenty, thirty years. In the event, she got herself a fancy lawyer, and he bargain-pleaded it down to eight.

"Twenty-sixteen she was released. She'd hidden her money in all sorts of places of course, so she wasn't ever going back to being that girl with a suitcase. We resumed where we'd left off, me working for her. And here we are. Me talking to you in the mountains with a rifle in my room."

We looked ominously at each other. The hissing of the oil lamps was all I heard. Then a gale whistling dismally through the trees.

Julia chuckled. "That's the wackiest story I've ever heard. Having said that, I'm pretty confident we're not in the slightest danger. Harlinne Vobrosky's eighty-nine. If she was going to kill anyone, she'd have done so long before now. She's a counterfeiter if she's anything. She's not in the business of murder."

"What about the Hell's Angels?" Charlotte asked.

"She got in with a really bad crowd," Julia said. "They probably influenced her. She's wealthy now, and, despite the fact that she's on the run, she's nobody's puppet. Plus, she caught up with us at Walmart. If she was going to kill us, she'd have done something there."

"In full view of everyone in Lancaster PA?" I said. "I doubt it."

"She'd have put in a personal appearance," Julia replied. "Menaced us. That's how revenge tends to work. You tell your victims what's about to happen, and you relay the information faster than they can do anything about it. You fill them with the misery of anticipation."

I wasn't convinced. But then, I knew Julia wasn't saying half of what was on her mind.

What Julia *Actually* Thought

The defendant had been tried and exonerated and it was bedtime. Soraya was the first to turn in, then Charlotte, then Rudolph. Julia and I went to our room at the south end of the cabin. The floor and walls were all unvarnished wood. A window with curtains occupied the centre of one side. The bunk beds took up exactly one half of the floor space, and a separate ladder stood at the head, ready to use. A wooden chair and a rug occupied the other side of the room. As we undressed, Julia said what was also on my mind.

"I badly need a shower. But I'm not up for freezing water. Not at this time of night."

"Top bunk or bottom?" I asked.

She went to the bedroom door, opened it slightly, peered out, then closed it again. "Top, please."

"What were you looking for?"

She closed the curtains. "Rudolph."

"He's gone to bed, hasn't he?"

"Apparently, yes. What did you think of his story?"

"Like you said, wacky."

She chuckled. "Understatement of the year. Pozzo and Lucky from *Waiting for Godot*, except Harlinne and Rudolph keep swapping places. You don't think there's more to it than meets the eye?"

"In what sense?"

We both got into bed, her on top, me beneath. "Whisper," she said.

"Okay."

"Here's the thing. Someone followed us to Walmart in that limo. Was it Harlinne Vobrosky? We don't know, but Rudolph says so, and I'm sure he's right."

"And?"

"She must have followed us all the way from New York City. How?"

I was tired, but obviously, this was important. "I'm guessing she was shadowing him while we were still there. He's got a fixed address. He can't be difficult to find. If you're Harlinne, you might stand on the corner outside, incognito, and follow him at a distance when he emerges. You see him hire a car. You might even put some kind of tracking device underneath, see where it goes. Especially if you've contacts in the underworld who can get that sort of thing for you."

"Roughly my conclusion. Now, ask yourself, why isn't it *Rudolph's* conclusion? What does *he* think happened?"

"He's ninety-six and probably shattered. He's been driving a lot of the day. Maybe he doesn't think anything."

"Let's not underestimate him. He was pretty lucid in there. At the very least, he knows she has an amazing ability to track us down, wherever we might be."

"When I spoke to him in New York, he actually compared her to Lord Baltimore."

I heard her sit up slightly in bed. "When? You mean, from *Butch Cassidy and the Sundance Kid?*"

"I'm impressed you knew that. I didn't." *University Challenge.*

"Wait a minute, Hannah. First of all, he told you she's on the run and you didn't tell the rest of us, now you're telling me he compared her to Lord Baltimore, and you didn't tell any of us *that,* either?"

"Unfortunately, I met him right after you got drunk and climbed in bed with Soraya. All that day, you weren't speaking to anyone, as I remember. You had a 'hangover' and you 'felt ill', so you did what people always do when that happens: you went to the park with a book, and sat there, famous-novelist-spotting."

She sighed. "Okay, fair enough. Sorry."

"It put us *all* on edge. I wasn't even sure if you were still coming with us."

"Friendly question, then: is there anything *else* you haven't told us?"

I thought hard. "No, I genuinely don't think so." I paused (mainly, I admit, for effect). "There isn't."

"Okay, here's my theory. Rudolph's actually in league with Harlinne. He's been feeding her information about our whereabouts and, pretty soon, she's going to turn up here. Probably tomorrow. We've nothing to be scared of. The limo's appearance at Walmart was meant to prepare us. Present the possibility."

"Why?" I asked.

"Because she wants to co-opt us."

I scoffed. "To what? Her counterfeiting business?"

"To her staying free. Think about it: if you're on the run, where's the one place the police aren't going to look for you? Answer: in company with the very people who reported you; the ones you're supposed to have wronged. And if you happen to make *friends* with those people, perhaps they'll drop their pesky charges against you."

"We didn't press any."

"She doesn't know that."

"She must do," I said. "Forging passports is a criminal offence. I don't know much about American law, but my guess is it's FBI business. Maybe even CIA, depending on whether she's getting migrants into the country."

"If it had been that sort of level investigation, we'd have found out about it in that police station in Avon."

"Not necessarily. I think we've probably seen enough US cop shows to know things are different here."

"What do you mean?" she asked.

"What happens is, it starts as a county issue, and the local cops set about investigating. Then, sometime later, the FBI gets wind of it, and they swoop in with a *You've done a great job so far, guys, but we'll take it from here.* And this one local cop – let's call her Hernandez – "

"Okay…"

" – She gets angry. She argues. All that work she's put in, and these guys just *show up?* Who the hell do they think they are?"

"You're right. Harlinne might have considered this a good hideout in any case."

"It's almost certainly *her* log cabin. Rudolph was cagey enough when we asked him."

"So what are we going to do?" she asked.

"I think we should just behave as if nothing's amiss. Probably the limo will pull up outside, very quietly, about four am. Rudolph will be waiting for her at the front door. He'll sneak her into his room. In the morning, she'll be sitting in the living room, possibly even in a dressing gown, hoping to give us a shock. I think we should just say, 'Hi, Harlinne', as if she's been here all along. That'll faze both of them. They need to know we're not stupid."

"So just act normally?"

"Why not?" I said. "She could be dangerous. If so, we don't want to antagonise her. I'm not saying I believe every word of what Rudolph said. Far from it. He's a man, and he'll present things from a man's perspective. But even apart from that, there are two sides to every story."

"Equally, there's no smoke without fire."

"If we're going for the pretence of nonchalance, we need to get a message to Soraya and Charlotte. Make sure they're on board. Maybe even arrange to all get up at exactly the same time in the morning, so we can present a united front. Normally, I'd say, text them. But that's not possible here."

"*You* need to take that message then," Julia said. "I'm not sure how Soraya will react if she finds me sneaking into her room in the middle of the night."

I yawned and threw my legs over the side of the bed. "If I'm not back in ten minutes, grab your things and run like the wind."

Suspiciously Like Breakfast

None of us heard a car pull in, we were too fast asleep, but we'd agreed to get up together at 10am. We'd make a common assault on the living room and occupy it in threes while the fourth used the bathroom. Ten o'clock would have the advantage that, even without Harlinne, Rudolph might have risen and got things ready for us – refuelling the generator, doing whatever checks and repairs were needed – so we wouldn't have to do any work. This was his 'friend's' place, after all: presumably he knew the visitors' drill. And we hadn't asked to come here.

Probably, once we were washed and dressed, we'd need to find a convenience store of some kind, get provisions. At least, if we were actually staying here. We might not be. It wasn't up to us. Right now, Rudolph was in charge.

When Julia shook me awake, I had no idea what time it was. I hadn't heard my alarm go off. It was light in the room. She'd opened the curtains.

She shushed me. "Can you smell anything?" she asked before I could speak.

She hadn't changed out of her pyjamas, so it couldn't be that late. "What time is it?" I said.

"Nine-thirty. Someone's cooking something. It smells suspiciously like bacon and egg."

I sat up. She was right.

And also, tobacco.

"It's not ten yet," I said. "But yes, it does. And what's more, like someone's smoking a cheroot. What do you want me to do?"

She climbed blearily up the ladder and got back in bed. "I don't even know. I just wanted to check I wasn't dreaming. It's bloody freezing, by the way. Don't get up."

I turned over, went back to sleep, and what seemed like a minute later, my alarm and hers sounded together. We switched them off together, groaned together, got out of bed together, rooted in our luggage for our dressing gowns together, and stood by the exit together.

"Cover me," she said.

I opened the door. "Go."

We walked along the short corridor in step and entered the living room. Charlotte and Soraya sat facing each other at the table, hair in towels, eating. In between them: toast, pancakes, honey, bread buns, a jar of marmalade, tomato ketchup, Branston pickle and HP sauce, a teapot, milk jug, sugar bowl and a full coffee press.

Soraya looked at us. "Sorry," she said, speaking with her mouth full. "We were hungry."

Harlinne appeared in the kitchen doorway. She wore a pink fur-trimmed nightie, and had her hair in curlers. She took a drag of her cheroot and blew the smoke back into the kitchen. "Sit down, ladies," she said. "Lovely to see you again, and I really mean that. What can I get you?"

Rudolph appeared behind her, looking miserable. Or pretending to. He wrung his hands and looked at the floor. "I couldn't stop her," he said.

"We'll have tea with milk, no sugar," Julia said. "And the full English breakfast, please."

We'd expected her to be thrown by the sheer insouciance, but she wasn't.

"With or without black pudding?" she asked amiably.

Sort of Friends Kind of Reunited

Julia went in the shower first. I got my towel and sat with Charlotte and Soraya while they cleared their plates like seagulls in a patisserie. In the kitchen, out of view, Harlinne and Rudolph spoke in low, conspiratorial tones. When

Julia emerged from the bathroom, she walked straight to our room and closed the door. I showered, combed my hair, tied a topknot, then got dressed. Julia was right: it was bloody freezing. I put on two vests, my Odetta T-shirt, a grey hoodie, jeans and two pairs of socks. The clothes I'd taken off last night had gone.

When I came back into the living room, Julia, Harlinne, Charlotte and Soraya were sitting together on the sofa, absorbed in what was obviously an affectionate conversation. Rudolph sat opposite them on an armchair, deep in a newspaper. Soraya hooted at something and clapped her hands. Harlinne leaned across Charlotte to pat her knee endearingly.

Bloody hell. This wasn't how I'd planned it. Even worse, I was the outsider.

Not for long, though. Harlinne had clearly been waiting for me. Our eyes met and she stood up.

"Sit down at the table, honey," she said. "You must be ravenous. I put your breakfast in the oven to keep it warm. Rudolph, switch the heating up. Can't you see everyone's cold?"

He grunted and shuffled after her into the kitchen.

She was right about me being starving. Add to that the fact that I didn't really know what was going on, and you'll appreciate I was in the perfect frame of mind for obeying orders unquestioningly. I sat at the table and picked up my knife and fork like I was five years old and a good girl, really.

Harlinne reappeared holding a plate with a tea-towel. "Don't touch it," she told me. "It's hot."

"Thank you," I said. I was about to add something, but the possibilities were endless, and they all got trapped trying to clear the exit at the same time. Things like, *You didn't have to do this* and, *We didn't hear you arrive last night* and, *Is everything okay between you and the police?* and, *Is this your log cabin?* and even, *Where did you learn about the existence of black pudding?*

"Why are you here?" I asked eventually.

She smiled. "You know I followed you, right?"

"We saw the limo in Walmart car park."

"I know this is going to sound like simply the biggest lie, but you're just going to have to trust me. Try not to interrupt. Just eat. The truth is, you paid me ten thousand dollars each to give you a good road trip, and I take that very seriously. I know the police are after me, so maybe I should have other priorities, and I do. But I made you a promise, and I'm eighty-nine and I really care what my Maker thinks of me. After all, we'll be seeing each other face to face before long. What good's forty thousand dollars going to do me then? *Thou fool, this night thy soul shall be required of thee: then whose shall those things be which thou hast provided?*"

"You're offering to pay it back?"

She reached into the pocket of her dressing gown, took out a thick billfold tied with an elastic band, and pushed it across the table.

Now, I know it's next to impossible to forge US banknotes, but I've read *Killing Floor*, so I know there are probably ways and means. If I took it, I'd have to get it checked before I did anything with it, and that would look suspicious. I'd likely have the FBI on my back sooner than you could say Jack Robinson.

"Keep it," I said, pushing it back.

She sighed and returned it to her pocket. "I know what Rudolph's probably told you. He always tells everyone the same thing. Most of it's made-up."

"It was the police who said you were into forgery, not Rudolph."

"Some friends of mine were, several years ago. I did time for it, I admit, but mainly because I'm a woman, and I'm old, and so I'm an easy target. The police have been trying to pin something more serious on me ever since, all because they didn't like my lawyer. Or rather, they didn't think that, in a perfect world, a two-bit piece of white trash like me should have an expensive attorney. True, those passports I gave you in New Jersey were forged, obviously they were. But they were just bits of flotsam I had left over from before my spell in jail. I got them out of storage, dusted them up some. I thought they'd add a bit of magic to your trip. I wanted it to be fun, you see. And to really have fun, you've got to be a bit scared. I didn't mean any harm."

She was a pretty good cook, I had to admit. People think anyone can do the full English, but it's very easy to get wrong. "It's in the past now," I told her.

"I'm here partly because you're going too fast," she said.

I looked at her. "How do you mean?"

"Well, you started yesterday in New York City, now you're in the Monongahela Forest. Carry on at this rate, you'll be in California in less than a fortnight. I thought you wanted to take it leisurely."

"We do."

"Then you should stay here a few days, 'chill', as the expression is nowadays. In fact, I insist on it. I'll do the cooking and cleaning. I'll organise the excursions. In fact, I've already started. I knew you wouldn't let me reimburse you, you see. This afternoon, I'm taking Charlotte and Soraya out to meet some real live Native Americans. Tomorrow, we're going to see a few Civil War sites: Cheat Summit Fort, Greenbrier River, Droop Mountain. I know that wasn't on your itinerary, but really, honey, what was? You can't come to the USA without finding out about the Civil War. It's what defined us as a nation. For better or worse, it still does."

I'd finished eating. I put my knife and fork together, said thank you again and poured myself a cup of tea. My disorientation hadn't diminished.

"I took the liberty of gathering your laundry up while you were in the shower," she said. "It's in the washing machine. I'll get it back to you tonight, so you can wear it tomorrow."

Panic Attack!

Overnight, thanks to Charlotte, Soraya had become an expert on crystals and auras and the healing power of aromas, and she genuinely wanted to go and meet the Native Americans. I kissed her on the forehead as she set off and told her to be good, and she said Yes Mum. Julia and I had elected to stay home with Rudolph. A pile of logs needed chopping, then the two of us were going to explore while he watched TV.

We went out front to wave the excursion off. Somewhere along the way here, Harlinne had ditched the limo – driven it into a lake somewhere, perhaps – and she now had a small red hatchback. I noticed our hire car was hidden from the road behind a grassy mound and underneath two pine trees with low hanging branches. That couldn't be an accident.

As soon as Soraya, Charlotte and Harlinne rounded the corner, I had a minor panic attack. I hadn't been thinking so far: events had crowded on each other so fast – getting here, hardly knowing where we were, last night's conflab, the uncertainty of this morning, the weirdness of being served black pudding by someone who, a few hours earlier, I'd been assured was an arch-criminal, the affectionate reassurances and offer of a refund, Soraya's enthusiasm for the Age of Aquarius – that I'd had no time to think. I swallowed hard, turned round, went into the bedroom and sat down on the bottom bunk. I trembled.

Julia came in and shut the door behind her. "What's wrong?" she asked me.

"I just had this horrible feeling: a kind of, *what if we never see them again?*" I cupped my hands over my eyes. The shaking increased. "Oh, my God. Oh, my God."

This wasn't like me, not at all. But everyone's got a *nothing like them* when it comes to seeing their loved ones driven off into possible oblivion.

"What if she kills them?" I said, unnecessarily. "I mean, what the hell do *we* know about where she's taking them? She was definitely short on specifics! 'Visit some Native Americans.' I don't know anything *about* Native Americans. I mean, *are* there any round here? Obviously, there must be. This used to be their country. Is. Used to be. Is. I don't know. They must be *everywhere*, mustn't they? "

"Let's not jump to conclusions, Hannah." Julia sat down and put her arm round me. "I'm sure they'll be fine. And actually, you're scaring me."

"Sorry. I'm sorry."

She hugged me hard and laughed. "We're being silly. Correction: *you* are. Think: Harlinne and Rudolph would have to be in it together. Don't you think that, if they were going to murder us, they'd have done it last night? They could easily have killed us in our sleep."

"Except the FBI would bring forensics in, and they'd discover the blood splatter. They always do."

"They could have gassed us. I suppose. Maybe. Or killed us and burned down the cabin. No splatter there."

I scoffed. "Have you never seen CSI Miami? Arson can't hide murder. Oh my God. What if that's why we've been asked to chop logs? We're outside. There could be a whole bucketful of splatter and they'd just turn the soil over."

"If Rudolph was going to do that, he'd probably have left the rifle in the trunk. He wouldn't have made a point of taking it out and showing us. And he wouldn't have told us that Harlinne's potentially lethal."

"Yes, but then Harlinne herself arrives and the plan gets updated."

Julia stopped hugging me and sat back, but not in a relaxed way. "Funnily enough, I do see what you're saying. The pair of them are like something from an Elmore Leonard novel. Okay, we need to keep an eye on him. I'm not saying you're right, but it's probably best not to take chances. When we chop logs, we take turns, we don't do it together. One of us stands guard, holding something heavy to throw at him if necessary – "

"One of us – *me, I'll* do it – needs to sneak into his room and get the rifle."

"It may not be his only gun."

I hand-combed my hair. "How did we get ourselves *into* this? How was it even possible? I wish to God we'd stayed in England."

"I live in Norway, you may recall."

"Stop splitting hairs. You distract him. I'll get his gun."

The Waiting Game

It began to rain hard. A gale swept the tops of the pine trees further down the slope. We told Rudolph we were going out for a walk, even though we weren't remotely dressed for it. Just in case we needed to run for our lives sometime, we took all four of our passports, credit cards and driving licences and buried them under a rock where two red pines stood exactly opposite each other on the track leading west. An eagle soared overhead. When we returned, soaked through, we approached the cabin stealthily from different directions. Thunder crashed. No sign of Rudolph. Julia beckoned me over. I ran to her, keeping as low as possible. She gestured at the logs. They'd been chopped.

I went inside first, looked left and right quickly, ready to spring back at any sign of danger to where Julia stood braced to catch me. Rudolph was asleep on the sofa. He jumped awake. He asked if I'd enjoyed my walk. Julia followed me in. She and I got changed and made a pot of tea. Our hearts still pounded. Our teeth chattered. No sign of that gun, though. Rudolph switched the TV on. "I chopped those logs," he said.

"Thank you," we both replied together.

"Least I could do," he said. "Sorry again about Harlinne."

End of conversation. It gradually sank in that he wasn't going to execute us – yet – and we began to relax. But not totally. Everything hung on whether Harlinne brought Charlotte and Soraya back. There was nothing much on TV, just a repeat of *The Real Housewives of Beverly Hills*. Julia went into the bedroom and came back with a book. She registered my look of curiosity and held it up. *Meditations* by Marcus Aurelius.

"I thought you were reading Emerson," I said.

"I'm alternating."

I wasn't being nosey. Julia likes you to ask what she's reading, mainly because she wants you to read it afterwards. The truth is, I think she's essentially lonely. Novelists don't exactly congregate in herds.

"Is this part of that 'spiritual journey' you mentioned yesterday?" I asked.

She nodded. "I couldn't carry on being a Christian."

"Why not?" Rudolph asked, in the same, slightly disappointed, tone he'd used at the airport when Charlotte said we all needed to visit the toilet.

"Jesus is the Son of God," Julia said. "He died to save us all from sin. He's part of the Trinity. He's the ultimate sacrificial lamb. He's the new Adam, except he came to undo Adam's transgression. I mean, how does that last idea even *work*, given that Adam's a made-up person? Too much metaphysics. One day, I just thought, 'That's it, I'm out of here.'"

"Don't let Harlinne hear you say Adam's made-up," Rudolph said. "Have you tried Islam?"

"I've had it with the whole Judaeo-Christian-Islamic tradition," she replied. "If there *is* a God, He or She or It has better things to do with eternity than write books."

"Don't you think The Lord *cares* how you live?" he asked.

"Whether I'm a good person or not, maybe," Julia said. "Not whether I swear an oath of allegiance to him and his book every week."

"What about Buddhism?" I asked. "That's supposed to be calming."

"I tried that for, oh, about five minutes," she replied. "You do good things, you get good karma, then good things happen to you; you do bad things, the opposite. Funny, because there's no Creator God. You might say it's too good to be true. Anyway, the Humanists are mostly sanctimonious know-alls, and most of me still believes there's a God, so I'm with the Stoics now."

"Best of luck with them," I said, holding up crossed fingers.

Julia grinned, returned the gesture, then removed her bookmark and read. I still needed something to take my mind off Charlotte and Soraya. *Real Housewives* wasn't ideal, but it was better than nothing. It occurred to me that, with Charlotte and Soraya somewhere so uncertain, maybe this wasn't the right time to be questioning the Christian – or any – God.

After half an hour, I turned to Julia. "Could I borrow your Emerson?"

She seemed pleased. "Absolutely!"

She went to get it. For the millionth time, my mind wandered to Harlinne.

I thought back to Venice, that hotel on the seafront. My God, to think I'd been worried about my *playlist!*

Holiday Snaps of Various Happenings

At five o'clock, Harlinne's car pulled onto the grassy forecourt in front of the cabin. By now, Julia and I were listening anxiously for any sound whatsoever. Rudolph was reading *USA Today* for the umpteenth time, and didn't notice us jump slightly. We both went to the window – thank God, Soraya was in the front seat, next to Harlinne; Charlotte sat safely in the back – then to the front door.

Harlinne got out, then Charlotte and Soraya. All three went round to the trunk/boot and strode towards us with carrier bags.

"We found another Walmart," Soraya said, as if it was an achievement.

"How was your day out?" I asked as casually as I could.

"Fantastic," Charlotte said. "We went to look at the remains of the Monongahela culture. There's not too much to see nowadays – they all died out in the seventeenth century – but it's really atmospheric. A village complex and a stone burial mound at LaPoe."

"Seriously spooky," Soraya said. "And it wasn't even dark."

"Then afterwards, we had lunch at the house of a real-life Shawnee man and his wife," Charlotte continued. "Salmon and cumber sandwiches, really nice, and he showed us his big collection of Native American artefacts. He actually had this grinding stone that was eight thousand years old. And two shell pendants that were well over a thousand years old. I Skyped Marcus from Morgantown. I told him to ring Tim and Knut, let them know we're safe and we might be out of contact for a while."

"That's great," I said. "I did tell Tim not to expect to hear from us every night, so he should be okay."

"He is okay," Soraya said. "I Skyped him and spoke to Lek."

Charlotte turned to her. "You never said."

"I didn't know you were Skyping Marcus," Soraya replied.

"True, I should have told you. Sorry, I still haven't got used to Lek having two mums. I didn't mean, 'You never said' to sound critical."

"No offence taken," Soraya said.

"Did you just say Morgantown?" I broke in. "Joni Mitchell? As in *Morning Morgantown*?"

"I can take you there if you're a fan," Harlinne said.

Julia chuckled. "*Is* Hannah a Joni Mitchell fan? *Do* bears defecate in the woods?"

Soraya looked askance at her. "'Defecate'," she said, thoughtfully. "Anyway," she continued, "this Native American guy had an Elkhound called Pecan. Really friendly."

Charlotte lifted her bags onto the table. "Mr Aquashequa's one of Harlinne's oldest friends. Did you know that Harlinne herself's actually a Native American?"

"*Part* Native American," Harlinne corrected her. She laughed derisively. "Like dear Elizabeth Warren."

This was news to me. Last night she'd referred to herself – only half-seriously, I admit – as 'white trash'.

"Half Sioux," Rudolph said. He chuckled. "Also: half white, half black, half Jewish, half Irish, half Egyptian – "

"That's *enough!*" she snapped.

A moment's discomfiture, then she turned to me. "Sorry," she said gathering her composure, "but when you've heard that kind of remark as often as I have, it stops being funny. And I've been hearing it since we first met in nineteen fifty-four."

I shot a querying look at Rudolph – according to him, they'd met in '47 – but he avoided eye-contact.

"Anyway," Charlotte went on, "in the car on the way back, we listened to some Native American chants and the entire soundtrack from *Dances with Wolves*."

"I'm really into the Native Americans now," Soraya said. "On another subject entirely, guess what we bought in the supermarket? Six bottles of bourbon."

French Revolutionaries

We stayed in that log cabin for a week. The day after the non-abduction of Charlotte and Soraya, we all went out in the blue hire-car, and Harlinne gave us a guided tour of local Civil War sites. She always seemed to sympathise with the Confederates, although "Lincoln was a Republican and you can't argue with that." We visited Morgantown for my benefit. On the way back, she played *Music of the Civil War*, a 3 CD boxset, then the soundtrack from the Ken Burns series, then Joni Mitchell's *Ladies of the Canyon*. During the latter, I regarded Charlotte through the corner of my eye. This was one of Dad's favourite albums, and probably something he'd played to us during that lock-in. She caught me looking. "I know what you're thinking," she said neutrally, "but I'm fine." That night, Harlinne made us clam chowder and an apple pie.

Things began to go downhill afterwards, slowly at first, but then more drastically. Harlinne and Rudolph argued, at first in low voices, but then, as the days went on, more audibly. They seemed to become increasingly irritated by us too.

Julia and I latched on to each other in the same way we had when we were teenagers. We shared the same political views, and we'd drink too much and start egging each other on like all we had to do was link arms, get marching, and we could change the world with a song and a flag. No more poverty, no more greed, no more prejudice or discrimination, no cruelty to animals, no climate change: the Kingdom of Hannah and Julia. It wasn't good for us. I remember a few years back when John brought his then girlfriend to meet the family at Christmas, and Julia and I had leapt down her throat because she was a Brexiteer. And ultimately, how much like bullies we'd felt afterwards.

We'd vowed not to mention Brexit or Donald Trump. But that still left us lots to complain about. The global retreat of liberalism was something we kept coming back to. Charlotte and Soraya usually went to bed when we got too fired up, and that didn't help. Once they'd gone, there was nothing and no one to apply the brakes.

Julia had an interesting theory about the rise of the right. She said it began with the failure of the Arab Spring. "That was when a lot of people in the West finally woke up to the fact that the rest of the world has no interest whatsoever in universal human rights. We simply can't export BBC-style tolerance and diversity overseas, not yet anyway. We can't even implement it where we are. Give most people the choice, they'll nearly always plump for a Morsi. They don't think women should be equal, and they certainly don't like gays. Then came the Syrian war and all those refugees, and we suffered a major crisis of confidence. Suddenly, it was all about pulling up the drawbridge."

I followed up with Putin. She threw Erdogan in. I added the fall of Mugabe in Zimbabwe and what a waste of time *that* was. She stirred the pan with Venezuela. She said that social media was like the French Revolution everywhere: sans-culottes baying for blood. We became more and more angry and depressed and when we went to bed, we lay there in silence, wanting to sleep but knowing we were too worked up.

"We need to stop doing this," Julia whispered the fifth time it happened. "Tomorrow, we'll swap rooms. One of us can go in with Charlotte."

"Good idea," I said.

Much as I missed Soraya at night, I thought it might be best for her to be with Julia for a while. Since that episode in New York when they'd got into bed together, there was still a residue of unease between them.

Unfortunately, I wasn't sure whether Soraya would want to be with *either* of us, given how choleric we both were; and also, that she and Charlotte were getting along like a house on fire.

Which was sweet, really.

I was just about to drop off to sleep when Julia started talking again. "Sorry I'm so bitter. God knows what Marcus Aurelius would say. He'd totally disown me."

"We were only talking. No one got hurt."

"It's not helpful for either of us. We should try to see the good in everything. Or at least, look at other people's stupidity as a matter of indifference. I'll read you something from the *Meditations* tomorrow. It's really good."

"I look forward to it."

"Sorry, I know I'm drunk. I'll shut up now."

I turned on my side. I felt myself drifting into sleep for the second time.

"Hannah?"

I turned on my back. "Yes?"

"I'm really, really homesick."

I took a second to digest this. "You can go home whenever you want. We won't feel offended. We'll miss you, obviously, but there's no point – "

"I don't mean for *Norway*. I love Norway, don't get me wrong. But it's not my home. I'm British. I'm homesick for England. Northumberland. I have been for some time."

I was awake now. The merest sniff of a family problem was enough to do that to me. And Julia was my younger sister. Younger: more vulnerable. That's how it had begun in 1986, me just five years old. That's how it had continued, *University Challenge* and all her other achievements notwithstanding. That's how it would always be.

"Have you told Knut?" I asked.

"Knut can't leave Norway, not permanently. Health reasons. I know that for a fact. It's not even something he told me. I think if I said I was homesick, he'd actually propose moving to England together. And he can't. Which is why I can't."

"What's so great about England?"

"Nothing. I don't know. When I said I was on a spiritual journey the other day… I think it's a bit more than that. Like a full-blown identity crisis. I don't know what I believe any more, and I'm not even sure who I am. Norwegian? British? I'm half-tempted to get Harlinne to forge me a US passport and just fade into the background here, get a job serving coffee in some small town diner somewhere, live in a trailer. I'm deadly serious."

"So you'd try to cure your homesickness for England by relocating to America?"

"I realise it sounds mad but – "

"Knut would come and find you. Or try to. So would I. So would Charlotte. So would Mum and Dad."

"I'm just warning you, in case I have a total meltdown. Forewarned is forearmed, as they say."

"I'll keep an eye on you."

We didn't say anything more. I was wide awake now. I couldn't have slept if I'd wanted to – which I did, obviously.

A few minutes later, I heard her lightly snore.

The *Snowflake* Song

Two days later, early, Rudolph took Soraya and Charlotte to Walmart again. They returned with an acoustic guitar, six dresses, four jumpers, a newspaper, eight magazines and a pile of sweets and pastries. While they were out, Julia and I made a packed lunch; ham sandwiches, potato salad, orange juice, fairy cakes. We picnicked at Spruce Knob, swam in the lake there, and got back to the cabin at four pm. Harlinne had lost all interest in entertaining us now. She spent most of her time in bed or arguing with Rudolph. When we got back, we showered, changed, and Charlotte and I watched TV for an hour while Julia read and Soraya composed tunes outside. At five, Charlotte made a shepherd's pie. I helped, and we talked as we worked. She said Harlinne and Rudolph reminded her of Theresa May and Jeremy Corbyn, or Margaret Thatcher and Michael Foot: 'what they'd be like if they lived for ever.' After we'd all done the washing and drying, we sat on the sofa, working our way through the magazines. At eight, Soraya unscrewed our second bottle of bourbon in three days and we passed it between us.

We'd switched sleeping arrangements the night before, and Julia had taken so unexpectedly and enthusiastically to Soraya that I half thought it might be something to panic about, especially given what she'd confided. Things like *I REALLY like Soraya, she's got SUCH hidden depths!* and *I completely misjudged her! She's SO original!* and *I've never just – clicked with anyone like that in my entire life!* Disturbing stuff in its own right but, given that Charlotte was also totally sold on Soraya, perhaps even an indication that reinforcement storm clouds were brewing in an entirely separate part of the sky.

"My agent tried to get me to write about this trip," Julia said. "But I said no. I'm not up to writing a 'how is America coping in the age of The US President we're Not Allowed to Mention on this Holiday' piece. I don't think I'm that entitled, apart from anything else. What right do I have to comment on their system?"

"Everyone comments on everyone else's country," Charlotte said. "I bet the Americans talk about The British Separation from the European Continent We're Not Allowed to Talk About on this Holiday all the time."

"I doubt that," I said.

"In any case, writing a book about it is different," Julia said. "There's an implication that you've some kind of prerogative. Imagine Chad Harbach or Toni Morrison coming to Britain, hiring a car, and writing a book about The British Separation from the European Continent

We're Not Allowed to Talk About on this Holiday. How do you think *that* would go down in South Tyneside?"

I couldn't think of a witty reply, and it was probably a rhetorical question anyway. Soraya picked up the guitar and strummed a chord.

"Hannah, tell Julia about the snowflake song," she said.

Julia looked from Soraya to me then back to Soraya again. "What's 'the snowflake song'?"

"It hasn't been written yet," Soraya replied.

I explained it as well as I could. It'd be a *zeitgeist* song, taking the notion of the snowflake – according to the stereotype, someone fragile, inexperienced and unworldly who's actively on the hunt for politically incorrect things to get outraged by – and turning it on its head and firing it back the way it came.

Julia raised her eyebrows. She laughed. "Sorry to sound sceptical, but that's one hell of a challenge you've set yourselves!"

"Which is why we need your help," Soraya said. "You've written poetry. That's what we need. Someone who understands words."

"Unfortunately, I'm also someone who knows my own limitations," Julia said.

"You mean, you can't do it," Soraya said.

"I doubt anyone can," Julia said.

"How do you know?" Charlotte asked. "Unless you've tried?"

Julia sighed. "Okay, say I agree to help you, it'd be on the understanding that it *just might not be remotely possible*, and that, in that case, no one's allowed to take it out on me. What we're talking about is a concept that's almost entirely negative; that *no one* uses in a positive way. I mean, okay, sometimes an entire culture *can* pick up certain abusive words – 'queer', for example – and own them, or try to: 'queory', that sort of thing. But it's not easy. Go more or less anywhere outside the metropolitan intelligentsia, and 'queer' is still seen as offensive. But what you're asking for is something vastly more than that. You're asking for three individual people to turn a hate-word one hundred and eighty degrees in the space of, what? this holiday?"

"We just want a catchy song with some cool lyrics," Soraya said.

"You can't make words mean whatever you want them to," Julia said. "Words exist in pre-configured networks, and they're fixed by matrices of social conventions."

"Right," Soraya said. She strummed another chord.

Julia ignored her. "Okay, if you're actually serious about this, and I can see you are, you need to start by picking off all the stuff that really *is* bad about 'snowflakes'. But don't be surprised if you end up with nothing."

"We all know what's negative about it," I said. "Why can't we just start by saying what's positive about it?"

"That's not going to subvert it," Julia replied. "What'll happen is that you'll get fixated on the tiny one percent you consider worth keeping. You'll sit there singing, 'I'm a snowflake', and your countless enemies in the tabloids – and most of them really *loathe* you, in case you hadn't already noticed – will think all their Christmases have come at once. That's actually where you'll get most of your exposure: from your enemies. And whoever in this sorry world still believes there's no such thing as bad publicity will have to do a serious re-think. You'll be buried. Or rather, you'll have buried yourselves."

I sighed. "I still think there's a good idea in there."

"I'm not denying it's *possible*," Julia said. "The trouble is, right now, the snowflake label's superglued to identity politics, and identity politics is the stupidest thing there is."

"Don't you think it's important that people's identities should be right at the centre?" Charlotte said. "I thought you'd be all for that. You're a feminist, and obviously you're against racism – "

"Spare me that," Julia said.

"Spare you what?" Soraya said.

Julia rounded on her. "Feminism and anti-racism have been around since long before any of us were born. Identity politics is new. It's a product of social media. It's Twitter and Instagram politics. Your 'identity' isn't your real identity. It's shot through with victimhood and self-pity and resentment. And 'snowflake' is a deserved term of abuse for those who indulge in it." She turned to me. "Maybe it's not that I don't think your idea will work, after all. Maybe it's because I don't think it's worth the effort."

"I've a proposal," Charlotte said.

I shrugged. "Let's hear it then."

"You make it so that the verses are all about big issues in the world – I don't know, global warming, war, genocide, that sort of thing – but your choruses are just, 'I'm a snowflake, I'm a despicable little snowflake.' You let the listener make the connection; you don't do it for them. And there's an implication that comes out of the link, once it's been made: that the media's trying to deflect attention from all that really terrible stuff out there by focusing on a few harmless but outspoken twentysomethings."

I took a breath. "That's actually pretty good," I said.

Soraya nodded. "If the verses were angry enough, it could work."

"What if people ignore the verses?" Julia said. "We're back to you two singing about being snowflakes." She laughed – and then kept laughing. She tried three times to stop, then got hiccups. "I need a glass of water," she said, getting up.

"So what's so funny?" Charlotte said.

"Just the thought of Hannah and Soraya sitting on barstools with an acoustic guitar singing, 'I'm a snowflake, I'm a despicable snowflake.' Come on," she said. "You've got to admit, that it's a *bit* funny." She laughed again. "Scratch that. It's a *lot* funny. In as much as professional suicide can ever be funny."

"It doesn't have to be those *exact* words," Charlotte said.

Now Soraya was laughing.

Charlotte didn't look happy. "Well, I'll just go to bed then," she said.

"I didn't mean it like that," Julia said. "It's a good idea. Relatively. But no one can make a silk purse out of a sow's ear." She turned to me. "The band's going through a bit of a crisis. It's tempting to make a high-stakes gamble. Take my advice and don't. Just let things ride for a while, see where you end up."

She turned to look at Rudolph's bedroom. We all did. There was an argument going on in there, had been for some time, though we'd only just consciously registered it. The volume was increasing.

The Big Fit Up

This wasn't the first time we'd been blindsided by a furious row from that quarter. And it was getting more frequent. Harlinne and Rudolph hardly spoke to each other civilly any more.

Suddenly, something inside the bedroom smashed. A bottle or a vase. The door burst open. Rudolph strode out carrying a travel-bag. He looked straight ahead without acknowledging our existence. He went directly to the exit and out into the night. A second later, we heard the hire-car pull away.

We looked at each other. *One of us should find out if Harlinne's all right, or maybe all of us together*. I could hear her moving about in there.

"I'll go," I said.

But she came out, dressed in her worsted skirt-suit and carrying a small suitcase. She brushed past me without making eye-contact and left the log cabin in exactly the way Rudolph had, except she left the door open behind her. A deathly pause, then we heard her drive away at speed, as if she thought we might give chase.

I went into the bedroom.

Two made-up bunk beds, an open wardrobe with nothing inside…

My God, they'd gone. This was a clear out. They'd abandoned us.

Shards of green glass littered the floor. A sealed envelope lay on the bed. I tore it open and looked at it.

I say 'looked at' rather than 'read' because it was one of those letters I'd only ever seen in films, where the words are made up from letters cut from magazines.

Then I read it.

Time to commend yourselves to the care of the open road again, ladies. Do you know the one thing necessary to make a road trip really enjoyable? Being chased by the police. Stay here as long as you like, but the FBI's on its way, and you'll surely have some explaining to do when they arrive. By the way, your documents are still in the woods between those two pine trees, where you buried them. Unlike Rudolph, I have your best interests at heart. There's a Greyhound bus station in Weston, about 40 miles from here. It's ten miles from this log cabin to the edge of the forest. Have fun! Call me if you need anything. But try not to. Lots of love, Harlinne.

What the – ?

Julia had brought a broom in. She swept the glass into a pile in the corner then leaned over my shoulder.

"Oh my God," she said.

Part of me felt relieved. "At least we're rid of them."

She'd propped the broom against the wall to put her fingertips on her temples. She walked out of the room and came back in again. Charlotte and Soraya had joined us now. Soraya strummed a chord. Only then did *the FBI's on its way* sink in.

"We've got to get out of here," I said.

Soraya read the letter. "She's bluffing."

"About what?" I asked.

"She's framed us!" Julia said, in the kind of half-laugh, half-vociferation people use when they're on the edge of panic. "Don't you see? She's wanted by the police. We're the people who set the investigation going. Now we've been staying here with her. Our fingerprints and hers will be literally all over the cabin. Even if we give the place a deep clean – and who knows how much time we've got before the FBI arrive, assuming they're even coming: or they could be outside the front door right now – there'll be footage of us at bloody Walmart, not to mention that place you went to look at Native Americans and that town where you went on Joni Mitchell pilgrimage, and those civil war sites. In the eyes of the law, we're about to go from being victims to being collaborators."

"Even if we clean the fingerprints, we'll still leave DNA," Soraya said.

"They might not care about DNA," I said. "I mean, no one's been murdered."

"This isn't the British police force," Julia said. "This is the FBI. If they want an all-over DNA test, they probably get one."

Soraya grabbed my sleeve. "Hannah, what are we going to do?"

They all turned to me. I was the older sister/ band manager again.

I blinked slowly. My mind raced. Thankfully, this was the kind of situation in which I always functioned best. An all-out emergency.

"We can't leave," I said at last. "It's night. We've no idea what's out there. We could end up getting ripped apart by a grizzly bear or a pack of wolves or a bobcat. Besides, we don't even know what direction to go in. There's no phone signal. We could end up walking round in circles. Here, we've got food and water and the generator's probably got at least some fuel in. I suggest we just bolt the front door and stay put. If the FBI arrives, we'll just have to tell the truth, ridiculous though it sounds."

"But we leave at first light, yes?" Julia said.

"Depends what time the wolves turn in," Soraya said. "I doubt they're like, 'Well, that's it for the night, guys. The sun's just peeped over the horizon.'"

"Eight o'clock then?" Julia said.

They were still looking to me for guidance. I sat down. "Maybe nine," I said. "The thing is," I went on in response to their expressions, "I'm not sure Rudolph's actually gone. Yes, we know he had a row with Harlinne. We know he left in a foul mood. My guess is he'll go to a bar somewhere, have a few drinks, put up at an inn for the night – because he won't be able to drive – and he'll cool down. He'll realise it's not our fault. In the morning, he'll be back for us."

"And yet, we're pretty sure he brought Harlinne here," Julia said. "They may have planned this all along. *Go to their hotel, ask to see that nice Lexingwood lady, beg for your job back, bring them to the middle of nowhere, incriminate them, abandon them in the dead of the night, hope they'll read the letter, hope they'll panic, hope they'll run for their lives, hope they'll get eaten by wolves, they're easily dumb enough."*

"If it'd had been that," I said, "they'd probably have sneaked out earlier. At some point tonight we'd have realised they weren't there, then we'd have gone into the bedroom and found the letter. *Then* we'd have panicked, etcetera. At the very least, they didn't have to stage a row and flounce out in a pretend rage."

"Hannah's right," Soraya said. "We should have faith in Rudy. He was angry with Harlinne, not us. And we're paying him. Without us, he's just a ninety-six-year-old car thief. How's he going to eat?"

"Sell the car?" Charlotte said.

"He may not be thinking long term," Julia added.

"We'd be leaving no later than eight in any event," I said. "According to that letter, and I've a feeling it's no lie, we've got a ten mile walk at least before we even reach the edge of the forest. And that's assuming we don't get lost."

"We could be trapped here for ever," Soraya said. "Among the *Blutbaden* and the *Fuchsbaus.*"

"Don't," Charlotte said.

I went on: "My proposal is that Julia and I set off at eight and retrieve our papers from where we hid them. You and Soraya stay here. We'll be back for nine. If there's still no sign of Rudolph, we bail out and make for Weston."

"What if you get back to find the FBI here?" Soraya said.

"They'd have picked us up anyway," I replied. "In any case, we just tell them the truth. Julia and I seeing their cars and vans outside, then not running away, might count for something."

"You've an admirably intense faith in human nature," Julia said. "Unfortunately, however, I haven't any better ideas."

"We should use tonight to clean up then," Charlotte said. "We might not be able to get rid of all traces of DNA, but we can wipe away fingerprints. It needn't look like we're trying to cover our tracks. If we wash the curtains and the bedding and do some really deep housework, we can just claim we were trying to leave the place as we found it, so the next set of visitors wouldn't complain."

"What if Harlinne's hidden some microphones in here?" Soraya said. "What if she's recording our conversations? What if a redacted version of those falls into the hands of the FBI?"

"Let's not think about that," Julia told her.

"If we clean the place thoroughly enough, we'll find anything like that," Charlotte said. "Although I agree: it might be too late if the recording device is elsewhere."

Julia's expression lit up. She gave a relieved smile. "How *can* it be? There's no wireless signal, remember!"

Soraya chuckled grimly. "Finally: good news."

Exit Stage Left

Contrary to all our expectations, that night was one of the best of the entire trip. There were four of us and we were hard workers, so it didn't take long till we'd given the cabin a thorough purge. We made ourselves some sandwiches and drinks for tomorrow, then washed up, brushed the carpet, swept the floors, laundered the bedding, plumped the cushions, polished the surfaces, dusted, wiped, sluiced, scoured, disinfected. We agreed to leave everything we couldn't carry, providing it could be anonymised. By midnight, we were finished. And shattered.

Yet we couldn't sleep. Not with the FBI hanging over us. We set to work on the snowflake song (Julia had finished objecting now) and I played a few tracks from our first album, *Magic War Melodies*. Julia read selections from Marcus Aurelius (gist: get ready to die, there's nothing to be scared of and not much reason to live), then Charlotte took us outside to connect with nature. She said trees knew how to communicate and they learned from the past and prepared for the future. "Read *The Hidden Life of Trees*," she told us. "It's all perfectly scientific." Julia went inside and fetched Emerson. "The greatest delight which the fields and the woods minister," she read, "is the suggestion of an occult relation between the man and the vegetable. I am not alone and unacknowledged. They nod to me, and I to them." We passed the bourbon round again, but none of us got sleepy, just… communal. As we went indoors, just before daybreak, we brushed ourselves and one another off, and left our shoes outdoors. We fell into a light sleep, in a huddled group, on the sofa.

My alarm went off at 7.45. I awoke immediately, Julia likewise. I grabbed a carrier bag, put on a bit of makeup, tied my hair, and we set off briskly for our papers' hiding place. We didn't talk. We were single-mindedly focused on the task ahead, and full of a sense of danger, half expecting to find we'd been robbed and a trap set for us.

But everything was just as we'd left it. We unearthed everything without the slightest hitch and set off back the way we'd come, having hardly paused for breath let alone for the excavation.

When we got back to the cabin, Soraya and Charlotte were waiting for us, fully dressed and ready to go. No sign of Rudolph. 8.45 am.

"I want to wait till nine," I said.

"Hannah, you're *totally OCD!*" Soraya said pleadingly. "I want to get out of here. We've made it this far. Let's not push our luck, *please*."

"It's just fifteen minutes," I replied. "You go ahead, if you like. I'll catch up."

Something in them seemed to fold. We all sat down on the sofa.

"When we *do* get going," Charlotte said to me, "we'll need to be walking at a brisk pace. You might not be able to catch up. And what if there's a fork in the road?"

"I don't want to spend the rest of my life in an orange jumpsuit," Soraya told me. "We probably wouldn't be together. They'd make sure of that. Different penitentiaries. It'd be part of the punishment. And I couldn't look after you any more. You'd have to learn the ways of the homosexuals, and when you came out – "

"We'll wait here with you, Hannah," Charlotte said. "Like you just said: only fifteen minutes."

"Cast us a spell," Soraya told her. "For luck."

"I already have," Charlotte said.

Soraya turned back to me. "Did you hear that? We've got to get out of here now, before it wears off." Disturbingly, there was no irony in her voice.

A car pulled up outside. We all heard it simultaneously and it jarred us like a strong electric shock. We got up in unison and looked through the window.

Not Rudolph. Not remotely a blue hire-car. A black SUV with tinted windows. Do I need add that it looked sinister? Probably not.

"Shit," Soraya said, articulating every thought in the whole cabin. "It's too late."

"What are we going to do?" Charlotte said. She swallowed.

I got up. "Let me handle it. Let me do the talking, in other words. After they separate us, tell the truth. The truth's the truth. Four people telling a fib hasn't a snowball's chance in hell with this lot... or anywhere, really. Remember, however hard they grill us, we haven't done anything wrong."

"The angels are on our side," Charlotte said. "We've all got one." I felt her hand slip into mine. "Holy Mary, mother of God – "

Julia chuckled. "So you're a Roman Catholic now?"

"I'm an everything," Charlotte replied. "'All creeds contain something of the divine.' Holy Mary, mother of God, pray for us sinners now and at the hour of our death. Amen."

"Hail Mary," Soraya said, slipping her hand into my other hand. "The Lord is with thee. Blessed art thou amongst women, and blessed is the fruit of thy womb,

Jesus. Holy Mary, Mother of God, pray for us sinners, now and at the hour of our death, Amen." She crossed herself.

"What the – heck?" I said. Things were getting surreal.

"My family's Catholic," Soraya responded. "I don't usually believe it."

"But there are no atheists in foxholes," Julia said.

The car doors opened. Instead of four men in dark suits, natty hairstyles and shades, a family got out. A man of about fifty, crew cut, overweight, in shorts and a GOP elephant T-shirt; a woman of about the same age, blonde bob, small, in velvet slacks and a button-up white blouse; two teenage girls: the older about seventeen, tall, slim, with dyed black hair, heavy eye-liner, a pale complexion, and wearing a long overcoat; the other about fifteen, equally thin, dressed in pale blue hoodie, a red miniskirt, and flip flops. They unloaded the boot together and argued.

"That's not the FBI," Charlotte said.

"Okay, we need to look decisive," I said. I picked up my bag, went to the door and opened it.

The family froze. They'd finished with the trunk and they were on their way over. They dropped their cases. They looked scared.

"Hi," I said. "It's okay, we're just leaving. We've left some fuel for the generator, and we've tidied up a bit."

"What – what're you doing in our property?" the man said.

"We've been staying here," I replied. "A mutual friend said it was okay."

I came out as I spoke to show I wasn't dangerous. I beckoned the others to follow me. We stood alongside each other like an identity parade. Charlotte gave the family a little wave. "Hi, everyone," she said.

I could see the man was about to say, 'Velma, go to the trunk and bring me my gun'. Which meant I had no choice but to try them with Harlinne's name, which, yes, could be incriminating, but –

"Hey, wait a minute," the older girl said, as if a light had dissolved the murky gloom of conventional Gothdom, "you two look like… And you're British…?"

"I'm Hannah," I said. "These are my two sisters, Julia and Charlotte. This is Soraya, my best friend, and a singer by profession."

The younger girl looked from me to Soraya and back again. She dropped her fishing net and put her hands over her mouth and said Oh my God, as they always do at that age. It needn't mean anything good.

However, it did. It was the OMG of recognition. It probably helped that Soraya had an acoustic guitar slung over her back and looked characteristically surly.

"I saw you'd been in jail in New Jersey," the older girl said to me. "I saw the photos. Those are great haircuts, by the way. You two are *so* cool."

"Marlene, get me my gun," the man said. "It's in the trunk."

The girls screamed. Their arms flew about. If it had been possible for them to wrestle their parents to the ground, they probably would have.

"Don't you understand who they *are?*" the younger yelled. She pulled her hoodie off to reveal a Fully Magic

Coal Tar Lounge T-shirt, and stood between her mum and the car, daring her to take another step forward.

I'm not joking when I say it was one of the most moving moments of my entire life.

PART SIX:

WEST VIRGINIA TO MISSISSIPPI

Steve and Family

THERE'S A LIMIT TO HOW FAR YOU CAN INGRATIATE yourself with a couple based solely on belonging to their daughters' favourite band. They were called Steve and Marlene; their kids, Sadie and Lisa. Fully Magic Coal Tar Lounge was enough to get Steve not to shoot us, and for Marlene to make us coffee, but it was never going to stop them demanding to know why we'd been living in their log cabin. I had no choice but to name names. To my relief, however, Harlinne and Rudolph were far from unheard-of.

"Not so keen on Rudolph," Steve said. "Nothing specifically wrong with him, but he's never going to be my kind of guy. Harlinne's a different matter. She's had a few run-ins with the law in her time, I believe, but that doesn't mean anything to me."

"This country needs pioneers," Marlene said. "Always has, always will. You can't be a ground breaker if you're shackled by rules and regulations. There's too much kowtowing at the moment. It's people like Harlinne who'll make America respected again. Assuming it's not too late for that."

They'd met Harlinne through a great friend of theirs, 'Senator Seth Shawcross of South Carolina'. (Like the song... maybe?) Afterwards, they learned Harlinne was friends with lots of other senators, and even more members of Congress. That made them like her even more.

"God broke the mould when He made Harlinne Vobrosky," Steve said, finishing his coffee. "Any friend of hers is a friend of mine. Now, no offence, but I need you four out of here, so me and the family can start enjoying our vacation. We've only got a week, but I don't mind telling you, Hannah, that you gave us quite a scare back there, so I'll probably need to spend the rest of the day recovering. Where are you headed? I'll give you a ride anywhere within reason."

"Oh, that's fine," I said. "We like walking."

I got the strong impression he didn't like me. Nothing personal (until he looked me up in detail later, perhaps): like all fathers, he probably considered it a safe assumption that any friend of his teenage children was *ipso facto* opposed to everything he hoped they'd one day become.

"Don't be silly," Marlene told me. "Lisa and Sadie aren't going to let you walk. They'll find ways to come with you."

"We need to get you at least ten miles away," Steve said. "Give you a head start."

While we were talking, Soraya was outside, singing to the girls. Steve and Marlene were only about ten years older than me, so they must have grown up with Van Halen and Black Sabbath at least somewhere in the background, but I could tell they'd never heard anything like this. They wouldn't be rushing to buy one of our albums any time this vacation. From one perspective – say, if you had a penchant for Michael Bublé or Katherine Jenkins – it really *was* uniquely awful. But that's what made it so exciting. It was primal. Teenagers get that. No one else does.

Suddenly, the front door opened. Lisa came in, obviously ready to ask a question. "Dad, could you drive us all over to Weston?"

I liked the way she didn't beat about the bush. Here was a girl used to getting her own way.

"Weston?" Steve said. "That's quite a long way, honey."

"We'll pay for the gas," Lisa said. "Me and Sadie. We'll go halves."

I laughed amiably. "If any paying for gas is going to be done, I'll do it. But – "

I paused for her to take a step back, hold up her phone, and take a selfie, me and her parents in the background.

"Lisa, don't do that, please," Marlene said. "It's very rude."

"My friends will totally like freak out when they find out about today," Lisa said. "I've just recorded like *a live performance*. This'll never happen again!"

"I don't mind being photographed," I told Marlene. "I'm used to it. I was just about to say, Lisa, we'd planned to walk. We don't need a lift."

"We'll walk *with* you then," Lisa said.

"What's at Weston?" Steve asked me. "If you don't mind me asking?"

"A bus, I believe," I said.

"You going north or south?" he asked.

"South," I said.

He turned to Marlene. "You know what? Why don't we *all* take a trip to Weston? It'd be a family day out."

Marlene drew her chin back. "There's nothing *there*," she said. She caught his look. "But… yeah, okay." Then she had a brainwave. "We're not all going to fit in the car, though. Not eight people."

"We insist," Steve snapped at me, before I could speak. He swivelled to face his wife. "You're right, Marlene. We'd get five in, max. You and the girls would have to stay here."

Lisa did a double-take. *"What?"*

"It's not possible to fit seven people in, sugar," Steve said. "And it's not legal."

"You'd have to say goodbye to Hannah sooner or later anyway," Marlene said.

"Could we swap numbers?" Lisa asked me. "I know we've only just met, but I'd really like to. I could send you pictures. I wouldn't stalk you or anything."

"I'm happy to swap numbers," I said, "but please don't tell anyone where we are, or that we're headed for Weston."

"No problem," she said. "We haven't switched on the signal-booster yet."

Steve shrugged. "We always bring a signal-booster. Such is the modern work place. You're never really on vacation nowadays."

Weston and Beyond

We left the girls and Marlene behind in the log cabin, while Steve drove us to Weston. I sat in the front passenger seat. Either he was in no hurry, or he was a very careful driver, because we never got above 40mph. After we left the national forest, the road became wider, hedged in on either side by forest and low, unobtrusive hillocks. Leadsville, Crystal Springs, Buckhannon. The landscape got progressively flatter and less interesting. Cows grazed on the grass verges, a gentle breeze brushed the tree tops and the sun shone. What I mainly noticed was the miles of telegraph poles in the towns, the large number of traffic lights and the way they all hung suspended from flimsy-looking wires, and the 'Laurel Hill Civil War Battlefield' sign, which reminded me briefly of Harlinne.

By way of conversation, Steve told us about a conference he'd been to in London, about a year ago. On the third day, he'd got the afternoon off. He'd seen Buckingham Palace, Nelson's Column and St Paul's Cathedral, and then he'd been on the London Eye. "I was pretty tired with all that walking around and the subway rides. I had to stand in line for over an hour to get aboard, but I figured if I went high enough, then I could say I'd seen everything, and call it a day."

Somehow, he segued to the President. Trump, he said, had reset the agenda in a way no one had previously believed possible; the next step was for someone intelligent to carry on where he left off; 'and there are plenty of good folk in politics lining up to do that.' None of us argued. It seemed rude when Steve was going so far out of his way to help us. We didn't like to sit in silence though, and Julia eventually discovered common ground in the alleged spuriousness of the 'democratic' (good) vs. 'populist' (bad) contrast, and the importance of free speech.

Internet service resumed before we left the national forest. As we passed through Buckhannon, Steve stopped talking politics to tender practical advice. "Download the Greyhound app and buy your tickets now. You probably won't be able to buy them at the stop. Sometimes, you get a reduction if you book early, though I doubt you'll get one this late, assuming you're travelling today."

"It says here the bus doesn't go till twenty-five past seven," Soraya said. "That's, like, eight hours' time." In an uncharacteristic attempt to soften the blow of her last remark, she added: "Which is great. We'll have time for lunch and for a bit of sightseeing."

"Keep your hand luggage where you can see it," Steve said. "Put it in the baggage-holder above your head, or tuck it under your seat. You never know who's on one of those buses. Keep tight hold of your ticket. Don't drink too much water before you get on, and if you have to go to the restroom, don't sit on the seat. A lot of those people have serious bowel issues, and some of them have got infectious skin conditions."

"That's useful to know," I said.

"If you have to line up to get aboard, make sure you're at the front of it. You might stand a chance of sitting together, but I doubt it. Weston's just a stop. It'll probably be pretty full before it even arrives."

He gave us the choice between being dropped in Weston itself or at the bus stop, which was about three miles out of town. After he'd waved aside our, *Whatever's easiest for you*, we had a brief conference and a vote.

"The town, please," I said.

Ten minutes later, we found ourselves standing somewhere that looked like a cross between a provincial suburb and an empty car-park, as if someone had taken all the buildings in a typical urban square mile, then spread them at random over a much bigger area and filled the gaps with superstores and places to leave your vehicle. The houses were very American: large, detached, with wooden-railed verandas, gables and neat gardens in front. There was a river, a warehouse with a shop front – 'Swisher Feed and Supply' – a clutch of silos, a neat row of clapped-out tractors in a dirt compound, a Baptist church, a picturesque former lunatic asylum. The sun had gone in and the sky was a uniform grey.

We were dressed for an excursion: travel bags, sunglasses, acoustic guitar, pumps. Julia wore her star and stripes baseball hat. Obviously, there was a Greyhound bus station here, but it definitely didn't feel like a tourist hot-spot. Everywhere we went, people looked at us a little bit longer than they did each other.

We didn't want a repeat of Sadie-Lisa, so we all bought shades at the Shop 'n Save Express. Charlotte purchased aspirin, mints, makeup, a copy of *O: The Oprah Magazine*, and four sets of earphones, one for each of us. Julia bought a lettuce, and ate it outside like it was an apple – just straight bites and swallows: I'd never seen anyone do that before, and she didn't seem to consider it odd. Afterwards we went for tacos and chilli at a fast-food place called Flying Dogs on West 2nd Street. We sat adjacent to two men in their late forties. They wore Spartans sweatshirts and shared a plateful of what looked like hot dogs with cream cheese, chatting amiably with their mouths full and nudging each other and laughing. A thin, twentysomething woman sat in front of us with a toddler and a milkshake in between them. She looked anxious. Behind the counter, two middle-aged women brewed coffee and called orders into the kitchen.

An hour later, we were sitting on the grass in City Park, which sounds much grander than it was. We'd bought our tickets for Tennessee now, and booked a hotel in Downtown Nashville, and killing time till our bus arrived looked set to become a problem. Even finding somewhere to sit wasn't easy. We'd walked alongside the river until it became obvious it wasn't taking us anywhere interesting. We turned round after the most exciting find of our visit: half a dozen yellow school buses parked in a patch of concrete at the roadside. We were tired and dispirited.

"No sign of Rudolph," Julia said. "Ten-thirty when we set off from the log cabin. I think you should probably ring the hire company and tell them the car's been stolen."

"It's not due back for a while yet," I said. "I don't want to prejudge matters."

Charlotte hooted. "You're not still imagining he'll *turn up*? Even if he did, how could he find us?"

"I asked Marlene to tell him to meet us in Nashville," I said.

Soraya laughed. "He must know Harlinne left a letter with the intention of scaring us away. He probably thinks it's worked."

"Harlinne's got my phone number," I said. "If he wants to find us, he can call her and she can call us."

"Last time we saw them, they weren't on speaking terms," Charlotte replied.

"They've been together since the late nineteen-forties or the early fifties," I said. "Depending on whose story you believe. However final it may have looked, I doubt that was the end of their relationship."

"What are we going to Nashville for?" Soraya asked. "I mean, what's actually there? Apart from the obvious fact that it's the home of Country, do any of us know anything about it?"

We didn't. We were doing a road-trip, and we knew about it had a musical connection, and it had sounded interesting, that's all. We wouldn't even recognise the skyline when the bus approached, which it would around 8.35am, after a fourteen hour journey. Stupid me, I'd looked at a map of American states I'd downloaded and, without thinking, imagined it'd take roughly three hours. I should have Googled it. Armed with the right information, we might have decided to stop off somewhere nearer first. Once again, we were racing, racing, like there was no time to lose.

We wandered around Weston for the rest of the afternoon like someone was forcing us to stay on our feet. For some reason – maybe it just seemed appropriate – I had Satie's *Gymnopédie No.1* going through my head, and I couldn't shake it. We spent another hour in Shop 'n Save Express – mostly with mothers and pre-school kids and old folks, all looking like they had lists and weren't, and never had been, impulse buyers – and drank coffee for forty-five minutes in Spanky's, just across the road from the river. We'd stopped talking to each other at about two o'clock. We shared a single donut in silence and stared fixedly at the table top.

We set off for the bus stop at five-thirty so we could queue if necessary. From what I could tell from Google Maps, the pick-up point was on a slight elevation, between an ice-cream shop, a pizza joint and a gas station with an attached supermarket. There was a Walmart supercentre a bit further along, but we decided against that, tempting though it was. What if the bus arrived slightly early? What if we lost track of time? What if we got to the departure point with minutes to spare and the queue was a mile long? What if, what if, what if. We were nervous now. Steve's warnings had spooked us a little, and we knew we almost certainly wouldn't be sitting together.

We were hungry when we arrived at the stop. We bought salads in plastic bowls from the supermarket and drank water, but not too much. We still weren't talking. We weren't even listening to music, though we still had power in our batteries. Saving it for the journey, maybe. Meanwhile, Erik Satie chipped away at my brain like a sadistic French maniac. Lisa texted me: *Hey, W'sup*. I sent her a photo of us in the gas station forecourt. *It's not all glamour*, I wrote. *Just about to get on the bus*. I wanted a shower. Thinking about it, that was probably one of the things that was making me so withdrawn.

The bus – navy blue with a long metallic stripe beneath the windows – came up the incline and pulled in by the garage. It hissed. We were the only ones waiting, so we got straight on. The driver politely indicated for Soraya to get off again. We all accompanied her. While the driver put the guitar in the under-bus baggage compartment, I asked Julia if I could borrow one of her books. She shrugged and gave me *Meditations*. We re-boarded. The bus wasn't full, but all the window seats were taken. It'd be night soon, anyway, so nothing to see out there. Charlotte sat down first, then Julia and Soraya, then me, separated by at least four places, so with no possibility of talking. At least I could see the others. I couldn't see who they were sitting next to.

All in all, I was bitterly disappointed. The seats were far too comfortable, with way too much leg room beneath. Everything oozed business class. I'd anticipated bog-standard upholstery and faulty suspension: a kind of tin can adventure ride in the company of dead beats and drifters. In my world, Greyhound buses were supposed to be an endurance test. You might or might not emerge from one unstabbed and in good mental health. When Steve told us to keep an eye on our bags in case they got stolen, he'd inadvertently raised my hopes. But bloody hell, I wasn't even sitting with a dead beat. The woman next to me looked to be in her mid-thirties. She wore an expensive jumper and smart trousers. She had an equally well-dressed baby asleep on her chest. She read a Kindle. For obvious reasons, she wasn't going to want a conversation.

Each seat came with an electrical socket. Talk about depressing. And yet, thank God: I could plug my phone in.

Then I looked at the screen. Lisa: *Not very glamorous here either*. A photo of Steve smoking a cigar in his underwear.

Delete. I'd have to write back to her sometime, though.

No time like the present. She *had* saved our lives, after all. I sent a simple *Whoa*.

When the bus got to the bottom of the drive, it turned right and followed the river as if taking us back into town, then it did a wide loop and joined a motorway.

Funny how things you don't particularly think you're enjoying at the time – occasionally, things you consider downright boring – sometimes stick with you. If I'd been American, I doubt I'd have given Weston a backwards look. It took a foreigner to notice the unselfconscious national signifiers: the wide streets, the look of the houses, the shop layouts, the fast food, the packaging of goods, the moulds of the vehicles, even the way people deported themselves: everything whispered 'America'. I wanted to go back.

And then I *really* wanted to go back.

Although no, that wasn't right. I didn't. I just didn't want to go to Nashville. Soraya was right: what was in Nashville? Well, a hotel and a tourist trail. No way could you get to know a city that big in less than half a lifetime. And where would we go afterwards? Jackson to Little Rock? Then maybe Dallas, Santa Fe, trawling the state capitals, staying in hotel after hotel. The kind of road trip a travel club for nonagenarians might plan for members who couldn't manage without a walking-frame. If that was the plan, even touring with the band would be preferable. Or buying a selection of postcards and looking through them on the plane home.

No disrespect to Nashville, but what we needed was more Westons. An entire trip of Westons. I needed to talk to the others.

As soon as I'd diagnosed the malaise and made a decision, I started to consider other things. Homesickness, for example. It wasn't just why were we going to Nashville? It was, why were we even in America?

Ostensibly, so I could talk to Charlotte; but that had more or less resolved itself. Charlotte wasn't half as bothered as we'd all imagined. Any talking to Dad (and I accept we still needed to clear the air) could as easily be done in Hexham as in California.

Or to inspire some sort of solution to the problems thrown up by *Top of My Tower*. Well, we'd got that: 'The Snowflake Song.' Either the greatest or the stupidest idea I'd ever had; time would tell. Anyway, it didn't need us to be in America.

So what were we doing here? I wanted to go home. Hampstead. I texted Tim. *I love you, how is Lek?*

I didn't expect to hear back from him for at least six hours. It was something like 2am in England.

To my surprise, he replied ten minutes later, just as I was falling into a doze.

I love you too. Lek's fine. We probably need to talk when you get home.

My stomach dropped onto the bus's immaculate floor. *What about?* I replied. 'Talk' was the sort of word men used when they were owning up to an affair and wanted a divorce.

Another ten minutes passed, during which time all my customary *You're an awful wife and mother* thoughts stood over me and jabbed swords into my neck, chest, eyes, stomach and legs.

I'm seriously thinking of giving up work, he replied. *Becoming a house-husband, pure and simple. You're right: Lek needs a full-time parent, and you're the bigger earner by a million miles. I know I've always resisted that in the past, but it needn't be a complete giving up, just a break. We're not poor.*

I had to read it twice before it sank in. I almost burst into tears. I gathered myself from the floor only because I had to compose a coherent reply.

I love you! I love you! I love you! Do it NOW!

Greyhound Bus Blues

I couldn't wait to tell Soraya. I'd wanted Tim to give up work for years, and he'd finally agreed. I could have texted her, or forwarded Tim's message, but I wanted to see her face. She'd definitely be as over the moon as I was.

I felt euphoric for about half an hour. I opened the *Meditations* at random just as it was wearing off.

> *IV. 40. Constantly think of the universe as one living creature, embracing one being and one soul; how all is absorbed into the one consciousness of this living creature; how it compasses all things with a single purpose, and how all things work together to cause all that comes to pass, and their wonderful web and texture.*

I kept reading. I could see why Julia liked it: a person's highest goal lay in being a good member of society. It was both dour and tantalising: *Every individual's mind is of God and has flowed from that other world.* Roughly how everyone probably felt sometimes, and it might well be true.

Tiredness crept up on me again. After about half an hour, we stopped at Sutton, WV. A few people got off, including the woman next to me and the guy next to Julia – a student-type guy with a fledgling beard and a green Tennessee Tigers sweatshirt. I was about to go and fill the vacant place, but Soraya beat me to it. I unplugged my phone and moved one place disconsolately along from where I'd been to the window. I half expected Charlotte to join me, but of course I'd positioned myself where she couldn't see me. I began to text her, but an old man with a walking stick plonked himself next to me before I could hit send. On the plus side, he looked refreshingly like a deadbeat: frayed denim jacket, wild hair, bare feet with plimsolls. On the minus side, he smelt of rancid sweat, had a hacking cough and, every five minutes on the dot, he spat into a tissue. He greeted me with a hoarse, "Hi, babes", which, although creepy, was more than the woman with the baby had managed. I said hello back, but didn't accept his offer of a handshake. I went to my phone. Old people accept that: they think millennials live in there. They don't like it, but they've grown used to it.

Music, music. I got the earphones Charlotte had bought me and scanned my playlist.

There had to be five hundred albums on here and yet I couldn't find anything. Something folk-y and timeless, perhaps. I considered Kathryn Tickell for a moment, or Holy Moly & the Crackers, but that'd be a cop out. No, it had to be something American. The Handsome Family? Christine Lavin? Suzanne Vega? Joan Baez? Shawn Colvin? All associated in my mind with specific times and places, not here. *Woody Guthrie.* Clichéd, I know, but it had to be him, if only because I'd only listened to his music once or twice before, and I'd admired more than enjoyed it. I tapped 'Sourwood Mountain' and lay back. Once I've started on an album, I don't skip around: I've got to reach the end, whatever I think of it. Nineteen tracks to go after this, which should see me to the next stop at least. The guy next to me sneezed. I pretended to be asleep. I heard him apologise in a crackled voice.

I suddenly felt sorry for him. What kind of a louse was I, faking sleep? I opened my eyes and smiled. "That's okay," I said.

In one way, no, it wasn't: I was probably going to catch something. In another, though, he was old, he had to get to wherever he was going, he had to sit somewhere, and it wasn't his fault he'd caught whatever he had. So it was my turn next; so what? I could almost hear Marcus Aurelius murmuring, just accept it.

Outside, I could make out the dim shapes of cars and lorries speeding in the opposite direction. Going home to Weston, perhaps.

I looked up the aisle. Charlotte sat next to a middle-aged guy in a brown suit with a respectable side-parted haircut. They were obviously enjoying each other's company.

A few rows further up, Soraya and Julia ditto. They were laughing.

But they weren't just enjoying each other's company. Somehow, it looked more than that. They were having a party.

A sudden wave of jealousy hit me – not something I was accustomed to – specifically directed at Soraya. Looking back, she hadn't even turned back to see if there was a vacant place next to me. She'd just made an instant bee-line for Julia, like they couldn't bear another moment's separation. And now there they were, thick as thieves.

I mentally reviewed their behaviour today. Actually, yes, they'd made a point of sitting together in both Flying Dogs and Spanky's, and at the park. They'd gone round Shop 'n Save Express together... on each of our visits. They'd probably planned to sit together on the bus. Secretly. Neither had ever anticipated sitting with me, much less wanted to. Charlotte probably didn't want to sit with me either. At least, not now.

Not that Charlotte mattered in the same way. Given the grand plan Soraya had divulged to me in New York, a Soraya-Julia hook-up might be imminent. Which wouldn't be good for anyone. I'd learned enough this holiday to know Julia was currently in a weird place. Homesick, she'd called it. Big time. And Soraya was always in a weird place.

Bloody hell, life.

I looked at them again, trying to interpret their body language. Soraya's was simple and direct and repetitive. *You're hot.* Julia's said, *You're an exciting, original person and I really like you, but I'm married – aren't I?* If it could have giggled like a besotted teenager, it probably would have.

That surge of jealousy again. But directed at who?

Soraya, obviously. I didn't care about Julia in the same way. Soraya was my sister-mother-employer-employee-best friend-collaborator. Julia had Knut and novel writing and Norway.

Nevertheless, worst case scenario: I might end up having to cut ties with both of them. Whatever they might be about to embark on, it couldn't end well, and they might each come to associate me with the other. And I might feel betrayed by both of them. Soraya would have to have access to Lek, obviously, if she wanted it –

My mind was racing way into the future. I picked up my phone and sent Julia a message. *Keep your hands off my girlfriend*, plus a growly face.

I was only half serious. But only half joking. Above all, I wanted to gauge her reaction. I couldn't see much of her, but I could see her left cheek. She stopped talking for a moment, looked at her phone, and blushed. She turned round to look at me. Our eyes met. Neither of us smiled. Her expression: a disturbing mixture of guilt and defiance.

Then she turned away and continued her conversation. I don't know whether she showed Soraya what I'd written. I couldn't see.

I immediately felt stupid. She didn't text back, which redoubled it.

Maybe I could retrieve the situation. I began to write, *Sorry, it was just a joke*, but I was only halfway through when my phone rang.

God, please let her not be in full *How very dare you* mode.

"Hi, Hannah," the voice on the other end said.

It didn't sound like Julia.

Because it wasn't.

"This is Sadie," the caller continued. "You might remember we met at my parents' log cabin this morning?"

Bloody hell. But there was no point in sounding unpleasant. Just let her talk herself out, then claim to be tired, and maybe buy a new phone tomorrow.

"Of course I remember," I said blandly. It wouldn't pay to put too much enthusiasm into my voice.

"I'm in Elkins. In case you don't know where that is, it's a small town just outside the national forest. I had to come here to buy a phone that I can throw away afterwards. I'll cut to the chase. We've had a visit from the FBI."

I sat up. "Oh, my God."

"Which is cool," she said, as if to make it clear I hadn't disappointed her. "They were looking for Harlinne. They couldn't find her, obviously. But they couldn't find any fingerprints either. Anyway, they're looking for *you* now. Dad denied Harlinne had ever been here, but he couldn't deny you'd ever been here, because they'd picked up footage of him taking you to Weston. Now they've got your fingerprints, I think. Anyway, they say they only want to *talk* to you, not to arrest you. But then, they always say that, don't they? They won't necessarily tell you the truth."

"No... No, maybe not."

"Anyway, Dad pretended he didn't know which way you were headed – he's gutsy like that, and he probably didn't want to look too much like a snitch in front of his daughters. The good news is, they think you've gone to Chicago."

"*Chicago?*"

"Because there's a bus there from Weston at 12.25 pm. Think about it. They weren't to know the reason Dad took you to Weston at half eleven was because he wanted to get rid of you. They assumed he was taking you to meet an imminent connection. Plus, no one in their right mind spends eight hours in Weston unless they want to end up in that lunatic asylum of theirs. What the hell did you find to do there?"

My mind wasn't on the conversation. "Oh, you know, this and that."

"The cameras can't have seen you get on the Chicago bus, obviously, but the Feds are probably thinking you're in disguise. Anyway, it's only a matter of time before they work out you're not where they think you are. They might start looking into other journeys you might have taken. Maybe they'll even check the online booking system, assuming they can get a warrant for something that paltry. My guess is they're pretty slow on the uptake, so that won't happen for a while. But I thought you'd appreciate the heads up."

"This is the second time today you and your sister have saved my life."

She laughed. "*Dad* was going to kill you. I don't think the FBI are! In any case, I'd better go now. Mom will be freaking out. I'll have to call her on my real phone, get them to pick me up. I'll probably be grounded for a month.

Take care, Hannah. And *keep in touch*. Me and Lisa can be more help than you think. We know this country."

She hung up.

SOS

There was no way we were going to Nashville now, and it being a cliché was the least of my reasons. Two other, much bigger, ones had arisen. Firstly, a city that size gave Julia and Soraya ample opportunity to wander off alone to a large number of romantic locations. Secondly, we had to get off the bus before the FBI found us. They only wanted to talk to us, supposedly, but given that telling the truth was always the best policy (true, in the present instance it was shit, but even so, better than any alternative), we'd have to tell them about Harlinne. That would incriminate Steve too. And given that we'd spent an entire night cleaning the log cabin – ?

Actually, how *had* the FBI recovered our prints?

Obviously because we'd left new ones in the interval between Steve's arrival and our departure later that morning. We'd been off guard. I know I had. I'd been tired, and a roller-coaster of emotions had made leaving fresh evidence the least of my concerns. I hadn't even considered it.

All that work for nothing. Mind you, they also had CCTV footage of us with Harlinne, so it was probably irrelevant.

I had a new text from Julia. *For your information, we're talking about the snowflake song.*

And one from Soraya. *Who are you on the phone to? xxx*

I hadn't time for that now. I scrolled down my list of contacts till I came to Harlinne, and pressed 'call'. I don't know whether I expected her to pick up or not. Nothing she did made any sense, so nothing was predictable.

It rang twice. "Hello, Hannah," she said. "Lovely to speak to you again."

It took me a second to adjust. "We got your note," I replied.

"That was just my little joke… Or *was* it? … Anyway, what's the problem? I hope you're not ringing to tell me off, because that would be yellow-bellied. I'm doing my absolute best to make your road trip interesting. If you want value for money – "

"Look, we know what you were trying to do at the log cabin."

She laughed. "What was I trying to do at the log cabin?"

"You wanted to mingle our fingerprints with yours, so when the FBI came, it'd look like we were your collaborators. Maybe that way, the charges against you might be undermined."

"What do you want from me?" she asked.

"We spent the entire night wiping that log cabin clean. The FBI have been and gone now, but the only prints they discovered were ours. They're looking for us because they want to 'talk' to us. If they do, we'll have to tell them we were staying there with you. Given that there's no evidence compelling us to divulge that, and that Steve – who's a really nice man, by the way – has actually kept schtum about you,

I think we'll get a million brownie points for a confession freely rendered. Once again, you'd be their sole target."

"Don't kid yourself, sweetie. They've been after me for as long as I can recall, and they've got nowhere. I'm used to it. Everyone knows the truth about the police and the Feds nowadays. They make things up to cover their asses and get a good conviction rate. So you won't find it completely beyond credibility when I say *I'm being framed*. It's a witch hunt, pure and simple."

"I don't know about that, and I don't care. I need your help."

"And I'm happy to give it, honey. But don't flatter yourself that you've blackmailed me with your 'confession freely rendered' spiel. You're not that smart. And I don't need you. I've got powerful connections: state attorneys, retired chief justices, state governors, senators, congressmen, the list goes on. If you doubt me, ask yourself: how did I get you that booking with *Harper's Bazaar?* Connections, that's all. I wanted a trip to Venice and I knew being linked to you and Harper's would make it easier, so I pulled the appropriate strings. Anyway, the FBI knows it hasn't a hope of bringing me to trial at present, no matter how much phoney evidence it plants. It's waiting till 2020, hoping against hope my strongest supporters will be swept from power in the presidential elections. Obviously, things might not pan out as they expect, though. Or I might die – after all, I'll be ninety next birthday – which would be a real disappointment for them, given how eager they are to see me *really suffer*. In a nutshell, they're in no hurry – they know they don't have that option – and so neither am I. Right now, I don't need you or anyone. So I'll ask you again: what exactly do you want?"

"Nothing," I said bitterly. "Nothing at all." Perhaps I should have hung up right there and then, but it seemed too theatrical. I was thirty-eight, not fifteen. "Actually," I went on, "even if – worst case scenario – the FBI pressures us into confessing to being with you, there's no need for us to implicate Steve. From their point of view, he might know nothing about it at all."

"I don't do handouts," she told me. "But I like the idea that you're concerned for Steve. That's the opposite of being yellow-bellied, in my view. So instead of saying, 'What do you want from me?' I should probably have said, 'How can I assist you?' Technically, I am still working for you, after all. And I did tell you to contact me if you needed help."

"Ideally, I'd like you to get us off this bus as soon as possible."

She chortled. "You'll have to be a little more specific than that, I'm afraid."

"We're on a Greyhound bus from Weston to Nashville. It left at 7.25 pm."

"Okay, hold the line for a few seconds, dear."

I half expected piped music. Instead, a slight clatter, presumably as she put her phone down somewhere. After three minutes I began to imagine she'd done a runner.

"Hello, Hannah," she said, at last. "Okay, according to my calculations, you should be about to pull in to Charleston, West Virginia. You're scheduled to transfer to another coach. If the FBI are looking to intercept you, they might do it there, but I doubt it. You're not a major issue in their book, and they probably think you're unaware that they want to speak to you. They'll be waiting in Nashville if they're waiting anywhere. On the other hand, getting off the bus *would* suggest someone's alerted you. And they'd probably conclude it was Steve; which presumably it was, am I right?"

"It was Sadie, one of his daughters. She used a disposable phone, then threw it away."

She laughed. "My goodness, how melodramatic of her! And how endearing. She must really like you to waste a perfectly good telephone like that. But then, she's a teenager and you're a pop idol, so it's not too outlandish, I suppose."

"Anyway, they won't be able to prove Steve alerted us. And since Sadie almost certainly hasn't told him, I'm sure he can produce a very convincing impression of being unjustly accused."

"So all's well that ends well. Give me five minutes. I need to ring around a little, speak to a few friends. I'll call you back and give you further instructions. Is that okay?"

"It's good."

I knew exactly how stupid I'd been the moment she hung up. She'd probably recorded the whole conversation, attached the audio file to an email and sent it to the FBI. Part of me didn't think she'd stoop that low, but obviously she'd tried to frame us once, so why not? I'd also been wrong about Rudolph. The refusal of my faith in human nature to lay down and die, in the wake of repeated shootings in the head, said everything about me and nothing whatsoever about the world. Perhaps I should text the others, let them know I'd dropped us all in an almighty vat of shit.

No, I still believed in her.

So I was a *knowing* idiot. In any case, what would telling the others achieve?

My phone rang. I almost threw it in the air in surprise.

"I'm sending Rudolph to meet you at Charleston," Harlinne said. "As chance would have it, he's actually somewhere round about where you are right now. He went back to the log cabin about an hour ago, hoping to find you; one of Steve's girls let him know you were heading south. He was hoping to connect with you some place, and he'd gambled on Nashville. I've directed him to Charleston. He'll be there before you, which should be about 9.20. He's in your hire car, obviously. Get straight in, but don't run. Act casual. You're not felons." She cackled. "Not yet, anyway."

She hung up.

Nope to Nashville

I outlined the situation to the others as we disembarked, and they didn't raise any objections. The thought that they might end up in jail if they didn't cooperate seemed to be enough. Rudolph awaited us in the parking lot on Reynolds Street. We couldn't see anything that looked like it might have FBI personnel inside, but then we had to act like we weren't looking. We loaded our bags and the guitar into the trunk. I manoeuvred Charlotte in between Julia and Soraya on the back seat, got in the front next to

Rudolph, and we set off at a leisurely 20 mph. As far as any of us could tell, we weren't followed.

"Where did you go last night?" I asked Rudolph as non-confrontationally as I could, once I was certain there was no turning back.

"Sometimes Harlinne does that to me," he said. "And I spent all this morning answering questions in a police station. Some people don't like seeing a ninety-six-year-old black guy driving a nice car like this. They don't see how it makes sense. Maybe it doesn't. Anyway, that's why I wasn't back earlier."

"Apology accepted," I said sarcastically.

"I'm a sucker for her, I know. I realise I've let you down."

I shrugged. "We're quits now. And I quite like the fact that you still love her. I'll be seventy-nine some day, maybe. I hope someone still loves me at that point."

He laughed. "It's not love exactly. Or maybe it is. I don't know. In any case, where are we headed? Still want to go to Nashville?"

"Not with the FBI waiting for us."

"I wouldn't believe any of that, if I were you. It's just Harlinne's way of adding a little frisson to your trip."

"I'd tend to agree," I said, "only I've got it on the authority of Steve's daughter, Sadie, that the FBI turned up at the log cabin today, looking for us."

"Steve Rogers's girl?"

"I don't know his second name. The guy who owns the log cabin."

"Sheesh. Maybe you *are* in trouble. Steve's not exactly my kind of guy – "

"Exactly what he said about you."

"He's into all that hunting and fishing stuff, killing things to eat. I'm no vegan, but I don't like watching things die. Which I guess makes me a hypocrite."

"No more than me. I was fighting climate change before I came here. A road trip across America's the last thing I should be doing. And I don't like seeing things die any more than you do, but I like a hot dog. Maybe it's time I thought seriously about that."

"Don't let Harlinne hear you talk that way. Principles are secondary, far as she's concerned. What matters in her world is two things only: appetite and imagination. Which is why people warm to her. She's fun to be with. Whereas I'm a killjoy, so they say. Too prissy for my own good. You still haven't told me where we're going."

"Somewhere small town, south west."

Julia leaned over from the back seat. "I've been listening to what you've been saying, Hannah, and it makes no sense at all. You're obviously tired out and not thinking clearly. You and I are famous: we've both got New York agents who can contact us whenever they want to. They've got our phone numbers. If the FBI really wanted to find us, they wouldn't chase us across the continent. They'd just go to the British embassy, and the embassy would do a bit of asking around, and someone would call us. Celine, for example, my literary agent. Or Nora from your PR firm. Or anyone. Or the FBI might just contact us directly. *Hi, this is Agent Dale Cooper here. Would you mind staying wherever you are? We'd like to talk to you.*"

"Or they could look at our credit card activity," Charlotte put in.

Rudolph shook his head. "Depends how badly they want to talk to you if they'd start rattling those sorts of cages. If I was a hunting man like Steve Rogers, I'd say your best method of catching a deer isn't necessarily to go crashing through the forest in a Sherman tank. Adverse publicity: you might well take offence, and Harlinne's got friends in Washington who'd bend over backwards to use that. There's no love lost between the administration and the FBI nowadays, not since Comey got fired, and Mueller started probing, and Andrew McCabe said his two cents worth. No, they'll be biding their time, waiting for a one on one with you, and they'll try their darndest to make it as pleasant as possible. Earl Grey from a silver teapot, scones with strawberry jelly and heavy cream, pink salmon sandwiches with the crusts removed, the whole British works. Leave you eternally grateful and totally disinclined to complain. Pass through invisible, as the saying goes."

"We know for sure they've been to see Steve," I told Julia. "Explain that."

"If they want to talk to us and they're going to be nice about it," Charlotte said, "why don't we just give them a call, get it over with?"

"Raise your hands everyone who wants to help them bust Harlinne," I said.

Rudolph laughed. "That's not a British word."

"We all know what it means, though."

"Point taken," Charlotte said. "About Harlinne, I mean. Not 'bust.'"

"Put it another way," Rudolph said. "They're probably not anticipating getting that much from you. You might end up surprising them. I mean, *delighting* them. I mean, incriminating yourselves. You strike me as the kind of people who, when the pressure's on, prefer the *Father, I cannot tell a lie, it was me who chopped down your cherry tree* approach. Which isn't so wise, nowadays."

"But the truth is," Julia said, "we've done nothing wrong."

Rudolph scoffed. "Sometimes it's not what the truth *is*, it's what they can *do* with it. It's raw materials, so to speak. You get picked up by mistake, which no one on their side wants to admit, so they get to work re-writing a tiny bit of history, just enough to put you in jail. Happens to black people all the time. And not just in this country, before you accuse me of being unpatriotic. Britain's got its problems that way too, from what I hear."

"Okay," I said. "It's decided. We keep 'running', in inverted commas, till we get a formal invitation to give ourselves up, which we probably will at some stage. We use the intervening time to get our story straight."

"You mean, our *lie*," Soraya said.

"Yes," I replied.

"That's my girl," she told me. "Love you, by the way."

"Long live rock and roll," Julia said jadedly.

"Put another dime in the jukebox, baby," Charlotte said.

"Two different songs," I told her.

"Rainbow and Joan Jett," Soraya said. We casually high-fived and I let out a big internal sigh of relief. Julia's *You're obviously tired out and not thinking clearly* had been designed to belittle me; to make me look like a fool in front of Soraya. Or more likely, make her look like the sharper sister. It had backfired.

Nevertheless, I had the distinct feeling this was just the beginning of all that.

Or maybe I was just tired. And paranoid. And stupid.

Racing Again, Naturally

Down we went, through Kentucky, Tennessee, Alabama – hardly seeing anything at all, unfortunately, in our pointless quest to put as much space as possible between ourselves and the FBI (as if geographical 'space' meant *anything at all* in a world in which all that mattered was the cellular network, and that was everywhere) – and ended up, fourteen hours later, and completely shattered, in Durant, Mississippi.

The Americans don't have villages, they have 'small towns' and this was one. The houses were wide, low and colourful, mostly wooden, with elaborate porches out front and verandas at the back. Trees old and young, and well-cut grass – everywhere actually – filled the broad spaces between the dwellings and the offices. Unpretentious roads led nowhere in particular. Its commercial centre comprised an insurance office, at least three diners, a wine and spirits shop, a bank and one or two general stores. I counted seven churches. The landscape was flat on all sides, and, as far as anyone standing at any point in the town could tell from looking at the horizon, it might have been the only place in the entire world. Haphazard but beautiful.

There was a motel somewhere in town called the Oak Tree Inn, but Rudolph already knew where we were going to stay. He'd organised another fully-furnished house, on broadly the same pretext as Steve's log cabin: owners away, they were 'friends' (of Harlinne, this time), they were happy about us being there, etc. We *could* have gone to the motel, I suppose, but that would have been playing it safe. *Steve hadn't shot us, so no owner of any property Rudolph installed us in ever would:* I'm pretty sure that was our subconscious, screwed-up logic.

We arrived just before midday. Rudolph showed us round the house like it was his. It was all on one floor. A big kitchen with windows on each side, views of grass, other houses, and telegraph wires, three bedrooms, one with a double bed, the second (presumably the children's, but there was no confirmatory juvenilia) containing three single beds, the third furnished as an office with a table and PC. Then a large living room containing two huge sofas and a TV, plus a bathroom and a laundry room.

"Are you sure the owners are okay about us being here?" Soraya asked. "Because Steve definitely wasn't. He nearly cut us down with an M14."

"Phone them," Rudolph said. "Or call Harlinne, if you prefer."

I absolutely wasn't going to decline his invitation. I was nervous. "What's the proprietor's number?" I asked.

He supplied it, apparently from memory. It rang twice and I had a ten minute conversation with a woman called Maggie who gave me instructions as to how the various appliances worked and the contents of the different cupboards. "It's two thousand a week," she said, before she hung up. "Payable in cash. But I guess you knew that. Try and leave things roughly as you found them. Rudy'll let me know when you're leaving, then I can come home. Have a good stay."

She hung up before I could ask what she meant. Had we somehow forced her out?

I turned quizzically to Rudolph. "She said, 'let me know when you're leaving, then I can come home.'"

He shrugged. "You're paying her rent and a good bit more. She's staying with her sister right now. How much did she say you should pay?"

"Two thousand a week," I replied.

He whistled. "You should have beat her down."

"I didn't know that was the point of the conversation." I sighed. "Anyway, I don't care. I just want to be able to sleep at night knowing the owner's not going to turn up with a rifle."

"She only pays Harlinne two hundred a week," he said.

"Well, in that case," I said, "I'm pleased. Everyone wins. We might even stay here a fortnight if it's a nice town and she's happy to let us."

He hooted. "I don't think there's much chance of her saying no to *that!*"

"Is there a Walmart nearby?" Soraya asked.

Julia's Brilliant Idea

As soon as I'd spoken to Maggie, we all went to sleep for the afternoon. We thought Rudolph might crash down on one of the single beds alongside Julia and Charlotte, but he said he lived nearby, and wanted to spend time with his great nieces and nephews. Nevertheless, while we were asleep, he brought us tea, coffee, milk and eggs from the local store, plus a ten-pack of bread rolls, a jar of apricot jelly, some cooking oil and a big bottle of sun cream. We all awoke fairly simultaneously at six in the evening. We made ourselves and him omelette sandwiches, then he left, taking the car. We sat in our pyjamas on the two sofas, drinking tea and watching a Don Lemon interview with Amy Klobuchar. By ten, we were bored. We showered, got dressed and went out to look round the town. We ended up wandering farther than we intended. In fact, we only found our way home because Durant was the sort of place where, if you continued walking long enough and kept changing direction, and didn't stray too far beyond the houses, you'd always return to where you started. Since it'd been dark throughout, we'd no real idea where we'd been (in terms of ever replicating the experience). At one point we stumbled across 'Durant Package Store', an off-licence behind a gravel parking lot. Closed. When we got in, we were dead beat. We went to bed a second time and slept soundly till eight the next morning.

We ate breakfast in silence. Julia and Soraya looked annoyed about something. I guessed (correctly) they'd been banking on a luxury hotel in Nashville. Charlotte ate three slices of toast and jam and asked what we had planned for today, as if she didn't really care where in the world we were.

Julia looked at her. "You mean, what can we conceivably do today that we didn't do last night? That was it, Lottie. That was Durant."

"Well, we didn't get much of a feel for it," Charlotte said. "I mean, we didn't meet anyone."

"On what footing are we supposed to 'meet people'?" Julia continued. "We're probably the only tourists within twenty miles. Everyone else actually lives here. What are we supposed to do? Offer ourselves for hire as farmhands? Because that's what this is: it's a farming and rural community. I looked it up on Wikipedia a few minutes ago. Population two thousand and something, lots of unemployment. And you know two nuns were murdered here a few years ago, right?"

"I didn't know that," I said. I thought I might as well chip in. Although Julia seemed to be talking to Charlotte, her comments were directed at me. She'd done it all the time when we were children, as if an oblique confrontation was easier than a direct one.

"We're supposed to be in Nashville now," Soraya said. "I mean, no disrespect to the Durantians, but this is just the same as Weston."

"If you want to go to Nashville, then go," I told her. "I won't stop you."

Soraya and Julia looked at each other. For the briefest of seconds, I could actually see them considering it. For all I knew, they might already have discussed it.

"We'll stay here," Julia said. "But only out of a sense of loyalty. All for one and one for all."

"Oh, shut up, Julia," I said. "Stop being so patronising. I told you why we came here."

"And you think the FBI can't find us here?" she said. "Not that they're after us anyway. How long are we planning on staying?"

"I've paid for a week," I said. "You heard me on the phone to Maggie last night."

"We don't have to *stay* a week, though," Soraya said.

I got up and went to sit on the sofa in the living room. I switched the TV on, flicked a few channels, watched the news. No one came to ask why I'd flounced out. After a few minutes, Julia and Soraya came to sit on the edge of the other sofa. They faced me. I ignored them.

"Julia had a dream last night," Soraya said.

"I had a dream last night!" Julia intoned, doing an unfunny impression of Martin Luther King Junior.

"Really," I said. I switched the volume up.

"I dreamed Louisa May Alcott was standing over me in bed," Julia went on, raising her voice slightly. "A bit like what I imagine it was like for Joseph Smith, the Mormon prophet, when he had a vision of the angel Moroni. Have you ever heard that story?"

"What do you want?" I asked her.

"Just let her tell the story, Hannah," Soraya said.

"There was Louisa May Alcott," Julia continued, "the author of *Little Women* – "

"I may not have been on *University Challenge*," I said, "but I do have a rudimentary education."

"Hovering above me in the air," Julia continued. "I was sitting up. And she said, 'You, Julia, *you* will write The Great American Novel!' And I said, 'I can't! I'm British! And I'm only here on holiday!' But she kept on repeating those same words, over and over again. 'You, Julia, *you* will write the Great American Novel.'"

For a second, I was tempted to retort with something monosyllabic and withering. But I stopped myself.

What she was saying was just too weird for derision. Why was she telling me this? Why make a special journey from the kitchen to sit facing me? Why the intensity?

I looked at her. I'd started out feeling angry, but now I was a tad concerned. I remembered her homesickness spiel in Steve's cabin.

"What are you trying to say?" I asked. "Are you – ? You're not thinking of applying for US citizenship, are you?"

"I'm not ruling it out," she replied.

"Why not just say that, then?"

"She hasn't finished," Soraya said. "She's got a great idea. Equally as good as your snowflake idea. And we've made great strides on that song, by the way. Tell her, Julia. Or shall I?"

I noticed them link hands.

"I'll tell her," Julia said. 'Her': the third person, like I wasn't fully present. "I'll begin at the beginning, shall I? When my literary agent, Celine, heard I was coming to America, she thought it'd make a marvellous idea for a book. We tossed a few ideas about. I wasn't keen on the 'visit every state' approach, I think I may have mentioned that already. It's based on the pretext that Americans love to read about what foreigners think of them, so you put in something for everyone, a kind of scattergun tactic. No depth, just breadth. Luckily, that was never going to be an option, because it was your road trip, not mine. Anyway, then we discussed the possibility of a memoir-stroke-biography. Premise: I come to

America and research the life and journeys of Elise Cowen, one of the original Beat women. I write about my findings, and I also undergo a 'spiritual journey' of kinds as I find out more and more about a personal hero of mine. That idea had legs, but I wasn't sure about the 'spiritual journey' bit. What if I wasn't changed by my findings? Should I pretend to be? The problem is, there are far too many nonentities like me droning on about their 'inner journeys'. It's an even bigger cliché than 'visit every state'. Anyway, after Louisa May Alcott spoke to me last night – "

"Hang on," I said, waving my hands just below the level of my face. "Just put it on pause a minute. Can you please stop saying, 'Louisa May Alcott spoke to me' like you think it really happened? It was a dream. Just a dream, that's all. Tell me you don't think it actually occurred, because you're starting to freak me out."

"I'm not saying it actually occurred," Julia said. "At least, not in the literal way in which yesterday's bus journey, or our stay in the Monongahela National Forest, actually happened. But there are other kinds of truths. Charlotte's right when she says – "

I rolled my eyes. Luckily, Charlotte was in the kitchen. From what I could hear, she was washing the dishes – I kept hearing the pipes hammer as she ran the hot tap – and listening to Alicia Keys on the CD player. "For God's sake," I said. "Either Louisa May Alcott came to visit you last night, or she didn't. And since she's been dead since…"

"Eighteen eighty-eight," Julia said.

"Correct," Soraya said. "Okay teams, fingers on buzzers again."

Julia laughed. They high fived, but without taking their eyes off me. It struck me for the first time that Soraya had completely bought into the derangement.

I sighed. "I think we can safely assume she was also dead last night."

"Of *course* she's dead," Julia said. "But my subconscious isn't. And that was what was speaking."

"Can we cut to the chase now?" I asked. "Firstly, where's the 'great idea' in all this? Secondly, what has any of it got to do with me?"

"Julia's going to ghost write the story of our trip across America for us," Soraya said. "It'll be an *actual literary work of art*. We come to America looking for redemption, and we find it."

"Americans love happy endings," Julia said. "By and large, they're not bitter, negative, self-centred trolls like the British."

"Julia'll write it free of charge," Soraya said. "It'll make us look good and, more importantly, it'll make us look deep."

Julia nodded. "I thought I'd divide it into, say, twenty or thirty first-person chapters, alternating each of our perspectives. Charlotte-Hannah-Julia-Soraya then back to Charlotte. It needn't be that mechanical, obviously."

"It'll be called 'The Snowflake Song,'" Soraya said. "It'll be the story of us writing the song and, indirectly, the story of all millennials everywhere. We won't read Marcus Aurelius, obviously. We'll read something a bit more relevant and up-to-date."

"I was thinking Aziz Ansari's *Modern Romance*," Julia said. "Although Emerson would still work. He might even be necessary." She giggled slightly, in excitement. "We'd have to resist all film offers till we had complete creative control, though. They'd turn it into a comedy: the cautionary tale of four slightly dippy, but endearing women."

The last three exchanges weren't even directed at me. They were talking to each other now, filling in the details on a done deal. And they'd come in here not to ask my permission, but to tell me what was happening.

Julia put her hand on my knee. "I'm sorry I was a bit snarky back there at breakfast. I didn't sleep as well as I should have." She lowered her voice, leaned over and whispered, "Charlotte was snoring." She sat up again. "To be honest," she said, "I couldn't care less about Nashville. Durant's perfect."

I'm Going Sadly Down

I was still watching TV half an hour later when Soraya poked her head round the door. She and Julia were going out, would I like to come? I knew they didn't want me around – Soraya's shrug and 'okay' was proof enough of that – and I didn't want to be where I wasn't wanted. I heard them chatting excitedly as they left. Charlotte called in on me thirty minutes later. She was going in town to see what was there, did I want to join her? I was depressed now; I couldn't see myself being any kind of company, so I said no. Two minutes later, I heard the front door close as she let herself out.

The first thing I do when I'm in anyone's house alone is check the owner's taste in music. More of a habit than anything, and I wasn't really in the mood for it now. But curiosity's stronger than misery. Most people have CD's lying around, even nowadays when they're largely defunct. Maggie's were on the top shelf in the cupboard above the fridge.

All rap and hip hop. Which suited me fine. I took an album out at random and put it on. Megan Thee Stallion, *Tina Snow*. I lay back on the sofa and switched the TV off. Pointless wasting electricity: the planet was in enough trouble, and we hadn't exactly helped the situation, fatuously driving and bussing hundreds of miles.

The road trip was over. At least, for me. Resolving Charlotte's 'crisis' aside, it had been a catastrophic failure. I'd lost Soraya and there hadn't even been a struggle. Julia had just shaken her supermodel-grade booty and flashed her cover-girl eyes and seductively whispered her pseudo-intellectual bullshit, and Soraya had swooned.

It wouldn't end well, because Soraya wasn't what Julia wanted. I didn't know what Julia wanted. Novelists often act as if they're on a plane above the rest of us. In my experience (and I've met more than a few), they're at least one level below. The difference between them and other lowlifes is mainly their stronger self-delusion, and that no one dares challenge them. Being 'literary' entitles them to an automatic halo.

What did Soraya want? Obviously, something physical, of the kind I couldn't supply. Julia looked willing at the moment, but that probably wouldn't last. She was mixed up and on vacation; looking for a holiday romance, but too self-important to admit it. Back in Norway, she'd see things differently. Assuming she ever returned. But even without that. Sometimes truth has a nasty habit of finding you wherever.

God knows how Knut would react to the prospect of losing her. I couldn't exactly warn him. Nothing had happened yet, and, if pressed on the matter, I couldn't explain how I knew it would.

My biggest concern right now was whether Soraya would still want me after Julia dumped her. It'd be a consolation (just) to know she was happy, but that didn't seem a likely outcome. Ironic that I was losing her just as Tim was becoming a house husband. Maybe I didn't deserve too much happiness.

God, I was so mixed up. I was actually crying now. To the sound of *Freak Nasty [Explicit]*, of all things. I went into the kitchen and turned it up.

Maybe I should just walk out and go home. The band was finished, Julia had purloined all rights to the Snowflake Song, Charlotte had resolved her problems with Dad. I wasn't needed.

What I needed was Tim and Lek.

My life as I'd constructed it over nearly twenty years was insane. Jetting from continent to continent with barely time for coffee or a loo-break while people threw money at me to stay locked indoors? I had a wonderful daughter, and a fabulous husband. What was I doing anywhere else? It looked like time to throw in the towel; draw a deliberate line under the days of being young; go home and stay home. We had money, enough to last us several lifetimes. We could buy ourselves an island in the

Pacific if we wanted. We need never see anyone else again. We could become completely self-sufficient.

Only Lek wasn't my daughter.

There it was. The problem, in a nutshell. And if I'm honest, Soraya – her 'real' mother – was everything I hoped Lek would become. And I loved her. I'd always love her.

How was that possible? How was that degree of love possible without sex?

I don't know.

I needed to get out of Durant, find an airport.

But I couldn't. I couldn't just run off. I had to wait. I had to see with my own eyes what I knew was coming. I had to be able to say to myself, afterwards, 'You were right.'

'Tis the Final Countdown

The next eight days can be summarised fairly briefly. We didn't see Rudolph again till we were leaving. In the meantime, we lived three parallel lives, Julia-Soraya, Charlotte, Me. We came together in the morning for breakfast and the obligatory Skype home, and dinner (sometimes), or, failing that, supper, in the evening. Soraya and I continued to sleep in the same bed. We didn't exactly avoid talking but there was a taciturnity-inducing awkwardness, concealed by the polite lie that we were both 'tired'. We stopped saying I love you. Which might not sound like much, given that we were only in Durant for just over a week, but it was. To me.

Soraya and Julia sallied out together every morning at about nine and returned every evening at seven. They talked excitedly about what they'd done: laid on their backs cloud-watching by Indian Creek, had lunch at the Küche restaurant (they seemed to spend a lot of time at the Küche restaurant), walked the old railway line, picnicked on the western bank of the Big Black River, skinny dipped in Odum Lake, hitchhiked to Walmart in Kosciusko nearly twenty miles away, sitting in the back of this guy's truck all the way, and they didn't know whether that was even legal – *it probably wasn't!* – and bought two *huge* milkshakes from McDonald's and drunk them in the park, where Soraya had played Regina Spektor songs on her guitar, and would you believe it, the Snowflake Song was almost finished!

While all this was going on, Charlotte made friends in town. I don't know how, but part of her philosophy was to be open to her angels or fate or the universe or whatever she called it that week. She never brought her new acquaintances home, but she started going round to their houses, or for coffee, from the second day onwards. Millicent, one was called; I think there was an Emily, and a third whose name I can't recall. They'd sometimes meet up at the Liberty Hill AME Zion Church, because all her new buddies were churchgoers. I think, looking back, they may have been hoping to convert her. And maybe it was the other way round too. She never put on airs: wherever she went, she was always upfront about her crystals, the healing power of chakra meditation and the Spirit in the Sky. Or maybe she and her new pals just liked each other pure and simple, I don't know. Sometimes people don't care about dogmatic differences. Why should they?

The third parallel life was mine, of course. It involved sitting in the house all day, listening to hip hop. There was a Whistle Stop Wine & Spirits shop nearby, and I could probably have spent all day every day drunk. I would have liked to... I think. But the last thing I wanted was for Julia to find me in that condition. She was stealing my girlfriend. That made me pathetic enough already. I didn't need her pity as well.

I'd never had much time for rap or hip hop before. I didn't like the misogyny or the homophobia or the ostentatious super wealth: gold-plated this, diamond-encrusted that, fur coats, Gucci, Prada, Chanel, luxury cars. But I liked the anger. Anger's quite difficult to pull off convincingly in popular music. Bob Dylan could do it. He was probably the first. Joni Mitchell's a better poet than him, and sometimes her lyrics are angry, but her delivery never is. The Sex Pistols managed it. Few others have.

Soraya knew all about rap and hip hop. I've lost count of the number of tracks that have 'feat. Soraya S' next to them. I don't take much notice. The artists know more than I ever will, so they're in charge. My job's simply to sign the contract and make sure Soraya gets on and off the plane safely. I don't even know why they want her, really. She's a rock singer, not a rapper. But she can do anger.

I suppose listening to Pharoahe Monch and Public Enemy and Onyx made *me* angry too. It certainly helped define my mood. 'Angry' is how people often describe gathering storm clouds. And incidentally, Durant was almost levelled by a typhoon a few years ago. It knows all about angry weather.

In my case, of course, the storm clouds were Julia and Soraya. One day very soon – as early as tomorrow maybe, or the day after – I expected a handwritten letter propped against the toaster in the kitchen. Or they might do it by phone. But that was less likely, because Julia took too much pride in her prose. It'd be stylistically perfect. *Dear Hannah, Please forgive me for what I'm about to say. Believe me, if I thought there was any other way... I'm in love ... We're in love... I've never felt anything like this. It's like that typhoon that hit Durant a few years ago, only much, much stronger...*

No, it wouldn't be anything like that. That was hackneyed. It'd be something worthy of *The Collected Letters of Julia Mordred, vol. II*, because I knew for a fact she already had one eye on professors and the critics a hundred years from now. Still, no room in the 22nd century for *Hot novelist leaves distraught husband for hot singer. Both at the top of their games.* Soraya's version would last a decade at most then be discreetly shelved.

I became aware of my own mortality in a way I hadn't since my long, hard brush with cancer, in 2013. I thought of those two murdered nuns, then dwelt morbidly on all the school shootings in America. Horrible. Yet life was limited. Sooner or later, whatever happened, we were all going to die. I was probably about half way through my allotted threescore years and ten now, the best bit behind me. You could only live once. You made your choices, and certain things implicitly got rejected, because no one can be everywhere, doing everything. When you decided to live in London, you also chose not to live in

Washington, or Paris, or Berlin, or Durant. You couldn't go back and change that. You might go and live in one of those places in the future sometime, but it wouldn't be those places. Like this road trip. *This* was it. It wouldn't come back. We'd already missed Maine where the witches were; we'd omitted wherever Edith Wharton used to live, the Woodstock museum, Timothy Leary's mansion, Philadelphia, Nashville. We wouldn't do it again, not this way. It sounds like a cliché, but there are moments when you realise everything's slipping through your fingers, and you're powerless to stop it. I say 'realise': you become aware of the truth. Things are disappearing for ever. Good things. Irreplaceable things. I had lots of those moments right now. And to help me make the most of my existential angst, I had an ear worm: ABBA's *Slipping Through My Fingers*. Since I had rap on almost continuously in the background, it felt like The Notorious B.I.G. *feat.* the cast of *Mama Mia*.

On Day 4 of all this, Charlotte apparently noticed there was something wrong. After Julia and Soraya left the house, she came into the living room. I was lying on one of the sofas in my nightie, holding the remote and watching a man on TV make strawberry pancakes. She was dressed to go out: dark skirt, button-up blouse and pumps. She sat opposite me.

"Soraya and Julia seem to be spending a lot of time together," she said.

"I'd noticed."

"Why don't you go with them?"

"I think they'd rather I stayed here."

"I'm sure that's not true. Have you tried asking them?"

I laughed miserably. "*I'd like to come with you. Would you prefer me not to, though?* How do you think that sounds? Because I'd call it a bit desperate."

"Don't be silly. Do you want them to insist?"

"I want them to have a good time. They're happy going out; I'm happy staying in. I'm discovering new music."

"Hip hop? It all sounds the same to me."

"That's what it means to belong to a genre. All pop sounds the same, all rock sounds the same, all folk sounds the same. It's what makes genres, genres."

"Would you like to come out with me? I could introduce you to my friends."

"It's a kind offer, but I'm fine."

She looked cautiously around herself as if she might be overheard, then lowered her voice. "I don't know whether it's just me, but… Well, Soraya and Julia seem pretty close. Do you think they could be having some sort of relationship? I mean, Soraya is gay, isn't she? I know Julia's married, but she might be bi."

I sighed. "The thought had occurred to me. There's nothing we can do if they are. They're adults."

She did something she'd never done before. She got off the sofa, knelt down in front of me and put her arms round me. I hadn't been close to crying until now. This did it, though.

After five minutes, she went into the kitchen. I heard her ring her friends and cry off whatever she had planned. Ten minutes later, she came into the living room in her nightie and lay on the other sofa. She grinned sheepishly at me.

"Let the hip hop roll," she said.

The Sound of Thunder Overhead and Sweet Refreshing Rain on Earth

This went on for days. The clouds got bigger and thicker. I could almost feel the moisture. I could avoid Soraya and Julia when they got up to go out in the morning – I could almost hear them tiptoeing, like they didn't want to wake me – but evenings were another matter. For some reason, they always felt duty-bound to describe whatever half-arsed thing they'd done that day, while I sat there with a frozen smile, trying to pretend I was enjoying listening to them, and looking at the corny pictures they'd taken. Luckily, Charlotte really *was* interested. She asked all sorts of questions and examined the snaps like they were mesmerising. There'd always come a point at which they'd ask me what I'd done. After a few days, I realised 'I listened to rap' was evoking concern. I took to wandering the streets like someone in a Carson McCullers novel just to have something to say that evening. To pad out the deception, I took up photography. To put it another way, I pretended to be interested in photography. I took pictures of insects, trees, a horse, a row of garages, a 'Stop' sign on Hamilton Street, the front of Hugh Carl's Mobile Home Parts, a flock of starlings on a chapel lawn. I covered my face in sun cream and tramped the streets this way for about two hours every morning. Then I went home, made myself a fried egg sandwich, and listened to songs about gangland violence in South Central LA. Later, at dinnertime, I'd don my rictus smile, listen to everyone's adventure stories, and show my photos. We'd spend ages cropping them and applying filters, trying futilely to make them interesting, then we'd post them to Instagram, where the reaction was consistently 'Duh?' The next morning, Charlotte would say, 'That one of the row of shovels was really good', or 'The dead cat one really made me think.'

I knew the time had come when she hugged me on her way out one morning. She obviously knew something I didn't (yet), and it wasn't good. She held me a little too tightly, a little too long, and she stroked my back. When she finally drew back, she looked like she was on the brink of tears, and if she said anything, it'd be the final straw. She let herself out of the house without looking back.

God, I know not everything I've done today has been good or had any point, but look after those I love and please don't let go of me. Your servant, Hannah.

Julia and Soraya had left about an hour earlier. They'd been unusually quiet in their morning preparations, and I had the definite feeling this was it. A relief, of sorts. I got up and had a bowl of cornflakes a few moments after they'd gone and went to watch TV. I heard Charlotte in the kitchen, like she too had been waiting to be alone. She didn't come and see me until she was on her way out. Then the weepy hug already described.

I switched the TV off. It didn't occur to me to put the CD player on. If this was what I thought it was it needed to be met with dignity. I had Tim. I had Lek. I still had two living parents. Life went on. I dressed, returned to the sofa and sat upright with my hands folded in my lap. After a week of non-stop rap, the silence was overwhelming.

A clock ticked somewhere. I hadn't even registered its existence till now.

I sat and I sat, waiting patiently for the axe to fall. And it seemed to be taking forever.

After ten minutes, it occurred to me I could check the accuracy of my analysis. I hadn't noticed Soraya packing her things, but she might have. She could have done it yesterday morning, while I was being Documentary Photographer of the Year, and hidden the bag outside somewhere. But I definitely wouldn't have noticed Julia packing because she was in the other bedroom. I should check.

Soraya's clothes were still here, but that needn't mean a thing. She travelled light and didn't own sentimental knick-knacks. And she'd grown used to me clearing up after her. She might easily just dump everything, never consider coming back for it, and never miss it.

Julia was a different matter.

And, oh God, when I looked, there was no trace of her ever having been here. She'd taken everything she owned.

And not only that, *Charlotte's* things had all gone too. Their room was just as we'd found it when we arrived. I hadn't seen her holding a travel bag, but then, *she'd* come in to see *me*, not the other way round. And I hadn't gone into the kitchen to wave her off. Why would I? She could easily have left carrying all her belongings.

I was seriously spooked now. My God, they'd *all* left!

It was my fault. I'd just become too needy and pathetic. Maybe I'd become unbearable.

But even so! How could they *do* that to me? I'd tried hard, *really* hard, not to sulk; not to wreck the good time everyone else but me was having! I'd been as good as I could!

I suddenly felt really sorry for myself and welled up. Maybe –

Somewhere in the living room, my phone was ringing. I panicked. Where – ? The sofa. I'd left it on the sofa.

I almost fell over in my rush to get to it. *Julia*.

"Hello?" I said. I sounded breathless, even to myself, but I didn't care.

"Hi," Julia said. "Are you okay?"

"I'm fine. I – what – What's going on? Where are your clothes? I mean – "

"I'm wearing them, and, as you've rightly surmised, I'm ringing to say goodbye. At least for a few weeks. I bought a second-hand car this morning, and Charlotte and I are going to Portland. We'll see you there in a few weeks, then we'll go and meet Mum and Dad in California."

"But – I don't know what you're talking about." Which was a lie, but not entirely. "Is Soraya with you?"

She laughed dismissively. "What? You think the three of us would just *leave you alone*? No, I think you'll find Soraya's sitting outside on the veranda, strumming that guitar of hers. We've finished the Snowflake Song, by the way. Get her to play it to you. I think you'll like it."

I was experiencing the biggest hot flush of my life. I began to say something, but didn't know what words to use. Julia waited till just before my speechlessness became an awkward pause.

"I finally had an 'Aha' moment," she said. "I genuinely thought you were joking when you sent me that text on the bus: *Leave my girlfriend alone,* or words to that effect. Then yesterday, the penny dropped. All that sitting in the house; all that listening to rap; all that Baudelairian strolling with your phone camera: it's because you suspect something's happening that *actually isn't.* Let me remind you, Hannah, friendship can be intense. It doesn't necessarily, nor even usually, shade into sexual attraction. Put it this way. Imagine *you* going on holiday somewhere with Mum and Dad when you were younger. You don't much like where you're staying: superficially it's boring. But then you meet this other kid your own age, and everything changes. You start having fun. I mean, *real* fun. Fun like you don't have that much of at home. And despite your first impressions, the *place* starts to be fun too. None of that means you and your new friend are going to have *sex* at any point, does it? For your information, I love my husband. Okay yes, I know Soraya's gay, and yes, she's upfront about being attracted to me – in a superficial way – but the fact is, *she* doesn't want us to have sex either. Or run off with me. Or anything else that might have occurred to you. It's only in TV soaps and trashy novels that it's not possible to consider someone attractive and still control your behaviour. In the real world, it's not even that difficult. The bottom line is, she loves you, and so do I, and you love us. In other words, we're all fully-grown adults. Now, I realise you've been trying hard not to show what you've been going through this past week, and I appreciate that; but you need to start enjoying yourself. Stop taking crappy photos of centipedes and pebbles, go and talk to your girlfriend, and have a day out at Walmart or something."

I sighed like I was groaning. "Okay, yes, I suppose… I admit, yes, that is what I was thinking." Thank God she couldn't see me. My face probably looked like a tomato. "Obviously, I want you both to be happy, and … I don't know. Saying I've been a 'fully grown adult' may be too generous. Perhaps I just didn't have enough evidence to start flinging accusations."

"But you didn't go looking for it, did you? The trashy novel thing to do would have been to spy on us."

"Maybe I'm just not very good at that sort of thing. Spying."

"Or maybe it's not in your nature. Come on, Hannah, be nice to yourself."

"Why are you going to… Where was it you said?"

"Portland, Oregon. Reputed to be the World Capital of Weird. Don't try chasing us down either. We won't be taking a direct route – Lottie's got a list of Native American sites we simply *must* visit without delay – and neither of us can take any more bullshit about being chased by the Federal Bureau of Investigation. You and Soraya are quite intense: you know that, don't you? And I think you've both fallen in love with small town America, which is fine, but it's not for me, and I'm pretty sure it's not for Lottie either. Frankly, I've got cabin fever. I desperately need to find somewhere with a robust literary scene and at least one major bookshop, preferably on two floors."

"So we'll …?"

"Call me in a month and we'll rendezvous somewhere in Portland. Also, obviously, get in touch if there's an emergency. Have a great time in the intervening. Good luck with the FBI. And give my regards to Soraya."

"Yeah, bye," came a voice from behind me, making me jump.

I hung up. Soraya walked round and sat on the sofa opposite me. She wore a green Florence + the Machine T-shirt, white shorts and flip-flops. She propped her guitar against the armrest, and pulled her feet onto the sofa so her knees were under her chin. She grinned.

"Feeling okay?" she said.

I nodded.

"You're a complete dork," she said. "I was starting to get seriously bummed, wondering why the hell you weren't coming out with us. Luckily, Julia knows you of old, what a deranged freak you are, so she was able to explain. Made me feel a hell of a lot better. For a while there, I thought I'd lost you to Jay-Z."

"You said you thought Julia was hot. And that plan of yours, in New York – "

"Don't make it *my* fault! You're the neurotic loser!"

"Sorry. No, you're right. I just thought… I don't know…"

"Come right out and say it. You just thought, 'Soraya's not getting enough sex.' That's what was going through your head, right? 'I'm hetero, she's gay. I've got a husband, maybe she needs a wife.'"

I shrugged. "I doubt Julia's gay wife material, but roughly that, yes. Maybe you do."

She picked up the guitar and strummed a minor chord. "I grew up on a council estate in Rotherham. I went to the local comprehensive. Just after I left, OFSTED put it in special measures. It survived with a name change and a new head teacher. Last year, we had a school reunion. *Ebenezer Elliot High, Class of 2006.* It didn't get advertised, because they didn't want the press getting in."

"I remember you telling me about that, yes."

"I didn't tell you everything. Nearly all the girls I knew back then are married, or living with partners, or they're single mums. They're not really that bothered about sex any more. A few of them spend their time trying to avoid it. Which sounds sad till you realise that, hey, it's actually *not:* we routinely see it like that only because the media's so hung up on celebrities, useless people who don't ever do much except sit home tweeting and looking at porn. The women of Ebenezer Elliot had kids they loved, jobs they worked hard at for virtually nothing, and major problems they couldn't always solve. Sex is good, or it can be. But there's about twenty or thirty things in life that aren't worth cashing in for it." She strummed another chord. "And that's what I learned from that evening."

"Whoa."

"I've got a kid too, that's my point. And we can have others, because Tim's ready and willing. We talked about it while you were at Paddington, picking up Charlotte. And that's my future. I don't want a wife. I've already got one. I've got you."

"*Oh, my God!* You talked to Tim about having another baby?"

"Same deal as before. Is there a problem?"

I almost leapt off the sofa. "It's – it's *the opposite!* It's *wonderful!* I thought you'd taken Lek to the park with Eva that day!"

"I'm capable of multi-tasking. And incidentally, don't imagine I never have sex. I do. Only I don't buy into all the BBC-Netflix bullshit about lesbianism. *In the highly unlikely event that you don't meet a sophisticated, witty, attractive, intelligent lesbian, hey, all women are potential lesbians. Just find yourself a suitable heterosexual and convert her. Simple!* The truth's nothing like that. Only a tenth of the population's gay. Those you're likely to meet, some of them are going to be fascists or morons, because there's no necessary connection between being gay and being smart or liberal or even kind. Last month, I had sex with Lissah La T – the self-styled 'Drum and bass queen of South Bermondsey'? It was nice, before you ask. But I couldn't love her. She's nothing like me: different tastes, different politics, different values, and her trousers smelt of fried onions. The way I see it, dissociating sex and love can be a good thing. It can help keep things in perspective."

I didn't hear any of this. I'd stopped listening at 'What's wrong with that?' It put Tim's decision to become a house husband in a new light. It had been good to begin with. It had become ten times better.

"And another thing," Soraya went on. "After this road trip, we're never leaving Lek at home again, okay? This is our coming of age. No more Skyping. That's crap parenting. I don't care about the band any more. I care about you and Tim and me and Lek, that's all. It's time both of us grew up."

Bad Bolt from the Blue

If Julia had been ghost writing this book – an idea she never mentioned again – she'd have ended the last section with something like, 'And that's the story of why we millennials don't put a premium on sex', or maybe even, 'That's why we've all gone off sex'. Her own view was rather different to Soraya's, and much kookier. I won't go into it here. She's got a lot of weird ideas, incidentally. If you ever meet her, get her to explain how the British actually won the American War of Independence. That's always good for a two-hour argument.

It wasn't till an hour later that I remembered what she'd told me. The Snowflake Song was finished. Soraya and I lay on the sofas, watching an old episode of *Chicago Med*. I waited till the credits appeared, then switched it off.

"What are we going to do now?" Soraya said.

"I just thought, while you've got that guitar to hand…"

"I was wondering when you'd ask."

"Right now."

She grinned and sat up. "Okay, all the lyrics are Julia's. No, that's not quite right. Okay, most of them. You and I wrote the tune, but I've been working hard on it. Ready?"

I nodded. I admit, I was a bit nervous.

It started softly. It was the story of our journey, with the frustrations tied to current events. It referenced about ten different songs, and the chorus changed key, switched unexpectedly from minor to major and back again, but kept enough of the refrain to be recognisable. There were fourteen verses. It was catchy like a good folk song, angry like rap, complex as Björk or Lucinda Williams.

When it finished, I had both hands over my mouth. "I can't believe it!" I laughed. "Julia's a bloody *genius!* We're going to blow everyone and everything *away!*"

Soraya laughed. "That's what I said!"

After we'd eaten lunch in the kitchen, I arranged with Maggie to extend our stay another week. That afternoon, we explored Holmes County State Park. The day after, we rowed a boat on Lake English, and planned the route from Durant to Portland on Google Maps – or tried to: we learned the hard way that a five-inch phone screen just doesn't work when you're planning a journey of two and a half thousand miles. On Thursday, we took a three-hour Greyhound bus to Memphis and stayed there overnight. We could probably have got Rudolph to drive us, but we anticipated leaving Mississippi soon, and he was old, so we wanted him to spend as much time with his family as possible. He might not have many more years to live. In any case, we knew we could contact him through Maggie whenever we wanted. We didn't take our route-planning endeavours very seriously, because firstly, it seemed too boring – the non-boring way would just be to point the bonnet northwest and drive – and secondly, it was too difficult (see above), but thirdly, Rudolph knew the country better than we ever could, and he'd be our best advisor. All we had to do was wait. At the time, it didn't strike us as odd that we hadn't heard from him in all the time we'd been there. We assumed he was giving us space to enjoy our sojourn.

Which was a mistake, in retrospect, though an understandable one. The day before we were due to leave, Soraya and I were eating lunch in Subway on Highway 12 when my phone rang. *Maggie.*

I'd expected this. Presumably, she wanted to know what time we'd be gone, so she could send word to Rudolph and make preparations to move back in.

"Hi," I said.

"I've got bad news," she told me. "I didn't tell you before because he asked me not to. He didn't want to ruin your time in Mississippi, and he says you don't know each other that well anyway. But now he's changed his mind. He wants to see you."

"Are you talking about Rudolph?" I asked. "What do you mean, he's – ?"

"He's dying," she said. She was upset now. "He probably hasn't got long. Maybe I should have let you know earlier, but like I just said, he told me not to. And as I also said, he's changed his mind. He wants to see you. Please. Come quickly."

PART SEVEN:

MISSISSIPPI TO IDAHO

We May Have Outstayed Mississippi…

Rudolph's niece, Rosalie, was sixty-seven and lived within walking distance, on Bain Street, on the outskirts of town. The house was all on one floor, painted brown with a low roof, and had a car on the lawn. She was waiting for us at the front door. She came outside long before we reached the garden path to introduce herself.

"Thank you for coming," she said. "He wants to talk to you alone. Which one of you is Hannah?"

"That would be me," I replied.

"He particularly wants to talk to you." She swivelled briefly to Soraya. "No disrespect to you, Miss – you're Soraya, right? – but" – turning back to me – "I understand you're the one paying his wages. Or was."

"I'm sorry we haven't been in touch," I said. Two other women appeared in the doorway and regarded us suspiciously. "He told us he wanted to spend time with his family," I added, "and we've been trying to respect that. There have been days when we could have used a driver – "

"No one's accusing you of *anything*, honey," Rosalie said. "The fact is, he's old. He's had – well, I don't know whether I'd call it a *happy* life, but a long one. And there are worse ways to go. He loves to drive, and he was doing just that till just a few days ago. He's almost in the hands of the Lord now, and since he's always been a good, upright Christian gentleman, I figure he's got lots to look forward to. We don't necessarily mourn death in this family. You feel sorry for yourself, obviously: sorry to lose them. But you console yourself with the thought that, in the grander scheme, it's actually a rejoicing occasion. I lost my father, Rudolph's brother, three years ago. Bitterly sad for me, seeing as I was left without my Pop. Wonderful for him, though, being back with Mom and Cissy and finally meeting Jesus face to face."

We were inside the house now. The two women who'd watched us approach came forward to greet us, shook our hands and said thank you for coming. Maggie was in the kitchen, with four other middle-aged women and two teenage girls. They sat silently, and turned to nod a solemn greeting at us.

Rosalie stood looking at us, her expression dark. I wasn't sure precisely what was coming, but I could see she was poised to add a new level of bad news.

"I'm going to tell you something before you go in to see him," she told me. "And I need you to be okay about it. If you're not, that's fine. You're entitled to be angry, and no one here'll hold it against you. Only don't go in and see him if you don't feel you can forgive him. It's partly what I'm about to tell you that caused him to get struck down, so to speak."

Soraya and I exchanged glances. Before we could say anything, Rosalie went on:

"Your car got stolen. I'm really sorry. We had it out front. We had it locked and everything, but it got taken yesterday night. The police know, and we thought we might get it back today, but they're making out there's less and less chance of that. The investigating sergeant told us this morning it might actually be in a different state by now, maybe resprayed or even in pieces."

"It's not our car," I said. "It's a hire car. It's insured and I can more than afford the excess. Of course we forgive him. It's not his fault. These things happen. No one can – "

"Rudolph took it real bad. The shock – "

"I'll tell him it's okay," I said. "It really is! It could happen to anyone!"

"*Thank* you," Rosalie said. "He said you were good people, but he wouldn't let us tell you yesterday. Kept thinking it'd be okay, it'd come back." She led us three paces across the hallway, opened a door and beckoned someone out. "The English girls are here," she said.

An old woman came out. She said thank you for coming and went through to the kitchen. Rosalie gestured for us to go in. "Let us know when you're finished," she said. "And thank you again."

She closed the door behind her, leaving us alone with him.

He lay on his back, propped up in a low bed in pyjamas. He stared glassily at the cornice on the opposite side of the room. He'd been thin when we met him, but he looked like he'd lost a lot of weight sometime in the last week. Each of the pale blue walls had a painting of a tropical scene in the middle, and there was a bedside table, empty except for a wind-up alarm clock. A pair of royal blue curtains had been drawn. Two chairs had been placed next to the bed, one on either side. I took his hand.

"We came as fast as we could," I said.

He turned to look at me and recognition dawned. He blinked slowly. "I lost your car," he said. "I mean, it got stolen. It's gone."

"Your niece told me," I said. "And you mustn't worry. It doesn't matter. It could have happened to any one of us, or another driver. Cars get stolen all the time. The hire firm budgets for that. We'll pay a little bit extra, they'll claim on the insurance, and in a week's time, no one'll remember it ever occurred. That's how it works nowadays."

"I was supposed to be taking care of it."

"Well, I was supposed to be taking care of my passport, driving licence and phone. It didn't stop me losing them in Shark River. I didn't blame myself. I just put it down to experience."

He laughed hoarsely and patted my hand. "Just say you actually forgive me, though. In those exact words. I mean, in case Jesus asks. The way I understand it, he likes things like that to be made explicit."

"I forgive you," I said.

We sat in silence. I thought I'd fulfilled my role, and was about to go and get Rosalie, when he turned looked at me again.

"I need to ask a favour," he croaked, "I know me saying that is one hell of a liberty – "

"Anything you want," I said quickly.

"I'm going to die, I know that now. Someone needs to tell Harlinne. Nobody out there's on speaking terms with her – "

"Consider it done," I said.

"Wait till I'm, you know, actually dead, though. I don't want to see her in person."

"Understood."

He chuckled sadly. "When I told you how ancient I was, back there in that hotel of yours in New York City, you said you wanted a Forrest Gump; a guy who could tell you all about the history of this country because he'd lived it. Rock and roll, soul, Rosa Parks, Malcolm X, Martin Luther King Junior, John Kennedy, Vietnam, Watergate, nine-eleven, President Obama, all that." He let out a long, weary sigh. "Truth is, I knew, even when I agreed, I couldn't be that guy. I just didn't say anything. You see, all me and Harlinne ever had was each other. My dove and her hawk. The real America was always something happening outside us. Me, I even arrived at that big old Washington March too late." He nodded gravely. "If it's any consolation, I regret not having lived more. But I probably didn't have a choice."

"We hired you to drive a car," I said. "You did a good job."

He closed his eyes and seemed to subside slightly. We sat with him for five minutes to see if he'd rally, but he didn't. I got Rosalie.

The women from the kitchen brought chairs in and sat down facing him. It turned out the old lady who'd been with him when I arrived was a doctor. I stood to let her take my seat and she checked Rudolph's pulse and felt his forehead. Someone brought me another chair. We sat for six hours saying nothing while the light slowly ebbed. At seven, snacks arrived: buttered bread rolls with ham and coleslaw. We ate in silence and resumed our vigil.

At 9.05, he stopped breathing. The doctor felt his wrist, looked at her watch, then applied two fingers to his carotid. She turned to Rosalie and announced that he'd passed away. No one cried, perhaps because he'd gone somewhere better, but even so, the room was full of grief.

Another Car

The funeral took place the next day. I tried calling Harlinne several times, but got no answer. From what Rudolph had told me, she wouldn't be welcome at the internment anyway, and it may have been one reason it occurred so fast.

We had another day in Maggie's house and just over five weeks before Mum and Dad arrived in California for what might or might not be a showdown meeting, depending on Charlotte. There was lots to do. First up, call Maxwell Clunes's New York office, tell them the hire car had been stolen and get them to arrange a replacement. Then learn how to drive all over again. Both Soraya and I had full driver's licences, but we hadn't used them for years. Nowadays, we got chauffeured, or we rode in chartered coaches, or, when we were in big cities, we disguised ourselves and used public transport. Considering this, I felt more disturbed than ever by my total ecological crappiness. Just one more way in which I was a complete fraud.

Soraya went into the kitchen with her phone and a notepad to do more work on our route. I sat on the sofa in the living room, scrolled down my list of Contacts and pressed Call. Sheena on Maxwell Clunes's switchboard took my request for a substitute car, and tried to put me through to Nora in London. I said I didn't need to talk to her. I tried to make it tactful ('I'm sure she's very busy'), but ten minutes later, Nora called back anyway. I'd begun to watch TV, but I switched it off.

"What are you doing in Durant Mississippi, of all places, Hannah?" she asked. "We've been worried. We haven't heard from you for an age."

"Don't exaggerate. I'm fine and so is Soraya."

"Sheena tells me you're heading to California via Portland, Oregon."

I didn't like her probing. "Is that a problem?" I said.

"According to what I've just learned, you don't have your two sisters with you any more. That makes you and Soraya a couple of lone women travelling through a country you barely know. Now I don't mean to sound sexist, but you're vulnerable. You've already had your car stolen. We've arranged a replacement obviously, but there's a whole world of other things that could go wrong. You could break down, or lose your way, or have a nasty accident, or get abducted by rednecks, or bitten by a snake. It happens. If you suddenly disappear, it'd help enormously to know your last location."

"Have the FBI been in touch?"

"Is that a serious question?"

"I've been told they're looking for Harlinne Vobrosky. And she also seems to think it's possible."

"Well, no one's contacted us. Which I'm sure they would have had there been any truth in that. Anyway, back to the main topic. As I say, we've got you a car. It's awaiting you at the Ford dealership on North Jackson Street. From what the manager tells me, anywhere in Durant's within walking distance of anywhere else in Durant, but we can tell her to bring it to you if you supply your address. You've still got your documentation – licences, passports – I assume? I mean, they weren't stolen too?"

"We always keep them close."

"Very wise. You don't have to like the car, incidentally. The manager says she'll get you another if it doesn't appeal. It's a convertible. I thought you'd like that."

"Is it electric? I mean, how eco-friendly is it?"

"Not at all. I can't have you in a green car. I don't know how well they're catered for in the mid-West, and I'd rather not worry about your battery running out in the middle of the Mojave Desert."

I sighed. "Okay. I'm not even sure if we're going that way. Or precisely where it is."

"After this, you can drive any green car you like for the rest of your life. Just not on my watch."

"What's the sound system like? I mean, has it got Bluetooth? Can we play our phones through it?"

She paused. "I don't know. I didn't ask."

"We'll check when we get there. And we'll walk. It's a nice day."

"Where are you going next, if you don't mind me asking? I mean, not another small town?"

"We haven't decided."

"Ironically, you'll probably be safer in a big city," she said. "You've got plenty to choose from. Nashville's nice. But there's also Jackson. And Memphis. New Orleans is less than four hours away: why not go there? I mean, I know it's in the opposite direction, but not much. And you've *got* to see it. In any case, please – I'm asking this as a friend: I'm not trying to control you – keep in touch."

"Will do," I said. "And thank you for your help."

We hung up. She was wrong, of course. New Orleans? No way. I'd seen it on TV. Everyone had. A presenter wandering up a high street marvelling at French balconies and Creole cottages: *there's absolutely nothing like this in England, nor is there any voodoo in England, nor do people have funerals with jazz bands, etc.*

They didn't make travel documentaries about Durant. Nor about the thousand other insignificant places I already sensed we were headed.

Yes, we'd get lost, what of it?

What kind of a wasted life was it where you never got lost?

Soraya's Shopping List

While I'd been speaking to Nora, Soraya was in the kitchen, route-planning. She sat at the table with a notepad and pen and a numbered list. I put the kettle on to boil and pulled up a chair opposite her.

"We've got a car," I told her.

"The thing is, neither of us has driven for about... Well, I haven't been behind a steering wheel for over ten years. What about you?"

"I sometimes drive Mum's car when I go to stay in Hexham. The last time was about a year ago."

She nodded. "Given that we're probably going to be rubbish drivers then, we don't want to be doing big chunks of driving. We need to stay safe, for Lek's sake. If we're going to do that, I reckon we shouldn't be doing any more than six hours a day. We've got thirty days to get to Portland. That means we can stay in each place five days max before we need to move on again."

"So where are we heading today?" I asked.

"We're leaving *today?*"

"No time like the present."

"We've got to get one of those steering wheel locks from Walmart."

"Other people must sell them. Why does it need to be Walmart?"

She laughed as if she couldn't believe I had to ask. "Because we need *all sorts of provisions, Hannah!* America's bloody massive! What if we get lost? What if we drive into a forest at night and go round and round in circles for hours? In that case, we'd need a gas stove and a box of matches and baked beans and a camping pan. And we'd definitely need a tent. And a knife, in case we're attacked. We need tinned food, lots of water, and a can opener. Where else do you know that's got all that under one roof?"

I looked at what she'd been writing in her notepad. I'd assumed it was a route plan. It was a shopping list. *1. Sleeping bags (two or one big one?) 2. Calor gas stove 3. Matches 4. Knives/ baseball bats 5. Cutlery 6. Tent 7. Camping pans 8. Tin opener 9. Torch 10. Spare batteries 11. Baby wipes 12. Soap 13. Teabags*

I stopped reading at *14. Powdered milk.*

"What about a jerry can for spare petrol?" I said.

She wrote it down.

Heading Out of Durant

Rudolph had put us both in mind of our dads. I hadn't thought much about what I'd say to mine in California, and I was fairly sure Charlotte didn't want to confront him any more. Yet part of me felt she had to: keep burying a problem and it'll repeatedly pop up again; the only way to deal with it is to hold it up by the hair, and get everyone to look hard at it, and make them declare for or against it and say why. Another part of me thought, no, let sleeping dogs lie. This bit of me held that sometimes, if you keep burying a problem, it kind of rots away, until one day it hasn't sufficient energy to pop out of the ground any more. Then it stays there until the decomposition's complete, and eventually, there's nothing left of it. Try digging it up and all you'll find is soil.

We'd invited Soraya's dad to California too, and now we were on our way to get the replacement hire-car, we were put doubly in mind of him. He'd actually taught her to drive in a second-hand car when she'd been eighteen. Two years later, she'd told him she was gay, and he'd sold it ('to stop me networking with other lesbians,' she later claimed). Six months later, she'd moved to London with the band, which is where I'd discovered her. Nowadays, father and daughter were back on speaking terms. He even spoke to me, but only in a remote way. He knew Lek was his granddaughter, and he understood how that had come about, but he couldn't seem to decide what attitude to adopt. He settled on being civil.

Both our dads would be dead soon, and we talked about that. I don't know how the good people of Durant felt about two women walking down the street holding hands, but no one seemed put out.

Thankfully, Pam, the dealership manager – a short woman with blonde curly hair, a double chin and a happy expression – was a Coal Tar fan, and *over the freaking moon* to make our acquaintance. She took four selfies with us and promised not to post them on social media till the day after tomorrow, when we'd be long gone. Then she gave us each a free one-hour refresher driving lesson, which was just as well, because we'd completely forgotten the steering wheel was on the 'wrong' side of the car. The sound system was outstanding. Afterwards, we went to Walmart in Kosciusko and loaded up with survivalist kit. We both felt emotional to be leaving Durant.

I mean, really, unexpectedly emotional.

Come 'N' Drive with Me

Mississippi: Durant, Lexington, Belzoni. Arkansas: Lake Village, Dermott, Monticello, Star City, Pinebergen.

Names that, in conjunction, sounded like a poem. White Hall, Prague, Sheridan, Prattsville, Poyen, Malvern, Lake Catherine State Park, Hot Springs. Eight hours, including detours and wrong turns. We kept off the motorways as much as we could, although we knew that would make the journey longer. Safety, primarily: we did it for Lek. This way, if we crashed, it'd be on a D road with nothing hurtling towards us. True, we might also be in the middle of nowhere, but we had a good tent, a can opener, ten days' worth of food and water, and a bottle of Wild Turkey.

Hot Springs was a medium size town with a motorway through the centre, and on the edge of a national park. It put me in mind of a 1950s film where the girls all have saddle shoes, ponytails and textbooks, and the boys have ironed trousers and zits. We stayed in a hotel the first night, because we needed a shower, and, after all that driving, a campsite – of which I'm sure there were many – would have been too much: all the setting up, queueing outside cubicles, towelling yourself down in miniscule space, the long walk to and from the tent, no thanks. Right now, we weren't up for roughing it.

The second night, yes, we were. We left the car in the hotel car park and set off for the Ouachita Mountains. I don't know what the rules are about spur-of-the-moment camping in America – they probably differ from state to state – and I didn't know whether there were cougars or bears to hand, but we'd had enough playing it safe. One thing we hadn't bought in Walmart was a compass, but we figured if we just found a track and followed it, we'd be okay for the return route. Since we didn't want to risk a forest fire, we took the camper stove. An hour later, we found a clearing behind the trees and beneath the shade of a small crag. It looked like other campers had been here before us: marks on the ground indicated the remains of a fire. We set the tent up – I say 'set': it just kind of popped into being – and 'made' beans and sausages, by which I mean, we opened the can, transferred the contents to a skillet and applied heat. Afterwards, Soraya played her guitar.

And in retrospect, that was where it all began to go wrong.

As I said somewhere earlier in this book, Soraya's voice is pretty unique. Three minutes later, it sucked in a young couple from the undergrowth. A man and a woman, both about college age, dressed in hiking gear. They looked more than pleased to see us. The man's first sentence was, 'Oh, my *God*, you're *Hannah and Soraya!*' The woman's, 'We *heard* you were in America, oh my God, this is *amazing!*' We shook hands, but that wasn't enough for them. They hugged us like we were old friends. They sat down, though we hadn't invited them to (it was, I guess, their country), and began to tell us about themselves, and inquire how we'd got here.

Even though Soraya had put the guitar to one side, six more trekkers arrived. They wore lumberjack jackets and denim trousers and hiking boots and carried professional-grade backpacks. Soon we were surrounded by thirty people, all the same age, laughing and joking and generally having a wonderful time. They didn't look like they were moving on anytime soon; rather, they gave every indication of wanting to spend the entire night talking. One of them had a Bluetooth speaker, so we had music. Luckily, he had good taste. I recognised Kathryn Williams's *Old Low Light*. One tall guy with a bobble hat and a blond beard down to his stomach kept taking pictures of us and saying, 'Oh my God, you're going to be on every billboard telegraph pole within a two hundred mile radius!' The first time he said this, it was vaguely funny. The second, creepy. The third, fourth and fifth times, well…

None of the others were that in-your-face but, being college age, they had more in common with each other than Soraya and I. For some reason (I can't recall what led up to it), an argument broke out about *Making a Murderer*. After five minutes, it had become much more general. They all agreed about the problem – the proverbial swamp needed draining – but were poles apart about how to address it. Half seemed to favour a top-down remedy, including, for a vocal few, a 'disruptor' who'd fly in the face of people's expectations. The others preferred a bottom-up fix: people power. Soraya and I didn't participate. When you're guests in someone else's country, you keep schtum in that sort of discussion.

It gradually heated up and became acrimonious, people raising their voices and gesticulating. One or two got to their feet and leaned forward into each other and pointed. Then – in the space of about five seconds – something surreal happened. A deep hush fell. One by one, they stopped arguing and turned their heads in the same direction.

For a moment, I thought the park ranger had arrived. It was as if a polar wind had just passed through.

In fact, it was the audio speaker.

Tracy Chapman: *Talkin' Bout a Revolution*.

Their enraged expressions gradually turned desolate. At the time, I had no idea why. It was only later that I saw. The bitter irony in the lyrics. *There never will be a revolution. The powers that be are just too strong. Things will stay the same forever, everywhere. At a certain level of insignificance, your hopes and dreams count for nothing whatsoever.*

Soraya and I surreptitiously packed our haversacks, grabbed the guitar, snuck into the bushes, and made our way back to the hotel. The next day at noon, we returned for the tent and the stove, mainly because we didn't want to litter. The clearing was exactly as we'd left it, only deserted, and with a carpet of cigarette butts. We gathered our belongings, took them back to the car and drove northwest.

Hot Springs, Crystal Springs, Mount Ida, Oden, Acorn and into Oklahoma. Heavener, Wister, Spiro, Sallisaw, Vian, Warner, Martin, Muskogee, Winchester, Mounds, Kellyville, Silver City, Jennings, Glencoe, Morrison, Sumner, Garber. It probably wasn't the most rational route, but we didn't care. The land gradually levelled and the towns became more like stopping points than places to spend a lifetime: a few intersecting suburban-style roads with widely separated houses and two or three stores. We saw places that sold catfish steak, flea markets, casinos, a 1940s station wagon, a museum made from a WWII submarine, dozens of churches and chapels, a herd of wild horses, four eighteen-wheeler lorries, Betty's Beauty

Store. We finally achieved Soraya's ambition and watched an American football game: Stillwater vs. Muskogee at Indian Bowl, whilst eating fajitas in tinfoil. In Kellyville, for some reason, we walked round a cemetery. We spent an entire day listening to Willie Nelson, Loretta Lynn and Dolly Parton. We ate a lot of burgers in a lot of similar diners. Everywhere we went looked new – like it hadn't been built any more than fifty years ago – and flat. Garber, our final stopping point on that leg, somehow summed it up: a small grid of roads, just down at heel enough to feel enigmatic. We ate at Simple Simon's Pizza and slept in the car.

By this time, I'd tried unsuccessfully to ring Harlinne eighteen times. It didn't even go to voicemail, not once. I began to suspect something bad had happened. If Rudolph hadn't burdened me with the entire responsibility for telling her he'd died, I might not have been so unsettled. As it was, though, if I never spoke to her again, she might never find out.

In the car, the night after we stayed in Garber, I dreamed about Julia. She'd gone back to New York. When I asked what she was doing there and if she had Charlotte with her, she said she'd been sitting Central Park all day, every day, looking for novelists. She didn't know where Charlotte was, but that didn't matter because so far she'd seen Jonathan Franzen, Dave Eggers, Joan Didion and Donna Tartt. We had an argument and I awoke with a start after she threw something down the phone at me. Anyway, I didn't read any kind of psychic insight into it. I was missing them, that's all.

The next town along was called (I kid you not) Kremlin, and it was there I consciously noticed something that had been bugging me for a while. Once you got out of your car, there wasn't much privacy. The houses were all widely separated with huge unbounded lawns in front, and when you walked down the street, often you were the only two people out. It was difficult to shake the feeling you were being watched.

In every town there was at least one house with an Old Glory out front. In most countries raising a big national flag in your own property might be seen as jingoism. Within a federal system like the USA, it felt like more of a reaching out: we're Americans first; Oklahomans or Kansans afterwards. A quaint stab at universalism.

I'd started to play a lot of tunes of my own in the car: Queen, T-Rex, Joy Division, The Clash, Bob Dylan, Bruce Springsteen, Billie Holiday, Joni Mitchell, Gil Scott-Heron, Tom Petty, K.D. Lang, Leonard Cohen. Soraya didn't seem to mind. I comprehended what I never had before, that she was a music connoisseur. She could easily have crushed it on *Never Mind the Buzzcocks*. The only two groups she knew nothing about were Pickettywitch and Rainbow Ffolly. When they came on, she sat up and listened.

Strange insight: I didn't even like a lot of what was in my collection. I'd heard it too often. I was actually focussed on meeting Dad, and the music got mixed up in my mind with that. I made a decision: it didn't matter what Charlotte thought, he had to be confronted. I didn't want to go to my grave wondering exactly what the hell he'd been thinking all those years ago.

The one thing I definitely *wasn't* sick of was The Snowflake Song. I don't know whether you've ever been in a position where you've felt irrationally protective of something? You keep imagining it *could* get stolen even though it's not the sort of thing that really *can*? That's how I felt.

All of this together – the morbid disappearance of Harlinne, the anonymous terrain in which a seemingly everlasting succession of small towns came and went, and when they were behind you, you couldn't recall which was which, or even how many there'd been, the perpetual thinking about Dad – put me in a strange mood. Melancholy, I'd probably call it, with unexpected panic-attacks, but also backlit with opaqueness, like there was a big secret out there in the wilderness and we were passing through the country too quickly to learn it.

After Kremlin, we went to Cherokee, then Tegarden, then Lookout. I drove. Soraya sat in the passenger seat with her bare feet on the dashboard, playing Minecraft or Fortnite offline. We crossed the state line into Kansas, then it was Sitka, Minneola, Ensign and Pierceville. Four hours. We were aiming for somewhere big enough to stop in and not feel you were being watched, but Pierceville was the opposite: too small to contain enough people to do the watching. There was an abandoned elementary school and a railway line running through a huge gravel expanse with a couple of windowless warehouses and several metal towers like upright torpedoes, probably meant for something agricultural. There was supposed to be a Walmart here, but we couldn't find it.

Small town America seemed to be fading out of existence, with nothing but empty horizons replacing it. Even on the maps, there didn't look to be anything but small/ miniscule/ microscopic settlements around for miles. Luckily, we had provisions to keep us going in an emergency, but we badly needed a shower. Denver, where the nearest five-star hotel was – God, how I longed for one now: I felt truly sorry for dissing them – was a good six-hour drive away. Closer to eight, the number of inadvertent detours we were taking.

But the map was deceptive. Thanks to the advice of a helpful Piercevillian, we ended up staying at a Boarders Inn in Syracuse, just over an hour away. We'd ditched our qualms about motorway driving now: we reasoned we'd never get anywhere otherwise. We took a room with an *en suite* and three armchairs. We showered then ate chicken sandwiches with coca cola while watching TV. It felt good to eat anything that wasn't fried. Afterwards, Soraya went out to stock up at the Food Center while I lay on the bed and looked at my hundred or so latest photos, hoping to put the best ones on Instagram. I was sunburned, but that was easily fixed for posterity. No one looks like themselves on Instagram.

While I was cropping and filtering, my phone rang. *Nora.*

"Where are you?" she asked, when we'd exchanged the usual pleasantries.

"Syracuse, Kansas."

"I'm calling to ask you whether you're behind the *Wanted Dead or Alive* thing. I assumed since I hadn't heard from you, and the photos look like genuine originals, it must be something you're okay with. Which is fine, but *we're* supposed to be handling your PR." She cleared her throat nervously. "We could help you make a better job of it, that's all I'm saying."

"I've no idea what you're talking about," I said. "What 'Wanted Dead or Alive thing'?"

"Okay. So you know nothing about it, right? In that case, I'm going to give you a call back in about ten minutes. In the meantime, I'd like you to do a quick search on social media, see what you can find. My guess is, that'll be much more effective than me telling you."

She hung up before I could protest.

Okay, so Twitter was the obvious place to start: *#Wanteddeadoralive*. I opened the app and was about to type it in. But I stopped at my own feed. I'd been tagged three and a half thousand times.

Oh my God.

That long-bearded kid at Hot Springs. ... *on every billboard and telegraph pole within a two hundred mile radius!* He'd used the photos to make posters.

Shit, shit, oh shit.

At that precise moment, Soraya came in. She held a shopping bag in one hand, and what looked like – and was – one of the posters in the other. She tore off her sunglasses, tossed them on the sofa, dropped the bag and leaned on the closed door, as if confirm we were safe for the moment. She looked as close to traumatised as I'd ever seen her. She held up the poster.

"Have you seen this?" she said.

I had. All over the internet; all over the Midwest, by all accounts. It was just bigger than A4 size, printed on sepia paper. The banner at the top read, 'Wanted Dead or Alive', then a black-and-white photo of Soraya and I (not a bad one, if I'm honest), then, 'Reward $100', and finally, at the bottom, in smaller font: *These two gals are extremely dangerous. If you spot them, call the sheriff's department on 123456. Do not approach them.*

The sort of thing a student would mock-up if he thought he was being funny.

The trouble was, not everyone in the world knew who we were. Quite a lot of people had never even heard of Fully Magic Coal Tar Lounge. One or two couldn't even pronounce it. Some of those people most likely had guns.

"I've got it in hand," I said. I pointed to my phone. "Nora's just told me."

"A hundred dollars?" Soraya said. *"A measly hundred bloody dollars?"*

True Outlaw Gals

"Find anything interesting?" Nora said coolly when I called back.

"This is serious," I said. "Soraya and I are on our own out here. It's not like we've any protection at all. Someone might kill us on the perfectly understandable assumption that it's all real."

"That thought had occurred to me. Have you any idea who might be behind it?"

"More than that: I'm fairly sure I *know*. The day before yesterday, we were in Hot Springs – "

"In?"

"Kansas. Somewhere in Kansas. No *Arkansas*, that's right. Arkansas."

"I'll check both."

"Soraya and I went camping in the woods, or tried to. Over the course of about an hour, we were joined by roughly thirty students. At least, I think that's what they were. Anyway, one of them had a really long beard and he was tall and he wore a bobble hat and he kept saying, 'Oh my God, you're going to be on every billboard and telegraph pole within a two hundred mile radius!' I mean, he must have said that about ten times."

"And did he – sorry, I'm just trying to put myself in the shoes of the police, here – did he do this... *furtively*, would you say?"

"As I recall, he was perfectly upfront about it." I sighed. "When I think back, yes, it's odd, but I don't suppose he meant any harm. You know how kids are. We've all been young at some point. Nora, I really don't want to get the police involved... unless he turns out to be some neo-Nazi freak with a grudge against us. But then, all the others were *nice kids*. What would he be doing with them if he wasn't a nice kid himself?"

"Point taken: we shouldn't rush in where angels fear to tread. If he was that outspoken at the campsite, he's probably not keeping a low profile now. In fact, he may even be bragging. Look, I'll do a bit more digging around, assign our tech experts to it *right now*, see what I can uncover. I'll get back to you in a couple of hours. In the meantime, I want you to gather your things, put some sunglasses on, and make for Denver. You should be safe there. I've said it before: these small towns aren't always predictable. I'll book you a hotel, send you the address, get someone to meet you, and we'll make sure you're okay from there on."

"That sounds super, but Nora, don't go to the police, please. Not until you've run it past me."

"I wouldn't think of it. Have a pleasant journey. Speak again soon."

She hung up. I tossed the phone on the bed and prepared myself for Soraya's barrage of questions.

But it never came. She didn't even look at me. She sat repeatedly swiping her phone.

"This is *so cool!*" she said. "I regret what I said now. A hundred dollars was probably a hell of a lot of money in Cowboy and Indian days. That long-bearded kid's a genius. We need to hire him."

I drew my chin back about two miles and spluttered a laugh. "Are you *joking?* Nora's trying to find out who he is! She'll tell us what she's come up with in two hours. I've told her not to go to the police without my say-so. In the meantime, she wants us to pack our things and make for Denver."

She stopped swiping and regarded me with an expression I'd grown used to over the years. *You're insane.*

"Nora's a complete douchebag," she said when she'd recovered. "And we're definitely *not* going to Denver. Not yet, anyway."

"So next time someone knocks on the door, are you going to answer it? If so, best of luck, because it could easily be some trigger-happy halfwit with a Smith and Wesson."

"In that case, I'll just put my hands up. He'll call the sheriff on 123456, then he'll discover there's no such number, then he'll call the real sheriff, then he'll discover it's all a practical joke. End of."

"At which point, he'll be so pissed off, he'll shoot us."

"Okay, put it another way. The long-bearded guy is called Aaron Gates. He does engineering at the University of Arkansas, where he's vice-president of the Fully Magic Coal Tar appreciation society. He's got two younger brothers, and a girlfriend called Kathleen. His hobbies are listening to music, photography, and building model planes. He was born in Earlham, Iowa."

My chin returned to its point of origin. I tried to look like I wasn't fazed. "How did you find all that out?"

"I've got a phone."

"Maybe use it to ring Nora then. Save her a bit of time."

"I will." She swiped down and put the phone to her ear. "Hello, Nora. It's me, Soraya. Hannah's being a bit of a jerk and so are you. This guy actually organises his college Coal Tar fan club, and he's definitely not out to spike us."

She held the phone away from her ear while Nora spoke. She hadn't put it on speaker, so I couldn't hear her.

"We'll go to Denver if you want us to," she said when she'd finished. "But we need to capitalise on this, not run away from it like delicate little dormice. And we need to act quickly, before it all blows over and everyone loses interest."

"What have you got in mind?" I asked, when she'd hung up.

"Remember when we were in Verona and I said we should be guerrilla musicians? That."

I grinned. It hadn't taken long. Our wavelengths had experienced a bit of mutual interference, but now they were in accord. "Go on," I said.

"It's yonks before we're due in Portland, so we can afford to take at least ten days out. Tonight we write twenty great songs, then we tour the local ghost towns with a drummer – ideally, a woman: that'll put Elliot's back up, the idea that we might be about to go rogue – and a film crew. We perform in twenty different locations, then upload the videos in different places: YouTube, Instagram, Facebook, Vimeo, the lot. Keep everyone guessing: firstly, about where we are; secondly, where our next video's going to appear; thirdly, about where we'll actually appear next. A kind of *Catch Us If You Can*."

"The Dave Clark Five? I didn't think you knew about them."

She rolled her eyes. "Just because I wasn't born then? I wasn't born during Shakespeare's time either. The question is, are you up for it?"

"Me on the guitar? I wouldn't have to sing would I?"

"Not likely. And we tie the whole thing in with 'Wanted Dead or Alive'. A kind of thank you to Aaron Gates for bigging us up."

"Writing twenty songs in one night's quite a challenge."

"They don't have to be any good."

*

Actually, though, they were. We occupied that special zone – looming deadline, inspired ideas, high ambitions, whiff of danger, pinch of transgression, euphoric optimism, ten bottles of beer – where creativity blossoms.

We aimed for a collection in the vocal vicinity of Bob Dylan's *Girl from the North Country* or Tina Turner's *Nutbush City Limits* or Loleatta Holloway's *Love Sensation*: a compendium perfect for Soraya's voice. Since we only had an acoustic guitar, we were in unknown, maybe even uncharted, territory. In retrospect, that might have helped.

By 3am, we had fifteen songs, most of them directly or indirectly about our journey through America. We discussed the possibility that it might be the booze and our lack of sleep that made them sound so great. Okay, we may have concluded it wasn't a little too quickly, but, hey, talk about inbuilt critical reflection.

Nevertheless, something here was bugging me. At 3.30, I realised what. By that time, we'd written song number sixteen, *Washing My Hair*, in which a vigorous shampooing serves as a metaphor for moral and spiritual renewal.

"We agreed in Verona that we didn't want the band to split up," I said. "Aren't the guys likely to look at this and see it as a non-too-subtle springboard to you launching a solo career?"

She gave me the Insane look again. "What are you saying? That we ought to ask their *permission*? What kind of a feminist are you?"

"There's a difference between seeking their permission as *men* because they represent the patriarchy and asking for it because they're our *friends* and we don't want to alienate them. If we go ahead with this without giving them any warning, it's kind of aggressive. How would *you* feel if it was them, and you suddenly saw them doing something like this, and they hadn't at least run it past you first?"

She took a deep breath. "Fair point, you're right. Maybe we should ring them then. Or you should. You're more diplomatic than me."

"It'll be about 9.30 in the morning in the UK. I'll ring them in a minute. But there's another problem. If we put out a series of videos of you singing and me playing the guitar, it could look desperate. People might think: she's the manager; what's she doing out front?"

"You came on stage that time in Jersey. You even sang."

"That was totally different. Look, imagine the England football team's going to play the Italians, and everyone knows there's been a little bit of trouble in the England dressing room, and when England finally runs on to the field, there's Whatshisname, the manager: he's in *goal*. Don't you think fans on both sides might go, bloody hell, England must be in deep shit?"

"Okay, so what are you saying?"

"In order not to look like a couple of sad sacks, we need to put you out front and keep me out of the way."

"But that wouldn't work, because it's the two of us on those posters, and they're what we're supposed to be building on."

"Okay then, *keep* me, but make it look like we don't *need* me. Get another guitarist, and put her in the forefront. Make it look like she's doing all the work. We could even get the other members of the band out here, if they're up for it. I mean Gaz, Elliot, Paul, Olly."

"*That* wouldn't be building on the posters, either. On the other hand, you might not be able to stop them. They might insist."

"I doubt it. Elliot's our songwriter. If the band's playing songs that you and I have written, that might signify a demotion. He wouldn't want to make a precedent out of that."

"Heads we win, tails they lose. Ring them now."

The Twenty Songs in Ten Days Tour

Elliot was fine to sit out our tour, but I could see he was pissed we'd written our own songs. When I told him about The Snowflake Song, scepticism turned to cynicism: he couldn't see how anything of that kind could possibly work; it sounded suspiciously like a professional suicide note. At most, he'd allow us to play it to him so he could make suggestions for improvements. Implication: if that's the best you've got, the band's already finished. I declined whilst suppressing the temptation to tell him where to go.

"The patronising jerk," Soraya said when I told her. "He'll be sorry. He's not half as talented as he thinks he is."

I waited two hours before I rang the others. I calculated Elliot would be on the phone to them pronto, one by one, encouraging them to present a united front and stay on message: *his* message. Sure enough, when I called each in turn at 6.30 am Kansas time, no, they didn't want to join Soraya and I, but they wished us the best of luck. Elliot had probably told them we were begging for their participation, and therefore about to crack. Because in general – and I'm not saying it's always the case – that's how men view long-term differences of opinion: in terms of interrogation rooms and sweating it out.

We'd already decided where we'd go on tour. We'd begin in Coolidge, Kansas, and end in twenty days' time at Holbrook Summit, Idaho. At each location, it'd literally be straight in, straight out, with just enough time to play the song. We'd rehearse by the car, or cars, somewhere in a wood or a field for about twenty minutes beforehand, but we didn't expect to have to do much of that, because Soraya's voice was the central deal and it had the effect of carrying all before it like a tsunami.

I still had to get us a local drummer, but I'd had an idea for the guitarist too. I called Nora and asked her to contact Aaron Gates. Surely, I added, there must be lots of kids at Arkansas University who could play guitar and drums? We wanted a different pair for each video, and please could she also sort out the musicians' union stuff? And could she also organise someone to manage our Twitter accounts, keep the world updated? And get us a good photographer, make the tweets look nice?

Afterwards, Soraya and I slept for eight hours. We awoke because my phone rang. Nora had organised a film crew, a photographer, two British tweeters, twenty drummers, twenty guitarists and a harmonica player. Like something from *The Twelve Days of Christmas*. The harmonica player made my day: I'd forgotten to ask for that. Aaron himself could play the guitar and he was going to join us at our second tour location in Hartman, Colorado. Everyone involved would make their own way there.

We reviewed the twenty songs we'd written. Since we'd had a good morning's sleep, we might be more objective. We'd recorded them on my phone.

"The music's okay," Soraya said after we finished listening. "The lyrics aren't bad, but they're not outstanding either. I wonder if we could get Julia in on an emergency basis, help us mend them."

"I'd rather not. I'd actually like a conversation with Julia, see how she's getting on, but I'm worried she might be in the area. Then we meet up, then we decide to get back together as a four again, and she and Charlotte accompany us on tour, then we start arguing. It's going to be stressful enough as it is, twenty gigs in ten days. So many things can go wrong. Besides, a day isn't enough for her to come up with lyrics to twenty songs. It's a miracle she even wrote the words for The Snowflake Song. Some poets take an entire year to accomplish anything worth reading."

The next day, the first quota of musicians came to our hotel in Syracuse. We rehearsed briefly before checking out. We wouldn't be back: this was officially it: we were now on tour. For the next ten days, we'd be grabbing a bit of sleep where we could, probably in the car most times. We made Coolidge, played like a dream at the T-junction between Main Street and Manchester Avenue, and left.

Fifteen minutes later we were in Hartman. Aaron Gates was waiting for us in front of the Post Office, and introduced us to a completely new set of guys. Another short rehearsal, another performance, this time on County Road 29S, with a flat horizon, a grain elevator, a dirt track, a level horizon, and louring clouds. Afterwards, we drove to Bristol, where there was virtually nothing except scrubland and farm buildings. Another 'unincorporated town', as they're called. We weren't due to play till tomorrow, so Soraya and I drove south to the Arkansas River, where we washed, read books, composed more songs (all of which we'd completely forgotten the next day), drank brandy, and slept in the open air. The musicians arrived at 8am the next morning. We played another audience-less gig in a gravel parking lot, this one in front of a row of white tankers. Afterwards, we walked up and down South Main Street. There was a big abandoned house with a veranda and peeling paint. We talked about one day buying it and settling down there, as if the universe where something like that could happen was actually the one we were in now.

Karval, our next stop, was two and a half hours away, and so similar to Coolidge (or the bit where we'd been) that, had it not been for the signs, we might think we'd driven round in a circle. As usual, it was minimalist in terms of the number of dwellings, and bounded by everlasting fields. The sky was blue and streaked with long clouds that seemed to emanate from a single point on the western horizon, as if they'd all decided to travel together, but somehow got separated and started losing touch in their effort to get away from whatever had set them flying.

The musicians were waiting for us, nervous but eager to get started. We taught them the tune. They got it right away.

That was it for that day, but we travelled on to Yoder, just under an hour away, drove onto the South Calhan Highway, parked, and set up our pop-up tent next to Big Springs Creek. Soraya read aloud from *The Onion* website ('Woman's Solo Hiking Trip Shockingly Doesn't Have To Do With Inner Journey Or Anything') and we laughed. We washed our clothes and ourselves in the stream, opened a big can of beans and sausages, toasted five slices of bread on the flame of the gas stove, and had lunch. We aimed to eat dinner at Big Joe's on Yoder Road, but when we got there, it only sold animal feed. We went back to the tent and ate two cans of Dinty Moore Beef Stew. We slept in the car that night, in close proximity, with the heater on intermittently. The next day the musicians arrived early. By now, we really looked forward to their company. Same pattern: we rehearsed, we played, we departed.

Peyton, our next stop, wasn't much bigger than the other places we'd been, but it did have a general store and a cemetery, and we got our first real view of the Colorado Rocky Mountains. We stocked up on food, beer, lemonade, toothpaste, water, bleach, soap. And make up: when you're filming every day, you need tons of it. Hal, behind the counter, was a fan. He took a selfie with us and closed the parking lot for ten minutes so we could perform.

All this and our periods. As always, Soraya and I were in sync. That evening, we pitched camp outside town. We set a pan to boil over a gas stove, sterilised our menstrual cups, and washed ourselves using bottled water and a tiny amount of bleach. The next morning, we walked five hundred yards and dug a hole for the vaginal waste. What followed: five days of boiling and re-boiling, intensive washing, surreptitious digging, which didn't end till we reached Jefferson. We drank loads. We scoffed acetaminophen. We rubbed each other's backs and got depressed. When things became too much, we 'cheated' and checked into a motel.

After Peyton, it was an hour northwest to Larkspur, the first vaguely urban stop on our tour. It had a pizzeria, a Mexican restaurant, a fire department, a general store, a dedicated liquor shop, an elementary school, and a mock medieval castle which I think they used for an annual festival of some kind. It looked a fun place to stay. We didn't find out whether there were any hotels. We'd grown used to our tent now. We set it up just out of town by Carpenter Creek and ate canned ravioli that we'd bought in Peyton. The next day, we performed *Washing My Hair* in front of Larkspur Butte.

We were heading into the mountains now. Time for astrakhan coats, leggings and long skirts, Doc Martens. We rendezvoused with our next contingent of musicians in front of Long Scraggy Peak, played, packed up, then drove twenty-two miles to Buffalo Creek.

I'd told myself I wouldn't look at the internet while we were touring and I'd persuaded Soraya to make the same commitment. We kept our phones turned off a lot of the time. We'd made a decision. The journey was going to be gruelling. The whole enterprise could easily bomb. We might end up being relentlessly mocked on *Saturday Night Live*; in Britain, the tabloids might have a jamboree: *World's Most Woke Middle-Class Leftie and Her Snowflake Sidekick Get Humongous Internet Thumbs-Down!* But cutting it short halfway through wasn't an option. If we were to stick it out, getting demoralised mid-point wouldn't help. We'd pick up the pieces, if need be, afterwards. Whatever happened, we always had each other.

Yet I couldn't help trying to glean tidbits of information. I got the impression it wasn't going well on more than a few occasions. The successive sets of musicians we met seemed to get less enthusiastic as the 'tour' – notice I'm putting it in inverted commas now – unfolded. Or it may have been my imagination. Grant, Jefferson, Avon. The semi-recognition with which complete strangers regarded us in the places we filmed seemed to become more derisory. Or maybe not. Gypsum, Meeker, Dinosaur. I started to recall my misgivings during the marathon song-writing session in the hotel in Syracuse. And honestly, how *could any* two people, no matter *how* talented (and, as far as I knew, we weren't at all, not at song-writing), really write twenty zingers in the space of a single night?

We crossed into Utah on the eighth day of our wandering – notice, that's what I'm calling it now: 'wandering' – and we were exhausted.

But we weren't demoralised. On the contrary, we were having the time of our lives. We didn't give a toss about *Saturday Night Live* or the British tabloids or any million-strong army of trolls. 'Intense', that's what Julia had called us. Yep. The ones who are mad to live, mad to talk, desirous of everything at the same time. We were in love with each other, that's the truth, as sometimes really old couples are: been together since the World's creation, always would be.

Everywhere we went, we kept seeing those Wanted posters on telegraph poles. But also on walls, fences, tree trunks, in rural bedroom windows. Enough to freak us out: a heady mixture of trepidation and pride.

We played at Naples, Utah. For the first time since Syracuse, we stayed in a hotel. Not in Naples itself, but in nearby Vernal, where a grinning brontosaurus stood holding the official town sign: *Vernal: Utah's Dinosaur Country*. We checked in at 3pm, showered, slept, ate, slept, showered, ate, slept, checked out, explored Vernal, got lost in Vernal, asked for directions in Vernal, worked out where we'd left the car in Vernal, left Vernal.

I'd given up ringing Harlinne now. In fact, I rarely thought about her. Depressingly, when I did, I knew I'd have to keep trying. Another two days, and the tour would be over. When that occurred, I'd call her again, though I wasn't optimistic. I guess there would come a time at which I'd *have* to throw in the towel. Not yet, though; after I'd left the USA.

Meanwhile, I was fed up of wearing sunglasses just about everywhere, and so was Soraya. Our next stop, Evanston, was in Wyoming, and an evening gig. We performed on a southern grassy slope that bordered the Lincoln Highway. We thought cars whizzing by would give it added realism. The journey was becoming much more urban now. Evanston had both a hotel (we didn't hesitate to check in, before you ask), and a Walmart. Since

Soraya had been suffering Walmart withdrawal symptoms for some time now, we spent two hours there. We ate at Don Pedro's Family Mexican.

We crossed Wyoming travelling southeast to northwest and re-entered Utah to play our penultimate gig at Plymouth. We were back in miniscule town territory now: a settlement with a post office, a farm equipment store and about ten or twelve intersecting roads. It reminded me a lot of Kansas, but with mountains in the background. The streets had names like *W20100 N Street* and *N 5000 W Street*. We played *Hell Hath No Fury Like Etta Place* out of town at Bishop Canyon, with Gunsight Peak in the background.

Our final stop was an hour away at Holbrook, Idaho. A long road, a few houses set back at a distance from it like they'd prefer to keep their own company, miles of flat fields, and mountain ranges sufficiently far in the distance on all sides to look deliberately aloof. Atmospheric in a very subtle way. The sort of place that gives you a feeling you can't describe for reasons you can't identify. We played our final number, *Mighty Sofa Dozing*, a slow, melancholy waltz, and then the drummer and the guitarist packed their instruments, said thanks for the opportunity, and drove off. The film crew did likewise.

And that was it: end of tour. No partying, no fireworks, no messages of congratulation from absent friends, no celebrities backstage, no nothing. We drove to Rupert in Minidoka County, where we checked into a hotel. Portland was a mere eight and a half hours away now, and we still had lots of time to kill before our appointment with Julia and Charlotte. We could do anything we wanted. Part of me was horrified, counting down to the confrontation with Dad.

After we'd checked in at the Excelsior in Rupert, we bathed, practised our yoga *asanas* for an hour, ate, and watched TV in our pyjamas. Soraya snacked on corn chips and looked half at the television, half at her phone. At 8pm, I tried to call Harlinne again. No reply.

"Oh my God," Soraya said. She laughed and sat up. "*Oh my GOD!*"

"What is it?" I asked, trying to see.

"It's – it's *Top of My Stupid Tower* – sorry, that's just *Top of My Tower* now! It's number one! On both sides of the Atlantic!"

I looked at her screen. "Bloody *hell*."

My head span for a few seconds. Then there was a knock at the door.

"I'll get it," I said manically. I fell off the bed and hurt my elbow.

I expected maybe the manageress. She'd found out who we were and sent up a magnum of champagne? It happens. We'd probably invite her over with a few of her staff, help us celebrate. Then we needed to go out somewhere -

I opened the door to find two middle aged men in suits. They didn't look happy; quite the contrary: they glowered at me like they knew me.

"Excuse the intrusion, ma'am," the first one said. "We're with the FBI. We need to ask you some questions."

PART EIGHT:

IDAHO TO CALIFORNIA

Really Outlaws?

EVERYTHING WE'D DONE ON THAT TOUR OF OURS HAD gone viral. Not that it matters much when you're in the hands of the FBI. I know I've harped on a bit about it, but *Making a Murderer* came to mind: the fact that once the establishment puts you somewhere, you tend to stay there, and sometimes neither justice nor truth has the slightest power to change that. Agents Tom Preston and Mike Neal weren't here to arrest us. They'd been 'looking to ask us a few questions' for a while now. They'd been in touch with our UK contact, as they called Nora, and asked her not to warn us: they didn't want to ruin the tour, which they were very pleased to learn had gone well.

Tom was about forty-five, square-jawed, with receding black hair and a knobbly chin. Mike looked to be slightly older. His eyes were brown and close set; he wore wire-framed spectacles and had a close cropped tawny beard. They took us to the police station on Fremont Avenue. A small middle-aged woman with glasses processed us at the main desk. Tom politely ushered Soraya along a corridor on the left; Mike equally courteously invited me to follow him straight ahead. He transferred me to a small windowless room with a coffee table and magazines (*Magic Values Shopper & Auto Trader* and *AG Weekly*), where he left me alone. A woman in a short-sleeved uniform brought me some tea. Mike came back with a smile. He took me up a flight of stairs and into a detergent-smelling room with a table, a cassette recorder and a TV-video. We sat opposite each other. He apologised again for the inconvenience.

As I think I've already said in this book, I never formulate a strategy for these situations. I've been taken into police custody countless times for all sorts of reasons. I try to relax and tell the truth. If you're at peace with your conscience, then you've no cause to lie, and when the investigators try to goad you into inconsistency, they can't. This occasion was slightly different, because I didn't yet have much of a notion what I was going to be asked. In law enforcement terms, Steve's log cabin was a long time back. If our being there and then running away had been the FBI's main concern it'd have caught up with us well before now. Still, my policy hadn't changed.

Tom said he'd like to record my statement for the file ('it makes things easier afterwards: we don't have to keep coming back to you to check details'), and asked me if that was okay. I said yes, of course. He pressed play and record, and stated our names and the time and date.

"Mrs Lexingwood – "

"Hannah, please."

He nodded a perfunctory thanks. "Can I begin by asking you why you think you're here?"

"You're looking for Harlinne Vobrosky. As I recall from New Jersey, she's wanted for forging passports, and you think I might know where she is."

"Do you?"

"No."

"You haven't been in contact with her recently?"

"I've tried, but she's not answering her phone."

"What about your two sisters? Have you spoken to them?"

Whoa. I felt like I was in a car and it had just taken a corner too fast and too soon. "Er, no. Not since we separated in Durant, Mississippi. I haven't even tried ringing them. We agreed to split up and meet again in Portland, Oregon, in a few weeks. Why?"

"What's in Portland?"

"Hang on. Can we go back a bit? What have my sisters got to do with anything?"

"I can tell you that in a moment. Let's take this one step at a time, and not get too much off track. Why Portland?"

"It was Julia's idea. Because it's 'reputed to be the World Capital of Weird.' That's what she said. She's not making that up. Have you ever seen a TV series called *Portlandia?* Or, um, *One Hundred Dollars and a T-Shirt?*"

"Okay, so you're all heading for Portland? When do you expect to arrive there?"

"Two weeks' time."

"Any idea where your sisters might be now?"

"Okay, sorry, I need you to tell me what's going on. I'm not under arrest, I've been very cooperative, and I'm happy to truthfully answer any questions you care to ask, but these are my sisters and you're getting me seriously worried. Put yourself in my shoes."

He smiled. "Okay, I'll write my last question down and we'll come back to it later."

He took out a notepad from his inside jacket pocket, wrote down 'Why did you split up' (not the question he'd just asked!), put it away, then interlaced his fingers on the desk. He looked at his watch, recited the time and date again and turned off the cassette recorder.

"Rudolph Williams, who I believe was your driver for a while, died recently – "

"I know," I said. "We were there."

"You *know?*"

"I was present at his deathbed. So was Soraya. He asked me to tell Harlinne. That's why I've been calling her."

"Why were you there at his deathbed?"

"I'll tell you in a minute. Can we just get back to my sisters? I mean, you just switched off the tape. We might as well make good use of the interval."

It wasn't clear now which of us was actually in charge. He wanted information from me, and for the moment, I was being cooperative. That gave me power. But he also had power. His problem was that using it might make me much less helpful. His confliction appeared in the form of an almost imperceptible facial twitch, then he backed down.

"Rewind," he said, "Rudolph Williams died recently. Now I don't know the whys and the wherefores – theory is, it was some kind of tax avoidance scheme – but at some point just over twenty years ago, he and Harlinne Vobrosky buried the hatchet sufficiently to sink their joint earnings into a trust fund for the benefit of one Cecelia Vobrosky, their great-great niece, who at that time was a mere two years old. Notice, Hannah, I said 'tax avoidance' not 'tax evasion': there's no suggestion of anything illegal here. The FBI's got a lot on Harlinne Vobrosky, but her whole dossier's become heavily politicised over the last couple of years, and we don't anticipate even being able to bring a charge against her till at least 2024. That's not the issue here. The issue's that the trust fund grew exponentially. When one or the other of the couple died, everything was supposed to go to Cecelia. Now, for some reason, there's a lot of people in Washington eager to see that happen: Harlinne's been trying their patience for some time now and, though they'll continue to stand behind her, ideally they'd like her to fade permanently away. Obviously, we've got no particular interest in facilitating that outcome. Anyhow, it appears she found out about Rudolph's death right bang as soon as it happened; we don't know how. I accept you didn't tell her: apart from anything else, you'd have no reason to deny it. At the time of his decease, she was domiciled in Buffalo, Texas. She packed a suitcase and left home very, very quickly. We know that because she abandoned most of her belongings and left a note to the neighbours pinned to her open front door, telling them to take whatever they wanted. Good way of covering her tracks perhaps? Again, we don't know precisely. What we do know is that she took some document that prevents the trust fund being activated. We don't know what it is: you might be starting to notice, Hannah, that there are a hell of a lot of unknowns in this case. Cecelia apparently knows, but she's not saying. She's covering her anxiety about the document beneath a show of concern, real or not, about her great-great aunt. Now, normally, someone like Harlinne Vobrosky goes on the road, it's no concern of the police. This is a free country: everyone's entitled to go anywhere as and when they please. But what if you – this is Cecelia we're talking about here – could plausibly claim she'd been abducted? I'd like you to watch this, Hannah, if you please."

He switched the TV on and pressed 'play' on the video.

CCTV footage of a major road, cars speeding by in both directions. Suddenly, from the bottom right, an old woman appears on the hard shoulder, lugging a suitcase. A car passes her, indicates, slows down, stops some way in front of her. A woman gets out of the driver's seat.

My God, Julia. Charlotte gets out of the passenger side. Both rush over to Harlinne. Charlotte takes the suitcase, opens the boot/trunk swings it in. Julia opens the rear door, helps Harlinne into the car. Charlotte closes the boot, gets back in the car. Julia looks around her, gets back in the car, indicates, pulls out. Mike presses 'stop'.

"Would you believe that's the *only* CCTV footage we have of them?" he said. "It's kind of unbelievable, almost like there's been some kind of meddling somewhere along the line."

My heart thumped. "Have you any idea where they were heading?" I asked. "I mean, where did that road lead to?"

"We believe they were on their way to Austin."

I felt like my chair was levitating. "Er, where's Austin? Sorry, I don't know as much about America as you do. I mean, is it… in the same *direction* as Portland?"

"From Durant? No, ma'am. It's in Texas, and it's in the opposite direction."

"Then… what…?"

"We've no idea, ma'am. As I say, we're in a sea of conundrums here. We were hoping *you* might be able to tell *us*."

I shook my head. "I swear I'm not lying: I don't know. They must have prearranged it, mustn't they? Sorry, I'm thinking aloud now. They must have. But why didn't they say anything to me?"

"I don't know, ma'am."

I was almost crying now. "Please, stop calling me 'ma'am'. My name's Hannah." It came out as pleading. I didn't care.

He smiled sympathetically. "Listen, Hannah, I'm actually glad you made me switch the tape recorder off. I need to tell you something."

He produced a box of tissues from the desk drawer. I took one and blew my nose. "Go on," I said.

"Cecelia Vobrosky and her husband are on their way over here. Not our doing. I probably shouldn't say this since it's probably 'unprofessional', but since we're person-to-person here, and I can see you're a decent lady, I don't mind telling you: prepare yourself. She's what I'd call *a piece of work*."

I'm always sceptical when men tell me that. It usually means they're not used to dealing with powerful women. But this was America. Most men were. Weren't they?

"Let's switch the tape recorder on again," he said. "We can go back to where we were before we pressed 'stop.'"

I shrugged. "Okay."

He pressed play and record, said the time etc. then took the notepad from his jacket pocket. "Why did you split up?"

"That wasn't your last question," I said. "Your last question was, Have you any idea where they are now?"

He smiled. "Why don't we address both?"

The Proverbial "Wire"

The obvious thing for me to do now was ring Julia or Charlotte or both. When Agent Mike switched off the cassette recorder for the last time, he handed me my phone. By now, I wasn't just willing to make those calls; I was eager. I really, really wanted to know what was going on. We agreed I'd put it on speakerphone.

Julia first. It rang five times than went to voicemail.

I called Charlotte. The same.

I called Julia again, and sat out the automatic response and the beep.

"Hannah here," I said. "Look, this isn't a joke. I'm sitting in Rupert police station in Idaho, with an FBI agent called Mike Neal, being interviewed about Harlinne Vobrosky. I've just watched a video of her getting into your car somewhere on the road to Austin. I'm really, really worried about both of you, and you need to call me, and also speak to Mike. You're not in any trouble yet, although that may change. There's been a suggestion that you abducted Harlinne. It's going to be hard to prove from the CCTV evidence, but it's not going to go away if you don't get in touch."

I passed it to Mike.

"Hi, Julia," he said. "This is Agent Mike Neal of the FBI. We'd just like to talk to you in connection with Harlinne, check you and she are okay. Please give me a call on 298-434-27761."

He hung up and passed the phone back to me.

"Now we wait," he said. "There's a car waiting to take you and Ms Snow back to The Excelsior. If it's okay with you, we've arranged for someone – a female officer – to wire you up. That okay?"

"I – er, I suppose so. Cecelia will be coming to the hotel?"

"You're a public figure, Hannah, and she'll know how to find you. Likely she'll check in at reception sometime in the next twelve hours and ask to speak to you. You've got nothing to gain from denying that request, and we'd like to see how it pans out. I'll send one of our agents to attach the listening devices. Thank you for your help. You're free to leave. Obviously, give me a call if you hear anything from your sisters."

We shook hands. He escorted me back to reception where Soraya sat waiting for me on one of the foldaway chairs opposite the duty officer. We went outside, got into a police car, held hands but didn't speak.

When we got back to the Excelsior, FBI Agent Letitia Coombes was waiting for us in the lounge. About thirty-five years old, five foot five, dressed casually, with dyed black hair. We all went to my room. I read and signed four forms. I stripped to the waist, Letitia attached the wires, like a scene from *Goodfellas*. Soraya looked at me as if she wanted to laugh then went into the bathroom. I felt like a snitch, but if Julia and Charlotte were in danger, I'd need the FBI's help. That meant making compromises (if that's what they were: I had no reason to feel allegiance to Cecelia Vobrosky, no reason to believe she'd incriminate herself, and no real cause to believe she was even suspected of anything).

"I'm staying in the room next to yours," Letitia said. "My cover, if it's needed, is that I'm with the film crew that accompanied the tour you've just completed. If you get any contact at all, either from Cecelia Vobrosky or your sisters, then knock on my door or call me. Anything else you need, please do likewise."

We exchanged phone numbers.

"How long do I have to stay like this?" I asked. "I mean, suppose she decides not to come? At what point do we decide to cut our losses?"

"That'll probably be tomorrow morning sometime, but I'll need to consult with Tom. It shouldn't be too uncomfortable, but if you have any issues, say, undressing or peeing, or anything comes loose, or you're in discomfort, just give me a call."

She asked a few more questions then made her excuses and left. Soraya came out of the bathroom. We sat on the bed, opened another bag of corn chips, and watched *The Ellen DeGeneres Show*, mainly to take our minds off the disappearances. After half an hour, I forgot I was wearing a wire. I certainly wasn't concentrating on the TV.

My phone rang. I jumped and looked at the screen. *Unknown caller*.

"Hello?" I said.

"Is this Hannah Lexingwood? This is Cecelia Vobrosky." A mid-western accent, refined and casual. "You don't know me, but I know you. You're the lady my great-great aunt arranged a road trip for. And now your sisters have gone away somewhere with her. I understand you've already talked to the FBI. Do you know where they are?"

"I'd have told them if I did." I was gesturing for Soraya to go and knock on Letitia's door. She got up and left.

"I think we should meet," Cecelia said. "You're staying at the Excelsior in Rupert, right?"

"How did you know that? And how did you get my phone number?"

"I'll meet you down in the hotel bar in thirty minutes. And bring Soraya. I'm a big fan. I'd love to meet both of you. The drinks are on me."

The Replacement Couple

The bar was mainly armchairs and sofas around low tables with the usual ugly long counter along one side of the room. Soraya and I were already seated when Cecelia walked in. About 5'8 with long dark hair, she wore a burgundy skirt-suit and matching heels. She was accompanied, two paces behind, by a man in denim dungarees who looked to be the same age as her, thin, clean shaven, sunken eyes and large feet. This, we later learned, was Leopold, her husband. He and she didn't look very well matched, and at first, I mistook him for some sort of blood relative, the sort you agree to chaperon because someone unreasonable in the family insists, and all you want is a quiet life.

I introduced myself and Soraya. Cecelia returned the courtesy, and asked what we were drinking. Soraya and I ordered Martinis; she had a Jack Daniels and coke, Leopold a Pepsi with ice. I'm not sure whether that was actually his choice, because I never saw him speak. Throughout our meeting he looked gloomily at the floor. Cecilia didn't appear to notice. When it was over, and he followed her out of the hotel, he left his drink untouched.

She sat down, crossed her legs and looked hard at me. She had a thin, quarrelsome-looking face; sunken cheeks and large blue eyes. "How's your road trip going?"

"Apart from the disappearance of my two sisters," I replied, "fine, thank you. To be honest, though, the whole thing's been pretty unpredictable from the outset. Harlinne threw our passports off a bridge in New Jersey, or pretended to."

Cecelia sighed, as if this wasn't the first time she'd ever heard this kind of report, but Lord help her, she'd tried. "Harlinne's had a good life," she said. "Yes, it's had its ups and downs, but I know she and Rudolph loved each other. Now I'm sorry she inconvenienced you. She believes in – a hackneyed phrase I'm sure you've heard her use often enough – 'throwing yourself on the mercy of the open road'. Well, now, that might have been a good idea sixty or seventy years ago, but this country's not what it was. It's a dangerous place to be nowadays. People shooting each other, rape, drugs, theft, you name it. I really don't think it's too big an exaggeration to say we live in a cesspit. I won't say what I think's to blame – I guess it's probably a variety of things – but it badly needs fixing."

"I'm not sure it's *that* bad," I said.

"Much as I love Harlinne," she said, "she's part of the problem, not part of the solution. Your sisters, by all accounts, are nice women and I'm confident they're trying to do what they think's best for her, but she's eighty-nine years old, and she's not right in the head. Probably never was, but it's got a lot worse recently. She needs to be in a home, and she's got friends in high places that would be more than happy to take care of that. She'd get the best treatment imaginable."

I didn't want to talk about Harlinne; I wanted to focus on Charlotte and Julia. "If my sisters have picked her up, they may have taken her somewhere she asked to go. Have you no idea where that may be?"

She smiled. "None whatsoever. Unless it's back to the crossroads where she signed that deal with the devil sixty-odd years ago, see if he's in the mood for a bit of clemency. I do believe she's carrying the very document they both signed."

Obviously, this was a quip, but she didn't deliver it like that. She spoke matter-of-factly, like this was one more inconvenience Harlinne had inflicted on her, and, heaven help her, she was tired, just so tired of it all.

We finished our drinks and Cecelia ordered more. We sat together for half an hour in total, and she held court for most of it. Soraya was almost as quiet as Leopold. Cecelia showed no interest in her, much less made any attempt to draw her out, despite her claim to be a 'fan'. She spoke mainly about how radically Harlinne had failed everyone, and what a much better job she'd do (of *what*, she never said) once she got her hands on the crucial documentation. Not that she absolutely *needed* it, I must understand, but it would make things a whole lot *easier* in the short term. She kept breaking off mid-sentence to look at her phone – sometimes texting or tweeting for an embarrassingly long time – and she contradicted herself more than twice. But what she lacked in intelligence, she clearly made up for in self-belief. When she finally decided to leave, she simply announced that she'd got what she came here for and said I must call her if I heard anything. She walked out with long, brisk strides as if she was late for an appointment. She didn't look back.

Soraya finished her Martini. "Well, that was weird," she said.

I was really tired now. The worrying wasn't helping. At the police station, I'd imagined that Julia and Charlotte might just have their phones turned off for a while, and that later, they'd see I'd left a message, and they'd know I was worried, and they'd try and get back. Perhaps I shouldn't have told them about the FBI. Maybe they were in serious trouble someplace. If Cecelia was right, and Harlinne was losing her mind, she might even have attacked them. *People shooting each other, rape, drugs, theft, you name it. We live in a cesspit.*

Ten minutes later, Letitia helped me off with the wire and thanked me for my cooperation. When she'd gone, I sat down on the bed. Soraya put her arm round me. We talked about hiring a private detective, and agreed that we needed to get back to the FBI tomorrow morning early, find out exactly what they were doing about Julia and Charlotte, and how concerned *they* thought we should be. I was shattered, but I didn't think I'd sleep tonight. We switched the TV on again and watched *World News Tonight with David Muir*, just for something to fill the silence.

Why were they on the road to Austin? Why didn't they tell us they'd picked Harlinne up? The only answers I could come up with were scary ones. Perhaps the FBI actually suspected Cecelia had murdered them all. That would make a certain kind of sense. In that case, Cecelia would visit me to find out how much I knew, and, if they had nothing concrete on her, they couldn't prevent it. They'd given me a wire in case she made a slip of the tongue and gave a hint as to where the bodies were. *That's the only CCTV footage we have of them. It's kind of unbelievable…*

The next question was, at what point should I tell Mum and Dad?

I had to ascertain more facts first. It wouldn't pay to scare them before I knew enough to answer all their inevitable questions. At the moment, I wasn't remotely prepared. And it might all turn out to be nothing. Julia hadn't had *that* long to check her messages.

I suddenly remembered how she'd actually emailed me in Venice. I'd been through my email twice in the last hour, but that wasn't the point. The point was: *emailed*. I'd very plausibly deduced she wasn't much of a phone person. And Charlotte… ? Charlotte prided herself on her spirituality. Someone like that could easily be persuaded to put her phone out of reach, maybe even for days at a time, Marcus and Seth notwithstanding. Add Harlinne into the mix – the woman who'd dumped our phones in Shark River – and perhaps I had pretty good cause not to be too pessimistic. Individually, they weren't exactly normal. In combination, they might be completely unpredictable.

God, I know not everything I've done today has been good or had any point, but look after Julia and Charlotte and please don't let go of them. Your servant, Hannah.

I fell asleep with the TV in the background and the lights on. At some point, Soraya got up and switched both off.

I must have been clutching my phone, because when it rang, at 3am, I felt it in my hand before I knew what it was. I jumped, remembered what had happened, and looked at the screen.

Julia.

Would You Like Weird Facts With Your Reunion?

"Julia?"

"I got your message," she said.

Oh my God, it *was* her! Thank you, thank you, Lord!

"I had no idea you were so concerned," she went on. "Did the FBI catch up with you, or did you go to them?"

"Is Charlotte with you?"

"She's upstairs in our room. In Portland. We're both fine. Why didn't you call me earlier if you were so worried? I did *say* to get in touch if there was an emergency."

Soraya awoke and clambered to her haunches. I gave her a thumbs-up. She kissed my head and went back to sleep.

"The FBI came to *me*," I said. "Harlinne's got a great-great niece called Cecelia – "

"We've heard about Cecelia. In fact, that's *all* we've heard about, more or less since we left you."

"Why the hell were you going to Austin?"

"For the same reason we wanted to go to Portland, although it sounds trite now, I admit: because it's officially 'weird'. The two cities are conscious rivals in that domain. We thought we'd judge for ourselves. We spotted Harlinne on the road over there. Spooky, the way we picked her up – I mean, it's exactly like the story Rudolph told. I understand he's dead, incidentally. Well, so is Harlinne now."

I'd half expected this. "How?"

"I don't know exactly, and nor do the doctors. Shock, they think. We've had a fine time of it on the way up here, by the way. We've visited every Native American community there is, but not in a good way. I think it actually put Charlotte off. It certainly embarrassed both of us. Harlinne wanted to say *sorry* all the time. *Sorry for what America's done to you.* Well, you can imagine how that went down. The word 'excruciating' about sums it up. Even so, most of them were reasonably nice about it. She is – was – eighty-nine, after all, and there was clearly something not normal about her. From the moment we picked her up, actually. Scared is how I'd describe it. Terrified, even. Do you know what her last words were? 'I never expected to die this soon'. She was crying all the time till just before she lost consciousness. But then she came across all beatific. Against all the odds, it was a peaceful end."

"You need to call the FBI. They half-suspect you of abducting her."

"Charlotte's on the phone to them now. They'll have their work cut out proving we coerced her in any way, but I suppose anything's achievable if you're determined enough."

"They're not interested in you. They're more interested in Cecelia. Who I think is the one who accused you, but I'm not even sure it was that. She just raised a possibility with the intention of prodding the authorities into some kind of action. She wants Harlinne out of the way, and access to some kind of document she believes is in Harlinne's possession. She's probably got both now. She's the next of kin, I believe."

"Are you still in Rupert, Idaho? That's what you said when you called."

"I'm still here. With Soraya. Oh my God, I'm *so* pleased to hear from you! I thought something terrible had happened. I know it sounds wussy – well, no it doesn't – but I was really scared. I need to get some proper sleep now. We'll check out tomorrow morning and come and see you in Portland. It's only eight hours away."

"That'll be too late for Harlinne's funeral. They're looking to get it done and dusted tomorrow. Not that it matters. I'm not even sure they're doing invitations. Listen, there's no need to rush over here. It's pointless – "

"But I'd like to see you again. And so would Soraya."

"Take your time. I'll expect to hear from you in three or four days. If you give me a call before that and tell me you're in Portland, fine: we'll meet up. If not, that's also good. You've been saying all through this trip that you don't want to take things too fast."

"Understood."

We hung up. The next day, after a long lie in, Soraya and I set off again, this time for Portland. We stopped for lunch in a city called La Grande, with mountains in the distance. We watched a girls' soccer game in Candy Cane Park. I called ahead to book a hotel room in Portland and rang Julia and Charlotte to let them know. They were waiting for us in the hotel lounge when we arrived. We all went upstairs. I ordered club sandwiches and white wine. Naturally, we spoke about the funeral.

There wasn't much to tell. Harlinne apparently knew she was dying before she got in Julia's car. She visited the reservations, as described, embarrassing and offending everyone, and wired some of her friends in Washington. She collapsed in Gresham, just outside Portland, two hours after a visit to the Warm Springs Reservation in Oregon. They got her back into the car and a passer-by accompanied them to the hospital. An hour later, she lost consciousness for the last time, and twelve hours later, she died.

Her funeral was short and functional and took place in a chapel somewhere ('don't ask me where,' Julia said) in the city suburbs. Nine important-looking elderly men in expensive overcoats, possibly her Washington friends, filled the two front pews, looking genuinely sad. Cecelia and Leopold didn't appear until the internment at the Multnomah Park Cemetery. They held hands and smiled as the undertakers filled the grave in.

Portland to the Pacific

The FBI never got back to any of us. It was as if Rupert, Idaho hadn't happened, which was fine by me. I assume Mike and Tom sorted matters out with Cecelia and her powerful friends (whoever they were) and discreetly closed the investigation, or at least put it on ice. They'd probably worked out that we couldn't help.

Once the four of us reunited in Portland, I half-expected Julia and Soraya to resume their Best Buddies Ever thing. However, I think it had run its course. How much of that was down to them feeling awkward about me, I didn't know. Selfish as it sounds, I didn't much care. It was preferable to being alone indoors all day depressed.

In any case, it wasn't *all* down to me. Julia was an author and she was interested in literary stuff. Soraya wasn't. Nor was I.

Soraya and I stayed in Portland three days, then continued on to the coast alone. Julia spent that period almost exclusively hobnobbing with book people. After our initial rendezvous at the hotel, she and I met just once, for lattes and a muffin, in Extracto Coffee Roasters on NE Killingsworth Street. We sat outside, and she told me about fabulous meetings with (or, to put it less politely, she name-dropped) people I'd never heard of: Susan DeFreitas, Paul Collins, Carlton Mellick III, Walt Curtis. Whoa, she *might even* have seen *Kathleen Flenniken*, whilst she'd been eating a baguette in Alberta Park!!! (Suspiciously, she seemed to accomplish a lot of her most spectacular author sightings in urban parks. Or maybe she was just very 'lucky' in that regard.) Meanwhile, she'd been invited to speak at a symposium devoted to the life and work of Ursula K Le Guin. Two days' time, Concordia University. Tickets were selling like hot cakes. (NB. She didn't use those exact words: that would have been a cliché-crime.)

In that exact moment, I made an executive decision: we had to leave Portland fast. Soraya, I lied, couldn't wait to swim in the Pacific. Soraya herself was out with Charlotte at the time, sightseeing. When I later told her what I'd fibbed, she thanked God and got packing.

As for Charlotte, she carried on in Portland as she'd left off in Durant, which is to say she made lots of local friends, got to know them close up, and spent nearly all her time in their company, drinking coffee, shopping, going to charity events, watching TV, babysitting, walking dogs, communing with nature in the evenings. I don't know how she bonded with hitherto complete strangers so effectively. I genuinely wish I *did:* I could use that kind of superpower. In the meantime, California, and Dad showdown, was closing in, and she showed not the slightest nervousness. I knew why: she'd given up on the idea. In her mind, it wasn't going to happen.

But it was. I wasn't going back on the resolution I'd forged a hundred or so miles back. When some advance choice you've made fills you with reluctance, you shouldn't ask yourself, Would it make my life easier to drop it? only,

Is the *me* who made that decision the best version of me? In other words, Is it the right thing to do? I know that sounds sanctimonious. I knew it at the time. That knowledge tugged at me, saying, Is the sanctimonious you really the right person to judge who's the best you? I had dreams in which I ruined everything for everyone I'd ever known. In one, I was actually responsible for the end of the world.

I believe it was partly my state of mind that turned me north (in the opposite direction to California, in other words). Soraya and I drove out of Oregon into Washington and a holiday house at Long Beach. It was cold here, and atmospheric, and beautiful, and very American. On our first night, a cat adopted us. He came into the house each afternoon we were there at 5pm precisely. We gave him water and canned tuna. He stayed with us till we went to bed at eleven. The next day, a middle-aged woman called Leona came round with a plate of cupcakes. She whispered that she knew who we were, and our secret was safe with her, and welcome to America. We invited her indoors for a large bourbon, and we all had whiskey and cakes. She seemed to expect something like that, and we aim to please.

Technically, the Pacific signals the end of your road trip, assuming of course you're doing the conventional east-west version. You're supposed to take off your shoes, climb barefoot onto the car roof, raise your arms and direct a huge *Whoo-hoo!* to the sun above and the ocean in front. Charlotte would have known that, and she'd probably have thrown herself into it. But I wasn't in the mood. When we got down to the beach, we took off our shoes and paddled in the sea. Later, Soraya went to Scoopers Market – a convenience store, in case you're wondering – and I played *Surfin' USA* on my phone, and cried with the cat asleep in my lap. Weird, yeah.

We were only in Long Beach for three days before leaving for San Francisco to meet Mum and Dad. After we dropped the holiday home keys off and drove onto the southbound highway, I had the distinct sense of Julia and Charlotte packing their things somewhere in Portland, solemn faces, preparing to appear at a hotel six hundred miles away where, unbeknown to them, it was distinctly possible I'd unleash a minor Armageddon.

San Francisco Bound

San Francisco was twelve hours away. We planned to cut the journey in two: Soraya would drive from Long Beach to Yreka, CA, where we'd crash overnight in the local Holiday Inn and maybe go for a last wander round Walmart, just for old times' sake; the next day, I'd take the wheel and we'd complete the journey, aiming to arrive in SF around noon in order to check out the hotel first-hand. I'd reserved six fifth-floor rooms in the Majestica, overlooking Ocean Beach, in the peninsula's northwest quarter. Tim, Soraya, Lek and I had one room; Knut and Julia another; then Charlotte, Marcus and little Seth; Colin, Soraya's dad, and Mandy, her step-mum (her birth mum had gone back to Liberia a couple of decades ago); John, my younger brother, and his wife, Phyllis; Mabel, my youngest sister, and Tom, her partner. The two families, Soraya's and mine, were due to arrive in San Francisco at 3pm, and we'd be there to greet them. That was the plan.

The journey south from Long Beach began mild and got hot. Soraya and I didn't believe in air con, even though the car was equipped with it: green issues aside, it just didn't seem very authentic to road trip down the West Coast with the windows wound up. As we passed through Seaside, Oregon, Soraya said she wanted some music on. We'd just finished a conversation about the best album of the 21st century. Soraya favoured Kanye West's *My Beautiful Dark Twisted Fantasy*; I argued for PJ Harvey, *Let England Shake*, but I wasn't totally confident. I never am about ranking music good-better-best. In any case, it seemed insane now that, back in Venice, I'd worried about Soraya's reaction to my playlist. She was infinitely bigger than that, and I had infinitely bigger problems.

It was unusual for us to drive without listening to tunes, which we did for the journey's first three-quarters of an hour, but I kept Soraya talking so I wouldn't have to think about the immediate future. I even allowed her to lecture me about the right way to listen to music ('know the track title, read the lyrics, turn it up loud, give it at least eight chances'), as if we weren't both in the high end of the business.

But all good things come to an end. Once she put music on, she always stopped conversing, which made sense because, to be honest, she usually switched the volume up to the point where talk became impossible. We agreed to alternate albums. Because I was in a very strange frame of mind, it was a unique blend. After her, *B'Day,* my *The Clangers Original TV Music*; after her *Back to Black*, my *Joseph and the Amazing Technicolour Dreamcoat*; her Riot Grrrl compilation, my *Gustav Holst: The Planets*, and so on.

My dad: whether I liked it or not, that's what I had to think about now. Just how well did I really know him? It was an important question. He'd actually been in San Francisco during the 1960s, I knew that. An English hippy who travelled to Haight-Ashbury for the summer of love, then left just before his visa expired, when it was obvious everything there was falling apart (contrary to received opinion, at least six months before the Manson murders). Much later, thanks to him, I'd seen all the best popular music artists of my day: The Stone Roses, Blur, Radiohead, Green Day, Snoop Dogg, Oasis, Rage Against the Machine, Whitney Houston, David Bowie, Joni Mitchell, Tina Turner, Beastie Boys, The Rolling Stones, Bruce Springsteen, Elton John, Bob Dylan, The Bee Gees, Public Enemy, The Clash, Siouxsie & The Banshees (just before they split – I must have been about twelve), U2 and many others I can't even remember. It's a pretty mean CV.

But it wasn't just me he took. Charlotte nearly always came with us. In fact she became a permanent fixture after she turned thirteen, Julia too.

The more I considered those few days of internment with pizza and non-stop music, the odder it seemed. Before Charlotte's bombshell in Venice, I'd thought about it only occasionally, and yes, I had it labelled 'odd' in my mind. But I hadn't *felt* it as such, certainly not in the way

I did now. What the hell *had* he been trying to achieve? It would have to have been something that taking us to every music concert under the sun couldn't. But what on earth would fit that description?

I think the whole family agreed that he'd been 'under a lot of stress at the time' – 1990s parlance for 'mentally ill'. To all appearances, he'd since recovered. But he might not even remember what he'd been aiming for. He might not remember anything about it whatsoever.

I was pretty sure he wouldn't lie. If he *did* recall anything, he'd admit it, then he'd try to be as honest with us as he could.

Unless I really didn't know him at all. Which is possible, I guess.

As for my forgiving him, the issues were many, but that wasn't one. How to broach the topic in the first place was the biggest, then how to avoid giving the impression that Charlotte and I had been waiting to challenge him and that we'd lured him to San Francisco specifically so we could do that (which was going to be especially tricky, given that we had), whether it would permanently damage our relationship, whether from his point of view, it would reopen old wounds, what Mum would make of it all, whether the rest of the family would find out, how they'd react if they did, whether the whole thing would get misinterpreted or blown up out of all proportion or both, whether events would spiral out of control downwards to the point where everyone considered it necessary to take sides, whether I'd become a pariah, whether Dad would become a pariah.

Obviously, there was the related business of telling John and Mabel I'd had cancer, and explaining why I hadn't told them, and that Lek was their niece in a lovely, unique way they probably hadn't remotely reckoned with. I wasn't too worried about that in itself, because both were indulgent, forgiving and broad-minded, but it might be a problem coming on top of a calamitous meeting with Dad.

And Mum and Dad were getting older. He was in his seventies now. What if the shock was too much? I thought of Rudolph, then Harlinne, then Rudolph again. They'd been much older than my parents, but there was often a link between old couples. When one went, the other quickly followed.

We played Vampire Weekend, then *Twenty Trumpet Greats*.

I started to re-evaluate my entire life. How the hell had I got to where I was now? Why all the stupid compromises? Why the PR machine and all the sordid rest of it?

Because the fans couldn't leave us alone, that's why. They chased us. Sometimes, they scared us. Anyone can like your music, they don't have to be nice people, and some of them aren't. And some people hated the music. And yet others were seriously warped. They'd post on social media saying they were going to rape and dismember you. After it happened for the tenth time, you stopped calling the police. And that's where people like Nora came in, and all the security. It wasn't particularly in keeping with the rock 'n' roll vibe, but it wasn't optional. Not if you wanted to sleep at night.

Soraya switched the music off, wrenching me out of my reverie. I looked out of the window. Pine trees. Distant mountains. Sunshine.

"Are we going to be taking drugs when we get to Frisco?" she asked.

I laughed. "I haven't thought about it. I'm too busy worrying about the possible family implosion."

"Well, we *are*," she said finally. "This is California. Marijuana's legal. You're a rock chick, so am I."

"I don't like that term."

"Rock mama, rock lady, rockette, rock sister, rock witch, rock sorceress, it's irrelevant."

"We'll see, then."

"We could *eat* some weed on the beach."

"You're not allowed to consume it in a public place, as I recall."

Okay yes, I knew I was being Lady Clenched Buttocks of Anal Hall, but I was depressed. Soraya gave an exaggerated, but genuine, sigh and switched the music on again. It was one of mine. We crossed the California state line to Louis Armstrong's *Cornet Chop Suey*. One of the greatest jazz tracks ever.

There's a Showdown in the Breeze

I didn't sleep that night, which might make me inclined to nod off on the road, so the next day, Soraya drove us to San Francisco. As planned, we arrived just before noon. We left the car in the hotel's underground parking lot, and I called the hire firm to pick it up. We wouldn't be using it again. We'd get around the city on foot, or by tram, and our next major stop, in about a week's time, would be the airport, either to go to Chicago or home to England, depending on whether I triggered a catastrophe or not.

The Majestica was more than up to scratch. I'd paid for all the rooms on the fifth, topmost floor, which meant that four rooms were vacant and would remain so throughout our stay. We had their use if we wanted it. The manager showed us round in person, obviously proud of his hotel. What to say about it? It had beds, armchairs, sofas, cupboards, wardrobes, *en suites*, low ceilings, televisions, adjustable lighting, and views of the Pacific. Minus the last item, pretty much every hotel room I'd ever been in. I used the word 'lovely' several times.

Julia and Charlotte arrived an hour later. We hugged, exchanged stories about driving and traffic jams and drank coffee. Still two hours to kill before everyone else arrived. After ten minutes of half-hearted catch-up, we fell silent. We were all completely knackered, to be honest, and the caffeine hadn't been entirely a social thing: we needed it. We sat in Charlotte and Julia's room. Julia sat on the bed, her arms by her side, not even reading a book; Charlotte lay low in an armchair with her feet stretched out in front of her; Soraya and I sat on the sofa, subtly propping each other up, trying to look like we weren't falling asleep. Someone needed to say something, or snap their fingers, or throw a bucket of cold water over us. We kept yawning and saying things like, 'Oh dear, it must be the sea air', or (jauntily) 'I could just go to sleep now', as if we were eighty. The truth was, if we carried on this way, we were poised to miss the arrival of flight BA 2273 from Heathrow. I took out my phone and set the alarm.

Suddenly, Charlotte broke the silence. "Hannah, you're not going to *say* anything, are you?"

"What do you mean?"

"To Dad. About what happened when we were kids."

I sat up. "Er… *yes*… That *is* why we're here, isn't it? I mean, partly."

"But I thought we agreed we wouldn't say anything."

I laughed humourlessly. "*When?* When did we agree that?"

"In New York, remember?"

I let out a long breath of air. "No, I don't. I don't remember that."

"Well, we did. And he's *old*, and it was *nothing*. I'd had a bottle of wine, and I wasn't thinking. *Please* don't say anything. What if he has a heart attack?"

"We've got to treat him like an adult. It's called respect. And he's not frail."

"Don't be so cruel, Hannah!"

"I'm not *cruel!*"

She hand-fanned her face. "Okay, I shouldn't have said that. Sorry, I didn't mean it. You're not cruel at all. But you *will* be, if you go through with this!"

I needed back up. I turned to Julia, although I had no idea whether she'd be on my side. "What do you think?"

But she was on the phone. She waved me contemptuously away, stood up and went outside.

Bloody hell.

"It could ruin our entire holiday," Charlotte continued. She was crying now. "I've had a fantastic time, thanks partly to you. I've got some lovely memories. I don't want them all wrecked by the fact that we drove Dad away. Seth needs a grandpa and so does Lek. Think about them. And if you can't do that, think of Mum. How do you think she'll feel if we imply that he was some kind of child abuser?"

"Come on, Charlotte. No one's suggesting that, not in the least."

"But what if he *interprets* it that way? He's difficult enough to talk to as it is. He's an old man. They're not like normal human beings – "

"Which isn't in any way ageist or sexist!"

"You know what I mean. Yes you do. They don't say much. They get the wrong end of the stick sometimes, and when that happens, they're often stubborn about hanging on to it."

"Sorry, you're over-generalising. That doesn't sound anything like *my* Dad."

"So *you* say. Are you willing to take the risk? Because I'm warning you, if you go ahead with this, and you're wrong, I'm going to find it very hard to forgive you. I'm not saying I won't, some day: you're my sister, and I love you, but you'll have been warned, and you'll have done the selfish thing."

"*Selfish?*"

"What *else* is it? Who are you doing it for, if not yourself?"

I ran my hands through my hair. "For *you*. For *both of us*. For *him*. We need to *know*."

"We don't."

"We *do*."

"We *don't*. The past's the past. It can't always be understood. Sometimes it's a waste of time raking it over, trying to make sense of it. Forgetting's always an option. The world would be a hell of a lot better if people did far more of that, instead of always priding themselves on their fabulous capacity to remember all the shit."

I'd noticed Soraya pretend to look at her phone about a minute ago. She'd got up and tactfully left the room, doubtless headed downstairs. Charlotte and I were alone.

"You don't have to be present when I speak to him," I said.

"I can't *not* be. I don't trust you."

"Great. Thanks."

A well of bitterness overflowed deep inside me. All I'd ever tried to do was look after the family, now I was Judas bloody Iscariot. I too was close to tears: but of fury, not grief. My phone rang. *Julia*.

After the look she'd thrown me on her way out, I considered not answering. I knew what it'd be. A hoity-toity *Don't you think we should be making our way over to the airport now?* A pathetic attempt to quash the argument rather than resolve it. Everyone was against me.

I glanced at the clock. Nowhere near time to leave yet.

"Yes?" I said as harshly as I could.

"Hannah?"

"What do you want? I'm slap bang in the middle of a serious conversation, in case you don't recall."

She didn't answer immediately. She seemed to be talking to someone – Soraya, I assumed – just out of range.

"This isn't Julia, love," she said eventually.

It took nearly a whole second for the penny to drop. "*Mum?*" Another breather. "What are you…? Are you calling from the plane? It said 'Julia' on my screen."

Charlotte leaned forward, looking appalled. "Put it on speakerphone," she said.

I obeyed.

"I'm downstairs in the hotel lobby," Mum continued. "Your dad's chatting to Soraya in the lounge, trying to find out what's going on, I think. The reason it said 'Julia' is because this is her phone. I wanted to surprise you."

"Hi, Hannah," Julia said flatly, in the background.

"She told me what's going on with you two girls," Mum continued. "That's why I'm here early. And you're quite right. It needs airing."

"You mean you… knew? All about it?"

She chuckled. "Your dad told me about it as soon as we got back from Auntie Jill's. I never realised you'd been so traumatised."

"We haven't," I said. "It's just… I don't know… A mystery. Something that needs explaining. Sorry, I'm not expressing myself very well."

"Dads do some idiotic things sometimes, Hannah. He loves all of you. He always has. From what he told me, it was a half baked attempt to make you more 'spiritual'. And Charlotte 'got' it, and I don't think you did. I'm sorry about that, love, but it was a long time ago, and you've achieved all sorts of fantastic things in your life. We're massively proud of you, you know that. Your dad and I have talked about it once or twice since. I don't know how much of it he remembers now, but I agree, he certainly owes you an explanation. Don't let Lottie tell you otherwise."

"Oh, God. Shit. Sorry. You mean he's on his way up?"

"I'm sending him to your room now. I haven't briefed him at all, but I'm fairly sure he knows there's something wrong. I think he's worried you've had a relapse. The big C. Anything other than that'll be good news, so I don't suppose it'll be a fraught conversation."

We hung up. Charlotte had risen to her feet. She had both hands over her mouth and her eyes bulged. She trembled. "Oh my God," she said. She clapped her hands twice and laughed. "I don't believe it! *I don't believe it! I'm the successful one!*"

I laughed too. I got up and wrapped my arms round her and then we cried a bit more. Then we laughed again. Mum was right. 'Idiotic' was how she'd described it. Mad, like the Mad Hatter or Professor Branestawm or Monty Python.

A minute later there was a knock at the door. I called *Come in* and Dad entered. An old man with curly grey hair, wire-rimmed spectacles, a lilac Oxford shirt and grey chinos. He smiled tentatively. Nothing he could say now would matter. We went over and hugged him and brought him in and made him coffee and told him I hadn't got cancer.

"So why have you been crying?" he asked.

"We've been laughing," I said.

Forget It

We didn't leave it at that, obviously. Nevertheless, the whole thing had been deprived of its nuclear warhead, so when we did broach it with him, five minutes later, we did it calmly, more from obligation to a stated intention than a desire for reparation.

"Look, Dad," I said. "Mum sent you up here for a reason."

"I know," he said. "What is it?"

I gathered my courage in both hands. I felt Charlotte tense the way people do when they sense an imminent crash. "We both need to ask you about something that happened when we were both children. When I was thirteen, and Lottie was eleven."

The colour drained from his face, slowly at first, then he seemed to twig. He put the fingertips of both hands in the little space between his eyebrows, and scrunched his eyes shut. Charlotte and I exchanged looks. The room filled with an oppressive silence.

"The time I locked you both in the house," he said eventually. "When your mum went to the Lake District with John and Julia and Mabel."

We nodded. Which he probably couldn't see, because he was looking at the carpet.

"All we want to know," Charlotte said softly, "is, what was it all about?"

"Mum's told us something," I said, "but we need your version."

"I'm sorry," he replied. "I was ridiculous. I'm *so* sorry."

More silence. I sensed that his brain was working overtime, not looking for any set of excuses, but for how to dig a hole big enough to jump into when there was no spade to hand.

"I'm sorry," he said again. His voice cracked. "I've – I've thought about it a lot since then. An awful lot. Part of me hoped you wouldn't remember. Part of me hoped the opposite – that you *would* remember – because not recalling something's sometimes a sign that you've been *really deeply* traumatised. Yet I didn't know how to raise the subject without embarrassing you. Or me. How, or when. In the end, I just left it hanging, like a pathetic coward."

"You trapped us both in the house, that's all," Charlotte said meekly. "There are worse things."

"*Thank God you brought it up!*" he suddenly exclaimed, making us both jump. "Sorry, sorry, I didn't mean to frighten you. My God, listen to me: 'frighten you'! I meant, neither now nor then!" He stood up, walked to the window at speed, then came back and faced us. His eyes bulged. "I'm not making any sense, I'm sorry. It's just – for years, I've wondered. Whether either of you…"

"Well, we both *did* remember," I said. "But on the plus side, you did feed us," I added, trying to introduce a lighter note. I sensed a possibility he might have a coronary if he went on this way. "The pizza was nice – "

"Don't make *excuses* for me, Hannah!" he replied angrily. "Sorry, I didn't mean to shout. What right have I to raise my voice? The pizza was awful, actually. I know, because I made it. Some sort of *cabbage* thing, with tomato. *Cabbage*, for God's sake! Oh, God, you must have been so frightened. True, I was blowing some kind of mental fuse, but it was still me, so I can't claim no responsibility. Your mum and I – I'd never really grown up – still haven't – she'd had enough – I knew I couldn't live without her – I wanted – possibly – to end it all – all I was trying to do – with those – "

"Thank God you didn't 'end it all,'" I said. Bloody hell, I hadn't expected a full on meltdown. What had happened to the diffident old man who'd put his head round the door ten minutes ago? Answer: he'd aged twenty years, and he was flapping about like a fish on a trawler.

"I was trying to inspire you with a feel for life's ultimate questions," he said quietly. He sat on the sofa and it looked like he was talking to himself. "Who are we? Why are we here? The music was unimportant, just a vehicle for the lyrics. *Dark Side of the Moon, Songs of Leonard Cohen,* and the like. I was bloody, *bloody* ridiculous! You didn't need *me* to teach you bloody cod philosophy! You'd have got there on your own. All teenagers do. All I did was scare you. And for that, I'm truly, truly sorry."

He apologised at least seven more times. We sat either side of him and each put an arm round him. We started making facetious remarks about the whole episode, beginning with the pizza. He wept a bit, but tried to conceal his face in what he probably considered a 'manly' way. I felt unbearably sorry for him, yet at no point did I regret bringing it up, and I'm pretty sure Charlotte didn't either. Women asserting their rights: a textbook example of how it's also good for men. And, yes, I realise how sanctimonious that probably sounds.

I don't remember how we got through the final ten minutes. What do you say to someone you've set your heart on confronting, when, before you can even read from the charge sheet, they plead guilty to everything you've got and throw themselves completely on your mercy? What next? Some people I know would be definitely: *just so we can be clear about what you're guilty of, I'm going to describe it in minute detail.* But that's not me. *Let he who is without sin cast the first stone*, that's more my approach. Charlotte too. Neither of us two was perfect. He'd been stupid, but now we'd confronted him, I could see he'd emerged from the whole thing damaged. Much more than we had. I didn't want to exacerbate that.

He didn't tell me, as Mum had, that I hadn't 'got' what he'd been trying to 'teach' us and Charlotte had, but when I reminisced later, in the light of what I learned that day, what became obvious was that, throughout our formative years, Charlotte had been his 'favourite child', not me or John or Julia or even Mabel.

Or maybe not, I don't know: maybe I'm erring in the opposite direction now.

Probably. It was a long time ago, all of it, and not worth spoiling the present for. Charlotte had been right: the world could do with a whole lot more forgetting.

We wiped our eyes, ate a few snacks and Soraya called me from downstairs. Time to go to the airport and meet Tim and Lek.

A few seconds later, we all left the room for the lift. I felt highly conflicted. I half wished I'd taken Charlotte's advice at the outset and let it go. There are no 'moral approaches' in situations like this, and no completely satisfying outcomes. I'd done the least wrong thing, that's all.

Even so – and I'm not sure what purpose my admitting this achieves – I was suffused with a strong sense of mission accomplished.

All's Well That Ends Anywhere in San Francisco

The road trip was officially over. Soraya paid a guy $20 to let us stand on the roof of his SUV and shout whoo-hoo to the Pacific while we listened to the greatest pop ballad ever written – Melanie's *Peace Will Come* – then we set about preparations for The Snowflake Song. One by one, I called Elliot, Gaz, Olly and Paul, and asked them if they wanted in. They didn't. Truth be told, they'd backed themselves into a cul-de-sac. They'd been utterly wrong about the twenty stops tour. But rather than admit it, they'd adopted a double or quits approach. The Snowflake Song, just from the very notion, looked to be such an obvious dud as to nullify all the critical and popular gains Soraya and I had just made. Afterwards, we'd be back to square one, only without a 'big idea'.

I finally realised they had no intention of resuscitating the band. They wanted to string us along in the hope that we'd fall over and give them the perfect excuse to walk away. Then they'd go head-to-head with us on solo projects. There were four of them, so they'd get four throws of the dice for every one of ours. Typical disgruntled band members: they always took their advice neat from Machiavelli.

Meanwhile, Julia had another of her good ideas. We should perform it in Haight-Ashbury. The hippy movement, she claimed, had been shot through with the values of white patriarchy, hence doomed to failure, but it hadn't *all* been a waste of time. Love really *was* important. It might even be all you needed. But you shouldn't indulge the hippies with any sentimental nods. Just perform it in Buena Vista Park, let people figure your location out. If they can't, it needn't matter. Bring in some of the musicians you met through Aaron Gates.

And a harpsichord, I knew it needed one of those. And we needed to accentuate the blues-y feel. Unknown to me, whilst I'd been listening to rap, Soraya and Julia had spent their time in Durant listening to Lead Belly, John Lee Hooker, Howlin' Wolf, and BB King. That had fed into the song in a way that, when Soraya finally revealed the fact, seemed obvious. I didn't know why I'd missed it. And we badly needed a harmonica player.

Nora organised everything. We roped in every musician who'd been with us on the mini-tour: about sixty people in total, all under the age of 25. Although they were pretty exclusively studying at Arkansas University, originally they came from every state and abroad. We piled into the studio on Union Street on Wednesday morning and finished recording that evening at seven. When we reunited at Buena Vista Park the next day to do the visuals, a thousand people turned up to greet us. That Friday, we released the track and the video together. By Tuesday, it was number one on both sides of the Atlantic. It stayed there a full ten weeks. I didn't call Elliot and crew. If they wanted to speak to me, let them do the running. I expect they will eventually. Depending on how things work out for them, they may have to. I'll be nice. But there'll be no Coal Tar reunion. Not in 2024, not ever.

Mum organised me telling John and Mabel I'd had cancer. She and Dad sat with us in my hotel room. Tim and Soraya and Lek sat on the sofa, looking nervous. I told my siblings about their niece. They wow-ed, but in a good way. Mabel said, "Soraya's an international superstar, so knowing you're related to her, even obliquely, is pretty awesome!" John never minds anything much. A human being's a human being as far as he's concerned. I suddenly saw how much he looks like Dad.

Soraya's parents had completely changed – Colin, anyway (Mandy never said much in my presence, but she always seemed perfectly affable). He was a lot happier than when I'd last seen him, and eager to prove he loved his daughter and Lek, and even me and Tim. I think you probably get like that if you've got any sense and you're getting older: more accepting, realistic, kinder. He and Tim and Knut, Julia's husband, went to see San Francisco Giants play Arizona Diamondbacks at Oracle Park. Then we played 'baseball' (I use the term loosely) – me, Julia, Knut, Mabel and Charlotte versus Colin, Mandy, Soraya, Tom and Tim – in Golden Gate Park with a kids' ball and bat.

On our final night we all went on to the beach. Soraya made friends with a fat Jack Russell called Karl. Charlotte built sandcastles with the children. Julia said she'd stopped feeling homesick. She'd realised the world was both bigger and smaller than she'd really ever sensed. An unlimited number of places, a brief lifespan, a few infinitely precious relationships. The point was to mine all three as fully as you could. After four hours of barbecue, wine, surfing and conversation, Mum and Dad went back to the hotel. Then Tim and Lek and Charlotte. Then everyone except me and Soraya. Soraya was still playing with Karl. I wasn't ready to leave yet.

I'd been a little drunk most of the evening. I was listening to *Oklahoma!* on my phone when Soraya returned. She leaned over me and put something in my mouth (well, okay, yes, I said she could). I sat for three minutes, experiencing nothing. Then I saw God. Angels came and went from her mouth. She felt an infinite pity for us which fell invisible on the sand and made the Pacific fizz like champagne. Even where we went wrong, she didn't abandon us. *You'll all reach paradise in the end*, she told me (though I hadn't asked): *the whole world*. No amount of approval or criticism could alter our value one bit. I wept. This was so much better than road tripping or being a parent or married or anything. And it couldn't last.

When I came down, I was lying on Soraya's chest and she was stroking my hair saying, 'There, there.' Karl licked my face. After about ten minutes, she hauled me to my feet and we walked blearily up the beach, closely followed by the dog.

Then, thank God, his owner called him, and he bounded away.

Because I don't think I could have abandoned Karl. Not with those beautiful, sad eyes of his. Not after what I'd just been through. I'd have had to look after him, right here on the beach, till he died of old age.

The Last Words in this Book

Since we returned to Britain, I've talked to one or two people about our trip. Their reaction's always the same. Once they realise we didn't see the Grand Canyon or Disneyland or Las Vegas or Hollywood, it's: *you didn't really see* America *then; you probably need to go back sometime.*

I get a moment's uncertainty. Like, maybe they're right. Perhaps we *didn't* do it properly…

But then I remember Harlinne. *Congratulations on throwing yourself on the mercy of the open road.*

At that point, I realise: we didn't just *see* America, we were actually *there*. In it up to our ears and eyes and noses. Swimming in it. And pretty ecstatic about the fact.

How many foreigners can honestly say that?

Oh, and before I write 'the end', another thing. You might think you live in a small town (and I'm not necessarily talking about America now: France, Germany, the USA, New Zealand, Canada, India, wherever). Don't be surprised if you come round the corner one day and find Soraya and I right in front of you, playing some song we just wrote. Hey, if you're nice to us, we might even give you a tambourine. Only, don't expect us to hang around for too long afterwards.

Because nowadays, that frontier just keeps on growing.

Other Books by James Ward

Romance

The House of Charles Swinter
The Weird Problem of Good
The Bright Fish

The Original Tales of MI7

Our Woman in Jamaica
The Kramski Case
The Girl from Kandahar
The Vengeance of San Gennaro

The John Mordred Tales of MI7 books

The Eastern Ukraine Question
The Social Magus
Encounter with ISIS
World War O
The New Europeans
Libya Story
Little War in London
The Square Mile Murder
The Ultimate Londoner
Death in a Half Foreign Country

The BBC Hunters
The Seductive Scent of Empire
Humankind 2.0
Ruby Parker's Last Orders

Poetry

The Latest Noel
Metals of the Future

Short Stories

An Evening at the Beach

Philosophy

21st Century Philosophy
A New Theory of Justice and Other Essays

For exclusive discounts on Matador titles,
sign up to our occasional newsletter at
troubador.co.uk/bookshop